DANGEROUS
C

The Selected Stories of

Elizabeth Taylor

Edited by Lynn Knight

virago

VIRAGO

Published by Virago Press 1997
Reprinted 2011

First published by Virago Press Limited 1995

This Selection and Introduction Copyright © Lynn Knight 1995

Thanks are due to Joanna Kingham for permission to quote from her
mother's letters and for her kind assistance.

Virago
An imprint of
Little, Brown Book Group
100 Victoria Embankment
London EC4Y 0DY

An Hachette UK Company
www.hachette.co.uk

www.virago.co.uk

Contents

Introduction

*Of recent years she had often tried to escape the
memory of two maiden-ladies who had lived near her
home when she and Melanie were girls. So sharp-
tongued and cross-looking, they had seemed then as
old as could be, yet may have been no more than in
their fifties, she now thought... In no time at all,
would they not be copies of those other old ladies?
The Misses Rogers, the neighbours would think of
them, feeling pity and nervousness. The elder Miss
Rogers would be alarmingly abrupt, with her sarcastic
voice and old-fashioned swear words. They won't be
afraid of me, Ursula decided; but had no comfort from
the thought. People would think her bullied and
would be sorry.*

Like all the best short stories, 'Summer Schools' conveys
much more than is stated. With the slightest of references,
Elizabeth Taylor traces an arc of denials that stretch from
late-night rides through summer darkness to the larger loss
of love and identity. The future which Ursula dreads (and
is all the more poignant for being convincing) is not the
story's focus: 'Summer Schools' encompasses two lives but
spans merely a holiday. Thoughts of Dorothea Casaubon
interleave with Ursula's own delayed rite of passage. Her
visit to an old school friend disappears in a fizz of drunken
bonhomie and hangovers; even the house is tipsy with
decoration. Within these vivid frames Elizabeth Taylor
skewers affectation and bad taste. The smallest touches
– 'fitful and exasperated' weather, a recalcitrant cat –
enlarge the story, while a deadpan humour underscores the
desperation at its heart. Deftly Elizabeth Taylor exposes
self-deceit. 'Melanie closed her eyes and thought how
insufferable people became about what has cost them too
much to possess... Lightly come or not at all, is what

1

I like, she told herself crossly.' 'Summer Schools' embodies many of the characteristics I love about Elizabeth Taylor's work: the intricate patterning of a scene; the darting glance that lets none of her characters off the hook, and a tone that tickles humour out of even the most difficult situation.

Elizabeth Taylor published her first story when she was thirty; some twelve years passed before *Hester Lilly*, her first collection, appeared in 1954. By then she was an established author with six of her twelve novels behind her. *Hester Lilly* was immediately acclaimed; *The Blush* (1958) and *A Dedicated Man* (1965) affirmed her success. The *New Yorker*, which had an option on her stories, helped to establish Elizabeth Taylor's transatlantic reputation; her work also featured in magazines such as *Harper's*, *Harper's Bazaar*, *Saturday Evening Post*, *Cornhill* and *Woman's Own*. Many critics felt that the short story was the form in which Elizabeth Taylor excelled. She shared their view: 'I feel happier about my stories than my novels,' she wrote to her agent Patience Ross in 1964. On the publication of her last collection, *The Devastating Boys* (1972), the *Times Literary Supplement* proclaimed: 'Elizabeth Taylor must surely now be among the four or five most distinguished living practitioners of the art of the short story in the English-speaking world.'

In compiling this selection I have attempted to choose themes and tones that characterise her work, to include the ironic laughter of 'Perhaps a Family Failing' as well as the lyrical keening of 'Miss A. and Miss M.'. There are some wonderful portraits: Mrs Allen in 'The Blush', blunted by disappointment; Harry, tethered by blindness in 'Spry Old Character'; Mrs Mason, of 'Sisters', a woman as smothered in self-satisfaction as she is in talcum powder, and the 'devastating boys' themselves. Again and again Elizabeth Taylor reveals herself to be an acute and accomplished stylist. These stories contain phrases that can wound or sing, and with little apparent effort.

I have omitted some stories I would have liked to see here, but my task was to select. The question of development between collections is not an easy one. Individual stories are not dated within their volumes and Elizabeth Taylor was already a mature writer when *Hester Lilly* was published. One of the paragraphs in 'Oasis of Gaiety' (I won't quote it here; it's unmissable) has nothing 'early' about it; the title story of *The Blush* never falters. However, the five stories from *The Devastating Boys* that feature in this selection are, as a group, my favourites.

Stories appear in the order in which their collections were published. They are followed by three stories which featured only in anthologies or magazines, and two early, unpublished ones. Of the uncollected stories, 'The Blossoming' (1972) and 'The Wrong Order' (1973)[1] were written too late for *The Devastating Boys*. One must assume, however, that Elizabeth Taylor decided to exclude the other stories from her early collections.

'A Responsibility' was written at Penn Cottage, the Taylors' home from Boxing Day 1945 to 1956 and, despite some pleasing images, is not fully developed. Compared with her other stories, speech is handled awkwardly. 'Violet Hour at the Fleece', full of hints but little explanation, is intriguingly oblique. Though undated, it is set at the end of the war and the male characters greet one another in 'symbols . . . strange half-savage noises', a reminder of the tribal Mess games in *At Mrs Lippincote's* (1945). (And, like Julia, Sarah weeps easily.) 'Husbands and Wives', published in the anthology *New Short Stories 1945–1946*, similarly exposes failures of communication and understanding. In a neat touch, one of Elizabeth Taylor's many uses of literary references, Alison restores her equanimity by reading *The Diary of a Nobody* after confronting the threat of violence. 'The Blossoming', a charming and light *Saturday Book Story*, tells of Miss Partridge who is emboldened by her mother's death to redecorate the house

3

– the first independent act of her life. She is elderly herself and has obviously known nothing but service, yet this is not a pathetic portrait, it is a blossoming.

In *Elizabeth and Ivy* Robert Liddell refers to a story Elizabeth Taylor wrote at St Joseph's nursing home in the summer of 1972 when she was recovering from an operation for the cancer which was to kill her three years later. 'The Wrong Order' is probably that story. This knowledge is not required for effect, although it certainly increases admiration for the author. Elizabeth Taylor does not tiptoe around death; instead she corners its hypocrisies – especially those paraded by Hilda who is terminally ill. It is this confrontation that gives 'The Wrong Order' its fine, albeit uncomfortable tension. Hilda's self-deceit is entirely forgivable but who would not also sympathise (and flinch) with those forced to share her continual, pointed gaze on all things lovely? The story shows remarkable candour and a wit that does not flinch.

'The Wrong Order' is a showcase for Elizabeth Taylor's greatest skill: her ability to pinpoint a significant moment that detonates understanding and strips pretence. While she reserves her sharpest glances for insincerity, she never withdraws compassion from those whose foibles she examines all too closely. Vulnerability is a key. 'Life persists in the vulnerable, the sensitive . . . *They* carry it on. The invulnerable, the too-heavily armoured perish . . . But the stream of life flows differently, through the unarmed, the emotional, the highly personal.' These words from Elizabeth Taylor's novel *A Wreath of Roses* seem to touch a primary chord in her stories, which so often reach into isolation and loneliness. And the short story itself, with its compressed, tight form, is ideally suited to an exploration of emotional solitude.

Perhaps this is why women are usually Elizabeth Taylor's concern. Often they are middle-aged, widowed or unmarried, with empty hours to fill. Here is little of the companionship that is one of the delights of her novels. In *The Sleeping Beauty* Isabella and Evalie greet middle age together, swapping tips on racing, calories and recipes. But in her short stories glasses of sherry and cups of tea are more likely to be sipped alone – to bolster confidence or cosset empty hours – than to cement friendships. Nevertheless, these women are busy keeping up appearances. In a letter to Robert Liddell, Elizabeth Taylor described a Beckett play: 'a middle-aged woman's gallantry (I see so much of it) signif[ies] the human tragedy'. The same could be said of her stories.

Being alone and middle-aged are not necessary ingredients of isolation. The couple in 'Hôtel du Commerce' whose relationship unravels before our eyes are on their honeymoon. The story, from the wallpaper patterned like 'embryos' onwards, exemplifies the way in which the seemingly insignificant triggers and drives large concerns. 'My God, I've got to walk upstairs and downstairs behind that bottom for the rest of my life' is a wonderful taunt one would rather read than hear. The timing and structure – the way mood is coaxed into annoyance and is then fanned into fury – make 'Hôtel du Commerce' a blueprint for an argument. Despite rich, concise phrases – 'Once in bed they had always been safe' – and its startling conclusion, Elizabeth Taylor did not think this story was very good and suggested to her agent that it be omitted from a reprint of *The Devastating Boys*. I am thankful she was obviously dissuaded.

'Hôtel du Commerce' shows how a relationship can crumble, but elsewhere the tentative growth of affection and desire holds Elizabeth Taylor's attention. She always writes compellingly about the fragility and intensity of emotion and manages to make uncertainty and excitement breathe on the page. 'Flesh' conjures tenderness and optimism in spite of circumstances, while 'Girl Reading' reveals youthful love – and the idea of love – in all its lights, with clarity, kindliness and humour.

In 'The Prerogative of Love' the desire and summer heat

she later evoked so headily in *In a Summer Season* (1961) is tangible. In that novel the character Arabella is transformed into Araminta and Mrs Hatton – one of Elizabeth Taylor's superb home helps – reappears as Mrs Meacock, but the story, subtle and understated, is no mere rehearsal. At its close, a vision of desire heightened by a recognition of loss – a husband's memory of his wife's youthful dive into a river, fully dressed – catches at the back of the throat. In response, William Maxwell, Elizabeth Taylor's editor at the *New Yorker*, sent the following telegram: 'I don't suppose you could give us the recipe for "Prerogative of Love". So we could pass it round. Then we'd really have a magazine.' (12 August 1959)

Elizabeth Taylor's territory is the Thames Valley where forced lilac, Michaelmas daisies and monkey-puzzle trees look out on whitened stones bordering the river's edge, and the noise of tyres on gravel signals an end to the daily round – of tea rooms, the butcher – and time to pour a drink. The very blandness of this setting attracted her: 'It has been a part of my life since my childhood; but it rarely enchants me. It simply has a banal reality, which disturbs me. In some lights and conditions I find it depressing, and sometimes the smooth affluence of river-bank life oppresses me; but the reality remains. One drifts along in a boat and gazes at the houses one passes, and wonders about life going on in them.'[2]

Background is vital to her work. 'I ought to have been a painter,' she explained in one of her rare interviews, 'I see everything in scenes as a painter would.'[3] She found it strange that neither Jane Austen nor Ivy Compton-Burnett, the writers she most admired, were interested in scenery. For her this was a particular charm of the short story, as well as a strength: 'The technique is so good,' Elizabeth Bowen wrote to her, on receipt of *The Blush*, 'the way you move right into the situation in the first paragraph and the brilliant solidity you give to scenes.'

'I am a great walker about strange streets and love to be alone in a town I have never visited before. When I was writing my last novel . . . I drank in the pubs where [my characters] would drink, and had awful teas in the awful teashops where they would meet.'[4] Her dialogue testifies to an extremely acute ear. Conversation crackles with insincerity and veiled combat in 'Nods & Becks & Wreathèd Smiles', while in 'The Benefactress' the use of clichés is telling: they are not an excuse for thought, but underline and emphasise personality. This aural and visual precision creates the feeling that circumstances could not possibly be other than how Elizabeth Taylor describes them. She makes understandable – and enlarges – the world one knows and, as Elizabeth Jane Howard has written, she increases one's sense of reality.

Elizabeth Taylor did not covet the literary world and was reticent about her own life. Her work does not draw attention to itself either. Part of her skill lies in the concealment of craft her characters affirm elsewhere: 'I hate those great agonised pictures, which say "I", "I", all the time' (Beddoes in *A Wreath of Roses*); 'One should really feel, how easy it must be! How effortless!' (Mrs Ingram in 'The Ambush'). A lack of flamboyance, an interest in motive rather than action, together with a focus on the middle classes – often judged unworthy subjects for literature – has led some critics to conflate territory with substance and think her genteel. Such criticisms are attendant upon those who make home truths their metier – as if morality did not begin at home. In her quiet concentration lies the poise of someone who targets hidden truths. The 'sharp claws' to which Angus Wilson famously referred, in his review of *A Dedicated Man*, are always at the ready.

No matter how many times one reads Elizabeth Taylor's work there is always an element of discovery. Elizabeth Bowen wrote, 'She makes one feel, "here really is something new; something that has not been perceived or said before".' A generation later Anne Tyler echoes that view: 'There's always an element of self-congratulation. Oh, what you've caught.' Elizabeth Taylor still dazzles and enthrals.

Lynn Knight, London 1995

Notes

1. I had assumed 'The Wrong Order' to be Elizabeth Taylor's last story, but a letter suggests otherwise. 'Here is a short story, if it can be called that,' she wrote to her agent on 8 March 1974. Sadly, further clues have eluded me.
2. 'Setting a Scene', *Cornhill*, No. 1045, autumn 1965.
3. Interview with Geoffrey Nicholson, *Sunday Times*, 1968.
4. 'Setting a Scene'.

from *Hester Lilly*

Spry Old Character

THE Home for the Blind absorbed the surplus of that rural charity – so much more pleasant to give than to receive – the cakes left over from the Women's Institute party, and concerts which could no longer tempt appetites more than satisfied by homely monologues and the post-mistress's zither. Fruit and vegetables from the Harvest Festival seemed not richer from their blessing, but vitiated by being too much arranged, too much stared at. The bread in the shape of a corn-sheaf tasted of incense, and, with its mainly visual appeal, was wasted on the blind.

No week went by without some dispiriting jollity being forced upon him. This week, it was a choir of schoolgirls singing 'Orpheus with His Lute'. 'Which drives me finally up the wall,' Harry decided, and clapped his great horny hands together at the end with relief. 'Your *nails*, Harry!' Matron had said earlier, as if he were a child; and, like a child, he winced each time the scissors touched him. 'You've been biting them again. I shall have to get very cross with you.' He imagined her irritating smile; false teeth

like china, no doubt; thin lips. He was on the wrong side
of her from the start; had asked her to read out to him the
runners at Newmarket. 'You old terror! I shall do nothing
of the kind. I'm not having that sort of thing here.' He was
helpless. Reading with his hands he regarded as a miracle
and beyond him. He had steered clear of books when he
could see, and they held even less attraction now that
tedious lessons, as well as indifference, stood in the way;
and the *Sporting Life* was not set in Braille, he soon
discovered.

His request had scandalised, for – he had soon decided –
only the virtuous lose their sight: perhaps as a further test
of their saintly patience. None of his friends – the Boys
– had ever known such a calamity, and rebelliousness, as if
at some clerical error, hardened his heart. Set down in this
institution after his sister's death, he was a fish out of water.
I'm just not the type, he thought, over and over again.

The great house, in its park; the village; the surrounding
countryside – which Harry called 'the rural set-up' – was
visually unimaginable to him. His nearest experience of it
was Hampstead Heath or the view (ignored) from Good-
wood race course. Country to him was negative: simply,
a place where there was not a town. The large rooms of
the Home unnerved him. In his sister's house, he could not
go far wrong, edging round the table which took up most
of the space; and the heat from the fire, the clock ticking
on the dresser had given him his bearings. When she
had died he was helpless. The Home had appealed to him
as a wonderful alternative to his own picture of himself
out in the street with a tray of matches and a card pinned
to his breast with some words such as 'On My Beam Ends'
or, simply, 'Blind'. 'You'll have the company of others like
you,' his neighbours had told him. This was not so. He
found himself in a society, whose existence he had never,
in his old egotism, contemplated and whose ways soon
lowered his vitality. He had nothing in common with these

faded seamstresses; the prophet-like lay preacher; an old piano tuner who believed he was the reincarnation of Beethoven; elderly people who had lived more than half a dim lifetime in dark drapers' shops in country towns. Blind they might not have been; for they found their way about the house, its grounds, the village, with pride and confidence. Indoors, they bickered about the wireless; for the ladies liked a nice domestic play and thought some of the variety programmes 'suggestive'. The racing results were always switched to something different, hastily, before they could contaminate the air.

'I once went to a race meeting,' Miss Arbuthnot admitted. She had been a governess in Russia in the Tsarist days and had taken tea with Rasputin: now she overrode her companions with her past grandeur. No one knew, perhaps she least of all, what bizarre experience might be related next. 'It was at Ascot after the last war. I mean the one before that. I went as chaperone to Lady Allegra Faringdon and one of the Ponsonby cousins.'

'Did you see the King and Queen drive down the course?' asked the sycophantic Mrs Hussey. 'What a picture that must be!'

'It is quite a pageant of English life. The cream of the cream, as one might say; but, dear, dear me! What a tiring way to spend a day! My poor feet! I wore some pale grey buckskin shoes, and how they *drew*. I dare say they would look very old-fashioned nowadays, but then they were quite *à la*.' She gave her silvery, trilling laugh. '"Well I have been once," I used to say. "I know what it is like, and I know that I give the preference to Henley, even if the crowd there is not so brilliant. Oh, yes, give me Henley any day."'

No one would be likely to give her any such thing ever again, but this occurred only to Harry.

'Did you have any luck – with the horses, I mean?' he asked, breaking his sullen silence with his coarse, breathy voice. Exasperation and nostalgia forced him to speak, although to do so invited ridicule. He was driven to broach the subject as lovers are often driven to mention the beloved's name, even in casual conversation with unworthy people.

'Do you mean betting?'

'What else do you go for?' he asked huffily.

'Well, certainly not for that, I hope. For the spectacle, the occasion – a brilliant opening to the London season.'

No one thought – their indignation was so centred upon Harry – that she spoke less as a governess than as a duchess. She coloured their lives with her extravagances; whereas Harry only underlined their plight; stumbling, cursing, spilling food, he had brought the word 'blindness' into their midst – a threat to their courage.

Cantankerous old virgin! he thought. Trying to come it over me. A spinster to him was a figure of fun; but now he, not she, sat humble and grumpy and rejected.

That evening at the concert, Miss Arbuthnot, with the advantage of her cultured life behind her ('Ah! Chaliapin in "Boris"! After that, one is never quite the same person again'), sat in the front row and led and tempered the applause. A humorous song in country dialect wound up the evening, and her fluting laugh gave the cue for broad-minded appreciation. Then chairs scraped back and talk broke out. Harry tapped his way to a corner and sat there alone.

The girls, told to mingle, to bring their sunshine into these dark lives, began nervously to hand round buns, unsure of how far the blind could help themselves. They were desperately tactful. ('I made the most frightful *faux pas*,' they would chatter in the bus going home. 'Dropped the most appalling brick. Wasn't it all depressing? Poor old things! But it doesn't bear thinking of, of course.')

One girl, obediently, came towards Harry.

'Would you like a cake?'

'That's very kind of you, missie.'

She held the plate out awkwardly, but he made no movement towards it.

'Shall I . . . may I give you one?'

'I should maybe knock them all on the floor if I start feeling about,' he said gloomily.

She put a cake into his hand and looked away as the crumbs began to fall on his waistcoat and knees, fearing that he might guess the direction of her glance; for the blind, she had been told, develop the other senses in uncanny ways.

Her young voice was a pleasure to him. He was growing used to voices either elderly or condescending. Hoping to detain her a little longer, he said: 'You all sang very nice indeed.'

'I'm so glad you enjoyed it.'

He thought: I'd only have run a mile from it given half a chance.

'I'm fond of a nice voice,' he said. 'My mother was a singer.'

'Oh, really?' She had not intended to sound so incredulous, but her affectation of brightness had grown out of hand.

'She was a big figure on the Halls – in more ways than just the one. A fine great bust and thighs she had, but small feet. Collins' Music Hall and the Met. . . . I dare say you heard of them?'

'I can't really say I have.'

'She had her name on the bills – Lottie Throstle. That was her stage name, and a funny, old-fashioned name it must sound nowadays, but they liked to have something out of the usual run. Louie Breakspear her real name was. I expect you've heard your mum and dad speak of Lottie Throstle.'

'I can't remember . . . '

'She was a good old sort.' (She'd have had you taped, he thought. I can hear her now . . . 'Ay can't say, ay'm sure'.)

'"Slip Round the Corner, Charlie", that was her song. Did you ever hear that one?' (No, ay can't say ay hev, he answered for her. No, I thought not. Orpheus and his sodding lute's more your ticket.)

'No, I haven't.' She glanced desperately about her.

'What colour dress you got on, miss?'

'White.'

'Well, don't be shy! Nothing wrong with a white dress at your age. When you're fat and forty I should advise thinking twice about it. You all got white dresses on?'

'Yes.'

Must look like the Virgins' Outing, he thought. What a sight! Never came my way, of course, before now. No one ever served up twenty-five virgins in white to me in those days; showing common sense on their part, no doubt.

His rough hand groped forward and rasped against her silk frock.

'That's nice material! I like nice material. My sister Lily who died was a dressmaker. . . . '

The girl, rigid, turned her head sharply aside. He smelt the sudden sweat of fear and embarrassment on her skin and drew back his hand.

'Now, young lady, we can't let you monopolise Mr Breakspear,' Matron said, coming swiftly across the room. 'Here's Miss Wilcox to have a chat with you, Harry. Miss Wilcox is the choir-mistress. She brings the girls here every year to give us this wonderful experience. You know, Miss Wilcox, Harry is quite the naughtiest of all my old darlings. He thinks we treat him so badly. Oh, yes, you do, Harry. You grumble from morning till night. And so lazy! Such a lovely basket he was going to make, but he lost all interest in it in next to no time.'

Sullenly, he sat beside Miss Wilcox. When coffee was brought to him, he spilt it purposely. He had no pride in overcoming difficulties as the others had. His waistcoat was evidence of this. He was angry that Matron had mentioned his basketwork; for a very deep shame had overtaken him when they tried to teach him such a craft. He saw a picture of his humiliation, as if through his friends' eyes – the poor old codger, broken, helpless, back to the bottom class at school. 'You want to be independent,' the teacher had said, seeing him slumped there, idle with misery. He thought they did not understand the meaning of the word.

'You haven't been here long?' Miss Wilcox enquired kindly.

'No, only since my sister, Lily, died. I went to live along with her when I lost my wife. I've been a widower nineteen years now. She was a good old sort, my wife.'

'I'm sure she was.'

Why's she so sure, he wondered, when she never as much as clapped eyes on her? She could have been a terrible old tartar for all she knows.

But he liked to talk, and none of the others would ever listen to him. He engaged Miss Wilcox, determined to prevent her escaping.

'I lost my sight three years ago, on account of a kick I had on the head from a horse. I used to be a horse dealer at one time.' Then he remembered that no one spoke about being blind. This apparently trivial matter was never discussed.

'How very interesting!'

'I made a packet of money in those days. At one time I was a driver on the old horse buses. . . . You could see those animals dragging up Highgate Hill with their noses on the ground nearly. I bought an old mare off of them for a couple of quid, and turned her out on a bit of grass I used to rent. Time I'd fed her up and got her coat nice with dandelion leaves and clover, I sold her for twenty pounds. Everything I touched went right for me in those days. She was the one who kicked me on the head. Francie, we called her. I always wished I could tell the wife what the doctors said. If I'd have said to her: "You know, Florrie, what they hold Francie did to me all those years ago" she would never have believed me. But that's what they reckoned. Delayed action they reckoned it was.'

'Extraordinary!' Miss Wilcox murmured.

'Now, you old chatterbox!' Matron said. 'We're going to sing "Jerusalem", all together, before the girls go home. And none of your nonsense, Harry. He's such an old rascal about hymns, Miss Wilcox.'

Once, he had refused to join in, believing that hymn-singing was a matter of personal choice, and not *his* choice. Now, he knew that the blind are always religious, as they are cheerful, industrious and independent. He no longer argued, but stood up clumsily, feet apart, hands clasped over his paunch, and moved his lips feebly until the music stopped.

In the first weeks of his blindness, he had suffered attacks of hysteria, as wave upon wave of terror and frustration swept across him. 'Your language!' his sister would say, her hand checking the wheel of the sewing machine. 'Why don't we go round to the Lion for a beer?' She would button up his overcoat for him, saying: 'I can't bear to see you fidgeting with your clothes.' When he had put on his old bowler-hat, they would go along the street arm in arm, 'Good evening, Mrs Simpson. That was Mrs Simpson went by, Harry.' She used no tact or Montessori methods on him. In the pub, she would say: 'Mind out, you! Let Harry sit down. How would *you* like to be blind?' They were all glad to see him. They read out the winners and prices for him. He knew the scene so well that he had no need to look at it, and the sensation of panic would be eased from him.

Now a deeper despair showed him daily the real tragedy of his blindness. This orderly, aseptic world was not only new to him, but beyond his imagining. Food and talk had lost their richness; central heating provided no warmth; he crouched over radiators with his hands spread over the pipes, his head aching with the dryness of the air. No one buttoned his coat for him. He tapped his way round with his stick, often hitting out viciously and swearing. 'There are ladies present,' he was told, and, indeed, this was so. They lowered the atmosphere with little jealousies and edged remarks and irritated with their arguments about birds ('I could not mistake a chaffinch's song, Mrs Hussey, being country-bred-and-born') or about royalty ('But both Lady Mary *and* Lady May Cambridge were bridesmaids to the Duchess of York'). They always remembered 'as if it were yesterday', although begging pardon for contradicting. Morale was very high, as it so often is in a community where tragedy is present. Harry was reminded of the Blitz and Cockney resilience and understatement. Although a Cockney himself he detested understatement. Some Irish strain in him allowed his mind to dwell on the mournful, to spread alarm and despondency and to envisage with clarity the possibilities of defeat. When he confessed to fear, the Boys had relished the joke. 'That'll be the day!' they said. He found the burden of their morale very tiring. The war's bad enough in itself, he had thought; as now he thought: Surely it's bad enough being blind, when he was expected to sing hymns and alter all his ways as well.

After the concert, his luck seemed to change; at first, though, to deteriorate. The still, moist winter weather drew the other inmates out on walks about the village. Only Miss Arbuthnot remained indoors with a slight cold. In the end, the sense of nervousness and irritation she induced in Harry drove him out, too. He wandered alone, a little scared, down the drive and out on to the high road. He followed the brick wall along and turned with it into a narrower lane with a softer surface.

The hedges dripped with moisture although it was not raining. There was a resinous scent in the air which was all about that neighbourhood and pronounced healthy by

Matron, who snuffed it up enthusiastically as if she were a war-horse smelling battle. Harry's tread was now muffled by pine needles and once a fir cone dropped on his shoulder, startling him wretchedly. Every sound in the hedgerow unnerved him: he imagined small, bright-eyed animals watching his progress. From not following the curve of the hedge sharply enough, he ran his face against wet hawthorn twigs. He felt giddiness, as if he were wandering in a circle. Bad enough being out by myself in the country, let alone being blind, too, he thought, as he stumbled in a rut.

He could imagine Matron when he returned – if he returned – 'Why, Harry, you naughty old thing, going off like that! Why didn't you go with Mr Thomas, who knows the neighbourhood so well and could have told you the names of all the birds you heard, and made it nice and interesting!'

The only birds, he, Harry, could recognise – and he did not wish to recognise any – were jackdaws (and they were really rooks), who seemed to congregate above him, throughout his walk, wheeling and cawing in an offensive manner; perhaps disputing over him, he thought morbidly; staking their claims before he dropped.

Then suddenly he lost hedge and ditch. He was treading on turf and the air had widened. He felt a great space about him and the wind blowing, as if he were on a sea cliff, which he knew he could not be in Oxfordshire. With a sense of being confronted by an immense drop – a blind man's vertigo – he dared not take a pace forward, but stood swaying a little, near to tears. He heard rough breathing and a large dog jumped upon him. In terror, he thrashed about with his stick, the tears now pouring from his eyes which had no other function.

He heard a woman's voice calling and the squelch of the wet turf as she ran towards him across what he had imagined to be the middle of the air. She beat the dog away and took Harry's arm.

'You all right, dear? He's plastered you up properly, but it'll brush off when it's dry.'

'I don't know where I am,' Harry said, fumbling for his handkerchief.

'It's the common where the bus stops.' She pulled his handkerchief from his pocket and gave it to him. 'That's our bus over there.'

'You a conductress then?'

'That's right, dear. You're from that Home, are you? It's on the route and we can give you a lift.'

'I don't have any coppers on me.'

'You needn't worry about that. Just take my arm and we're nearly there. It's a scandal the way they let you wander about.'

'The others manage better nor I. I'm not one for the country. It always gives me the wind-up.'

At the gates of the Home she helped him down, saying: 'Any time, dear. Only too pleased. Take care of yourself. Bye-bye!'

No one had noticed his absence and he concealed his adventure. One of the daily cleaners, with whom he felt more confidence than with the resident staff, brushed his coat for him.

After this, the lane which had held such terror, was his escape route. The buses came every hour, and he would sometimes be waiting there; or the drivers would see him stumbling across the common and would sound the horn in welcome. Sitting in the bus before it drew out, he could enjoy the only normal conversation of his day.

'A shilling each way Flighty Frances! That's not much for a man of your substance, Harry.'

'It's just I fancy the name. I had an old mare of the name of Francie. Time was, no doubt, I'd have had a fiver on it. Now I'm left about as free of money as a toad of fleas.'

He would try to roll his own cigarettes, but tore the paper and spilt the tobacco, until the bus drivers learnt to help him.

In their company he opened out, became garrulous, waggish, his old manner returning. He came to know one from another and to call each by his name. Their camaraderie opened up to him garage gossip, feuds at the depot, a new language, a new life. His relationship with them was not one of equality, for they had too much to give, and he nothing. This he sensed and, while taking their badinage and imagining their winks, he played up his part – the lowering role of a proper old character – and extracted what he could from it, even to the extent of hinting and scrounging. His fumblings with his cigarette-making became more piteous than was necessary.

'Oh, for goodness' sake, have a proper cigarette . . . messing about like that.'

'That's all I got the lolly for, mate.'

'Whose fault's that – if you've got to drink yourself silly every night.'

'I haven't had a pint since I come down here.'

'Well, where's your money gone to – wild living, I suppose? And women.'

'Now don't you start taking the mike out of me, Fred.' He used their names a great deal – the first pride he had felt since his blindness, was in distinguishing Fred from Syd or Lil from Marg. The women had more individuality to him, with wider variety of inflection and vocabulary and tone; and the different scents of their powder and their hair.

'Supposing Flighty Frances comes in, what are you going to do with your winnings, Harry? Take us all out for a beer?'

'I'll do that,' he said. 'I forget the taste of it myself. I could do with a nice brown. It's the price of it, though, and how to find my way back afterwards, and all them old codgers sitting round fanning theirselves each time I free a belch. Very off-hand they can be with their ways.'

'What do you do all day?'

The driver felt a curiosity about a life so different from his own, imagined a workhouse with old people groping about, arms extended as if playing Blind Man's Buff.

'We have a nice listen to the wireless set – a lot of music which I never liked the sound of anyway – and plays about sets of people carrying on as if they need their arses kicked. You never met a breed of people like these customers on the wireless; what they get into a rare consternation about is nobody's business. Then we might have some old army gent give a talk about abroad and the rum ways they get into over there, but personally I've got my own troubles so I lie back and get in a bit of shut-eye. The other night we had a wagon-load of virgins up there singing hymns.'

He played to the gallery, which repaid him with cigarettes and *bonhomie*. His repartee became so strained that sometimes he almost waited to hear Flo, his late wife, say sharply: 'That's enough now, Harry. It's about time we heard something from someone else.' He had always talked too much; was a bad listener; almost a non-listener, for he simply waited without patience for others to stop talking that he might cap their story. Well, hurry up, hurry up! he would think. Get a move on with it, man. I got something to say myself on those lines. If you go drivelling on much longer, chances are I'll forget it.

'No, what I'd do, say this horse comes in, bar the fact I'd only make about seven bob all told, but what I'd do is take the bus down to the fair on Saturday. I like a nice lively fair.'

'What, and have a go on the coconut shies?'

'I wouldn't mind, Fred,' he boasted.

'You can come along with me and Charlie, Saturday evening,' Fred said, adding with an ungraciousness he did not intend: 'Makes no odds to us.'

'Well, I don't know,' Harry said. 'Have to see what's fixed up for Saturday. I'll let you know tomorrow.'

'All right, Harry. We'll get one of the boys to pick you

up at the gates Saturday after tea, and we can put you on the last bus along with all those coconuts you're going to knock down.'

They left him at the gates. He lifted his white stick in farewell and then walked up the drive, slashing out at the rhododendron hedge and whistling shrilly. Now he was in for a spell of his old difficulty – currying favour. He would not have admitted to Fred that he could not come and go as he pleased, that for the rest of the day he must fawn on Matron and prepare his request. This he overdid, as a child would, arousing suspicion. He lowered himself in his own eyes by praising the minced meat and going into ecstasies over the prunes and custard. His unctuous voice was a deep abasement to him and an insult to Matron's intelligence. 'My, that's what I call a meal, quite a pre-war touch about it. Now, say I have another go at that basketwork, ma'am?'

'What are you up to today, Harry?'

'Me?'

'Yes, you.'

Later, the wind drove gusts of fair-music up the hill. Miss Arbuthnot complained; but Harry could not hear it. Missing so much that the others heard was an added worry to him lately; for, to lose hearing as well, would finish him as a person, and leave him at the mercy of his own thoughts which had always bored him. His tongue did his thinking for him: other people's talk struck words from him like a light from a match; his phrases were quick and ready-made and soon forgotten; but he feared a silence and they filled it.

Matron found him alone, after the basket-making class was over. He was involved in a great tangle of withies. His enormous hands engrained with dirt looked so ill-adapted to the task that Matron, stringent as she was about the difficulties of others, found them wretchedly pathetic. So few men of action came her way; the burly, the ham-handed ended up in other backwaters she supposed, with gout and dropsy and high blood pressure. She felt, as Harry himself felt, that he was not the type. He was certainly ill-matched to his present task of managing the intractable, and even dangerous, tangle of cane.

'When is your birthday, Harry?' she asked; for she was interested in astrology and quite surprised how many Cancer subjects came her way.

'April the twenty-first. Why?'

'Taurus the Bull,' she said.

He began to bristle indignantly, then remembered his purpose and bent his head humbly, a poor broken bull with a lance in his neck.

'You mean,' some instinct led him to say, 'I'm like a bull in a china shop?'

Her contrition was a miracle. He listened to her hurried explanations with a glow in his heart.

'I only thought you meant I was clumsy about the place,' he said. 'I don't seem to cotton on to half what the others say and I keep spilling my dinner.'

'But, Harry . . . '

'I've had my sight longer than them, and it takes more getting used to doing without it,' he went on, and might have been inspired. 'When you've been lucky to have your eyes so long as me, it takes some settling to.' You've still got yours hung in the air. He managed to insinuate the idea and seem innocent of the thought; but he had lost his innocence and was as cagey as a child. His late wife would have said: 'All right, you can come off it now, Harry.' Matron said: 'We only want to make you happy, you know; though sometimes you're such an old reprobate.'

After that, he had to endure the impatience of being coaxed to do what he desired, and coquetry was not in his line. He became unsure of himself and the trend of the conversation, and with a Cockney adroitness let the idea of the fair simmer in Matron's mind, undisturbed. Busy again with his basketwork, he let one of the osiers snap back and hit him across the face. 'I'm no spoilsport, Harry,' she said. This daunted him; in all his life he had found that sport was spoiled by those who claimed this to be their last intention. He awaited all the rest of the phrases – 'I should hate to be a wet blanket', and 'Goodness knows I don't want to criticise'. In his agitation, he took up the picking knife to cut an end of cane and cut into the pad of his thumb. At first, he felt no pain; but the neatness with which the blade divided his flesh alarmed him. He missed his sight when he needed to feel pain. Blood, crawling between his thumb and fingers put him into a panic and he imagined the bone laid bare, and his head swam. Pain, coming through slowly, reassured him more than Matron could.

For the rest of the evening, he sat alone in his corner by the radiator, and the steady throbbing of his bandaged thumb kept him company, mixed as it was – and, no doubt, in Matron's mind too – with the promise of the fair. 'I should insist on their bringing you back,' she had said. 'There's the rough element to contend with on a Saturday night.' In other years he had been – proudly – a large part of the rough element himself.

After supper, Miss Arbuthnot too, reminded by the distant sounds of the roundabouts, began to discuss the rough element – which, in her experience, as in all her experiences, was exaggerated beyond anything Harry had ever known. Spinster-like, she described a teeming, Hogarthian scene of pickpockets, drunkards and what she called, contradictorily, 'undesirable women'. 'Oh, once, I dare say, these fairs were very picturesque . . . the maypoles and the Morris dancing; and so vividly I remember the colourful peasants I saw at the fair at Nidjni Novgorod . . . such beautiful embroidery. But now, what is there left of such a life? So drearily commercial as all our pleasures are.'

She drove their inclinations into the corral: now no one cared to go to the fair; except Harry, worldly-wise, crouched over his radiator, nursing his poor hand, with his own inner vision still intact.

In the Home there was an aristocracy, never – from decency – mentioned, of those who had once, and even perhaps recently, seen, over those blind from birth. The aristocracy claimed no more than the privilege of kindness and of tact and was tempered by the deftness and efficiency of those who had had longest to adapt themselves. Miss Arbuthnot, blinded, Harry imagined, by her own needlework, was the eyes of them all: for she had great inventiveness and authority and could touch up a scene with the skill of an artist. Harry, finding her vision unacceptable, had nothing of his own to take its place; only the pig-headed reiteration. 'It isn't like that' – the fair, the races, the saloon bar.

'I used to like a roundabout when I was a girl,' Mrs Hussey said timidly.

'Well, there you have it!' said Miss Arbuthnot. 'All we have salvaged of the picturesque. The last of a traditional art, in fact. For instance, the carved horses with their bright designs.'

'It was going round, I liked,' Mrs Hussey said.

With a tug, as of a flag unfurling, an old memory spread out across Harry's mind. He recalled himself as a boy, coming home from school with one of his friends, along the banks of a canal. It was growing dark. His child's eyes had recorded the scene, which his busy life had overlaid and preserved: now, unexpectedly laid bare, it was more vivid than anything he had witnessed since. Sensually, he evoked the magic of that time of day, with the earth about to heel over into darkness; the canal steaming faintly; cranes at a menacing angle across the sky. He and the other boy walked in single file, on the muddy path which was hoof-printed by barge horses. The tufted grass on each side was untidy and hoary with moisture; reeds, at the water's edge, lisped together. Now, in his mind, he followed this path with a painful intensity, fearing an interruption. Almost slyly, he tracked down the boy he had been, who, exposed like a lens, unconsciously took the imprint of the moment and the place. Now, outside the scene, as if a third person, he walked behind the boys along the path; saw one, then the other, stoop and pick up a stone and skim it across the water. Without speaking, they climbed on the stacks of planks when they came to a timberyard. The air had seemed to brace itself against distant thunder. The canal's surface wrinkled in a sudden breeze, then drops of rain spread rings upon it. The boys, trying the door of a long shed, found it unlocked and crept inside to shelter, wiping their wet hands down their trousers. Rain drove against the windows in a flurry and the thunder came nearer. They stood close to one another just inside the door. The shapes which filled the shed, set out so neatly in rows, became recognisable after a while as roundabout horses, newly carved and as yet unpainted. Harry moved amongst them, ran his hand down their smooth backs, and breathed the smell of the wood. They were drawn up in ranks, pale and strange horses, awaiting their trappings and decorations and flowing tails.

The two boys spoke softly to one another; their voices muted – for the wood shavings and the sawdust, which lay everywhere like snow, had a muffling effect: nervousness filled them. Harry forced himself to stare at the horses as if to hypnotise them, to check them rearing and bearing down; and became convinced of their hostility. Moving his eyes watchfully, he was always just too late to see a nostril quiver or a head turn; though feeling that this happened.

The rain fell into the timberyard as if the sky had collapsed, drumming upon the roof of the shed and hissing into the canal. It was dark now, and they thought of their homes. When the horses were swallowed by shadows, the boys were too afraid to speak and strained their ears for the sound of a movement. Lightning broke across the shed, and the creatures seemed to rear up from the darkness, and all their eyes flashed glassily.

The boys, pelting along the footpath, slipping in the squelching mud, their wet fringes plastered to their foreheads, began after a while to feel their fear recede. The canal was covered with bubbles, sucked at the banks and swirled into rat-holes. Beyond the allotments was the first street lamp, and the boys leaned against it to take a deep breath and to wipe the rain from their faces. 'That was only their glass eyes,' Harry had said; and there, under the lamp post, the memory ended. He could not pursue himself home; but was obliged to take leave of his boyhood there – the child holding his wet jacket across his chest. The evening was lying vaguely before him, with perhaps a box on the ears from Lottie Throstle, for getting his books wet; or had she fetched the tin bath in from the wall in the yard and let him soak his feet in mustard water? She had had her moods and they defeated his memory.

Miss Arbuthnot was still talking of traditional art and craftsmanship and, rather to her vexation, was upheld in her views by the piano tuner.

Harry leaned sleepily against the radiator, tired from the mental strain of recollection – that patient stalking of his boyhood, tiring to one who had never dwelt on the past or reconsidered a scene. The intensity of the experience was so new to him that he was dazed by it; enriched; and awed by the idea of more treasure lying idle and at his disposal.

That night, nursing his throbbing hand to his chest, the pain easing him by giving a different focus to his distress, he slept his first deep and unbroken sleep since his sister's death.

On Saturday, as it grew dark, he waited for the bus at the top of the drive. His bowler hat was tilted forward, as if to match his feeling of jaunty anticipation; his scarf was

29

tucked into his coat. Muffled up, stooping, with his head thrust from side to side, his reddened, screwed-up eyes turned upwards, he looked like a great tortoise balancing on its hind legs – and one burdened by the extra carapace of blindness.

At tea, he had excited envy in some of the inmates when he at last overcame superstition enough to mention the fair. Miss Arbuthnot had doubled her scorn, but felt herself up against curiosity and surprise and the beginning of a reassessment, in most of their minds, of Harry's character. He had left behind a little stir of conjecture.

He heard the bus coming down the lane and stood ready, his stick raised, to hail it. The unseen headlights spread out, silhouetting him.

'You been hurting your hand?' the conductress asked, helping him into a seat.

'I just cut it. Is that old Fred up in front?'

'No, that's Evan. Fred's been on a different route, but he said to tell you he'd be waiting for you at the depot along with Jock and Charlie.'

Fred's heart sank when he saw Harry climbing down from the bus and smiling like a child. Saddling his friends with the old geezer for an evening was too much of a responsibility, and constraint and false heartiness marked the beginning of the outing. He had explained and apologised over and over again for the impulse which had brought Harry into the party.

'Why, that's all right, Fred,' they had assured him.

He thought that a beer or two at the Wheatsheaf would make them feel better; but Harry, after so much enforced abstinence, found the drink go to his head with swift effect; became boastful, swaggering; invited laughter and threw in a few coarse jests for good measure. Sitting by the fire, his coat trailing about him, he looked a shocking old character, Fred thought. The beer dripped on to his knees; his waist-coat bulged above the straining fly-buttons, looped with the tarnished chain of a watch he kept winding and holding to his ear although he could no longer read it. Every so often he knocked his bowler hat straight with his stick – a slick, music-hall gesture. Cocky and garrulous, he attracted attention from those not yet tired of his behaviour or responsible for it, as Fred was. They offered cigarettes and more drink. When at last he was persuaded to go; he lurched into a table, slopping beer from glasses.

Down the wide main street the fair booths were set out. Their lights spread upwards through the yellowing leaves of the trees. The tunes of competing roundabouts engulfed them in a confusion of sound. They stopped at a stall for a plateful of whelks and were joined by another bus driver and his wife, whose shrill, peacock laughter flew out above all the other sounds.

'How are you keeping, Harry?' she asked. She was eating some pink candy-floss on a stick, and her lips and the inside of her mouth were crimson from it. Harry could smell the sickly, raspberry smell of her breath.

'Quite nicely, thanks. I had a bit of a cold, but I can't complain.'

'Ever such a lot of colds about,' she said vaguely.

'And lately I seem to be troubled with my hearing.' He could not forgo this chance to talk of himself.

'Well, never mind. Can't have it all ways, I suppose.'

He doesn't have it many ways, Fred thought.

'You ought to take me through the Haunted House, you know, Harry. I can't get anyone else to.'

'You don't want to go along with an old codger like me.'

'I wouldn't trust him in the dark, Vi,' Fred said.

'I'll risk it.'

She sensed his apprehension as they turned towards the sideshow. From behind the canvas façade with its painted skeletons, came the sound of wheels running on a track, and spasms of wild laughter. Harry tripped over a cable and she took his arm. 'You're a real old sport,' she told him. She

31

paid at the entrance and helped him into a little car like a toast rack. They sat close together. She finished her candy, threw away the stick and began to lick her fingers. 'I've got good care of you,' she said. 'It's only a bit of kids' fun.'

The car started forward, jolting at sharp bends, where sheeted ghosts leant over them and luminous skulls shone in the darkness. Vi out-laughed everyone, screaming into Harry's ear and gripping his arm with both hands.

'It isn't much for *you*,' she gasped sympathetically at each horrific sight; but the jerking, the swift running-on, the narrow – he guessed – avoidance of unseen obstacles, had made him tremble. The close smell was frightening and when, as part of the macabre adventure, synthetic cobwebs trailed over his face and bony fingers touched his shoulder, he ducked his head fearfully.

'Well, you are an old baby,' Vi said.

They came out into the light and the crowds again, and she put up her raspberry lips and kissed his cheek.

Her behaviour troubled him. She seemed to rehearse flirtatiousness with him for its own sake – unless it were to excite her audience. She expected no consequence from her coquetry, as if his blindness had made him less than a man. Her husband rarely spoke and never to her, and Harry could not see his indifferent look.

With ostentatious care, Vi guided him through the crowds, her arm in his, so closely that he could feel her bosom against his elbow. He was tired now; physically, and with the strain of being at everybody's mercy and of trying to take his colour from other people. His senses, with their extra burden, were fatigued. The braying music cuffed his ears until he longed to clap his hands over them: his uncertain stumblings had made his step drag; drifting smells began to nauseate him – shellfish, petrol and Vi's raspberry breath.

At the coconut shy, she was shriller than ever. She stood inside the net, over the ladies' line, and screamed each time

she missed, and, in piteous baby-talk, when a coconut rocked and did not fall, accused the proprietor of trickery.

Her husband had walked on, yawning, heedless of her importunities – for she *had* to have a coconut, just as she had *had* to have her fortune told and her turn on the swing-boats. Jock and Charlie followed, and they were lost in the crowd. Fred stayed and watched Vi's anger growing. When he knocked down a coconut, she claimed it at once as a trophy. She liked to leave a fair laden with such tributes to her sexual prowess.

'Well, it's just too bad,' Fred said, 'because I'm taking it home to my wife.'

'You're mean. Isn't he mean, Harry?'

Fred, coming closer to her, said softly as he held the coconut to his ear and rattled the milk: 'You can have it on one condition.'

'What's that?'

'You guess,' he said.

She turned her head quickly. 'Harry, you'll get a coconut for me, won't you?'

She ran her hands up under the lapels of his coat in a film-actressy way and rearranged his scarf.

'That's right, Harry,' Fred said. 'You told me the other day you were going to have a try. You can't do worse than Vi.' Her fury relaxed him. He threw the coconut from one hand to the other and whistled softly, watching her.

Harry was aware that he was being put to some use; but the childish smile he had worn all the evening did not change: it expressed anxiety and the hope to please. Only by pleasing could he live; by complying – as clown, as eunuch – he earned the scraps and shreds they threw to him, the odds and ends left over from their everyday life.

Fred and Vi filled his arms with the wooden balls and led him to the front of the booth. Vi took his stick and stepped back. Someone behind her whispered: 'He's blind. How dreadful!' and she turned and said: 'Real spry old character,

33

isn't he?' in a proprietary voice. More people pressed up to watch, murmuring sympathetically.

'Aim straight ahead,' Fred was saying, and the man in charge was adding his advice. Harry's smile wrinkled up his face and his scared-looking eyes. 'How's that?' he cried, flinging his arm up violently. The crowd encouraged him, desperately anxious that he should be successful. He threw again.

Fred stepped back, close to Vi, who avoided his glance. Staring ahead, still whistling, he put his hand out and gripped her wrist. She turned her arm furiously, but no one noticed.

'You've been asking for something all the evening, haven't you?' he asked her in a light conversational tone. 'One of these days you're going to get it, see? That's right, Harry!' he shouted. 'That was a near one! Proper old character. You can't help admiring him.'

Vi's hand was still. She looked coolly in front of her; but he could sense a change of pulse, an excitement in her; and almost nodded to himself when she began to twist her fingers in his, with a vicious lasciviousness he had foreseen.

A cheer went up as Harry went near to his target. 'Next round on the house,' the owner said. Harry's smile changed to a desperate grin. His bowler hat was crooked, and all of his movements were impeded by his heavy overcoat. Noise shifted and roared round him until he felt giddy and began to sweat.

Insanely, the roundabout horses rose and plunged, as if spurred on by the music and the lateness of the hour; sparks spluttered from the electric cars. Above the trees, the sky was bruised with a reddish stain, a polluted light, like a miasma given off by the fair.

The rough goodwill of the crowd went to Harry's head, and he began to clown and boast as if he were drunk. Fred and Vi seemed to have vanished. Their voices were lost. He

could hear only the roundabout and the thud of the wooden balls as he threw them against the canvas screen, and he feared the moment when his act was over and he must turn, empty-handed, hoping to be claimed.

Nods & Becks
& Wreathèd Smiles

'I WAS *hours* with Jennifer,' Mrs Miller said, and she lifted the lump of sugar out of her coffee to see how much of it had melted. 'I went in at ten o'clock at night, and she didn't arrive until after tea the next day.'

Mrs Graham, not really attending, had a sudden vision of Jennifer, quite grown up, stepping out of a cab with all her luggage, just as it was getting dark. Such pictures were constantly insinuating themselves into her mind, were sharply visual, more actual than this scene in the teashop in the High Street among her friends, from whose conversation she often retracted painfully, to whose behaviour she usually reacted absurdly.

'... and dares to tell me there are no such things as labour pains,' Mrs Miller was saying. '"It's all psychology," he said, and I said, "So are too many things nowadays."'

Mrs Howard said, 'He told me just to relax. Well, I relaxed like mad and I still had to have seven stitches.'

Her voice had risen in her indignation, and Mrs Miller gave a little sideways warning glance at a man at the corner table, who had turned up his coat collar and was rustling his newspaper.

'Well, it was certainly the worst experience I ever had,' Mrs Howard said emphatically. 'I hope never to go through – '

'I thought neuralgia was worse,' Mrs Graham forgot herself enough to say.

At first, they were too surprised to speak. After all, *men* could have neuralgia. Then Mrs Miller gave her own special little laugh. It was light as thistledown. It meant that Mrs Graham only said that to be different, probably because she was a vegetarian. And was always so superior, so *right* about everything – had said that there wouldn't be a war at the time of Munich, when they were sitting in this very café surrounded by the dried fruit and the tinned food they had been so frantically buying, and the next year, when they *hadn't* bought the fruit, she *had*.

'My God, Dolly! What *have* you done?' Mrs Miller suddenly exclaimed.

Groping tragically before her, like Oedipus going into exile, Mrs Fisher came stumbling toward them, a bandage over one eye, her hat crooked.

They all scraped their chairs back, making room for her.

'Conjunctivitis,' she said faintly.

'You poor darling! Is it infectious?' Mrs Howard asked all in one breath.

'It's the same as pinkeye,' Mrs Miller said.

'In a more virulent form,' Dolly Fisher added. 'Coffee,' she said to the waitress. 'Nothing to eat. What's that you've got, Laura?'

'A scone, dear,' Mrs Miller said.

'I thought you'd given it up.'

'Oh, I did – for at least three weeks. It didn't do any good.'

'A scone and butter,' Dolly Fisher said to the waitress when she brought the coffee.

'Wherever did you *pick that* up?' Mrs Miller went on, and her voice made the affliction sound very sordid indeed.

'I've been run down,' Dolly said.

'You don't get it from being run down. You pick it up.' Mrs Miller spread margarine over half a scone and popped it into her mouth.

'Oh, I'm late!' said Mrs Liddell. She put down her empty shopping basket and pulled up a chair. 'I haven't started yet. I wonder is there any fish about?'

'There *was* some halibut,' Mrs Miller said. 'I went for mine as soon as I'd taken Arthur to the station.'

'Oh, dear! Wasn't there anything else?'

'I seem to remember some sprats.'

'But, Dolly, dear! What *have* you done?'

'She's picked up pinkeye from somewhere,' Mrs Howard said. From somewhere not very nice, she implied.

Oedipus sat munching her scone. 'It's the worst pain I think I ever had,' she said defiantly.

The man at the corner table stood up hastily and called for his bill.

'Now what are you hiding from us?' Mrs Miller asked Mrs Liddell, who blushed and said, 'Oh, of course, none of you've seen it. Hughie gave it to me.'

She had been hiding nothing but had turned her hand a great deal in the light and now laid it in the middle of the table, as if she were pooling it.

'What a lovely ring!' they cried.

'For my birthday.' She drew it off and let it lie in the palm of her hand.

'Oh, do let me!' Mrs Miller begged. 'If my poor old hands aren't too fat.'

The ring was, after all, rather loose on her.

'It's so unusual!' Mrs Howard said. 'I wonder where on earth he got it.'

'It really has character,' Mrs Miller announced, after long consideration and turning her hand this way and that to catch the light. 'Yes, it really has. And it's *your* ring.' She passed it back to Mrs Liddell. 'Clever Hughie!'

'That will be the day,' Oedipus said, 'when Sidney gives me a ring for *my* birthday.'

'It's a very old ring, he said,' Mrs Liddell began.

'What of it?' Mrs Miller said generously. 'You will often get far better value with second-hand things.'

'Last year, he gave me a set of saucepans we had to have anyhow.'

'Cheer up, Dolly, we're all in the same boat. None of *our* husbands gives us rings.'

'I shall have to go,' Mrs Liddell said, finishing her coffee quickly. She had had her little triumph and now must hurry with it to the fishmonger's.

'I must come, too,' said Oedipus. They left together, and Dolly went off down the High Street toward the hills of Cithaeron.

'Well!' Mrs Miller said. 'Fancy Hughie!' She gave her famous laugh.

They looked at one another.

'It was a very beautiful ring,' said Mrs Graham, who always liked to be different.

Mrs Miller put down her cup. 'I wouldn't have it as a gift,' she said. 'Personally.'

Oasis of Gaiety

———⟨❧⟩———

AFTER luncheon Dosie took off her shoes and danced all round the room. Her feet were plump and arched, and the varnish on her toenails shone through her stockings.

Her mother was sitting on the floor playing roulette with some of her friends. She was always called Auntie except by Dosie, who 'darlinged' her in the tetchy manner of two women living in the same house, and by her son, Thomas, who stolidly said 'Mother', a *démodé* word, Auntie felt – half insulting.

On Sunday afternoons, most of Auntie's ' set' returned to their families when the midday champagne was finished. They scattered to the other houses round the golf course, to doze on loggias, snap at their children, and wonder where their gaiety had fled. Only Mrs Wilson, who was a widow and dreaded her empty house, Ricky Jimpson, and the goatish Fergy Burns stayed on. More intimate than a member of the family, more inside than a friend, Fergy supported Auntie's idea of herself better than anyone else did, and, at times and in ways that he knew she couldn't mind, he sided with Dosie and Thomas against her.

In some of the less remote parts of Surrey, where the nineteen-twenties are perpetuated, such pockets of stale and elderly gaiety remain. They are blank as the surrounding landscape of fir trees and tarnished water.

Sunshine, especially blinding to the players after so much champagne, slanted into the room, which looked preserved, sealed off. Pinkish-grey cretonnes, ruched cushions with tassels, piles of gramophone records, and a velvet Maurice Chevalier doll recalled the stage sets of those forgotten comedies about weekends in the country and domestic imbroglio.

Auntie's marmoset sat on the arm of a chair, looking down sadly at the players and eating grapes, which he peeled with delicate, worn fingers and sharp teeth. His name was Rizzio. Auntie loved to name her possessions, everything – her car (called the Bitch, a favourite word of her youth), her fur coat, the rather noisy cistern in the w.c. Even some of her old cardigans and shawls had nicknames and personalities. Her friends seemed not to find this tiresome. They played the game strenuously and sometimes sent Christmas presents to the inanimate objects. In exchange for all the fun and champagne they were required only to assist the fantasy and preserve the past. Auntie thought of herself as a 'sport' and a 'scream'. (No one knew how her nickname had originated, for neither niece nor nephew had ever appeared to substantiate it.) 'I did have a lovely heyday,' she would say in her husky voice. 'Girls of Dosie's age have never had anything.' But Dosie had had two husbands already, not to count the incidentals, as Thomas said.

Thomas was her much younger brother, something of an incidental flowering himself. 'Auntie's last bit of nonsense,' people called him. Fifteen years and their different worlds separated brother and sister. He was of a more serious generation and seemed curiously practical, disabused, unemotional. His military service was a life beyond their imagination. They (pitying him, though recoiling from him) vaguely envisaged hutted sites at Aldershot, and boorish figures at football on muddy playing fields with mists rising. Occasionally, at weekends, he arrived, wearing sour-smelling khaki, which seemed to rub almost raw his neck and wrists. He would clump into the pub in his great army boots and drink mild and bitter at his mother's expense, cagey about laying down a halfpenny of his own.

He made Fergy feel uneasy. Fergy had, Auntie often said, an impossible conscience. Watching bullocks being driven into a slaughterhouse had once taken him off steak for a month, and now, when he saw Thomas in khaki, he could only remember his own undergraduate days, gilded youth, fun with fireworks and chamber pots, débutantes arriving in May Week, driving his red MG to the Beetle and Wedge for the Sunday-morning session. But Thomas had no MG. He had only the 7.26 back to Aldershot. If he ever had any gaiety, his mother did not discover it: if he had any friends, he did not bring them forward. Auntie was, Fergy thought, a little mean with him, a little on the tight side. She used endearments to him, but as if in utter consternation. He was an uncouth cuckoo in her nest. His hands made excruciating sounds on the silk cushions. Often, in bars, she would slip him a pound to pay his way, yet here he was, this afternoon, making as neat and secret a little pile as one would wish to see.

He played with florins, doubling them slowly, giving change where required, tucking notes into the breast pocket of his battle-dress, carefully buttoning them away as if no one was to be trusted. He had a rather breathy concentration, as he had had as a child, crouching over snakes and ladders; his hands, scooping up the coins, looked, Auntie thought, like great paws.

Only Mrs Wilson's concentration could match his, but she had none of his stealthy deliberation. She had lost a packet, she proclaimed, but no one listened. She kept putting her hand in her bag and raking about, bringing out only a handkerchief, with which she touched the corner of her mouth. The others seemed to her quite indifferent to the fortunes of the game – Fergy, for instance, who was the banker, pushing Thomas's winnings across to him with no change of expression and no hesitation in his flow of talk.

Auntie gave a tiny glance of dislike at her son as he slipped some coins into his pocket. She could imagine him counting them all up, going back in the train. In her annoyance, she added a brutish look to his face. She sighed, but it was almost imperceptible and quite unperceived, the slightest intake of breath, as she glanced round at her friends, the darlings, who preserved her world, drinking her whisky, switching the radio away from the news to something gayer, and fortifying her against the dreary post-war world her son so typified. Mrs Wilson, also, was a little dreary. Although trying gallantly, she had no real flair for recklessness and easily became drunk, when she would talk about her late husband and what a nice home they had had.

'Oh, Dosie, do sit down!' Auntie said.

Dosie was another who could not drink. She would become gayer and gayer and more and more taunting to poor Ricky Jimpson. Now she was dancing on his winnings. He smiled wanly. After the game, he would happily give her the lot, but while he was playing, it was sacred.

What Dosie herself gave for all she had from him was something to conjecture. Speculation, beginning with the obviously shameful, had latterly run into a maze of contradictions. Perhaps – and this was even more derogatory – she *did* only bestow taunts and abuse. She behaved like a very wilful child, as if to underline the fact that Ricky was old enough to be her father. Rather grey-faced (he had, he thought, a duodenal ulcer, and the vast quantity of whisky he drank was agony to him), he would sit and smile at her naughty ways, and sometimes when she clapped her hands, as if she pretended he was her slave, he would show that this was not pretence but very truth, and hurry to carry out her wishes.

Dosie, with one hand on the piano to steady herself, went through some of the *barre* exercises she had learned as a child at ballet class. Her joints snapped and crackled with a sound like a fire kindling.

'You are a deadly lot,' she suddenly said, and yawned out at the garden. 'Put ten shillings on *rouge* for me, Ricky. I always win if you do it.'

At least she doesn't lose if it isn't her money, Mrs Wilson thought, wondering if she could ever, in a rallying way, make such a request of Fergy.

The hot afternoon, following the champagne, made them all drowsy. Only Ricky Jimpson sat up trimly. Fergy, looking at Mrs Wilson's bosom, which her *décolleté* blouse too generously tendered, thought that in no time it would be all she had to offer. He imagined her placing it on, perhaps *zéro* – her last gesture.

Quite frightful, Auntie thought, the way Thomas's brow furrowed because he had lost two shillings. He was transparently sulky, like a little boy. All those baked beans in canteens made him stodgy and impossible. She hadn't visualised having such a son, or such a world for him to live in.

'We can really do nothing for young people,' she had once told Mrs Wilson. 'Nothing, nowadays, but try to preserve for them some of the old days, keep up our standards and give them an inkling of what things used to be, make a little oasis of gaiety for them.' That had been during what she called 'the late war'. Thomas was home from school for the Christmas holidays. With tarnished pre-war tinsel Auntie was decorating the Christmas tree, though to this, as to most things, Thomas was quite indifferent. He had spent the holidays bicycling slowly round and round the lawn on the white, rimed grass. In the evenings, when his mother's friends came for drinks, he collected his books and went noticeably to his room. The books, on mathematics, were dull but mercifully concerned with things as they were, and this he preferred to all the talk about the tarnished, pre-war days. He could not feel that the present day was any of his doing. For the grown-ups to scorn what they had bequeathed to him seemed tactless. He ignored those conversations until his face looked mulish and immune. His mother arranged for his adenoids to be removed, but he continued to be closed-up and unresponsive.

Dosie was so different; she might almost be called a ring-leader. She made her mother feel younger than ever – 'really more like a sister,' Auntie said, showing that this was a joke by saying it with a Cockney accent. Oh, Dosie was the liveliest girl, except that sometimes she went too far. The oasis of gaiety her mother provided became obviously too small and she was inclined then to go off into the desert and cry havoc. But Auntie thought her daughter mischievous, not desperate.

'Either play or not,' she told her sharply, for sometimes the girl irritated her.

But Dosie, at the french windows, took no notice. She could feel the sun striking through her thin frock, and she seemed to unfold in the warmth, like a flower. In the borders, lilies stood to attention in the shimmering air, their petals glazed and dusty with pollen. The scent was wonderful.

'I shall bathe in the pool,' she said, over her shoulder. The pool – a long rectangle of water thick with plants – was deep and Dosie had never learned to swim, had always floundered wildly.

Only Ricky Jimpson remonstrated.

'She can't swim,' Auntie said, dismissing her daughter's nonsense. 'Does anyone *want* to go on playing?'

Mrs Wilson certainly did not. She had never believed in last desperate flings, throwing good money after bad. In games of chance there was no certainty but that she would lose; even the law of averages worked against her.

What she wanted now was a cup of tea and aspirins, for champagne agreed with her no better than roulette. She felt lost. Her widowhood undermined her and she no longer felt loved.

But who was loved – in this room, for instance? Mrs Wilson often thought that her husband would not have dared to die if he had known she would drift into such company. 'What *you* need, darling, is a nice, cosy woman friend,' Fergy had said years ago when she had reacted in bewilderment to his automatic embrace. He had relinquished her at once, in a weary, bored way, and ignored her coldly ever since. His heartless perception frightened her. Despite her acceptance of – even clinging to – their kind of life, and her acquiescence in every madness, every racket, she had not disguised from him that what she wanted was her dull, good husband back and a nice evening with the wireless; perhaps, too, a middle-aged woman friend to go shopping with, to talk about slimming and recipes. Auntie never discussed those things. She was the kind of woman men liked. She amused them with her scatter-brained chatter and innuendo and the fantasy she wove, the stories she told, about herself. When she was with women, she rested. Mrs Wilson could not imagine her feeling unsafe, or panicking when the house emptied. She seemed self-reliant and efficient. She and Dosie sometimes quarrelled, or appeared to be quarrelling, with lots of 'But, *darling*!' and '*Must* you be such a fool, sweetie?' Yet only Thomas, the symbol of the post-war world, was really an affront. Him she could not assimilate. He was the grit that nothing turned into a pearl – neither gaiety nor champagne. He remained blank, impervious. He took his life quite seriously, made no jokes about the army, was silent when his mother said, 'Oh, *why* go? Catch the last train or wait until morning. In fact, why don't you desert? Dosie and I could hide you in the attic. It would be the greatest fun. Or be ill. Get some awful soldier's disease.'

Dosie was blocking the sunlight from the room, and Mrs Wilson suddenly felt goose flesh on her arms and cramp in her legs from sitting on the floor.

Ricky Jimpson put his winnings in his pocket without a glance at them. He sat, bent slightly forward, with one hand pressed to his waist. He smiled brilliantly if he caught anybody's eye, but his face soon reassembled itself to its look of static melancholy. The smile was an abrupt disorganisation. His eyes rarely followed Dosie. He seemed rather to be listening to her, even when she was silent. He was conscious of her in some other way than visually. His spirit *attended* to her, caught up in pain though he was.

The roulette cloth was folded and put away. The marmoset was busy tearing one of the cushion tassels. Then, to Mrs Wilson's relief, the door opened and a maid pushed in a trolley with a jazzy black and orange pottery tea-set and some rolled-up bread and butter.

Dosie wandered out across the gravelled path in her stockinged feet. The garden, the golf course beyond it, and all the other wistaria-covered, balconied Edwardian villas at its perimeter seemed to slant and swoon in the heat. Her exasperation weakened and dispersed. She always felt herself leaving other people behind; they lagged after her recklessness. Even in making love, she felt the same isolation – that she was speeding on into a country where no one would pursue her. Each kiss was an act of division. 'Follow me!' she willed 'them' – a succession of them, all shadowy. They could not follow, or know to what cold distances she withdrew. Her punishment for them was mischief, spite, a little gay cruelty, but nothing drastic. She had no beauty, for there was none to inherit, but she was a bold and noticeable woman.

When Fergy joined her in the garden, he put his arm across her shoulders and they walked down the path towards the pool. Water-lilies lay picturesquely on the green surface. The oblong of water was bordered by ornamental grasses in which dragonflies glinted. A concrete gnome was fishing at the edge.

They stood looking at the water, lulled by the heat and the beauty of the afternoon. When he slipped his arm closer round her, she felt herself preparing, as of old, for flight. Waywardly, she moved from him. She stripped seeds off a tall grass, viciously, and scattered them on the water. Goldfish rose, then sank away dejectedly.

'Let us throw in this bloody little dwarf,' Dosie said, 'and you can cry for help. They will think I am drowning.' She began to rock the gnome from side to side. Small brown frogs like crumpled leaves leapt away into the grass.

'Auntie dotes on the little creature,' Fergy said. 'She has a special nickname for him.'

'So have I.'

Together they lifted the gnome and threw him out towards the centre of the pool.

'I always loathed the little beast,' Dosie said.

'Help!' Fergy cried. 'For *God's* sake, help!'

Dosie watched the house, her face alight, her eyebrows lifted in anticipation. Rings widened and faded on the water.

Ricky Jimpson dashed through the french windows and ran towards the pool, his face whiter than ever, his hand to his side. When he saw them both standing there, he stopped. His look of desperation vanished. He smiled his brilliant, dutiful smile, but, receiving one of his rare glances, Dosie saw in his eyes utter affliction, forlornness.

That evening, Thomas, on his way back to Aldershot, met Syd at the top of the station subway; as per usual arrangement, Syd had said when they parted the day before. Their greeting was brief and they went in silence towards the restaurant, shouldering their way along the crowded platform. In the bar, they ordered two halves of mild and bitter and two pieces of pork pie.

Syd pushed back his greasy beret and scratched his head. Then he broke open the pie to examine the inside – the pink gristle and tough grey jelly.

'What they been up to this time?' he asked.

'The usual capering about. My mother was rather lit up last night and kept doing the Charleston.'

'Go on!'

'But I suppose that's better than the Highland fling,' Thomas said. 'Pass the mustard.'

Syd, whose own mother rarely moved more than, very ponderously, from sink to gas stove, was fascinated. 'Like to've seen it,' he said. 'From a distance.'

'What did you do?' Thomas asked.

'Went to the Palais Saturday night along with Viv. Never got up till twelve this morning, then went round the local. Bit of a read this afternoon, then went for a stroll along with Viv. You know, up by the allotments. Had a nice lie down in the long grass. She put her elbow in a cow pat. Laugh!' He threw back his head and laughed there and then.

'Same again,' Thomas said to the barmaid. 'Want some more pie, Syd?'

'No, ta. I had me tea.'

'I made thirty-four bob,' Thomas said, tapping his breast pocket.

'You can make mine a pint then,' Syd said. But Thomas didn't say anything. They always drank halves. He looked at Syd and wondered what his mother would say of him. He often wondered that. But she would never have the chance. He looked quite fiercely round the ugly restaurant room, with its chromium tables, ringed and sticky, thick china, glass domes over the museum pieces of pork pie. The look of the place calmed him, as Syd's company did – something he could grasp, *his* world.

'Don't know how they stick that life, week after week,' Thomas said. 'My sister threw a garden ornament in the

pond – pretended she'd fallen in herself. A sort of dwarf,'
he added vaguely.

'What for?' Syd asked.

'I think she was fed up,' Thomas said, trying to understand. But he lived in two irreconcilable worlds.

Syd only said, 'Rum. Could they fish it out again?'

'No one tried. We had tea then.' He gave up trying to
explain what he did not comprehend, and finished his beer.

'Better get a move on,' Syd said, using as few consonants
as possible.

'Yes, I suppose so.' Thomas looked at the clock.

'The old familiar faces.'

'You're right,' Thomas agreed contentedly.

from *The Blush*

The Blush

THEY were the same age – Mrs Allen and the woman
who came every day to do the housework. 'I shall never
have children now,' Mrs Allen had begun to tell herself.
Something had not come true; the essential part of her
life. She had always imagined her children in fleeting scenes
and intimations; that was how they had come to her, like
snatches of a film. She had seen them plainly, their chins
tilted up as she tied on their bibs at meal-times; their naked
bodies had darted in and out of the water sprinkler on the
lawn; and she had listened to their voices in the garden and
in the mornings from their beds. She had even cried a little
dreaming of the day when the eldest boy would go off to
boarding school; she pictured the train going out of the
station; she raised her hand and her throat contracted and
her lips trembled as she smiled. The years passing by had
slowly filched from her the reality of these scenes – the gay
sounds; the grave peace she had longed for; even the pride
of grief.

She listened – as they worked together in the kitchen –

to Mrs Lacey's troubles with her family, her grumblings about her grown-up son who would not get up till dinner-time on Sundays and then expected his mother to have cleaned his shoes for him; about the girl of eighteen who was a hairdresser and too full of dainty ways which she picked up from the women's magazines, and the adolescent girl who moped and glowered and answered back.

My children wouldn't have turned out like that, Mrs Allen thought, as she made her murmured replies. 'The more you do for some, the more you may,' said Mrs Lacey. But from gossip in the village which Mrs Allen heard, she had done all too little. The children, one night after another, for years and years, had had to run out for parcels of fish and chips while their mother sat in the Horse & Jockey drinking brown ale. On summer evenings, when they were younger, they had hung about outside the pub: when they were bored they pressed their foreheads to the window and looked in at the dark little bar, hearing the jolly laughter, their mother's the loudest of all. Seeing their faces, she would swing at once from the violence of hilarity to that of extreme annoyance and although ginger beer and packets of potato crisps would be handed out through the window, her anger went out with them and threatened the children as they ate and drank.

'And she doesn't always care who she goes there *with*,' Mrs Allen's gardener told her.

'She works hard and deserves a little pleasure – she has her anxieties,' said Mrs Allen, who, alas, had none.

She had never been inside the Horse & Jockey, although it was nearer to her house than the Chequers at the other end of the village where she and her husband went some-times for a glass of sherry on Sunday mornings. The Horse & Jockey attracted a different set of customers – for instance, people who sat down and drank, at tables all round the wall. At the Chequers no one ever sat down, but stood and sipped and chatted as at a cocktail party, and luncheons and dinners were served, which made it so much more respectable: no children hung about outside, because they were all at home with their nannies.

Sometimes in the evening – so many of them – when her husband was kept late in London, Mrs Allen wished that she could go down to The Chequers and drink a glass of sherry and exchange a little conversation with someone; but she was too shy to open the door and go in alone: she imagined heads turning, a surprised welcome from her friends, who would all be safely in married pairs; and then, when she left, eyes meeting with unspoken messages and conjecture in the air.

Mrs Lacey left her at midday and then there was gardening to do and the dog to be taken for a walk. After six o'clock, she began to pace restlessly about the house, glancing at the clocks in one room after another, listening for her husband's car – the sound she knew so well because she had awaited it for such a large part of her married life. She would hear, at last, the tyres turning on the soft gravel, the door being slammed, then his footsteps hurrying towards the porch. She knew that it was a wasteful way of spending her years – and, looking back, she was unable to tell one of them from another – but she could not think what else she might do. Humphrey went on earning more and more money and there was no stopping him now. Her acquaintances, in wretched quandaries about where the next term's school fees were to come from, would turn to her and say cruelly: 'Oh, *you're* all right, Ruth. You've no idea what you are spared.'

And Mrs Lacey would be glad when Maureen could leave school and 'get out earning'. '"I've got my geometry to do," she says, when it's time to wash up the tea things. "I'll geometry you, my girl," I said. "When I was your age, I was out earning."'

Mrs Allen was fascinated by the life going on in that house and the children seemed real to her, although she had never seen them. Only Mr Lacey remained blurred and unimaginable. No one knew him. He worked in the town in the valley, six miles away and he kept himself to himself; had never been known to show his face in the Horse & Jockey. 'I've got my own set,' Mrs Lacey said airily. 'After all, he's nearly twenty years older than me. I'll make sure neither of my girls follow my mistake. "I'd rather see you dead at my feet," I said to Vera.' Ron's young lady was lucky; having Ron, she added. Mrs Allen found this strange, for Ron had always been painted so black; was, she had been led to believe, oafish, ungrateful, greedy and slow to put his hands in his pockets if there was any paying out to do. There was also the matter of his shoe-cleaning, for no young woman would do what his mother did for him – or said she did. Always, Mrs Lacey would sigh and say: 'Goodness me, if only I was their age and knew what I know now.'

She was an envious woman: she envied Mrs Allen her pretty house and her clothes and she envied her own daughters their youth. 'If I had your figure,' she would say to Mrs Allen. Her own had gone: what else could be expected, she asked, when she had had three children? Mrs Allen thought, too, of all the brown ale she drank at the Horse & Jockey and of the reminiscences of meals past which came so much into her conversations. Whatever the cause was, her flesh, slackly corseted, shook as she trod heavily about the kitchen. In summer, with bare arms and legs she looked larger than ever. Although her skin was very white, the impression she gave was at once colourful – from her orange hair and bright lips and the floral patterns that she always wore. Her red-painted toenails poked through the straps of her fancy sandals; turquoise-blue beads were wound round her throat.

Humphrey Allen had never seen her; he had always left for the station before she arrived, and that was a good thing, his wife thought. When she spoke of Mrs Lacey, she wondered if he visualised a neat, homely woman in a clean white overall. She did not deliberately mislead him, but she took advantage of his indifference. Her relationship with Mrs Lacey and the intimacy of their conversations in the kitchen he would not have approved, and the sight of those calloused feet with their chipped nail varnish and yellowing heels would have sickened him.

One Monday morning, Mrs Lacey was later than usual. She was never very punctual and had many excuses about flat bicycle tyres or Maureen being poorly. Mrs Allen, waiting for her, sorted out all the washing. When she took another look at the clock, she decided that it was far too late for her to be expected at all. For some time lately Mrs Lacey had seemed ill and depressed; her eyelids, which were chronically rather inflamed, had been more angrily red than ever and, at the sink or ironing board, she would fall into unusual silences, was absent-minded and full of sighs. She had always liked to talk about the 'change' and did so more than ever as if with a desperate hopefulness.

'I'm sorry, but I was ever so sick,' she told Mrs Allen, when she arrived the next morning. 'I still feel queerish. Such heartburn. I don't like the signs, I can tell you. All I crave is pickled walnuts, just the same as I did with Maureen. I don't like the signs one bit. I feel I'll throw myself into the river if I'm taken that way again.'

Mrs Allen felt stunned and antagonistic. 'Surely not at your age,' she said crossly.

'You can't be more astonished than me,' Mrs Lacey said, belching loudly. 'Oh, pardon. I'm afraid I can't help myself.'

Not being able to help herself, she continued to belch and hiccough as she turned on taps and shook soap powder into the washing-up bowl. It was because of this that Mrs Allen decided to take the dog for a walk. Feeling consciously fastidious and aloof she made her way across the fields, trying to disengage her thoughts from Mrs Lacey and her troubles; but unable to. Poor woman, she thought again and again with bitter animosity.

She turned back when she noticed how the sky had darkened with racing, sharp-edged clouds. Before she could reach home, the rain began. Her hair, soaking wet, shrank into tight curls against her head; her woollen suit smelt like a damp animal. 'Oh, I am drenched,' she called out, as she threw open the kitchen door.

She knew at once that Mrs Lacey had gone, that she must have put on her coat and left almost as soon as Mrs Allen had started out on her walk, for nothing was done; the washing-up was hardly started and the floor was unswept. Among the stacked-up crockery a note was propped; she had come over funny, felt dizzy and, leaving her apologies and respects, had gone.

Angrily, but methodically, Mrs Allen set about making good the wasted morning. By afternoon, the grim look was fixed upon her face. 'How dare she?' she found herself whispering, without allowing herself to wonder what it was the woman had dared.

She had her own little ways of cosseting herself through the lonely hours, comforts which were growing more important to her as she grew older, so that the time would come when not to have her cup of tea at four-thirty would seem a prelude to disaster. This afternoon, disorganised as it already was, she fell out of her usual habit and instead of carrying the tray to the low table by the fire, she poured out her tea in the kitchen and drank it there, leaning tiredly against the dresser. Then she went upstairs to make herself tidy. She was trying to brush her frizzed hair smooth again when she heard the doorbell ringing.

When she opened the door, she saw quite plainly a look of astonishment take the place of anxiety on the man's face. Something about herself surprised him, was not what he had expected. 'Mrs Allen?' he asked uncertainly and the astonishment remained when she had answered him.

'Well, I'm calling about the wife,' he said. 'Mrs Lacey that works here.'

'I was worried about her,' said Mrs Allen.

She knew that she must face the embarrassment of hearing about Mrs Lacey's condition and invited the man into her husband's study, where she thought he might look less out of place than in her brocade-smothered drawing-room. He looked about him resentfully and glared down at the floor which his wife had polished. With this thought in his mind, he said abruptly: 'It's all taken its toll.'

He sat down on a leather couch with his cap and his bicycle clips beside him.

'I came home to my tea and found her in bed, crying,' he said. This was true. Mrs Lacey had succumbed to despair and gone to lie down. Feeling better at four o'clock, she went downstairs to find some food to comfort herself with; but the slice of dough cake was ill-chosen and brought on more heartburn and floods of bitter tears.

'If she carries on here for a while, it's all got to be very different,' Mr Lacey said threateningly. He was nervous at saying what he must and could only bring out the words with the impetus of anger. 'You may or may not know that she's expecting.'

'Yes,' said Mrs Allen humbly. 'This morning she told me that she thought. . . . '

'There's no "thought" about it. It's as plain as a pike-staff.' Yet in his eyes she could see disbelief and bafflement and he frowned and looked down again at the polished floor.

Twenty years older than his wife – or so his wife had said – he really, to Mrs Allen, looked quite ageless, a crooked, bow-legged little man who might have been a jockey once. The expression about his blue eyes was like a child's: he was both stubborn and pathetic.

Mrs Allen's fat spaniel came into the room and went straight to the stranger's chair and began to sniff at his corduroy trousers.

'It's too much for her,' Mr Lacey said. 'It's too much to expect.'

To Mrs Allen's horror she saw the blue eyes filling with tears. Hoping to hide his emotion, he bent down and fondled the dog, making playful thrusts at it with his fist closed.

He was a man utterly, bewilderedly at sea. His married life had been too much for him, with so much in it that he could not understand.

'Now I know, I will do what I can,' Mrs Allen told him. 'I will try to get someone else in to do the rough.'

'It's the late nights that are the trouble,' he said. 'She comes in dog-tired. Night after night. It's not good enough. "Let them stay at home and mind their own children once in a while," I told her. "We don't need the money."'

'I can't understand,' Mrs Allen began. She was at sea herself now, but felt perilously near a barbarous, unknown shore and was afraid to make any movement towards it.

'I earn good money. For her to come out at all was only for extras. She likes new clothes. In the daytimes I never had any objection. Then all these cocktail parties begin. It beats me how people can drink like it night after night and pay out for someone else to mind their kids. Perhaps you're thinking that it's not my business, but I'm the one who has to sit at home alone till all hours and get my own supper and see next to nothing of my wife. I'm boiling over some nights. Once I nearly rushed out when I heard the car stop down the road. I wanted to tell your husband what I thought of you both.'

'My husband?' murmured Mrs Allen.

'What am I supposed to have, I would have asked him? Is she my wife or your sitter-in? Bringing her back at this time of night. And it's no use saying she could have refused. She never would.'

Mrs Allen's quietness at last defeated him and dispelled the anger he had tried to rouse in himself. The look of her,

too, filled him with doubts, her grave, uncertain demeanour
and the shock her age had been to him. He had imagined
someone so much younger and – because of the cocktail
parties – flighty. Instead, he recognised something of himself in her, a yearning disappointment. He picked up his cap
and his bicycle clips and sat looking down at them, turning
them round in his hands. 'I had to come,' he said.

'Yes,' said Mrs Allen.

'So you won't ask her again?' he pleaded. 'It isn't right
for her. Not now.'

'No, I won't,' Mrs Allen promised and she stood up as
he did and walked over to the door. He stooped and gave
the spaniel a final pat. 'You'll excuse my coming, I hope.'

'Of course.'

'It was no use saying any more to her. Whatever she's
asked, she won't refuse. It's her way.'

Mrs Allen shut the front door after him and stood in the
hall, listening to him wheeling his bicycle across the gravel.
Then she felt herself beginning to blush. She was glad that
she was alone, for she could feel her face, her throat,
even the tops of her arms burning, and she went over to a
looking glass and studied with great interest this strange
phenomenon.

The Letter-Writers

AT eleven o'clock, Emily went down to the village to fetch the lobsters. The heat unsteadied the air, light shimmered and glanced off leaves and telegraph wires and the flag on the church tower spreading out in a small breeze, then dropping, wavered against the sky, as if it were flapping under water.

She wore an old cotton frock, and meant to change it at the last moment, when the food was all ready and the table laid. Over her bare arms, the warm air flowed, her skirt seemed to divide as she walked, pressed in a hollow between her legs, like drapery on a statue. The sun seemed to touch her bones – her spine, her shoulder blades, her skull. In her thoughts, she walked nakedly, picking her way, over dry-as-dust cow dung, along the lane. All over the hedges, trumpets of large white convolvulus were turned upwards towards the sky – the first flowers she could remember; something about them had, in her early childhood, surprised her with astonishment and awe, a sense of magic that had lasted, like so little else, repeating itself again and again, most of the summers of her forty years.

From the wide-open windows of the village school came the sound of a tinny piano. 'We'll rant, and we'll roar, like true British sailors,' sang all the little girls.

Emily, smiling to herself as she passed by, had thoughts so delightful that she began to tidy them into sentences to put in a letter to Edmund. Her days were not full or busy and the gathering-in of little things to write to him about took up a large part of her time. She would have made a paragraph or two about the children singing, the hot weather – so rare in England – the scent of the lime and privet blossom, the pieces of tin glinting among the branches of the cherry trees. But the instinctive thought was at once checked by the truth that there would be no letter-writing that evening after all. She stood before an alarming crisis, one that she had hoped to avoid for as long as ever she lived; the crisis of meeting for the first time the person whom she knew best in the world.

'What will he be like?' did not worry her. She knew what he was like. If he turned out differently, it would be a mistake. She would be getting a false impression of him and she would know that it was temporary and would fade. She was more afraid of herself, and wondered if he would know how to discount the temporary, and false, in her. Too much was at stake and, for herself, she would not have taken the risk. 'I agree that we have gone beyond meeting now. It would be retracing our steps,' he had once written to her. 'Although, perhaps if we were ever in the same country, it would be absurd to make a point of *not* meeting.' This, however, was what she had done when she went to Italy the next year.

In Rome, some instinct of self-preservation kept her from giving him her aunt's address there. She would telephone, she thought; but each time she tried to – her heart banging erratically within a suddenly hollow breast – she was checked by thoughts of the booby trap lying before her. In the end, she skirted it. She discovered the little street where he lived, and felt the strangeness of reading its name, which she had written hundreds of times on envelopes. Walking past his house on the opposite pavement, she had glanced timidly at the peeling apricot-coloured plaster. The truth of the situation made her feel quite faint. It was frightening, like seeing a ghost in reverse – the insubstantial suddenly solidifying into a patchy and shabby reality. At the window on the first floor, one of the shutters was open; there was the darkness of the room beyond, an edge of yellow curtain and, hanging over the back of a chair set near the window, what looked like a white skirt. Even if Edmund himself threw open the other shutter and came out on to the balcony, he would never have known that the woman across the road was one of his dearest friends, but, all the same, she hastened away from the neighbourhood. At dinner, her aunt thought she might be ill. Her visitors from England so often were – from the heat and sight-seeing and the change of diet.

The odd thing to Emily about the escapade was its vanishing from her mind – the house became its own ghost again, the house of her imagination, lying on the other side of the road, where she had always pictured it, with its plaster unspoilt and Edmund inside in his tidied-up room, writing to her.

He had not chided her when she sent a letter from a safer place, explaining her lack of courage – and explain it she could, so fluently, half touchingly yet wholly amusingly – on paper. He teased her gently, understanding her decision. In him, curiosity and adventurousness would have overcome his hesitation. Disillusionment would have deprived him of less than it might have deprived her; her letters were a relaxation to him; to her, his were an excitement, and her fingers often trembled as she tore open their envelopes.

They had written to one another for ten years. She had admired his novels since she was a young woman, but would not have thought of writing to tell him so; that he could conceivably be interested in the opinion of a complete stranger did not occur to her. Yet, sometimes, she felt that without her as their reader the novels could not have had a fair existence. She was so sensitive to what he wrote, that she felt her own reading half created it. Her triumph at the end of each book had something added of a sense of accomplishment on her part. She felt it, to a lesser degree, with some other writers, but they were dead; if they had been living, she would not have written to them, either.

Then one day she read in a magazine an essay he had written about the boyhood of Tennyson. His conjecture on some point she could confirm, for she had letters from one of the poet's brothers. She looked for them among her grandfather's papers and (she was never impulsive save when the impulse was generosity) sent them to Edmund, with a little note to tell him that they were a present to repay some of the pleasure his books had given her.

Edmund, who loved old letters and papers of every kind, found these especially delightful. So the first of many letters from him came to her, beginning, 'Dear Miss Fairchild'. His handwriting was very large and untidy and difficult to decipher, and this always pleased her, because his letters took longer to read; the enjoyment was drawn out, and often a word or two had to be puzzled over for days. Back, again and again, she would go to the letter, trying to take the problem by surprise – and that was usually how she solved it.

Sometimes, she wondered why he wrote to her – and was flattered when he asked for a letter to cheer him up when he was depressed, or to calm him when he was unhappy. Although he could not any longer work well in England – for a dullness came over him, from the climate and old, vexatious associations – he still liked to have some foothold there, and Emily's letters refreshed his memories.

At first, he thought her a novelist *manqué*, then he realised that letter-writing is an art by itself, a different kind of skill, though, with perhaps a similar motive – and one at which Englishwomen have excelled.

As she wrote, the landscape, flowers, children, cats and dogs, sprang to life memorably. He knew her neighbours and her relation to them, and also knew people, who were dead now, whom she had loved. He called them by their Christian names when he wrote to her and re-evoked them for her, so that, being allowed àt last to mention them, she felt that they became light and free again in her mind, and not an intolerable suppression, as they had been for years.

Coming to the village, on this hot morning, she was more agitated than she could ever remember being, and she began to blame Edmund for creating such an ordeal. She was angry with herself for acquiescing, when he had suggested that he, being at last in England for a week or two, should come to see her. 'For an hour, or three at most. I want to look at the flowers in the *very* garden, and stroke the cat, and peep between the curtains at Mrs Waterlow going by.'

He knows too much about me, so where can we begin? she wondered. She had confided such intimacies in him. At that distance, he was as safe as the confessional, with the added freedom from hearing any words said aloud. She had written to his mind only. He seemed to have no face, and certainly no voice. Although photographs had once passed between them, they had seemed meaningless.

She had been so safe with him. They could not have wounded one another, but now they might. In *ten* years, there had been no inadvertent hurts, of rivalry, jealousy, or neglect. It had not occurred to either to wonder if the other would sometimes cease to write; the letters would come, as surely as the sun.

But will they now? Emily was wondering.

She turned the familiar bend of the road and the sea lay glittering below – its wrinkled surface looking solid and without movement, like a great sheet of metal. Now and

then a light breeze came off the water and rasped together
the dried grasses on the banks; when it dropped, the late
morning silence held, drugging the brain and slowing the
limbs.

For years, Emily had looked into mirrors only to see if her
hair were tidy or her petticoat showing below her dress.
This morning, she tried to take herself by surprise, to see
herself as a stranger might, but failed.

He would expect a younger woman from the photograph
of some years back. Since that was taken, wings of white
hair at her temples had given her a different appearance.
The photograph would not, in any case, show how poor
her complexion was, unevenly pitted, from an illness when
she was a child. As a girl, she had looked at her reflection
and thought, No one will ever want to marry me, and no
one had.

When she went back to the living-room, the cat was
walking about, smelling lobster in the air; balked, troubled
by desire, he went restlessly about the little room, the pupils
of his eyes two thin lines of suspicion and contempt. But the
lobster was high up on the dresser, above the Rockingham
cups, and covered with a piece of muslin.

Emily went over to the table and touched the knives and
forks, shook the salt in the cellar nicely level, lifted a wine
glass to the light. She poured out a glass of sherry and
stood, well back from the window – looking out between
hollyhocks at the lane.

Unless the train was late, he should be there. At any
moment, the station taxi would come slowly along the lane
and stop, with terrible inevitability, outside the cottage. She
wondered how tall he was – how would he measure against
the hollyhocks? Would he be obliged to stoop under the
low oak beams?

The sherry heartened her a little – at least, her hands

stopped shaking – and she filled her glass again. The wine was cooling in a bucket down the well and she thought that perhaps it was time to fetch it in, or it might be too cold to taste.

The well had pretty little ferns of a very bright green growing out of the bricks at its sides, and when she lifted the cover, the ice-cold air struck her. She was unused to drinking much, and the glasses of sherry had, first, steadied her; then, almost numbed her. With difficulty, she drew up the bucket; but her movements were clumsy and uncertain, and greenish slime came off the rope on to her clean dress. Her hair fell forward untidily. Far, far below, as if at the wrong end of a telescope, she saw her own tiny face looking back at her. As she was taking the bottle of wine from the bucket, she heard a crash inside the cottage.

She knew what must have happened, but she felt too muddled to act quickly. When she opened the door of the living-room she saw, as she expected, the cat and the lobster and the Rockingham cups spread in disorder about the floor.

She grabbed the cat first – though the damage was done now – and ran to the front door to throw him out into the garden; but, opening the door, was confronted by Edmund, whose arm was raised, just about to pull on the old iron bell. At the sight of the distraught woman with untidy hair and her eyes full of tears, he took a pace back.

'There's no lunch,' she said quickly. 'Nothing.' The cat struggled against her shoulder, frantic for the remains of the lobster, and a long scratch slowly ripened across her cheek; then the cat bounded from her and sat down behind the hollyhocks to wash his paws.

'How do you do,' Emily said. She took her hand away from his almost as soon as she touched him and put it up to her cheek, brushing blood across her face.

'Let us go in and bathe you,' he suggested.

'Oh, no please don't bother. It is nothing at all. But, yes, of course, come in. I'm afraid . . . ' She was incoherent and he could not follow what she was saying.

At the sight of the lobster and the china on the floor, he understood a little. All the same, she seemed to him to be rather drunk.

'Such wonderful cups and saucers,' he said, going down on his knees and filling his hands with fragments. 'I don't know how you can bear it.'

'It's nothing. It doesn't matter. It's the lobster that matters. There is nothing else in the house.'

'Eggs?' he suggested.

'I don't get the eggs till Friday,' she said wildly.

'Well, cheese.'

'It's gone hard and sweaty. The weather's so . . . '

'Not that it isn't too hot to eat anything,' he said quickly. 'Hotter than Rome. And I was longing for an English drizzle.'

'We had a little shower on Monday evening. Did you get that in London?'

'Monday? No, Sunday we had a few spots.'

'It was Monday here, I remember. The gardens needed it, but it didn't do much good.'

He looked round for somewhere to put the broken china. 'No, I suppose not.'

'It hardly penetrated. Do put that in the waste-paper basket.'

'This cup is fairly neatly broken in half, it could be riveted. I can take it back to London with me.'

'I won't hear of it. But it is so kind . . . I suppose the cat may as well have the remains of this – though not straight away. He must be shown that I am cross with him. Oh, dear, and I fetched it last thing from the village so that it should be fresh. But that's not much use to you, as it's turned out.'

She disappeared into the kitchen with her hands full of lobster shells.

He looked round the room and so much of it seemed familiar to him. A stout woman passing by in the lane and trying to see in through the window might be Mrs Waterlow herself, who came so amusingly into Emily's letters.

He hoped things were soon going to get better, for he had never seen anyone so distracted as Emily when he arrived. He had been prepared for shyness, and had thought he could deal with that, but her frenzied look, with the blood on her face and the bits of lobster in her hands, made him feel that he had done some damage which, like the china, was quite beyond his repairing.

She was a long time gone, but shouted from the kitchen that he must take a glass of sherry, as he was glad to do.

'May I bring some out to you?' he asked.

'No, no thank you. Just pour it out and I will come.'

When she returned at last, he saw that she had washed her face and combed her hair. What the great stain all across her skirt was, he could not guess. She was carrying a little dish of sardines, all neatly wedged together as they had been lying in their tin.

'It is so dreadful,' she began. 'You will never forget being given a tin of sardines, but they will go better with the wine than the baled beans, which is the only other thing I can find.'

'I am *very* fond of sardines,' he said.

She put the dish on the table and then, for the first time, looked at him. He was of medium height after all, with broader shoulders than she had imagined. His hair was a surprise to her. From his photograph, she had imagined it white – he was, after all, ten years older than she – but instead, it was blond and bleached by the sun. And I always thought I was writing to a white-haired man, she thought.

Her look lasted only a second or two and then she drank her sherry quickly, with her eyes cast down.

'I hope you forgive me for coming here,' he said gravely.

Only by seriousness could he hope to bring them back to the relationship in which they really stood. He approached her so fearfully, but she shied away.

'Of course,' she said. 'It is *so* nice. After all these years. But I am sure you must be starving. Will you sit here?'

How are we to continue? he wondered.

She was garrulous with small talk through lunch, pausing only to take up her wine glass. Then, at the end, when she had handed him his coffee, she failed. There was no more to say, not a word more to be wrung out of the weather, or the restaurant in Rome they had found they had in common, or the annoyances of travel – the train that was late and the cabin that was stuffy. Worn out, she still cast about for a subject to embark on. The silence was unendurable. If it continued, might he not suddenly say, 'You are so different from all I had imagined', or their eyes might meet and they would see in one another's nakedness and total loss.

'I *did* say Wednesday,' said Mrs Waterlow.

'No, Thursday,' Emily insisted. If she could not bar the doorway with forbidding arms, she did so with malevolent thoughts. Gentle and patient neighbour she had always been and Mrs Waterlow, who had the sharp nose of the total abstainer and could smell alcohol on Emily's breath, was quite astonished.

The front door of the cottage opened straight into the living-room and Edmund was exposed to Mrs Waterlow, sitting forward in his chair, staring into a coffee cup.

'I'll just leave the poster for the jumble sale then,' said Mrs Waterlow. 'We shall have to talk about the refreshments another time. I think, don't you, that half a pound of tea does fifty people. Mrs Harris will see to the slab cake. But if you're busy, I mustn't keep you. Though since I am here, I wonder if I could look up something in your encyclopaedia. I won't interrupt. I promise.'

'May I introduce Mr Fabry?' Emily said, for Mrs Waterlow was somehow or other in the room.

'Not Mr *Edmund* Fabry?'

Edmund, still holding his coffee cup and saucer, managed
to stand up quickly and shake hands.

'The author? I could recognise you from your photo.
Oh, my daughter will be so interested. I must write at
once to tell her. I'm afraid I've never read any of your
books.'

Edmund found this, as he always found it, unanswerable.
He gave an apologetic murmur, and smiled ingratiatingly.

'But I always read the reviews of them in the Sunday
papers.' Mrs Waterlow went on, 'I'm afraid we're rather a
booky family.'

So far, she had said nothing to which he could find any
reply. Emily stood helplessly beside him, saying nothing.
She was not wringing her hands, but he thought that if they
had not been clasped so tightly together, that was what
would have happened.

'You've *really* kept Mr Fabry in the dark, Emily,' said
Mrs Waterlow.

Not so *you* to *me*; Edmund thought. He had met her
many times before in Emily's letters, already knew that her
family was ' booky' and had had her preposterous opinions
on many things.

She was a woman of fifty-five, whose children had grown
up and gone thankfully away. They left their mother almost
permanently, it seemed to them, behind the tea urn at
the village hall – and a good watching place it was. She had,
as Emily once put it, the over-alert look of a ventriloquist's
dummy. Her head, cocked slightly, turned to and fro between
Emily and Edmund. Dyed hair, she thought, glancing away
from him. She was often wrong about people.

'Now, don't let me interrupt you. You get on with your
coffee. I'll just sit quiet in my corner and bury myself in the
encyclopaedia.'

'Would you like some coffee?' Emily asked. 'I'm afraid it may be rather cold.'

'If there *is* some going begging, nothing would be nicer. "Shuva to Tom-Tom", that's the one I want.' She pulled out the encyclopaedia and rather ostentatiously pretended to wipe dust from her fingers.

She has presence of mind, Edmund decided, watching her turn the pages with speed, and authority. She has really thought of something to look up. He was sure that he could not have done so as quickly himself. He wondered what it was that she had hit upon. She had come to a page of photographs of tapestry and began to study them intently. There appeared to be pages of close print on the subject. So clever, Edmund thought.

She knew that he was staring at her and looked up and smiled; her finger marking the place. 'To settle an argument,' she said. 'I'm afraid we are a very argumentative family.'

Edmund bowed.

A silence fell. He and Emily looked at one another, but she looked away first. She sat on the arm of a chair, as if she were waiting to spring up to see Mrs Waterlow out – as indeed she was.

The hot afternoon was a spell they had fallen under. A bluebottle zig-zagged about the room, hit the window-pane, then went suddenly out of the door. A petal dropped off a geranium on the window-sill – occasionally – but not often enough for Edmund – a page was turned, the thin paper rustling silkily over. Edmund drew his wrist out of his sleeve and glanced secretly at his watch, and Emily saw him do it. It was a long journey he had made to see her, and soon he must be returning.

Mrs Waterlow looked up again. She had an amused smile, as if they were a couple of shy children whom she had just introduced to one another. 'Oh, dear, why the silence? I'm not listening, you know. You will make me feel that I am in the way.'

You preposterous old trollop, Edmund thought viciously. He leant back, put his fingertips together and said, looking across at Emily: 'Did I tell you that cousin Joseph had a nasty accident? Out bicycling. *Both* of them, you know. Such a deprivation. No heir, either. But Constance very soon consoled herself. With one of the army padres out there. They were discovered by Joseph's batman in the most unusual circumstances. The Orient's insidious influence, I suppose. So strangely exotic for Constance, though.' He guessed – though he did not look – that Mrs Waterlow had flushed and, pretending not to be listening, was struggling hard *not* to flush.

'Cousin Constance's Thousand and One Nights,' he said. 'The padre had courage. Like engaging with a boa-constrictor, I'd have thought.'

If only Emily had not looked so alarmed. He began to warm to his inventions, which grew more macabre and outrageous – and, as he did so, he could hear the pages turning quickly and at last the book was closed with a loud thump. 'That's clinched *that* argument,' said Mrs Waterlow. 'Hubert is so often inaccurate, but won't have it that he can ever be wrong.' She tried to sound unconcerned, but her face was set in lines of disapproval.

'You are triumphant, then?' Edmund asked and he stood up and held out his hand.

When she had gone, Emily closed the door and leant against it. She looked exhausted.

'Thank you,' she said. 'She would never have gone otherwise. And now it is nearly time for *you* to go.'

'I am sorry about Cousin Joseph. I could think of no other way.'

In Emily's letters, Mrs Waterlow had been funny; but she was not in real life and he wondered how Emily could suffer so much, before transforming it.

'My dear, if you are sorry I came, then I am sorry, too.'

'Don't say anything. Don't talk of it,' she begged him,

standing with her hands pressed hard against the door behind her. She shrank from words, thinking of the scars they leave, which she would be left to tend when he had gone. If he spoke the truth, she could not bear it; if he tried to muffle it with tenderness, she would look upon it as pity. He had made such efforts, she knew; but he could never have protected her from herself.

He, facing her, turned his eyes for a moment towards the window; then he looked back at her. He said nothing; but she knew that he had seen the station car drawing to a standstill beyond the hollyhocks.

'You have to go?' she asked.

He nodded.

Perhaps the worst has happened, she thought. I have fallen in love with him – the one thing from which I felt I was completely safe.

Before she moved aside from the door, she said quickly, as if the words were red-hot coals over which she must pick her way – 'If you write to me again, will you leave out today, and let it be as if you had not moved out of Rome?'

'Perhaps I didn't,' he said.

At the door, he took her hand and held it against his cheek for a second – a gesture both consoling and conciliatory.

When he had gone, she carried her grief decently upstairs to her little bedroom and there allowed herself some tears. When they were dried and over, she sat down by the open window.

She had not noticed how clouds had been crowding into the sky. A wind had sprung up and bushes and branches were jigging and swaying.

The hollyhocks nodded together. A spot of rain as big as a halfpenny dropped on to the stone sill, others fell over leaves down below, and a sharp cool smell began to rise at once from the earth.

She put her head out of the window, her elbows on the outside sill. The soft rain, falling steadily now, calmed her.

Down below in the garden the cat wove its way through a flowerbed. At the door, he began to cry piteously to be let in and she shut the window a little and went downstairs. It was dark in the living-room; the two windows were fringed with dripping leaves; there were shadows and silence.

While she was washing up, the cat, turning a figure-of-eight round her feet, brushed her legs with his wet fur. She began to talk to him, as she often did, for they were alone so much together. 'If you were a dog,' she said, 'we could go for a nice walk in the rain.'

As it was, she gave him his supper and took an apple for herself. Walking about, eating it, she tidied the room. The sound of the rain in the garden was very peaceful. She carried her writing things to the table by the window and there, in the last of the light, dipped her goose-quill pen in the ink, and wrote, in her fine and flowing hand, her address, and then, 'Dear Edmund'.

Summer Schools

SITTING outside on the sill, the cat watched Melanie through the window. The shallow arc between the tips of his ears, his baleful stare, and his hunched-up body blown feathery by the wind, gave him the look of a barn owl. Sometimes, a strong gust nearly knocked him off balance and bent his whiskers crooked. Catching Melanie's eye, he opened his mouth wide in his furious, striped face, showed his fangs and let out a piteous mew instead of a roar.

Melanie put a finger in her book and padded across the room in her stockinged feet. When she opened the french windows, the gale swept into the room and the fire began to smoke. Now that he was allowed to come in, the cat began a show of caprice; half in, he arched his back and rubbed against the step, purring loudly. Some leaves blew across the floor.

'Either in or out, you fool,' Melanie said impatiently. Still holding the door, she put her foot under the cat's belly and half pushed, half lifted him into the room.

The french windows had warped, like all the other

wooden parts of the house. There were altogether too many causes for irritation, Melanie thought. When she had managed to slam the door shut, she stood there for a moment, looking out at the garden, until she had felt the full abhorrence of the scene. Her revulsion was so complete as to be almost unbelievable; the sensation became ecstatic.

On the veranda, a piece of newspaper had wrapped itself, quivering frenziedly, round a post. A macrocarpa hedge tossed about in the wind; the giant hydrangea by the gate was full of bus tickets, for here was the terminus, the very end of the esplanade. The butt and end, Melanie thought, of all the long-drawn-out tedium of the English holiday resort. Across the road a broken bank covered with spiky grass hid most of the sands, but she could imagine them clearly, brown and ribbed, littered with bits of cuttlefish and mussel shells. The sea – far out – was staved with white.

Melanie waited as a bowed-over, mufflered man, exercising a dog, then a duffel-coated woman with a brace of poodles on leads completed the scene. Satisfied, she turned back to the fire. It was all as bad as could be and on a bright day it was hardly better, for the hard glitter of the sun seemed unable to lift the spirits. It was usually windy.

The creaking sound of the rain, its fitful and exasperated drumming on the window, she listened to carefully. In one place at the end of the veranda, it dropped more heavily and steadily: she could hear it as if the noise were in her own breast. The cat – Ursula's – rubbed its cold fur against her legs and she pushed him away crossly, but he always returned.

'A day for indoors,' Ursula said gaily. She carried in the tea-tray, and set down a covered dish on the hearth with the smug triumph of one giving a great treat.

I am to be won over with buttered scones, Melanie thought sulkily. The sulky expression was one that her face, with its heavy brows and full mouth, fell into easily. 'One of Miss Rogers's nasty looks,' her pupils called it, finding it not alarming, but depressing. Ursula, two years younger, was plumper, brighter, more alert. Neither was beautiful.

'Oh, sod that cat of yours,' Melanie said. He was now mewing at the french windows to be let out. Melanie's swearing was something new since their father had died – an act of desperation, such as a child might make. Father would turn in his grave, Ursula often said. Let him turn, said Melanie. 'Who will look after him while you're away?' she asked, nodding at the cat. Ursula put him outside again and came back to pour out the tea. 'How do you mean, look after him? Surely you don't mind. I'll order the fish. You'll only have to cook it and give it to him.'

'I shan't be here.'

The idea had suddenly occurred, born of vindictiveness and envy. For Pamela had no right to invite Ursula to stay there on her own. Melanie was only two years their senior; they had all been at the same school. Apart from all that, the two sisters always spent their holidays together; in fact, had never been separated. To Melanie, the invitation seemed staggeringly insolent, and Ursula's decision to accept it could hardly be believed. She had read out the letter at breakfast one morning and Melanie, on her way out of the room to fetch more milk, had simply said, 'How extraordinary,' her light, scornful voice dismissing the subject. Only a sense of time passing and middle age approaching had given Ursula the courage (or effrontery) to renew the subject. For the first time that either she or Melanie could remember, her energy and enthusiasm overcame the smothering effect of her sister's lethargy.

She means to go, Melanie told herself. Her sensation of impotence was poison to her. She had a bitter taste in her mouth, and chafed her hands as if they were frozen. If Ursula were truly going, though, Melanie determined that the departure should be made as difficult as possible. Long before she could set out for the station she should be worn out with the obstacles she had had to overcome.

'You can't expect me to stay here on my own just in order to look after your cat.'

And lest Ursula should ask where she was going before she had had time to make her plans, she got up quickly and went upstairs.

The cat was to stay in kennels and Ursula grieved about it. Her grief Melanie brushed aside as absurd, although she was at the same time inclined to allow Ursula a sense of guilt. 'A dog one can at least take with one,' she told her. She had decided that the cat reflected something of Ursula's own nature – too feminine (although it was a tom); it might be driven, though not led, and the refusal to co-operate mixed, as it was, with cowardice resulted in slyness.

The weather had not improved. They could remember the holidays beginning in this way so often, with everything – rain, flowers, bushes – aslant in the wind. It will be pretty miserable at Pamela's, Melanie thought. She could imagine that house and its surroundings – a parade of new shops nearby, a tennis club, enormous suburban pubs at the corners of roads. She was for ever adding something derogatory to the list. 'Dentists' houses always depress me,' she said. 'I don't think I could stay in one – with all that going on under the same roof.'

What awaited herself was much vaguer.

'It will be like being at school – though having to run to the bell instead of ringing it,' Ursula said, when she had picked up the prospectus for the Summer Lecture Course. 'A pity you can't just go to the discussions and not stay there. Breakfast 8.15,' she read. 'Oh, Lord. The Victorian Novel. Trollope. 9.30.'

Melanie, in silence, held out her hand for the prospectus and Ursula gave it to her. She did not see it again.

'Will you want Mother's fur?' she asked, when she began to pack. 'I just thought . . . evenings, you know, it might be useful . . . '

'I shall have evenings, too,' Melanie reminded her.

Their mother could not have guessed what a matter of contention her ermine wrap would turn out to be when she was dead.

'How is Melanie?' Pamela asked.

'Oh, she's well. She's gone on a little holiday, too.'

'I'm so glad. I should have liked to have asked her to come with you,' Pamela lied. 'But there's only this single bed.'

Ursula went over to the window. The spare room was at the back of the house and looked across some recreation grounds – a wooden pavilion, a bowling green; and tennis courts – just as Melanie had said there would be.

That evening, there was the pub.

All afternoon the front door bell had rung, and Pamela and Ursula, sitting in the drawing-room upstairs, could hear the crackle of Miss Potter's starched overall as she crossed the hall to answer it. Patients murmured nervously when they entered, but shouted cheerful goodbyes as they left, going full tilt down the gravelled drive and slamming the gate after them.

'I'm sorry about the bell,' Pamela said. 'At first, I thought it would send me out of my mind, but now it's no worse than a clock striking.'

Ursula thought it extraordinary that she had changed so much since their schooldays. It was difficult to find anything to talk about. The books they had once so passionately discussed were at the very bottom of the glass-fronted case, beneath text-books on dentistry and Book Club editions, and Ursula, finding Katherine Mansfield's Journal covered with dust, felt estranged. Perhaps Pamela had become a good cook instead, she thought, for there were plenty of books on that.

Melanie would have scorned the room, with its radiogram

and cocktail cabinet and the matching sofa and chairs. The ashtrays were painted with bright sayings in foreign languages; there were piles of fashion magazines that later – much later, Ursula guessed – would be put in the waiting-room downstairs. The parchment lampshades were stuck over with wine labels and the lamps were made out of chianti bottles. The motif of drinking was prevalent, from a rueful yet humorous viewpoint. When Pamela opened the cigarette box it played 'The More we are Together', and Ursula wondered if the clock would call *Prosit!* when it struck six.

'That's the last patient,' Pamela said. 'Mike will come up panting for a drink.'

Her full skirt, printed with a jumble of luggage labels, flew out wide as she made a dash to the cocktail cabinet. She was as eager to be ready with everything as if she were opening a pub.

Panic now mingled with the feeling of estrangement, as Ursula listened to the footsteps on the stairs. 'Hello, there, Ursula,' said Mike as he threw open the door. 'And how are you? Long time, no see, indeed.'

'Not since our wedding,' Pamela reminded him.

'Well, what will you be after taking?' Mike asked. He slapped his hands together, ready for action, took up a bottle and held it to the light.

I suppose he feels uneasy because I am a schoolmistress, Ursula thought; And perhaps also – lest I shall think Pam married beneath her.

Pamela put out the glasses and some amusing bottle-openers and corkscrews. Ursula remembered staying with her as a girl, had a clear picture of the gloomy dining-room: a dusty, cut-glass decanter, containing the dregs of some dark, unidentified liquid had stood in the centre of the great sideboard, its position never shifting an inch to the right or left. From that imprisoning house and those oppressive parents, Mike had rescued his betrothed and, though she had shed Katherine Mansfield somewhere on the way, she seemed as gay as could be that she had escaped.

Now she kissed her husband, took her drink and went downstairs – to turn the waiting-room back into a dining-room, she said. Mike's uneasiness increased. He was clearly longing for her to return.

'You must be a brave man,' Ursula said suddenly. 'I remember Pam's mother and father and how nervous I was when I stayed there. Even when we were quite well on in our teens, we were made to lie down after luncheon, in a darkened room for ages and ages. "And no reading, dears," her mother always said as we went upstairs. At home, we never rested – or only when we were little children, but I pretended that we did, in case Pam's mother should think badly of mine. They seemed so very stern. To snatch away their only daughter must have needed courage.'

For the first time, he looked directly at her. In his eyes was a timid expression. He may have been conscious of this and anxious to hide it, for almost immediately he glanced away.

'I girded on my armour,' he said, 'and rode up to the portcullis and demanded her. That was all there was to it.'

She smiled, thinking, So this room is the end of a fairy tale.

'Astonishing good health, my dear,' Mike said, lifting his glass.

Melanie took her coffee and, summoning all her courage, went to sit down beside Mrs Rybeck, who gave her a staving-off smile, a slight shake of her head as she knitted, her lips moving silently. When she came to the end of the row, she apologised, and jotted down on her knitting pattern, whatever it was she had been counting.

'What a stimulating evening,' Melanie said.

'Have you not heard George Barnes lecture before?' Mrs Rybeck was obviously going to be condescending again, but Melanie was determined to endure it. Then – what she had hoped – Professor Rybeck came in. She felt breathless and self-conscious as he approached.

'Darling!' he murmured touching his wife's hair, then bowed to Melanie.

'Miss Rogers,' his wife reminded him quickly. 'At Saint Winifred's, you know, where Ethel's girls were.'

'Yes, of course I know Miss Rogers,' he said.

His dark hair receded from a forehead that seemed always moist, as were his dark and mournful eyes. As soon as they heard his voice – low, catarrhal and with such gentle inflections – some of the women, who had been sitting in a group by the window, got up and came over to him.

'Professor Rybeck,' one said. 'We are beside ourselves with excitement about your lecture tomorrow.'

'Miss Rogers was just saying that she thought highly of George's talk this evening,' said Mrs Rybeck.

'Ah, George!' her husband said softly. 'I think George likes to think he has us all by the ears. Young men do. But we mustn't let him sharpen his wits on us till we ourselves are blunt. None the less, he knows his Thackeray.'

Melanie considered herself less esteemed for having mentioned him.

'How I love *Middlemarch*,' some woman said. 'I think it is my favourite novel.'

'Then I only hope I do it justice tomorrow,' Professor Rybeck said. Although he seemed full of confidence, he smiled humbly. Nothing was too much trouble.

Pamela had insisted that the three of them should squeeze into the front of the car and Ursula, squashed up in the middle, sat with rounded shoulders and her legs tucked to one side. She was worried about the creases in her skirt. The wireless was on very loud and both Pamela and Mike joined in the Prize Song from *Die Meistersinger*. Ursula was glad when they reached the Swan.

The car-park was full. This pub was where everybody went, Pamela explained; 'at the moment', she added. In the garden, the striped umbrellas above the tables had been furled; the baskets of geraniums over the porch were swinging in the wind.

'Astonishingly horrid evening,' Mike said, when some of his acquaintances greeted him. 'This is Pam's friend, Ursula. Ursie, this is Jock' – or Jean or Eve or Bill. Ursula lost track. They all knew one another and Mike and Pam seemed popular. 'Don't look now, the worst has happened,' someone had said in a loud voice when Mike opened the door of the saloon bar.

Ursula was made much of. From time to time, most of them were obliged to bring out some dull relation or duty-guest. ('Not really one of us'), and it was a mark of friendliness to do one's best to help with other people's problems – even the most tiresome of old crones would be attended to; and Ursula, although plump and prematurely grey, was only too ready to smile and join in the fun.

'You're one of us, I can see,' someone complimented her.

'Cheers!' said Ursula before she drank. Melanie would have shivered with distaste.

'We are all going on to Hilly's,' Pam called to Mike across the bar at closing time.

This moving on was the occasion for a little change round of passengers and, instead of being squeezed in between Pamela and Mike, Ursula was taken across the car-park by a man called Guy.

'Daddy will give you a scarf for your head,' he promised, opening the door of his open car. The scarf tucked inside his shirt was yellow, patterned with horses and when he took it off and tied it round Ursula's head, the silk was warm to her cheeks.

They drove very fast along the darkening roads and were the first to arrive.

'Poor frozen girl,' said Guy when he had swung the car

round on the gravelled sweep in front of the house and brought it up within an inch of the grass verge. With the driving off his mind, he could turn his attention to Ursula and he took one of her goosefleshy arms between his hands and began to chafe it. 'What we need is a drink,' he said. 'Where the hell have they all got to?'

She guessed that to drive fast and to arrive first was something he had to do and, for his sake and to help on the amiability of the evening, she was glad that he had managed it.

'You're sure it's the right house?' she asked.

'Dead sure, my darling.'

She had never been called 'darling' by a man and, however meaningless the endearment, it added something to her self-esteem, as their arriving first had added something to his.

She untied the scarf and gave it back to him. He had flicked on his cigarette lighter and was looking for something in the dash-pocket. For a moment, while the small glow lasted, she could study his face. It was like a ventriloquist's dummy's – small, alert, yet blank; the features gave the appearance of having been neatly painted.

He found the packet of cigarettes; then he put the scarf round his neck and tied it carefully. 'Someone's coming,' he said. 'They must have double-crossed us and had one somewhere on the way.'

'You drove fastest, that's all,' she said, playing her part in the game.

'Sorry if it alarmed you, sweetheart.' He leaned over and kissed her quickly, just before the first of the cars came round the curve of the drive.

That's the first evening gone, Ursula thought, when later, she lay in bed, rather muzzily going over what had happened. She could remember the drawing-room at Hilly's. She had sat on a cushion on the floor and music from a gramophone above her had spilled over her head, so that she had seen people's mouths opening and shutting but had not been able to hear the matching conversations. In many ways the room – though it was large – had seemed like Pamela's, with pub signs instead of bottle labels on the lampshades. Her sense of time had soon left her and her sense of place grew vaguer, but some details irritated her because she could not evade them – particularly a warming-pan hanging by the fireplace in which she confronted her distorted reflection.

There had seemed no reason why the evening should ever end and no way of setting going all the complications of departure. Although she was tired, she had neither wanted to leave or to stay. She was living a tiny life within herself, sitting there on the cushion; sipping and smiling and glancing about her. Mike had come across the room to her. She turned to tilt back her head to look up into his face but at once felt giddy and had to be content with staring at his knees, at the pin stripes curving baggily, a thin stripe, then a wider, more feathery one. She began to count them, but Mike had come to take her home to bye-byes he said, stretching out a hand. If I can only do this, I can do anything, Ursula thought, trying to rise and keep her balance. I was silly to sit so low down in the first place, she decided. 'I think my foot has gone to sleep,' she explained and smiled confidingly at his knees. His grip on her arm was strong; although appearing to be extending a hand in gallantry, he was really taking her weight and steadying her, too. She had realised this, even at the time and later, lying safe in bed at last, she felt wonderfully grateful for his kindness, and did not at all mind sharing such a secret with him.

Pamela had put a large jug of water by her bed. An hour earlier, it had seemed unnecessary, but now water was all she wanted in the world. She sat up and drank, with a steady, relentless rhythm, as animals drink. Then she slid back into the warm bedclothes and tried to reconstruct in her mind that drive with Guy and became, in doing so, two people, the story-teller and the listener; belittling his endearments, only to reassure herself about them. The sports car, the young man (he was not very old, she told herself), the summer darkness, in spite of its being so windy, were all things that other young girls she had known had taken for granted, at Oxford and elsewhere, and she herself had been denied. They seemed all the more miraculous for having been done without for so long.

Of recent years she had often tried to escape the memory of two maiden-ladies who had lived near her home when she and Melanie were girls. So sharp-tongued and cross-looking, they had seemed then as old as could be, yet may have been no more than in their fifties, she now thought. Frumpish and eccentric, at war with one another as well as all their neighbours, they were to be seen tramping the lanes, single file and in silence, with their dogs. To the girls, they were the most appalling and unenviable creatures, smelling of vinegar, Melanie had said. The recollection of them so long after they were dead disturbed Ursula and depressed her, for she could see how she and Melanie had taken a turning in their direction, yet scarcely anything as definite as this, for there had been no action, no decision; simply, the road they had been on had always, it seemed, been bending in that direction. In no time at all, would they not be copies of those other old ladies? The Misses Rogers, the neighbours would think of them, feeling pity and nervousness. The elder Miss Rogers would be alarmingly abrupt, with her sarcastic voice and old-fashioned swear-words. They won't be afraid of me, Ursula decided; but had no comfort from the thought. People would think her bullied and would be sorry. She, the plumper one, with her cat and timid smiles, would give biscuits to children when Melanie's back was turned. Inseparable, yet alien to one another, they would become. Forewarned as she was, she felt herself drifting towards that fate and was afraid when she woke at night and thought of it.

Her first drowsiness had worn off and her thirst kept her wakeful. She lay and wondered about the details of Pamela's escape from her parents' sad house and all that had threatened her there – watchfulness, suspicion, envy and capricious humours; much of the kind of thing she herself suffered from Melanie. Pamela's life now was bright and silly, and perhaps she had run away from the best part of herself; but there was nothing in the future to menace her as Ursula was menaced by her own picture of the elderly Misses Rogers.

'But *surely*,' insisted the strained and domineering voice. The woman gripped the back of the chair in front of her and stared up at Professor Rybeck on the platform.

At the end of his lecture, he had asked for questions or discussions. To begin with, everyone had seemed too stunned with admiration to make an effort; there were flutterings and murmurings, but for some time no one stood up. Calmly, he waited, sitting there smiling, eyes half closed and his head cocked a little as if he were listening to secret music, or applause. His arms were crossed over his chest and his legs were crossed too, and one foot swayed back and forth rhythmically.

The minute Mr Brundle stood up, other people wanted to. He was an elderly, earnest man, who had been doggedly on the track of culture since his youth. His vanity hid from him the half-stifled yawns he evoked, the glassy look of those who, though caught, refused to listen and also his way of melting away to one victim any group of people he approached. Even Professor Rybeck looked restless, as Mr Brundle began now to pound away at his theory. Then others, in disagreement or exasperation, began to jump to their feet, or made sharp comments, interrupting; even shot

their arms into the air, like schoolchildren. World peace
they might have been arguing about, not George Eliot's
Dorothea Casaubon.

'Please, please,' said Professor Rybeck, in his melodious
protesting voice. 'Now, Mrs Thomas, let us hear you.'

'But *surely*,' Mrs Thomas said again.

'Wouldn't it be time to say?' asked Mrs Wetherby – she
sounded diffident and had blushed; she had never spoken in
the presence of so many people before, but wanted badly
to make her mark on the Professor. She was too shy to stand
upright and leaned forward, lifting her bottom a couple of
inches from the chair. Doing so, she dropped her notebook
and pencil, her stole slipped off and when she bent down
to pick it up she also snatched at some large, tortoiseshell
pins that had fallen out of her hair. By the time she had done
all this, her chance was gone and she had made her mark
in the wrong way. The one and only clergyman in the room
had sprung to his feet and, knowing all the tricks needed
to command, had snatched off his spectacles and held them
high in the air while, for some reason no one was clear
about, he denounced Samuel Butler.

'I think, Comrade . . . Professor, I should say,' Mr
Brundle interrupted. 'If we might return but briefly to
the subject . . . '

Melanie closed her eyes and thought how insufferable
people became about what has cost them too much to
possess – education, money, or even good health.

Lightly come or not at all, is what I like, she told herself
crossly and, when she opened her eyes, glanced up at
Professor Rybeck, who smiled with such placid condescension as the ding-dong argument went on between clergyman
and atheist (for literature – Victorian or otherwise – had
been discarded) and then she looked for Mrs Rybeck and
found her sitting at the end of the second row, still knitting.
She gave, somehow, an impression of not being one of the
audience, seemed apart from them, preoccupied with her

own thoughts, lending her presence only, like a babysitter or the invigilator at an examination – well accustomed to the admiration her husband had from other women of her own age, she made it clear that she was one with him in all he did and thought; their agreement, she implied, had come about many years ago and needed no more discussion, and if the women cared to ask her any of the questions he had no time to answer, then she could give the authorised replies. With all this settled, her placidity, like his, was almost startling to other people, their smiling lips (not eyes), their capacity for waiting for others to finish speaking (and it was far removed from the act of listening), is often to be found in the mothers of large families. Yet she was childless. She had only the Professor, and the socks she knitted were for him. She is more goddessy than motherly, Melanie thought.

'We are summoned to the banqueting hall,' said the Professor, raising his hand in the air, as a bell began to ring. This was the warning that lunch would be ready in ten minutes, the Secretary had told them all when they arrived, and 'warning' was a word she had chosen well. The smell of minced beef and cabbage came along passages towards them. To Melanie it was unnoticeable, part of daily life, like other tedious affairs; one disposed of the food, as of any other small annoyance, there were jugs of water to wash it down and slices of bread cut hours before that one could crumble as one listened to one's neighbour.

One of Melanie's neighbours was an elementary school teacher to whom she tried not to be patronising. On her other side was a Belgian woman whose vivacity was intolerable. She was like a bad caricature of a foreigner, primly sporty and full of gay phrases. '*Mon Dieu*, we have had it, chums,' she said, lifting the water jug and finding it empty. The machine-gun rattle of consonants vibrated in Melanie's head long after she was alone. "*Oh, là, là!*" the woman sometimes cried, as if she were a cheeky French maid in an old-fashioned farce.

'You think "Meedlemahtch" is a good book,' she asked
Melanie. They all discussed novels at meal-times too; for they
were what they had in common. Melanie was startled, for
Professor Rybeck had spent most of the morning explaining
its greatness. 'It is one of the great English novels,' she said.

'As great as Charles Morgan, you think? In the same
class?'

Melanie looked suspicious and would not answer.

'It is such a funny book. I read it last night and laughed
so much.'

'And will read *War and Peace* between tea and dinner, I
suppose,' the elementary schoolteacher murmured. 'Oh dear,
how disgusting!' She pushed a very pale, boiled caterpillar
to the side of her plate. 'If that happened to one of our little
darlings at school dinner, the mother would write at once
to her MP.'

At Melanie's school, the girls would have hidden the
creature under a fork in order not to spoil anyone else's
appetite, but she did not say so.

'A *funny* book?' she repeated, turning back to the Belgian
woman.

'Yes, I like it so much when she thinks that the really
delightful marriage must be that where your husband was
a sort of father, and could teach you Hebrew if you wished
it. *Oh là, là!* For heaven's sake.'

'Then she did read a page or two,' said the woman on
Melanie's other side.

A dreadful sadness and sense of loss had settled over
Melanie when she herself had read those words. They had
not seemed absurd to her; she had felt tears pressing at the
back of her eyes. So often, she had longed for protection and
compassion, to be instructed and concentrated upon; as if
she were a girl again, yet with a new excitement in the air.

As they made their way towards the door, when lunch
was over, she could see Professor Rybeck standing there
talking to one or two of his admirers. Long before she drew

near to him, Melanie found another direction to glance in. What she intended for unconcern, he took for deliberate hostility and wondered at what point of his lecture he had managed to offend her so.

In a purposeless way, she wandered into the garden. The Georgian house – a boys' preparatory school in the term-time – stood amongst dark rhododendron bushes and silver birches. Paths led in many directions through the shrubberies, yet all converged upon the lake – a depressing stretch of water, as bleary as an old looking-glass, shadowed by trees and broken by clumps of reeds.

The pain of loneliness was a worse burden to her here than it had ever been at home and she knew – her behaviour as she was leaving the dining-room had reminded her – that the fault was in herself.

'Don't think that I will make excuses to speak to you,' she had wanted to imply. 'I am not so easily dazzled as these other women.' But I wanted him to speak to me, she thought, and perhaps I only feared that he would not.

She sat down on the bank above the water and thought about the Professor. She could even imagine his lustrous eyes turned upon her, as he listened.

'I give false impressions,' she struggled to explain to him. 'In my heart . . . I am . . . '

'I know what you are,' he said gently. 'I knew at once.'

The relief would be enormous. She was sure of that. She could live the rest of her life on the memory of that moment.

'But he is a fraud,' the other, destructive voice in her insisted, the voice that had ruined so much for her. 'He is not a fraud,' she said firmly; her lips moved; she needed to be so definite with herself. 'Perhaps he cannot find the balance between integrity and priggishness.'

'Is that all?' asked the other voice.

The dialogue faded out and she sighed, thinking: I wish I hadn't come. I feel so much worse here than I do at home.

Coming round the lake's edge towards her was the atrocious little Mr Brundle. She pretended not to have seen him and got to her feet and went off in the other direction.

By the afternoon post came a letter from Ursula, saying how dull she was and that Melanie had been so right about it all – and that comforted her a little.

Ursula was polishing a glass on a cloth printed with a chart of vintage years for champagne. Although she was drunk, she wondered at the usefulness of this as a reference. It would be strange to go home again to a black telephone, white sheets and drying-up cloths on which there was nothing at all to read, not a recipe for a cocktail or a cheerful slogan.

On the draining board two white tablets fizzed, as they rose and fell in a glass of water. The noise seemed very loud to her and she was glad when the tablets dissolved and there was silence.

'There you are,' Guy said, handing the glass to her. The water still spat and sparkled and she drank it slowly, gasping between sips.

'Pamela will wonder where I am,' she said. She put the glass on the draining board and sat down with a bump on one of the kitchen chairs. She had insisted on washing the two glasses before she went home, and had devoted herself to doing so with single-mindedness; but Guy had been right, and she gave in. Everything she had to do had become difficult – going home, climbing the stairs, undressing. I shall just have to sit on this chair and let time pass, she decided. It will pass, she promised herself, and it mends all in the end.

'Where did we go after that club?' she suddenly asked frowning.

'Nowhere,' said Guy. 'On our way back to Pamela's we stopped here for a drink. That's all.'

'Ah, yes!'

She remembered the outside of this bungalow and a wooden gate with the name Hereiam. It had been quite dark when they walked up the stony path to the front door. Now, it seemed the middle of the night. 'I think you gave me too much whisky,' she said, with a faint, reproachful smile.

'As a matter of fact, I gave you none. It was ginger ale you were drinking.'

She considered this and then lifted her eyes to look at him and asked anxiously: 'Then had I had . . . was I . . . ?'

'You were very sweet.'

She accepted this gravely. He put his hands under her arms and brought her to her feet and she rested the side of her face against his waistcoat and stayed very still, as if she were counting his heartbeats. These, like the fizzing drink, also sounded much too loud.

'I didn't wash the other glass,' she said.

'Mrs Lamb can do it in the morning.'

She went from one tremulous attempt at defence to another, wanting to blow her nose, or light a cigarette or put something tidy. In the sitting-room, earlier, when he had sat down beside her on the sofa, she had sprung up and gone rapidly across the room to look for an ashtray. 'Who is this?' she had asked, picking up a framed photograph and holding it at arm's length, as if to ward him off. 'Girl friend,' he said briefly, drinking his whisky and watching her manœuvres with amusement.

'Haven't you ever wanted to get married?' she had asked.

'Sometimes. Have you?'

'Oh, sometimes . . . I daresay,' she answered vaguely.

Now, in the kitchen, he had caught her at last, she was clasped in his arms and feeling odd, she told him.

'I know. There's some coffee nearly ready in the other room. That will do untold good.'

What a dreadful man he is, really, in spite of his tenderness, she thought. So hollow and vulgar that I don't know what Melanie would say.

She was startled for a moment, wondering if she had murmured this aloud; for, suddenly, his heartbeat had become noisier – from anger, she was afraid.

'You are very kind,' she said appeasingly. 'I am not really used to drinking as much as people do here – not used to drinking at all.'

'What *are* you used to?'

'Just being rather dull, you know – my sister and I.'

His way of lifting her chin up and kissing her was too accomplished and she was reminded of the way in which he drove the car. She was sure that there was something here she should resent. Perhaps he was patronising her; for the kiss had come too soon after her remark about the dullness of her life. I can bring *some* excitement into it, he may have thought.

Without releasing her, he managed to stretch an arm and put out the light. 'I can't bear to see you frowning,' he explained. 'Why frown anyway?'

'That coffee . . . but then I mustn't stay for it, after all. Pamela will be wondering . . . '

'Pam will understand.'

'Oh, I hope not.'

She frowned more than ever and shut her eyes tightly although the room was completely dark.

Melanie sat on the edge of the bed, coughing. She was wondering if she had suddenly got TB and kept looking anxiously at her handkerchief.

The sun was shining, though not into her room. From the window, she could see Professor Rybeck sitting underneath the Wellingtonia with an assortment of his worshippers. From his gestures, Melanie could tell that it was he who was talking, and talking continuously. The hand rose and fell and made languid spirals as he unfolded his theme, or else cut the air decisively into slices. Mrs Rybeck was, of course, knitting. By her very presence, sitting a little apart from her husband, like a woman minding a stall on a fairground, she attracted passers-by. Melanie watched the Belgian woman now approaching, to say her few words about the knitting, then having paid her fee, to pass on to listen to the Professor.

Desperately, Melanie wished to be down there listening, too; but she had no knowledge of how to join them. Crossing the grass, she would attract too much attention. Ah, *she* cannot keep away, people would think, turning to watch her. She must be in love with the Professor after all, like the other women; but perhaps more secretly, more devouringly.

She had stopped coughing and forgotten tuberculosis for the moment, as she tried to work out some more casual way than crossing the lawn. She might emerge less noticeably from the shrubbery behind the Wellingtonia, if only she could be there in the first place.

She took a clean handkerchief from a drawer and smoothed her hair before the looking-glass; and then a bell rang for tea and, when she went back to the window, the group under the tree was breaking up. Mrs Rybeck was rolling up her knitting and they were all laughing.

I shall see him at tea, Melanie thought. She could picture him bowing to her, coldly, and with the suggestion that it was she who disliked him rather than he who disliked her. I could never put things right now, she decided.

She wondered what Ursula would be doing at this minute. Perhaps sitting in Pamela's little back garden having tea, while, at the front of the house, the patients came and went. She had said that she would be glad to be at home again, for Pamela had changed and they had nothing left in common. And coming here hasn't been a success, either, Melanie thought, as she went downstairs to tea. She blamed Ursula very much for having made things so dull for them both. There must be ways of showing her how mistaken she had been, ways of preventing anything of the kind happening again.

'Miss Rogers,' said the Professor with unusual gaiety. They had almost collided at the drawing-room door. 'Have you been out enjoying the sun?'

She blushed and was so angry that she should that she said quite curtly, 'No, I was writing letters in my room.'

He stood quickly aside to let her pass and she did so without a glance at him.

Their holiday was over. On her way back from the station, Ursula called at the kennels for the cat and Melanie, watching her come up the garden path, could see the creature clawing frantically at her shoulder, trying to hoist himself out of her grasp. The taxi driver followed with the suitcase.

Melanie had intended to be the last home and had even caught a later train than was convenient, in order not to have to be waiting there for her sister. After all her planning, she was angry to have found the house empty.

'Have you been home long?' Ursula asked rather breathlessly. She put the cat down and looked round. Obviously Melanie had not, for her suitcase still stood in the hall and not a letter had been opened.

'Only a minute or two,' said Melanie.

'That cat's in a huff with me. Trying to punish me for going away, I suppose. He's quite plump though. He looks well, doesn't he? Oh, it's so lovely to be home.'

She went to the hall table and shuffled the letters, then threw them on one side. Melanie had said nothing.

'Aren't *you* glad to be home?' Ursula asked her.

'No, I don't think so.'

'Well I'm glad you had a good time. It was a change for you.'

'Yes.'

'And now let's have some tea.'

She went into the kitchen and, still wearing her hat, began to get out the cups and saucers. 'They didn't leave any bread,' she called out. 'Oh, yes, it's all right, I've found it.' She began to sing, then stopped to chatter to the cat, then sang again.

Melanie had been in the house over an hour and had done nothing.

'I'm so glad you had a good time,' Ursula said again, when they were having tea.

'I'm sorry you didn't.'

'It was a mistake going there, trying to renew an old friendship. You'd have hated the house.'

'You'd have liked *mine*. Grey stone, Georgian, trees and a lake.'

'Romantic,' Ursula said and did not notice that Melanie locked her hands together in rather a theatrical gesture.

'Pam seems complacent. She's scored over me, having a husband. Perhaps that's why she invited me.'

'What did you do all the time?'

'Just nothing. Shopped in the morning – every morning – the housewife's round – butcher, baker, candlestick maker. "I'm afraid the piece of skirt was rather gristly, Mr Bones." That sort of thing. She would fetch half a pound of butter one day and go back for another half-pound the next morning – just for the fun of it. One day, she said, "I think we'll have some hock for supper." I thought she was talking about wine, but it turned out to be some bacon – not very nice. Not very nice of me to talk like this, either.'

However dull it had been, she seemed quite excited as she described it; her cheeks were bright and her hands restless.

'We went to the cinema once, to see a Western,' she added. 'Mike is very fond of Westerns.'

'How dreadful for you.'

Ursula nodded.

'Well, that's their life,' she said, 'I was glad all the time that you were not there. Darling puss, so now you've forgiven me.'

To show his forgiveness, the cat jumped on to her lap and began dough-punching, his extended claws catching the threads of her skirt.

'Tell me about *you*,' Ursula said. She poured out some more tea to sip while Melanie had her turn; but to her surprise Melanie frowned and looked away.

'Is something the matter?'

'I can't talk about it yet, or get used to not being there. This still seems unreal to me. You must give me time.'

She got up, knocked over the cream jug and went out of the room. Ursula mopped up the milk with her napkin and then leant back and closed her eyes. Her moment's consternation at Melanie's behaviour had passed; she even forgot it. The cat relaxed, too, and, curled up against her, slept.

Melanie was a long time unpacking and did nothing towards getting supper. She went for a walk along the sea road and watched the sunset on the water. The tide was out and the wet sands were covered with a pink light. She dramatised her solitary walk and was in a worse turmoil when she reached home.

'Your cough is bad,' Ursula said when they had finished supper.

'Is it?' Melanie said absent-mindedly.

'Something has happened, hasn't it?' Ursula asked her, and then looked down quickly, as if she were confused.

'The end of the world,' said Melanie.

'You've fallen in love?' Ursula lifted her head and stared at her.

'To have to go back to school next week and face those bloody children – and go on facing them, for ever and for ever – or other ones exactly like them . . . the idea suddenly appals me.'

Her bitterness was so true, and Ursula could hear her own doom in her sister's words. She had never allowed herself to have thoughts of that kind.

'But can't you . . . can't he?' she began.

'We can't meet again. We never shall. So it *is* the end of the world, you see,' said Melanie. The scene gave her both relief and anguish. Her true parting with Professor Rybeck (he had looked up from *The Times* and nodded as she crossed the hall) was obliterated for ever. She could more easily bear the agonised account she now gave to Ursula and she would bear it – their noble resolve, their last illicit embrace.

'He's married, you mean?' Ursula asked bluntly.

'Yes, married.'

Mrs Rybeck, insensitively knitting at the execution of their hopes, appeared as an evil creature, tenacious and sinister.

'But to say goodbye for ever . . . ' Ursula protested. 'We only have one life . . . would it be wicked, after all?'

'What could there be . . . clandestine meetings and sordid arrangements?'

Ursula looked ashamed.

'I should ruin his career,' said Melanie.

'Yes, I see. You could write to one another, though.'

'Write!' Melanie repeated in a voice as light as air. 'I think I will go to bed now. I feel exhausted.'

'Yes, do, and I will bring you a hot drink.' As Melanie began to go upstairs, Ursula said, 'I am very sorry, you know.'

While she was waiting for the milk to rise in the pan, she tried to rearrange her thoughts, especially to exclude (now that there was so much nobility in the house) her own squalid – though hazily recollected – escapade. Hers was a more optimistic nature than Melanie's and she was confident of soon putting such memories out of her mind.

When she took the hot milk upstairs, her sister was sitting up in bed reading a volume of Keats' letters. 'He gave it to me as I came away,' she explained, laying the book on the bedside table, where it was always to remain.

We have got this to live with now, Ursula thought, and

it will be with us for ever, I can see – the reason and the excuse for everything. It will even grow; there will be more and more of it, as time goes on. When we are those two elderly Miss Rogers we are growing into it will still be there. 'Miss Melanie, who has such a sharp tongue,' people will say. 'Poor thing . . . a tragic love affair a long way back.' I shall forget there was a time when we did not have it with us.

Melanie drank her milk and put out the light; then she lay down calmly and closed her eyes and prepared herself for her dreams. Until they came, she imagined walking by the lake, as she had done, that afternoon, only a few days ago; but instead of Mr Brundle coming into the scene, Professor Rybeck appeared. He walked towards her swiftly, as if by assignation. Then they sat down and looked at the tarnished water – and she added a few swans for them to watch. After a long delicious silence, she began to speak. Yet words were not really necessary. She had hardly begun the attempt; her lips shaped the beginning of a sentence – 'I am . . . ' and then he took her hand and held it to his cheek. 'I know what you are,' he said. 'I knew at the very beginning.'

Although they had parted for ever, she realised that she was now at peace – she felt ennobled and enriched, and saw herself thus, reflected from her sister's eyes, and she was conscious of Ursula's solemn wonder and assured by it.

Perhaps a Family Failing

OF course, Mrs Cotterell cried. Watery-eyed, on the arm of the bridegroom's father, she smiled in a bewildered way to left and right, coming down the aisle. Outside, on the church steps, she quickly dashed the tears away as she faced the camera, still arm in arm with Mr Midwinter, a man she detested.

He turned towards her and gave a great meaningless laugh just as the camera clicked and Mrs Cotterell had his ginny breath blown full in her face. Even in church he had to smell like that, she thought, and the grim words, 'Like father, like son', disturbed her mind once more.

Below them, at the kerb's edge, Geoff was already helping his bride into the car. The solemnity of the service had not touched him. In the vestry, he had been as jaunty as ever, made his wife blush and was hushed by his mother, a frail, pensive creature, who had much, Mrs Cotterell thought, to be frail and pensive about.

It was Saturday morning and the bridal car moved off slowly amongst the other traffic. Mrs Cotterell watched until the white-ribboned motor disappeared.

The bridesmaids, one pink, one apple-green, were getting into the next car. Lissport was a busy place on Saturdays and to many of the women it was part of the morning's shopping outing to be able to stand for a minute or two to watch a bride coming out of the church. Feeling nervous and self-conscious, Mrs Cotterell, who had often herself stood and watched and criticised, crossed the pavement to the car. She was anxious to be home and wondered if everything was all right there. She had come away in a flurry of confused directions, leaving two of her neighbours slicing beetroot and sticking blanched almonds into the trifles. She was relieved that the reception was her own affair, that she could be sure that there would be no drunkenness, no rowdy behaviour and suggestive speeches, as there had been at Geoff's sister's wedding last year. One glass of port to drink a toast to the bride and bridegroom she had agreed to. For the rest she hoped that by now her kindly neighbours had mixed the orange cordial.

Mrs Cotterell cried again, much harder, when Beryl came downstairs in her going-away suit, and kissed her and thanked her (as if her mother were a hostess, not her own flesh and blood, Mrs Cotterell thought sorrowfully) and with composure got into Geoff's little car, to which Mr Midwinter had tied an empty sardine tin.

Then everyone else turned to Mrs Cotterell and thanked her and praised the food and Beryl's looks and dress. It had all gone off all right, they said, making a great hazard of it. 'You'll miss her,' the women told her. 'I know what it's like,' some added.

The bridesmaids took off their flower wreaths and put on their coats. Geoff's brothers, Les and Ron, were taking them out for the evening. 'Not long till opening time,' they said.

Mrs Cotterell went back into the house, to survey the

wedding presents, and the broken wedding cake, with the trelliswork icing she had done so lovingly, crumbled all over the table. Beryl's bouquet was stuck in a vase, waiting to be taken tomorrow to poor Grandma in hospital.

In the kitchen the faithful neighbours were still hard at work, washing up the piles of plates stained with beetroot and mustard and tomato sauce.

'She's gone,' Mrs Cotterell whispered into her crumpled handkerchief as her husband came in and put his arm round her.

'Soon be opening time,' Geoff said, driving along the busy road to Seaferry. He had long ago stopped the car, taken the sardine tin off the back axle and thrown it over a hedge. 'Silly old fool, Dad,' he had said fondly. 'Won't ever act his age.'

Beryl thought so, too, but decided not to reopen that old discussion at such a time. For weeks, she had thought and talked and dreamt of the wedding, studied the advice to brides in women's magazines, on make-up, etiquette and Geoff's marital rights – which he must, she learnt, not be allowed to anticipate. 'Stop it, Geoff!' she had often said firmly. 'I happen to want you to respect me, thank you very much.' Unfortunately for her, Geoff was not the respectful kind, although, in his easy-going way he consented to the celibacy – one of her girlish whims – and had even allowed the gratifying of his desires to be postponed from Easter until early summer, because she had suddenly decided she wanted sweet peas in the bridesmaids' bouquets.

To the women's magazines Beryl now felt she owed everything; she had had faith in their advice and seen it justified. I expect Geoff's getting excited, she thought. She was really quite excited herself.

'Now where are you going?' she asked, as he swerved suddenly off the road. It was perfectly plain that he was going into a public house, whose front door he had seen flung open just as he was about to pass it by.

'Well, here it is,' he said. 'The White Horse. The very first pub to have the privilege of serving a drink to Mr and Mrs Geoffrey Midwinter.'

This pleased her, although she wanted to get to the hotel as quickly as she could, to unpack her trousseau, before it creased too badly.

It was a dull little bar, smelling frowsty. The landlord was glumly watchful, as if they might suddenly get out of hand, or steal one of his cracked ashtrays.

Geoff, however, was in high spirits, and raised his pint pot and winked at his wife. 'Well, here's in anticipation,' he said. She looked demurely at her gin and orange, but she smiled. She loved him dearly. She was quite convinced of this, for she had filled in a questionnaire on the subject of love in one of her magazines, and had scored eighteen out of twenty, with a rating of 'You and Cleopatra share the honours'. Only his obsession with public houses worried her, but she was sure that – once she had him away from the influence of his father and brothers – she would be able to break the habit.

At six o'clock Mr Midwinter took his thirst and his derogatory opinions about the wedding down to the saloon bar of the Starter's Orders. His rueful face, as he described the jugs of orangeade, convulsed his friends. 'Poor Geoff, what's he thinking of, marrying into a lot like that?' asked the barmaid.

'Won't make no difference to Geoff,' said his father. 'Geoff's like his Dad. Not given to asking anybody's by-your-leave when he feels like a pint.'

Mrs Midwinter had stayed at home alone. It had not occurred to her husband that she might be feeling flat after the day's excitement. She would not have remarked on it herself, knowing the problem was insoluble. He could not have taken her to a cinema, because Saturday evening was sacred to drinking, and although she would have liked to go with him for a glass of stout, she knew why she could not. He always drank in the men-only bar at the Starter's Orders. 'Well, you don't want me drinking with a lot of prostitutes, do you?' he often asked, and left her no choice, as was his habit.

Beryl had never stayed in a hotel before, and she was full of admiration at the commanding tone Geoff adopted as they entered the hall of the Seaferry Arms.

'Just one before we go up?' he inquired, looking towards the bar.

'Later, dear,' she said firmly. 'Let's unpack and tidy ourselves first; then we can have a drink before dinner.' The word 'dinner' depressed him. It threatened to waste a great deal of Saturday evening drinking time.

From their bedroom window they could see a bleak stretch of promenade, grey and gritty. The few people down there either fought their way against the gale, with their heads bowed and coats clutched to their breasts, or seemed tumbled along with the wind at their heels. The sun, having shone on the bride, had long ago gone in and it seemed inconceivable that it would ever come out again.

'No strolling along the prom tonight,' said Geoff.

'Isn't it a shame? It's the only thing that's gone wrong.'

Beryl began to hang up and spread about the filmy, lacy, ribboned lingerie with which she had for long planned to tease and entice her husband.

'The time you take,' he said. He had soon tipped everything out of his own case into a drawer. 'What's this?' he asked, picking up something of mauve chiffon.

'My nightgown,' she said primly.

'Whatever for?'

'Don't be common.' She always affected disapproval when he teased her.

'What about a little anticipation here and now?' he suggested.

'Oh, don't be so silly. It's broad daylight.'

'Right. Well, I'm just going to spy out the lie of the land. Back in a minute,' he said.

She was quite content to potter about the bedroom, laying traps for his seduction; but when she was ready at last, she realised that he had been away a long time. She stood by the window, wondering what to do, knowing that it was time for them to go in to dinner. After a while, she decided that she would have to find him and, feeling nervous and self-conscious, she went along the quiet landing and down the stairs. Her common sense took her towards the sound of voices and laughter and, as soon as she opened the door of the bar, she was given a wonderful welcome from all the new friends Geoff had suddenly made.

'It seems ever so flat, doesn't it?' Mrs Cotterell said. All of the washing-up was done, but she was too tired to make a start on packing up the presents.

'It's the reaction,' her husband said solemnly.

Voices from a play on the wireless mingled with their own, but were ignored. Mrs Cotterell had her feet in a bowl of hot water. New shoes had given her agony. Beryl, better informed, had practised wearing hers about the house for days before.

'Haven't done my corns any good,' Mrs Cotterell mourned. Her feet ached and throbbed, and so did her heart.

'It all went off well, though, didn't it?' she asked, as she had asked him a dozen times before.

'Thanks to you,' he said dutifully. He was clearing out the budgerigar's cage and the bird was sitting on his bald head, blinking and chattering.

Mrs Cotterell stared at her husband. She suddenly saw him as a completely absurd figure, and she trembled with anger and self-pity. Something ought to have been done for her on such an evening, she thought, some effort should have been made to console and reward her. Instead, she was left to soak her feet and listen to a lot of North Country accents on the radio. She stretched out her hand and switched them off.

'Whatever's wrong, Mother?'

'I can't stand any more of that "By goom" and "Nowt" and "Eee, lad". It reminds me of that nasty cousin Rose of yours.'

'But we always listen to the play on a Saturday.'

'This Saturday isn't like other Saturdays.' She snatched her handkerchief out of her cuff and dabbed her eyes.

Mr Cotterell leaned forward and patted her knee and the budgerigar flew from his head and perched on her shoulder.

'That's right, Joey, you go to Mother. She wants a bit of cheering up.'

'I'm not his mother, if you don't mind, and I don't want cheering up from a bird.'

'One thing I know is you're overtired. I've seen it coming. You wouldn't care to put on your coat and stroll down to the public for a glass of port, would you?'

'Don't be ridiculous,' she said.

After dinner, they drank their coffee, all alone in the dreary lounge of the Seaferry Arms, and then Beryl went to bed. She had secret things to do to her hair and her face.

'I'll just pour you out another cup,' she said. 'Then, when you've drunk it, you can come up.'

'Right,' he said solemnly, nodding his head.

'Don't be long, darling.'

When she had gone, he sat and stared at the cupful of black coffee and then got up and made his way back to the bar.

All of his before-dinner cronies had left and a completely different set of people stood round the bar. He ordered some beer and looked about him.

'Turned chilly,' said the man next to him.

'Yes. Disappointing,' he agreed. To make friends was the easiest thing in the world. In no time, he was at the heart of it all again.

At ten o'clock, Beryl, provocative in chiffon, as the magazines would have described her, burst into tears of rage. She could hear the laughter – so much louder now, towards closing time – downstairs in the bar and knew that the sound of it had drawn Geoff back. She was powerless – so transparently tricked out to tempt him – to do anything but lie and wait until, at bar's emptying, he should remember her and stumble upstairs to bed.

It was not the first happy evening Geoff had spent in the bar of the Seaferry Arms. He had called there with the team, after cricket matches in the nearby villages. Seaferry was only twenty miles from home. Those summer evenings had all merged into one another, as drinking evenings should – and this one was merging with them. I'm glad I came, he thought, rocking slightly as he stood by the bar with two of his new friends. He couldn't remember having met nicer people. They were a very gay married couple. The wife had a miniature poodle who had already wetted three times on the carpet. 'She can't help it, can you, Angel?' her mistress protested. 'She's quite neurotic; aren't you, precious thing?'

Doris – as Geoff had been told to call her – was a heavy jolly woman. The bones of her stays showed through her frock, her necklace of jet beads was powdered with cigarette ash. She clutched a large, shiny handbag and had snatched from it a pound note, which she began to wave in the air, trying to catch the barmaid's eye. 'I say, Miss! What's her name, Ted? Oh, yes. I say, Maisie! Same again, there's a dear girl.'

It was nearly closing time, and a frenzied reordering was going on. The street door was pushed open and a man and woman with a murderous-looking bull terrier came in. 'You stay there,' the man said to the woman and the dog, and he left them and began to force his way towards the bar.

'Miss! Maisie!' Doris called frantically. Her poodle, venturing between people's legs, made another puddle under a table and approached the bull terrier.

'I say, Doris, call Zoë back,' said her husband. 'And put that money away. I told you I'll get these.'

'I insist. They're on me.'

'Could you call your dog back?' the owner of the bull terrier asked them. 'We don't want any trouble.'

'Come, Zoë, pet!' Doris called. 'He wouldn't hurt her, though. She's a bitch. Maisie! Oh, there's a dear. Same again, love. Large ones.'

Suddenly, a dreadful commotion broke out. Doris was nearly knocked off her stool as Zoë came flying back to her for protection, with the bull terrier at her throat. She screamed and knocked over somebody's gin.

Geoff, who had been standing by the bar in a pleasurable haze, watching the barmaid, was, in spite of his feeling of unreality, the first to spring to life and pounce upon the bull terrier and grab his collar. The dog bit his hand, but he was too drunk to feel much pain. Before anyone could snatch Zoë out of danger, the barmaid lifted the jug of water and, meaning to pour it over the bull terrier, flung it instead over Geoff. The shock made him loosen his grip and the fight began again. A second time he grabbed at the collar and had his hand bitten once more; but now – belatedly, everyone else thought – the two dog-owners came to his help. Zoë, with every likelihood of being even more neurotic in the future, was put, shivering, in her mistress's arms, the bull terrier was secured to his lead in disgrace, and Maisie called Time.

After some recriminations between themselves, the dog-owners thanked and congratulated Geoff. 'Couldn't get near them,' they said. 'The bar was so crowded. Couldn't make head or tail of what was going on.'

'Sorry you got so wet,' said Doris.

The bull terrier's owner felt rather ashamed of himself when he saw how pale Geoff was. 'You all right?' he asked. 'You look a bit shaken up.'

Geoff examined his hand. There was very little blood, but he was beginning to be aware of the pain and felt giddy. He shook his head, but could not answer. Something dripped from his hair on to his forehead, and when he dabbed it with his handkerchief, he was astonished to see water and not blood.

'You got far to go?' the man asked him. 'Where's your home?'

'Lissport.'

'That's our way, too, if you want a lift.' Whether Geoff had a car or not, the man thought he was in no condition to drive it; although, whether from shock or alcohol or both, it was difficult to decide.

'I'd *like* a lift,' Geoff murmured drowsily. 'Many thanks.'

'No, any thanks are due to *you*.'

'Doesn't it seem strange without Geoff?' Mrs Midwinter asked her husband. He was back from the Starter's Orders, had taken off his collar and tie and was staring gloomily at the dying fire.

'Les and Ron home yet?' he asked.

'No, they won't be till half-past twelve. They've gone to the dance at the town hall.'

'Half-past twelve! It's scandalous the way they carry on.

Drinking themselves silly, I've no doubt at all. Getting decent girls into trouble.'

'It's only a dance, Dad.'

'*And* their last one. I'm not having it. Coming home drunk on a Sunday morning and lying in bed till all hours to get over it. When was either of them last at chapel? Will you tell me that?'

Mrs Midwinter sighed and folded up her knitting.

'I can't picture why Geoff turned from chapel like that.' Mr Midwinter seemed utterly depressed about his sons, as he often was at this time on a Saturday night.

'Well, he was courting . . . '

'First time I've been in a church was today, and I was not impressed.'

'I thought it was lovely, and you looked your part just as if you did it every day.'

'I wasn't worried about *my* part. Sort of thing like that makes no demands on *me*. What I didn't like was the service, to which I took exception, and that namby-pamby parson's voice. To me, the whole thing was – insincere.'

Mrs Midwinter held up her hand to silence him. 'There's a car stopping outside. It can't be the boys yet.'

From the street, they both heard Geoff's voice shouting goodbye, then a car door was slammed, and the iron gate opened with a whining sound.

'Dad, it's Geoff!' Mrs Midwinter whispered. 'There must have been an accident. Something's happened to Beryl.'

'Well, he sounded cheerful enough about it.'

They could hear Geoff coming unsteadily up the garden path. When Mrs Midwinter threw open the door, he stood blinking at the sudden light, and swaying.

'Geoff! Whatever's wrong?'

'I've got wet, Mum, and I've hurt my hand,' Geoff said.

from *A Dedicated Man*

Girl Reading

ETTA'S desire was to belong. Sometimes she felt on the fringe of the family, at other times drawn headily into its very centre. At meal-times – those occasions of argument and hilarity, of thrust and counterstroke, bewildering to her at first – she was especially on her mettle, turning her head alertly from one to another as if watching a fast tennis match. She hoped soon to learn the art of riposte and already used, sometimes unthinkingly, family words and phrases; and had one or two privately treasured memories of even having made them laugh. They delighted in laughing and often did so scoffingly – 'at the expense of those less fortunate' as Etta's mother would sententiously have put it.

Etta and Sarah were school friends. It was not the first time that Etta had stayed with the Lippmanns in the holidays. Everyone understood that the hospitality would not be returned, for Etta's mother, who was widowed, went out to work each day. Sarah had seen only the outside of the drab terrace house where her friend lived. She had persuaded her elder brother, David, to take her spying there one evening.

They drove fifteen miles to Market Swanford and Sarah, with great curiosity, studied the street names until at last she discovered the house itself. No one was about. The street was quite deserted and the two rows of houses facing one another were blank and silent as if waiting for a hearse to appear. 'Do hurry!' Sarah urged her brother. It had been a most dangerous outing and she was thoroughly depressed by it. Curiosity now seemed a trivial sensation compared with the pity she was feeling for her friend's drab life and her shame at having confirmed her own suspicions of it. She was threatened by tears. 'Aren't you going in?' her brother asked in great surprise. 'Hurry, hurry,' she begged him. There had never been any question of her calling at that house.

She must be very lonely there all through the holidays, poor Etta, she thought, and could imagine hour after hour in the dark house. Bickerings with the daily help she had already heard of and – Etta trying to put on a brave face and make much of nothing – trips to the public library the highlight of the day, it seemed. No wonder that her holiday reading was always so carefully done, thought Sarah, whereas she herself could never snatch a moment for it except at night in bed.

Sarah had a lively conscience about the seriousness of her friend's private world. Having led her more than once into trouble, at school, she had always afterwards felt a disturbing sense of shame; for Etta's work was more important than her own could ever be, too important to be interrupted by escapades. Sacrifices had been made and scholarships must be won. Once – it was a year ago when they were fifteen and had less sense – Sarah had thought up some rough tomfoolery and Etta's blazer had been torn. She was still haunted by her friend's look of consternation. She had remembered too late, as always – the sacrifices that had been made, the widowed mother sitting year after year at her office desk, the holidays that were never taken and the contriving that had to be done.

Her own mother was so warm and worldly. If she had anxieties she kept them to herself, setting the pace of gaiety, up to date and party-loving. She was popular with her friends' husbands who, in their English way, thought of her comfortably as nearly as good company as a man and full of bright ways as well. Etta felt safer with her than with Mr Lippmann, whose enquiries were often too probing; he touched nerves, his jocularity could be an embarrassment. The boys – Sarah's elder brothers – had their own means of communication which their mother unflaggingly strove to interpret and, on Etta's first visit, she had tried to do so for her, too.

She *was* motherly, although she looked otherwise, the girl decided. Lying in bed at night, in the room she shared with Sarah, Etta would listen to guests driving noisily away or to the Lippmanns returning, full of laughter, from some neighbour's house. Late night door-slamming in the country disturbed only the house's occupants, who all contributed to it. Etta imagined them pottering about downstairs – husband and wife, would hear bottles clinking, laughter, voices raised from room to room, good-night endearments to cats and dogs and at last Mrs Lippmann's running foot-steps on the stairs and the sound of her jingling bracelets coming nearer. Outside their door she would pause, listening, wondering if they were asleep already. They never were. 'Come in!' Sarah would shout, hoisting herself up out of the bedclothes on one elbow, her face turned expectantly towards the door, ready for laughter – for something amusing would surely have happened. Mrs Lippmann, sitting on one of the beds, never failed them. When they were children, Sarah said, she brought back *petits fours* from parties; now she brought back *faux pas*. She specialised in little stories against herself – Mummy's Humiliations, Sarah named them – tactless things she had said, never-to-be-remedied remarks which sprang fatally from her lips. Mistakes in identity was her particular line, for she never remembered a face, she

119

declared. Having kissed Sarah, she would bend over Etta to do the same. She smelt of scent and gin and cigarette smoke. After this they would go to sleep. The house would be completely quiet for several hours.

Etta's mother had always had doubts about the suitability of this *ménage*. She knew it only at second hand from her daughter, and Etta said very little about her visits and that little was only in reply to obviously resented questions. But she had a way of looking about her with boredom when she returned, as if she had made the transition unwillingly and incompletely. She hurt her mother – who wished only to do everything in the world for her, having no one else to please or protect.

'I should feel differently if we were able to return the hospitality,' she told Etta. The Lippmanns' generosity depressed her. She knew that it was despicable to feel jealous, left out, kept in the dark, but she tried to rationalise her feelings before Etta. 'I could take a few days off and invite Sarah here,' she suggested.

Etta was unable to hide her consternations and her expression deeply wounded her mother. 'I shouldn't know what to do with her,' she said.

'Couldn't you go for walks? There are the Public Gardens. And take her to the cinema one evening. What do you do at *her* home?'

'Oh, just fool about. Nothing much.' Some afternoons they just lay on their beds and ate sweets, keeping all the windows shut and the wireless on loud, and no one ever disturbed them or told them they ought to be out in the fresh air. Then they had to plan parties and make walnut fudge and de-flea the dogs. Making fudge was the only one of these things she could imagine them doing in her own home and they could not do it all the time. As for the dreary Public Gardens, she could not herself endure the asphalt paths and the bandstand and the beds of salvias. She could imagine vividly how dejected Sarah would feel.

Early in these summer holidays, the usual letter had come
from Mrs Lippmann. Etta, returning from the library, found
that the charwoman had gone early and locked her out.
She rang the bell, but the sound died away and left an even
more forbidding silence. All the street, where elderly people
dozed in stuffy rooms, was quiet. She lifted the flap of the
letterbox and called through it. No one stirred or came. She
could just glimpse an envelope, lying face up on the doormat,
addressed in Mrs Lippmann's large, loopy, confident handwriting. The house-stuffiness wafted through the letterbox.
She imagined the kitchen floor slowly drying, for there was
a smell of soapy water. A tap was steadily dripping.

She leaned against the door, waiting for her mother's
return, in a sickness of impatience at the thought of the
letter lying there inside. Once or twice, she lifted the flap
and had another look at it.

Her mother came home at last, very tired. With an anxious
air, she set about cooking supper, which Etta had promised
to have ready. The letter was left among her parcels on the
kitchen table, and not until they had finished their stewed
rhubarb did she send Etta to fetch it. She opened it carefully with the bread knife and deepened the frown on her
forehead in preparation for reading it. When she had, she
gave Etta a summary of its contents and put forward her
objections, her unnerving proposal.

'She wouldn't come,' Etta said. 'She wouldn't leave her
dog.'

'But, my dear, she has to leave him when she goes back
to school.'

'I know. That's the trouble. In the holidays she likes to
be with him as much as possible, to make up for it.'

Mrs Salkeld, who had similar wishes about her daughter,
looked sad. 'It is too one-sided,' she gently explained. 'You
must try to understand how I feel about it.'

'They're only too glad to have me. I keep Sarah company
when they go out.'

They obviously went out a great deal and Mrs Salkeld suspected that they were frivolous. She did not condemn them for that – they must lead their own lives, but those were in a world which Etta would never be able to afford the time or money to inhabit. 'Very well, Musetta,' she said, removing the girl further from her by using her full name – used only on formal and usually menacing occasions.

That night she wept a little from tiredness and depression – from disappointment, too, at the thought of returning in the evenings to the dark and empty house, just as she usually did, but when she had hoped for company. They were not healing tears she shed and they did nothing but add self-contempt to her other distresses.

A week later, Etta went the short distance by train to stay with the Lippmanns. Her happiness soon lost its edge of guilt, and once the train had rattled over the iron bridge that spanned the broad river, she felt safe in a different country. There seemed to be even a different weather, coming from a wider sky, and a riverside glare – for the curves of the railway line brought it close to the even more winding course of the river, whose silver loops could be glimpsed through the trees. There were islands and backwaters and a pale heron standing on a patch of mud.

Sarah was waiting at the little station and Etta stepped down on to the platform as if taking a footing into promised land. Over the station and the gravelly lane outside hung a noonday quiet. On one side were grazing meadows, on the other side the drive gateways of expensive houses. The Gables was indeed gabled and so was its boat-house. It was also turreted and balconied. There was a great deal of woodwork painted glossy white, and a huge-leaved Virginia creeper covered much of the red brick walls – in the front beds were the salvias and lobelias Etta had thought she hated. Towels and swim-suits hung over balcony rails and a pair of tennis shoes had been put out on a window-sill to dry. Even though Mr Lippmann and his son, David, went to London every day, the house always had – for Etta – a holiday atmosphere.

The hall door stood open and on the big round table were the stacks of new magazines which seemed to her the symbol of extravagance and luxury. At the back of the house, on the terrace overlooking the river, Mrs Lippmann, wearing tight, lavender pants and a purple shirt, was drinking vodka with a neighbour who had called for a subscription to some charity. Etta was briefly enfolded in scented silk and tinkling bracelets and then released and introduced. Sarah gave her a red, syrupy drink and they sat down on the warm steps among the faded clumps of aubretia and rocked the ice cubes to and fro in their glasses, keeping their eyes narrowed to the sun.

Mrs Lippmann gossiped, leaning back under a fringed chair-umbrella. She enjoyed exposing the frailties of her friends and family, although she would have been the first to hurry to their aid in trouble. Roger, who was seventeen, had been worse for drink the previous evening, she was saying. Faced with breakfast, his face had been a study of disgust which she now tried to mimic. And David could not eat, either; but from being in love. She raised her eyes to heaven most dramatically, to convey that great patience was demanded of her.

'He eats like a horse,' said Sarah. 'Etta, let's go upstairs.' She took Etta's empty glass and led her back across the lawn, seeming not to care that her mother would without doubt begin to talk about her the moment she had gone.

Rich and vinegary smells of food came from the kitchen as they crossed the hall. (There was a Hungarian cook to whom Mrs Lippmann spoke in German and a Portuguese 'temporary' to whom she spoke in Spanish.) The food was an important part of the holiday to Etta, who had nowhere else eaten *Sauerkraut* or *Apfelstrudel* or cold fried fish, and she went into the dining-room each day with a sense of adventure and anticipation.

On this visit she was also looking forward to the opportunity of making a study of people in love – an opportunity she had not had before. While she unpacked, she questioned Sarah about David's Nora, as she thought of her; but Sarah would only say that she was quite a good sort with dark eyes and an enormous bust, and that as she was coming to dinner that evening, as she nearly always did, Etta would be able to judge for herself.

While they were out on the river all the afternoon – Sarah rowing her in a dinghy along the reedy backwater – Etta's head was full of love in books, even in those holiday set books Sarah never had time for – *Sense and Sensibility* this summer. She felt that she knew what to expect, and her perceptions were sharpened by the change of air and scene, and the disturbing smell of the river, which she snuffed up deeply as if she might be able to store it up in her lungs. 'Mother thinks it is polluted,' Sarah said when Etta lifted a streaming hand from trailing in the water and brought up some slippery weeds and held them to her nose. They laughed at the idea.

Etta, for dinner, put on the Liberty silk they wore on Sunday evenings at school and Sarah at once brought out her own hated garment from the back of the cupboard where she had pushed it out of sight on the first day of the holidays. When they appeared downstairs, they looked unbelievably dowdy, Mrs Lippmann thought, turning away for a moment because her eyes had suddenly pricked with tears at the sight of her kind daughter.

Mr Lippmann and David returned from Lloyd's at half-past six and with them brought Nora – a large, calm girl with an air of brittle indifference towards her fiancé which disappointed but did not deceive Etta, who knew enough to remain undeceived by banter. To interpret from it the private tendernesses it hid was part of the mental exercise she was to be engaged in. After all, David would know better than to have his heart on his sleeve, especially in this *dégagé* family where nothing seemed half so funny as falling in love.

After dinner, Etta telephoned her mother, who had perhaps been waiting for the call, as the receiver was lifted immediately. Etta imagined her standing in the dark and narrow hall with its smell of umbrellas and furniture polish.

'I thought you would like to know I arrived safely.'

'What have you been doing?'

'Sarah and I went to the river. We have just finished dinner.' Spicy smells still hung about the house. Etta guessed that her mother would have had half a tin of sardines and put the other half by for her breakfast. She felt sad for her and guilty herself. Most of her thoughts about her mother were deformed by guilt.

'What have you been doing?' she asked.

'Oh, the usual,' her mother said brightly. 'I am just turning the collars and cuffs of your winter blouses. By the way, don't forget to pay Mrs Lippmann for the telephone call.'

'No. I shall have to go now. I just thought . . . '

'Yes, of course, dear. Well, have a lovely time.'

'We are going for a swim when our dinner has gone down.'

'Be careful of cramp won't you? But I mustn't fuss from this distance. I know you are in good hands. Give my kind regards to Mrs Lippmann and Sarah, will you, please. I must get back to your blouses.'

'I wish you wouldn't bother. You must be tired.'

'I am perfectly happy doing it,' Mrs Salkeld said. But if that were so, it was unnecessary, Etta thought, for her to add, as she did: 'And someone has to do it.'

She went dully back to the others. Roger was strumming on a guitar but he blushed and put it away when Etta came into the room.

As the days went quickly by, Etta thought that she was belonging more this time than ever before. Mr Lippmann, a genial patriarch, often patted her head when passing, in confirmation of her existence, and Mrs Lippmann let her run errands. Roger almost wistfully sought her company, while Sarah disdainfully discouraged him; for they had their own employments, she implied; her friend – 'my best friend', as she introduced Etta to lesser ones or adults – could hardly be expected to want the society of schoolboys. Although he was a year older than themselves, being a boy he was less sophisticated, she explained. She and Etta considered themselves to be rather wordly-wise – Etta having learnt from literature and Sarah from putting two and two together, her favourite pastime. Her parents seemed to her to behave with the innocence of children, unconscious of their motives, so continually betraying themselves to her experienced eye, when knowing more would have made them guarded. She had similarly put two and two together about Roger's behaviour to Etta, but she kept these conclusions to herself – partly from not wanting to make her friend feel self-conscious and partly – for she scorned self-deception – from what she recognised to be jealousy. She and Etta were very well as they were, she thought.

Etta herself was too much absorbed by the idea of love to ever think of being loved. In this house, she had her first chance of seeing it at first hand and she studied David and Nora with such passionate speculation that their loving seemed less their own than hers. At first, she admitted to herself that she was disappointed. Their behaviour fell short of what she required of them; they lacked a romantic attitude to one another and Nora was neither touching nor glorious – neither Viola nor Rosalind. In Etta's mind to be either was satisfactory; to be boisterous and complacent was not. Nora was simply a plump and genial girl with a large bust and a faint moustache. She could not be expected to inspire David with much gallantry and, in spite of all the red roses he brought her from London, he was not above telling her that she was getting fat. Gaily retaliatory, she would threaten him with the bouquet, waving it about his head, her huge engagement ring catching the light, flashing with different colours, her eyes flashing too.

Sometimes, there was what Etta's mother would have called 'horseplay', and Etta herself deplored the noise, the dishevelled romping. 'We know quite well what it's instead of,' said Sarah. 'But I sometimes wonder if *they* do. They would surely cut it out if they did.'

As intent as a bird-watcher, Etta observed them, but was puzzled that they behaved like birds, making such a display of their courtship, an absurd-looking frolic out of a serious matter. She waited in vain for a sigh or secret glance. At night, in the room she shared with Sarah, she wanted to talk about them more than Sarah, who felt that her own family was the last possible source of glamour or enlightenment. Discussing her bridesmaid's dress was the most she would be drawn into and that subject Etta felt was devoid of romance. She was not much interested in mere weddings and thought them rather banal and public celebrations. 'With an overskirt of embroidered net,' said Sarah in her decisive voice. 'How nice if you could be a bridesmaid, too; but she has all those awful Greenbaum cousins. As ugly as sin, but not to be left out.' Etta was inattentive to her. With all her studious nature she had set herself to study love and study it she would. She made the most of what the holiday offered and when the exponents were absent she fell back on the textbooks – *Tess of the D'Urbervilles* and *Wuthering Heights* at that time.

To Roger she seemed to fall constantly into the same pose, as she sat on the river bank, bare feet tucked sideways, one arm cradling a book, the other outstretched to pluck – as if to aid her concentration – blades of grass. Her face remained pale, for it was always in shadow, bent over her book. Beside her, glistening with oil, Sarah spread out her body to the sun. She was content to lie for hour after hour with no object but to change the colour of her skin and with thoughts crossing her mind as seldom as clouds passed overhead – and in as desultory a way when they did so. Sometimes, she took a book out with her, but nothing happened to it except that it became smothered with oil. Etta, who found sunbathing boring and enervating, read steadily on – her straight, pale hair hanging forward as if to seclude her, to screen her from the curious eyes of passers-by – shaken by passions of the imagination as she was. Voices from boats came clearly across the water, but she did not heed them. People going languidly by in punts shaded their eyes and admired the scarlet geraniums and the greenness of the grass. When motor-cruisers passed, their wash jogged against the mooring stage and swayed into the boat-house, whose lacy fretwork trimmings had just been repainted glossy white.

Sitting there, alone by the boat-house at the end of the grass bank, Roger read, too; but less diligently than Etta. Each time a boat went by, he looked up and watched it out of sight. A swan borne towards him on a wake, sitting neatly on top of its reflection, held his attention. Then his place on the page was lost. Anyhow, the sun fell too blindingly upon it. He would glance again at Etta and briefly, with distaste, at his indolent, spreadeagled sister, who had rolled over on to her stomach to give her shiny back, criss-crossed from the grass, its share of sunlight. So the afternoons passed, and they would never have such long ones in their lives again.

Evenings were more social. The terrace with its fringed umbrellas – symbols of gaiety to Etta – became the gathering place. Etta, listening intently, continued her study of love and as intently Roger studied her and the very emotion which in those others so engrossed her.

'You look still too pale,' Mr Lippmann told her one evening. He put his hands to her face and tilted it to the sun. 'You shan't leave us until there are roses in those cheeks.' He implied that only in his garden did sun and air give their benefit. The thought was there and Etta shared it. 'Too much of a bookworm, I'm afraid,' he added and took one of her textbooks which she carried everywhere for safety, lest she should be left on her own for a few moments. '*Tess of the D'Urbervilles*,' read out Mr Lippmann. 'Isn't it deep? Isn't it on the morbid side?' Roger was kicking rhythmically at a table leg in glum embarrassment. 'This won't do you any good at all, my dear little girl. This won't put the roses in your cheeks.'

'You are doing that,' his daughter told him – for Etta was blushing as she always did when Mr Lippmann spoke to her.

'What's a nice book, Babs?' he asked his wife, as she came out on to the terrace. 'Can't you find a nice story for this child?' The house must be full, he was sure, of wonderfully therapeutic novels if only he knew where to lay hands on them. 'Roger, you're our bookworm. Look out a nice story-book for your guest. This one won't do her eyes any good.' Buying books with small print was a false economy, he thought, and bound to land one in large bills from an eye specialist before long. 'A very short-sighted policy,' he explained genially when he had given them a little lecture to which no one listened.

His wife was trying to separate some slippery cubes of ice and Sarah sprawled in a cane chair with her eyes shut. She was making the most of the setting sun, as Etta was making the most of romance.

'We like the same books,' Roger said to his father. 'So she can choose as well as I could.'

Etta was just beginning to feel a sense of surprised gratitude, had half turned to look in his direction when the betrothed came through the french windows and claimed her attention.

'In time for a lovely drink,' Mrs Lippmann said to Nora.

'She is too fat already,' said David.

Nora swung round and caught his wrists and held them

threateningly. 'If you say that once more, I'll . . . I'll just
. . . ' He freed himself and pulled her close. She gasped and
panted, but leant heavily against him. 'Promise!' she said
again.

'Promise what?'

'You won't ever say it again.'

He laughed at her mockingly.

They were less the centre of attention than they thought
– Mr Lippmann was smiling, but rather at the lovely evening
and that the day in London was over; Mrs Lippmann,
impeded by the cardigan hanging over her shoulders, was
mixing something in a glass jug and Sarah had her eyes
closed against the evening sun. Only Etta, in some bewilderment, heeded them. Roger, who had his own ideas about
love, turned his head scornfully.

Sarah opened her eyes for a moment and stared at Nora,
in her mind measuring against her the wedding dress she
had been designing. She is too fat for satin, she decided,
shutting her eyes again and disregarding the bridal gown
for the time being. She returned to thoughts of her own
dress, adding a little of what she called 'back interest'
(though lesser bridesmaids would no doubt obscure it from
the congregation – or audience) in the form of long velvet
ribbons in turquoise . . . or rose? She drew her brows
together and with her eyes still shut said 'All the colours of
the rainbow aren't very many, are they?'

'Now, Etta dear, what will you have to drink?' asked Mrs
Lippmann.

Just as she was beginning to ask for some tomato juice,
Mr Lippmann interrupted. He interrupted a great deal, for
there were a great many things to be put right, it seemed to
him. 'Now, Mommy, you should give her a glass of sherry
with an egg beaten up in it. Roger, run and fetch a nice egg
and a whisk, too . . . all right, Babsie dear, I shall do it
myself . . . don't worry, child,' he said, turning to Etta and
seeing her look of alarm. 'It is no trouble to me. I shall do

this for you every evening that you are here. We shall watch the roses growing in your cheeks, shan't we, Mommy?'

He prepared the drink with a great deal of clumsy fuss and sat back to watch her drinking it, smiling to himself, as if the roses were already blossoming. 'Good, good!' he murmured, nodding at her as she drained the glass. Every evening, she thought, hoping that he would forget; but horrible though the drink had been, it was also reassuring; their concern for her was reassuring. She preferred it to the cold anxiety of her mother hovering with pills and thermometer.

'Yes,' said Mr Lippmann, 'we shall see. We shall see. I think your parents won't know you.' He puffed out his cheeks and sketched with a curving gesture the bosom she would soon have. He always forgot that her father was dead. It was quite fixed in his mind that he was simply a fellow who had obviously not made the grade; not everybody could. Roger bit his tongue hard, as if by doing so he could curb his father's. I must remind him again, Sarah and her mother were both thinking.

The last day of the visit had an unexpected hazard as well as its own sadness, for Mrs Salkeld had written to say that her employer would lend her his car for the afternoon. When she had made a business call for him in the neighbourhood she would arrive to fetch Etta at about four o'clock.

'She is really to leave us, Mommy?' asked Mr Lippmann at breakfast, folding his newspaper and turning his attention on his family before hurrying to the station. He examined Etta's face and nodded. 'Next time you stay longer and we make rosy apples of these.' He patted her cheeks and ruffled her hair. 'You tell your Mommy and Dadda next time you stay a whole week.'

'She *has* stayed a whole week,' said Sarah.

'Then a fortnight, a month.'

He kissed his wife, made a gesture as if blessing them all, with his newspaper raised above his head, and went from the room at a trot. Thank goodness, thought Sarah, that he won't be here this afternoon to make kind enquiries about *her* husband.

When she was alone with Etta, she said, 'I'm sorry about that mistake he keeps making.'

'I don't mind,' Etta said truthfully, 'I am only embarrassed because I know that you are.' That's *nothing*, she thought; but the day ahead was a different matter.

As time passed, Mrs Lippmann also appeared to be suffering from tension. She went upstairs and changed her matador pants for a linen skirt. She tidied up the terrace and told Roger to take his bathing things off his window-sill. As soon as she had stubbed out a cigarette, she emptied and dusted the ashtray. She was conscious that Sarah was trying to see her with another's eyes.

'Oh, do stop taking photographs,' Sarah said tetchily to Roger, who had been clicking away with his camera all morning. He obeyed her only because he feared to draw attention to his activities. He had just taken what he hoped would be a very beautiful study of Etta in a typical pose – sitting on the river bank with a book in her lap. She had lifted her eyes and was gazing across the water as if she were pondering whatever she had been reading. In fact, she had been arrested by thoughts of David and Nora and, although her eyes followed the print, the scene she saw did not correspond with the lines she read. She turned her head and looked at the willow trees on the far bank, the clumps of borage from which moorhens launched themselves. Perhaps next time that I see them, they'll be married and it will all be over, she thought. The evening before, there had been a great deal of high-spirited sparring about between them. Offence meant and offence taken they assured one another. 'If you do that once more . . . I am absolutely serious,' cried Nora. 'You are trying not to laugh,' David said. 'I'm not. I am absolutely serious.' 'It will end in tears,' Roger had muttered contemptuously. Even good-tempered Mrs Lippmann had looked down her long nose disapprovingly. And that was the last, Etta supposed, that she would see of love for a long time. She was left once again with books. She returned to the one she was reading.

Roger had flung himself on to the grass near by, appearing to trip over a tussock of grass and collapse. He tried to think of some opening remark which might lead to a discussion of the book. In the end, he asked abruptly, 'Do you like that?' She sat brooding over it, chewing the side of her finger. She nodded without looking up and, with a similar automatic gesture, she waved away a persistent wasp. He leaned forward and clapped his hands together smartly and was relieved to see the wasp drop dead into the grass, although he would rather it had stung him first. Etta, however, had not noticed this brave deed.

The day passed wretchedly for him; each hour was more filled with the doom of her departure than the last. He worked hard to conceal his feelings, in which no one took an interest. He knew that it was all he could do, although no good could come from his succeeding. He took a few more secret photographs from his bedroom window, and then he sat down and wrote a short letter to her, explaining his love.

At four o'clock, her mother came. He saw at once that Etta was nervous and he guessed that she tried to conceal her nervousness behind a much jauntier manner to her mother than was customary. It would be a bad hour, Roger decided.

His own mother, in spite of her linen skirt, was gawdy and exotic beside Mrs Salkeld, who wore a navy-blue suit which looked as if it had been sponged and pressed a hundred times – a depressing process unknown to Mrs Lippmann. The pink-rimmed spectacles that Mrs Salkeld wore seemed to reflect a little colour on to her cheekbones, with the result that she looked slightly indignant about something or other. However, she smiled a great deal, and only Etta guessed what an effort it was to her to do so. Mrs Lippmann gave her a chair where she might have a view of the river and she sat down, making a point of not looking round the room, and smoothed her gloves. Her jewellery was real but very small.

'If we have tea in the garden, the wasps get into Anna's rose-petal jam,' said Mrs Lippmann. Etta was not at her best, she felt – not helping at all. She was aligning herself too staunchly with the Lippmanns, so that her mother seemed a stranger to her, as well. 'You see, I am at home here,' she implied, as she jumped up to fetch things or hand things round. She was a little daring in her familiarity.

Mrs Salkeld had contrived the visit because she wanted to understand and hoped to approve of her daughter's friends. Seeing the lawns, the light reflected from the water, later this large, bright room, and the beautiful poppy-seed cake the Hungarian cook had made for tea, she understood completely and felt pained. She could see then, with Etta's eyes, their own dark, narrow house, and she thought of the lonely hours she spent there reading on days of imprisoning rain. The Lippmanns would even have better weather, she thought bitterly. The bitterness affected her enjoyment of the poppy-seed cake. She had, as puritanical people often have, a sweet tooth. She ate the cake with a casual air, determined not to praise.

'You are so kind to spare Etta to us,' said Mrs Lippmann.

'*You* are kind to invite her,' Mrs Salkeld replied, and then for Etta's sake, added: 'She loves to come to you.'

Etta looked self-consciously down at her feet.

'No, I don't smoke,' her mother said primly. 'Thank you.'

Mrs Lippmann seemed to decide not to, either, but very soon her hand stole out and took a cigarette – while she was not looking, thought Roger, who was having some amusement from watching his mother on her best behaviour. Wherever she was, the shagreen cigarette case and the gold lighter were near by. Ashtrays never were. He got up and fetched one before Etta could do so.

The girls' school was being discussed – one of the few topics the two mothers had in common. Mrs Lippmann had never taken it seriously. She laughed at the uniform and despised the staff – an attitude she might at least have hidden from her daughter, Mrs Salkeld felt. The tea-trolley was being wheeled away and her eyes followed the remains of the poppy-seed cake. She had planned a special supper for Etta to return to, but she felt now that it was no use. The things of the mind had left room for an echo. It sounded with every footstep or spoken word in that house where not enough was going on. She began to wonder if there were things of the heart and not the mind that Etta fastened upon so desperately when she was reading. Or was her desire to be in a different place? Lowood was a worse one – she could raise her eyes and look round her own room in relief; Pemberley was better and she would benefit from the change. But how can I help her? she asked herself in anguish. What possible change – and radical it must be – can I ever find the strength to effect? People had thought her wonderful to have made her own life and brought up her child alone. She had kept their heads above water and it had taken all her resources to do so.

Her lips began to refuse the sherry Mrs Lippmann suggested and then, to her surprise and Etta's astonishment, she said 'yes' instead.

It was very early to have suggested it, Mrs Lippmann thought, but it would seem to put an end to the afternoon. Conversation had been as hard work as she had anticipated and she longed for a dry martini to stop her from yawning, as she was sure it would; but something about Mrs Salkeld seemed to discourage gin drinking.

'Mother, it isn't half-past five yet,' said Sarah.

'Darling, don't be rude to your Mummy. I know perfectly well what the time is.' (Who better? she wondered.) 'And this isn't a public house, you know.'

She had flushed a little and was lighting another cigarette. Her bracelets jangled against the decanter as she handed Mrs Salkeld her glass of sherry, saying, 'Young people are so stuffy,' with an air of complicity.

Etta, who had never seen her mother drinking sherry before, watched nervously, as if she might not know how to do it. Mrs Salkeld – remembering the flavour from Christmas mornings many years ago and – more faintly – from her mother's party trifle – sipped cautiously. In an obscure way she was doing this for Etta's sake. It may speed her on her way, thought Mrs Lippmann, playing idly with her charm bracelet, having run out of conversation.

When Mrs Salkeld rose to go, she looked round the room once more as if to fix it in her memory – the setting where she would imagine her daughter on future occasions.

'And come again soon, there's a darling girl,' said Mrs Lippmann, putting her arm round Etta's shoulder as they walked towards the car. Etta, unused to but not ungrateful for embraces, leaned awkwardly against her. Roger, staring at the gravel, came behind carrying the suitcase.

'I have wasted my return ticket,' Etta said.

'Well, that's not the end of the world,' her mother said briskly. She thought, but did not say, that perhaps they could claim the amount if they wrote to British Railways and explained.

Mrs Lippmann's easy affection meant so much less than her own stiff endearments but she resented it all the same and when she was begged, with enormous warmth, to visit them all again soon her smile was a prim twisting of her lips.

The air was bright with summer sounds, voices across the water and rooks up in the elm trees. Roger stood back listening in a dream to the goodbyes and thank-yous. Nor was *this* the end of the world, he told himself. Etta would come again and, better than that, they would also grow older and so be less at the mercy of circumstances. He would be in a position to command his life and turn occasions to his own advantage. Meanwhile, he had done what he could. None the less, he felt such dejection, such an overwhelming conviction that it *was* the end of the world after all, that he could not watch the car go down the drive, and he turned and walked quickly – rudely, off-handedly, his mother thought – back to the house.

Mrs Salkeld, driving homewards in the lowering sun, knew that Etta had tears in her eyes. 'I'm glad you enjoyed yourself,' she said. Without waiting for an answer, she added: 'They are very charming people.' She had always suspected charm and rarely spoke of it, but in this case the adjective seemed called for.

Mr Lippmann would be coming back from London about now, Etta was thinking. And David will bring Nora. They will all be on the terrace having drinks – dry martinis, not sherry.

She was grateful to her mother about the sherry and understood that it had been an effort towards meeting Mrs Lippmann's world half-way, and on the way back, she had not murmured one word of criticism – for their worldliness or extravagance or the vulgar opulence of their furnishings. She had even made a kind remark about them.

I might buy her a new dress, Mrs Salkeld thought – something like the one Sarah was wearing. Though it does seem a criminal waste when she has all her good school clothes to wear out.

They had come on to the main road, and evening traffic streamed by. In the distance the gas holder looked pearl grey and the smoke from factories was pink in the sunset. They were nearly home. Etta, who had blinked her tears back from her eyes, took a sharp breath, almost a sigh.

Their own street with its tall houses was in shadow. 'I wish we had a cat,' said Etta, as she got out of the car and saw the next door tabby looking through the garden railings. She imagined burying her face in its warm fur, it loving only her. To her surprise, her mother said: 'Why not?' Briskly, she went up the steps and turned the key with its familiar grating sound in the lock. The house with its smell – familiar, too – of floor polish and stuffiness, looked secretive. Mrs Salkeld, hardly noticing this, hurried to the kitchen to put the casserole of chicken in the oven.

Etta carried her suitcase upstairs. On the dressing table was a jar of marigolds. She was touched by this – just when she did not want to be touched. She turned her back on them and opened her case. On the top was the book she had left on the terrace. Roger had brought it to her at the last moment. Taking it now, she found a letter inside. Simply 'Etta' was written on the envelope.

Roger had felt that he had done all he was capable of and that was to write in the letter those things he could not have brought himself to say, even if he had had an opportunity. No love letter could have been less anticipated and Etta read it twice before she could realise that it was neither a joke nor a mistake. It was the most extraordinary happening of her life, the most incredible.

Her breathing grew slower and deeper as she sat staring before her, pondering her mounting sense of power. It was as if the whole Lippmann family – Nora as well – had proposed to her. To marry Roger – a long, long time ahead though she must wait to do so – would be the best possible way of belonging.

She got up stiffly – for her limbs now seemed too clumsy a part of her body with its fly-away heart and giddy head – she went over to the dressing table and stared at herself in the glass. I am I, she thought, but she could not believe it. She stared and stared, but could not take in the tantalising idea.

After a while, she began to unpack. The room was a place of transit, her temporary residence. When she had made it tidy, she went downstairs to thank her mother for the marigolds.

The Prerogative of Love

WHERE the lawn was in shadow from the house, the watering-spray flung dazzling aigrettes into the air. The scent of the wet earth, the sound of dripping rose leaves was delicious.

The round marble table was abandoned in the sun, a butterfly hovered above it, both blindingly white. Too hot, Lillah had decided, and had taken her chair and her sewing into the shade; but the damage was done, and she began to feel giddy. Mrs Hatton made her go upstairs and drink salt water and lie on her bed.

'It's a swine, isn't it?' the gardener said, meaning the weather. He was speaking to the postman, who crunched by on the gravel drive with letters in his hand.

'Too sudden,' the postman agreed, stopping for a moment, watching the other man work, the brown hand moving slow as a toad amongst the geraniums, tweaking up tiny weeds. 'A criminal colour, that bright red,' he said. 'Hurts my eyes to look at it. I always preferred the white ones.'

He continued slowly up the drive, hoping to be seen from the house by Mrs Hatton the cook, and offered tea.

No one saw him, for the curtains, hardly stirring, were drawn across the open windows. He stepped into the hall and laid the letters on the brass tray on the table. He suffered a fit of noisy coughing, stood with bowed head after it, listening, but heard not a sound and made off down the drive again.

The letters – what Lillah would call a tradesman's lot – stayed there until Richard came home. It was six o'clock then and hardly any cooler. The cats lay on the stone floor like cast-off furs. One of them got up and stretched and came towards him, its sides hanging, very thin, for it did not fancy its food in this weather. Listlessly, it rubbed its head against his leg, smelt the streets of London on his shoes and wandered, repelled, back to its place and flopped again.

Mrs Hatton, neat as a new pin, came down the back stairs to the kitchen, having napped and tidied up and now, ready for the fray, pinned a clean, folded napkin round her head, as if it were a Stilton cheese. She took the grey and white fish off the ice and, looking grim, began to fillet. All her movements were slow, so that she should not get hot. She even sang under her breath; although yearningly – for a Wiltshire woman – about Galway Bay.

'I'm afraid you'll have to hold the fort,' Lillah told her husband. 'I'll try again later, but at the moment I can't put my feet to the ground.'

She lay on the bed, wrapped in a white kimono. The bedroom was cool to Richard, after the hot pavements and the asphyxiating train. His clothes clung to him, he felt that this room was no place for him and longed to plunge into the river, a long dive between the silken, trailing weeds. But Lillah said there would not be time.

She had nothing to do all day but keep herself cool, he thought, and she had not even managed that. He held the curtain aside, so that at least he could look at the river. It flowed by at the foot of the garden, beyond the urns of geraniums where the lawn sloped down to the mooring stage. On the evenings when there was dinghy racing from the club, white sails clustered there, tipping and rocking, caught in the sheltered curve of river without wind. There was none tonight. There was no breath of air.

'Too late to put the Foresters off,' Lillah said. 'I suppose.'

Although actressy in so many other ways, she lacked the old trouper's temperament, and her audiences – even such a loyal one as the Foresters – were not considered first if she were out of humour.

'Do you mean you won't come down at all?' he asked in consternation.

'Of course, I'll try. I did a little while ago. You must leave me as long as you can, please, darling. Every minute I think it must get cooler, that the dizziness will go.'

She sighed and stirred, then stretched her arm towards him. It looked imploring, but as he moved towards her was withdrawn. She crooked it under her head, and stared up at the ceiling.

'A quick wash, then,' he said, turning to the door.

'Did Mrs Hatton put the wine on ice, I wonder,' Lillah said, not exactly giving him instructions to go and find out, but getting that effect.

Richard went to the kitchen as soon as he could, and found that Mrs Hatton had remembered the wine. She was well forward, she said. And it was certainly hot, she agreed, but nothing to the climate in some parts of the world.

Once upon a time, she had made what she called 'the round trip', on a legacy from an employer, and travel had changed her life. She had returned to another kitchen, but so enriched that her mind was forever roaming, as she stirred and whisked and sieved. 'Bermuda, you'd like, sir,' she once told Richard, as he was setting off for a short holiday in Suffolk.

'The heat's knocked Madam,' she remarked, and took up some steak and began to knock that. 'I got her to drink some salt water. We always did that in India, I told her. "It will put back what you've perspired," I said.' She had indeed told Lillah this and Lillah had disdained to listen, drinking quickly to prevent more of such homely hints. 'You learn to respect the sun when you've been in the tropics,' Mrs Hatton informed Richard.

'No doubt you do,' he said. 'I never was east of Biarritz in all my life.'

'If Madam wants help dressing, I can spare a minute. I'm quite nicely forward.'

'We can always rely on you,' he said hurriedly, looking about him in a flustered manner, forgetting what on earth it was that had suddenly come into his mind while she was talking.

'The ice is in the drawing-room on the tray,' she said.

She could even recapture and read thoughts that had flown from him. She was always more attuned to the master of the house than to the mistress. 'I laid it all out ready.'

'Yes, you think of everything.'

'It's simple enough when you're on your own. It's when there are two of you that things get overlooked.'

I could have swum, after all, Richard thought.

But that moment he heard a car coming up the drive, and went out to the hall door to greet the Foresters, relieved to know that at last Lillah had decided to get up again and dress.

A small, open car swung round the circle of gravel in front of the house and, alone in it, bare-shouldered, with hair knotted up on top, Lillah's niece, Arabella, looked as if she were naked, she might have been sitting up in her bath.

'I won't stop a second if you would rather not,' she said, as the car pulled up.

'I thought you were stark naked,' Richard said, opening the door and looking with interest at her small, white frock – which was sparsely patterned with strawberries – at her shining, tanned legs.

'I'll only come in for a minute,' she said, when she had jumped out of the car. She put her thin arms round his neck and kissed him. They were very long arms, he thought, and seemed to have been flung over his head like a lasso. Then she stepped back and hauled out of the car a large wicker hamper.

'Are you picnicking?' he asked.

She looked surprised. 'This is only my make-up,' she explained. 'Don't worry, darling. I shan't stay the night. But I must have it with me. My cigarettes are in it.'

'And your shoes?' he asked, for she was crossing the gravel barefoot.

'Maybe,' she said, nodding. 'Oh, it's cool!' She stood in the hall and let out a deep breath. 'I've been in some bogus-looking pub all day long wearing a chinchilla coat – one of those snobbish photographs; playing darts with the locals, draped in fur and choked with pearls and all the mates grinning and enjoying the joke. So hot.'

'Lillah's not been well all day.'

'Oh, poor old thing. I'll tell you what, Richard – though I promise not to stay one moment, can I just slake my thirst before I go? Oh, you've got people coming,' she said, passing the open dining-room door, seeing the table. 'That settles it. I'll run out the back way with my empty glass the minute they arrive.'

Richard wished that Lillah had been down to answer for him and he poured out the drink quickly and handed it to Arabella.

She picked up ice with her fingers and dropped it into her glass and took another piece and ran it round the nape of her neck and up and down the insides of her arms. 'What's wrong with her?' she asked.

'The heat, you know.'

'Oh, I *know*. A chinchilla coat, if you please. Oh, I told you. I'll just dash up and say goodbye to her. Who's coming?'

'The Foresters. John and Helen.'

'Well, do give them my love.'

She ran upstairs, still holding the lump of ice in her fist, and Richard stood staring in a disturbed way at her wicker basket lying on a chair.

Lillah, whose bedroom, at the back of the house, over-looked the river, had not heard the car and answered rather suspiciously when Arabella knocked on the door.

She was at the dressing table powdering her white shoulders, and turned, looking far from welcoming, to be kissed and then leant towards the glass again and wiped the lipstick off her cheek.

'What are you up to, Arabella?'

'I've been at Henley all day long, playing darts in a pub and wearing fur coats. I was just going home, when I thought that being in striking distance, I would look in for a drink.'

She sat down on a brocade-covered chair and sucked her ice cube. 'I'm not staying a minute, though.'

'How is your mother?'

'Oh, you're not well, Richard was saying. I'm so sorry. I was quite forgetting. I expect it's the heat. I know *I've* sweltered all day long. Guess what I had for lunch. A cheese sandwich. But not to worry, I'll be home in an hour and a half with any luck. You look so wonderfully cool, Lillah. It's the most elegant dress. The Poor Man's Lady Diana Duff Cooper, Mother and I always call you. Don't let me hinder you, but I must shake out my hair.'

She wandered round the room, looking for somewhere

to put the piece of melting ice and at last threw it out of the window. Then she took the pins from her bright hair and shook it against her bare shoulders.

'I like the colour of your hair today,' Lillah said.

'Oh, thank you. And I simply dote on yours.'

'Well, mine is always the same.'

Lillah leant close to the looking glass, fixing on some earrings.

'Yes, of course, darling,' her niece murmured, face hidden now under a tent of hair, rubbing her scalp. Before Lillah had put on the second earring, she saw Arabella stretch out a hand and take up one of her hairbrushes.

'You don't mind, to you?' she asked, and began to brush with great energy.

'Well, as a matter of fact, I do rather,' Lillah replied.

Back under her hair and brushing until it crackled, the girl seemed not to hear.

'Haven't you one of your own?' Lillah asked, making an impatient movement to gain the girl's attention. 'I thought that models carried the lot wherever they went.'

She felt giddy again – rage hitting her, as the sun had.

Arabella swept the hair back from her face and smiled at her aunt. 'I left the lot downstairs with Uncle Richard,' she replied.

'But you should have put us off,' Helen Forester protested.

'Of course you should,' her husband added.

'For goodness' sake, we're old enough friends by now . . . ' his wife went on.

'Lillah wouldn't hear of it. She says she feels so much better now and I shall be in trouble for ever having mentioned it. She'll be down in a moment. This is Arabella's, her niece's,' he explained, as he moved the wicker basket from a chair so that Helen Forester could sit down. 'She's a model in London and just looked in on her way home from some job.'

He thought that John Forester seemed to brace himself, and that well he might.

'Forgive me, please,' Lillah said, coming across the hall to the open door of the drawing-room. She stretched out her arms to them and put her cheek first to Helen's then John's, a heavy earring swung against each face in turn. 'I've felt so stupid all day long. I couldn't lift my silly head.'

'You should have put us off,' said Helen. 'I was telling Richard . . .'

'But I had looked forward to seeing you so much, and now I have seen you I'm myself again. Mrs Hatton' – she lowered her voice – 'insisted on my going to bed. She's a very strict disciplinarian.'

She saw John looking towards the door and turned round.

'This is my niece, Arabella, who's just dropped in,' she said, staring down at the girl's bare feet.

Arabella's hair was now looped smoothly against her cheeks, like the youthful Queen Victoria's. She had also, her aunt noticed, helped herself very liberally to Lillah's scent.

'We met when I was a little girl,' Arabella said demurely. 'I know you can't remember me, because I was fat and had pigtails and a great brace on my teeth. I must look different now.'

'You must indeed,' John Forester said.

She smiled and came farther into the room. 'You're the Labrador breeders, aren't you?' she asked.

'Where are your shoes, dear girl?' asked Lillah, trying to get a tone of asperity across to Arabella, but so that the Foresters would not detect it.

'It's hardly worth putting them on now when I'm just going. I don't care to drive with shoes on.'

'You left your drink,' said Richard, handing it to her.

'Thank you, darling, I'll thrust it down and be off. I promised to be out of the back door before you arrived,' she told John Forester.

'You silly girl,' said Lillah lightly. She took the drink that Richard had poured out quickly, before, he hoped, she could put them all in the wrong, as she often did, by asking for something without gin. She laid her hand on his shoulder for a moment, where it looked very pale against the dark cloth, and Richard covered it quickly with his own. He smiled questioningly and she nodded.

'Isn't that a beautiful dress of Lillah's?' Helen asked, slightly embarrassed to find herself caught staring at them.

'It's my beautiful wife in it,' Richard said.

'But I meant that, too,' Helen said, too willing for words to agree, not to seem restrained by hearing another woman praised.

Arabella was telling John Forester about the chinchilla coat and the game of darts and he seemed entranced. 'And guess what I had for lunch,' she asked.

'Isn't it a heavenly frock Lillah's wearing?' Helen asked him. 'Doesn't it suit her wonderfully?' To bring Lillah's beauty to the notice of her husband was even greater generosity, she thought, and she looked almost transfigured with the pleasure of finding her friend so lovely.

John's attention was turned from Arabella rather slowly, his eyes moved almost unseeingly to where they were directed. 'Perfect,' he said.

'A cheese sandwich,' said Arabella. 'Just imagine.'

'I suppose you live on air,' he said, his glance, enlivened, returning quickly to her. He was much taken by the rounded thinness of her arms, slim even where they joined the shoulders. If they had been alone, he would have made some excuse to touch them, perhaps patting her in a fatherly way as he begged her not to starve herself or, more youthfully, wondering if he could circle them between finger and thumb.

'I eat like a horse,' she said. 'Worse – for I'm carnivorous. And the bloodier the better.'

'What a gigantic cineraria,' Helen said in an admiring voice.

'It *is* rather ghastly, but dear Mrs Hatton gave it to me on my birthday and I have to have it about, not to hurt her feelings. It's just the sort of thing she adores.'

Helen decided not to like cinerarias in future.

John was looking at Arabella's diminishing drink with anguish. Evenings alone with Richard and Lillah were never so entrancing to him as they were to his wife. Admiration was such a large ingredient of Helen's simple good nature. She did not feel, as he did, that some attempt should be made on their own behalf. She basks in the shade, he thought. The tops of her arms, he suddenly noticed, were very freckled and their flabbiness flattened against her sides.

What would happen to them all if the girl didn't soon go, Richard wondered. Especially, he wondered, what would happen to him.

Then Lillah – not to be put in the wrong by this ravenous girl – warmly said, 'Arabella, may I ask Mrs Hatton to do a little concocting? You *will* stay?'

'I simply *couldn't*. I know only too well how it is in kitchens. Sometimes I take a man home to dinner without warning and there may be only two cutlets.' John seemed to have drawn her eyes back to his, and to his devouring attention she addressed herself. 'Mother and I hiss over them all the time they are cooking. "Let *me* be the vegetarian this time. You were yesterday." But Mother's so noble. She usually manages to get the poached egg for herself and makes long, long apologies for never eating meat. She goes into it rather too much. She went on and on to one man, and a lot later he came again and this time I had managed to get the egg, and Mother ate her cutlet with great enjoyment. "You've changed over, you two," he said.'

For some reason, John burst into sycophantic laughter, then he tilted his glass and finished his gin.

'You will think we live on cutlets,' Arabella said, a few seconds later and after that there was silence.

Well, nothing is settled, Richard thought. She hasn't

answered one way or another. He felt that their evening was nearly on the rocks. Adoration left the conversation in two – John's of Arabella, Helen's of Lillah – and he began to pour out more drinks, since the continuing silence and John's empty glass made it impossible not to. Lillah, thinking of Mrs Hatton and even more, no doubt, of social patterns she despised, would be impatient. 'Everyone drunk before dinner,' she had said so often, driving home from other people's houses. 'I have never known a claret so thrown away,' or 'That poor withered old soufflé.'

'I'll tell you what, Lillah,' Arabella said in her most childish voice, 'Let me go and reconnoitre. I'll see how things are with Mrs Hatton. It's for me to bear the brunt.'

Lillah moved quickly to prevent her, tried to say something to detain her, but the girl had sped across the hall. John was touched to see that the soles of her feet were dirty.

'Oh dear,' Lillah said. 'I'm so sorry.'

'Such a beautiful girl,' said Helen.

'That family has more than its fair share of looks, I always think,' Richard said, smiling at his wife. John looked at her, too, almost for the first time that evening – and saw resemblances between the two faces – the niece's, the aunt's. He had not known Lillah in the early years of her marriage, and he wondered if Richard had had such luck long ago – an Arabella-like bride, whom time had changed and paled and quietened, but whose erstwhile beauty still quite clearly bewitched him.

'Oh, dear,' Lillah said again. 'I hope she is not lifting the lids off the saucepans and asking questions.'

Richard, seeing Mrs Hatton crossing the hall with a grim stride, going to rearrange her table, closed the door.

'How are the roses this year, John?' he asked.

Having upset all but one of them under that roof, hindered dinner, made an awkward number at the table and talked too much, Arabella, towards the end of the meal, suddenly shivered. Leaning forward, chafing the tops of her arms, she studied the centrepiece of fruit and took out an apple from underneath, so that the pyramid collapsed, a peach rolled across the table and cherries were scattered.

'It will be a chilly run back,' she said. 'Perhaps I should make a start.' For at last the day was cool.

The others were still eating a kirsch-flavoured confection that Mrs Hatton had sampled in California. Much praised it had been by Helen, who spooned it up lovingly. She would describe it later to her humbler friends and would expect them to listen spellbound.

Arabella was up now and darted round the table with a kiss for each of them. Lillah, receiving hers last, kept her head bent, and John pushed back his chair, dropped his napkin, knocked a spoon and some cherries on the floor. Richard went to the door and opened it.

'Don't stir, anybody,' Arabella said.

'It's true that we haven't finished dinner,' Lillah said. ('And I consider she had every right to say it,' Helen told John afterwards.)

'Don't come out, Richard. Please not to. Lillah, may I borrow a sweater. I'll be frozen driving home.'

'There's a cardigan on the hall settle,' her aunt said, and seemed with the most delicate gesture to draw Richard's attention to his place at the table. He returned to it and passing Lillah's chair, patted her shoulder – with such a touch of understanding, Helen thought.

'There's lipstick on your face,' she told her husband.

'On all your faces, if I may say so,' Lillah said, having removed it from her own.

'Such a lively girl,' Helen said uncertainly. After all, it was Lillah's own sister's child and so had every claim to praise.

'Delightful,' John said in a more definite tone. 'She reminds me how scatter-brained I was myself when I was young.' He listened to the car being started, then throwing up gravel as it tore away.

We envy the young, that's what it is, Richard thought sadly. It is natural for us to harden against them.

'My poor sister was widowed at twenty-three,' Lillah said; as if this could be the explanation of her niece's behaviour. She gazed at the scattered cherries on the white cloth, then added: 'Her life was haphazard, at the best of times.'

'My aunt is a perfectionist,' Arabella had said a little while ago. She had spoken to Helen, and as if Lillah herself were not present.

This had often been said of her before, but now she would have liked to disclaim the label, seeing herself, in Arabella's eyes, too much absorbed by trifles, restricted and neurotic. 'It must be Mrs Hatton who is the perfectionist,' she had said. 'It was all left to her.' Helen had once more, boringly, been praising something.

Haphazard though her sister's life was, she had this daughter in it, and close enough they seemed to Lillah whenever she saw them together. And the Foresters had children, too, though grown-up now and gone away.

'Rather a disrupted evening,' Lillah said apologetically as her guests were going, and had hardly the patience to listen to their protestations, their expressions of delight. She and Richard went down the steps with them on to the dark drive and stood together as the car drove away, each lifting a hand briefly in farewell, then turning back towards the house, which still threw out from its walls the stored warmth of the day. He took her arm as they went up the steps.

'You were wonderful,' he said.

'Well, it is over.'

'You must feel exhausted.'

'That dreadful girl,' she said.

*   *   *

Helen looked back as the car turned into the lane, and saw Richard and Lillah at the top of the steps, in the light from the hall. Until they were out of the drive, she had said nothing, and even now kept her voice low, as if the still air might waft it back towards the house.

'How in love they are,' she said. 'Every time I see them they seem more so.' Which touched her most she hardly knew – Richard's gallantry, or Lillah, who inspired it. 'I loved the stuffed vine leaves. I've so often read about them in books. I suppose Mrs Hatton picked that up in the Middle East. What a pretty touch – those tiny flowers in the finger-bowls. What were they? I meant to ask. I don't think the niece was welcome. I'm sure I shouldn't have been so smooth about it as Lillah was. If Mrs Hatton complained, you couldn't blame her. I must try that with the vine leaves. See what I can do. I suppose you would need to blanch them first. I was longing to ask, but didn't quite like to.'

She was really talking to herself.

Those treasure hunts we used to go on, all about these very lanes, John suddenly remembered. Lovely summer evenings just like this one, tearing like demented things about the countryside, diving into the river in the early hours, parking cars at the edges of woods.

He kept his thoughts to himself, as if they were secrets of his own, and then he remembered that Helen had been there too. She had once swum across the river fully dressed, for a bet. It was difficult to believe.

'A really beautiful frock,' she was saying.

'Unusual,' he replied. 'Not much of it.' He suddenly laughed.

'I meant Lillah's.'

Presently she sighed and said: 'He's so wonderful to her always.'

John knew the pattern – the excited admiration invariably turned to dissatisfaction in the end – one of the reasons why these evenings ruffled him.

'I'm sure that to him she's as beautiful as on the day they married,' she went on.

'Still a very fine woman,' he replied.

'Is it because they've never had children, I wonder? The glamour wasn't worn off by all those nursery troubles. All their love kept for one another.'

'It is better to have children,' John said.

'Well, of course. Who ever'd deny it? You know I didn't think that. But I wondered if it had drawn them close together, *not* having them. They never seem to take one another for granted.' As we do, she left unspoken, though her sigh was explicit.

'Well, we mustn't compare ourselves with *them*,' he said rather smartly. 'And who are we to be talking about love? They're the ones. They're famous for it, after all. It's their prerogative.'

The Benefactress

FOUR widows lived in the almshouses beside the church. On the other side of the wall, their husbands' graves were handy. 'I've just seen to Charlie's,' Mrs Swan called out to Mrs Rippon, who was going down the garden path carrying a bunch of phlox.

They were four robust old ladies, and their relationship with one another was cordial, but formal. Living at close quarters, they kept to themselves, drank their own tea in their own kitchens, used surnames, passed a few remarks, perhaps, when they met by chance in the graveyard or weeding their garden plots or, dressed in their best, waiting for the bus to go the village and draw their pensions.

The almshouses were Elizabethan, with pretentious high chimneys whose bricks were set in a twist. In an alcove above the two middle front doors was a stone bust of the benefactor who had built the cottages and endowed them for the use of four old people of the parish. He wore a high ruff and a pointed beard, and rain had washed deep sockets to his eyes and pitted his cheeks so that he looked as if he were ravaged by some horrible disease. His name was carved in Latin below the alcove – a foreigner, the old ladies had always supposed.

Outside each front door was a wooden bench where they could have sat in the sun to warm their ageing bones, but this they never did. In fine weather it was much too public, with sightseers in and out of the old church taking photographs. They photographed the almshouses without asking permission, and once Mrs Swan, going down the garden to pick a few gooseberries, had been requested to pose within her porch wearing an old black apron. 'Saucy monkeys,' she had said to her niece's daughter, who was indoors visiting.

She was there again this afternoon, sitting in the greenish light that came through heavily leaded panes and slanted in from the open, leaf-fringed doorway. The path outside was shaded by a yew tree, and Mrs Rippon had passed by it carrying her bunch of phlox.

'That grave's a novelty to her,' Mrs Swan said to her grand-niece when her neighbour was out of hearing. 'It's only human, after all. I know I was over there every day when Charlie had just died.'

The niece, Evie, seemed to stiffen with disdain.

I wish I could bring her down to earth, Mrs Swan thought. What's wrong with going to the graveyard, I should like to know.

'I couldn't bring myself to grieve,' she went on. 'Poor man, he did suffer. From here to here they opened him.' She measured off more than a foot of her own stomach, holding her hands there.

'Yes, you've told me,' Evie said, refusing to look.

'"Its a fifty-fifty chance," the doctor said, before he operated.'

As if he would have, Evie thought.

Her mother had told her to take a present to her aunt, and on the way from work she had bought some purple grapes. They were reduced in price, being past their prime, and they lay now on the table in a dish shaped like a cabbage leaf. Dull, and softly dented, they gave a sweet, beery smell to the room. Tiny flies had already gathered round them. They rose for a moment when Mrs Swan waved her hand over the dish, but soon settled again. Grapes were for the dying, she had always believed, and 'deathbed grapes' she called the purple kind. She would rather have had a quarter of a pound of tea.

It was no use Evie glancing up at the clock every few seconds, she thought. The bus would come along no sooner than it was due, if then. It was a wasted afternoon for them both. Mrs Swan could imagine the argument at her niece's house. 'You really ought to go, Evie. No one's been near her for months.' 'Why pick on me?' Evie would ask, and be told that the others had their families to occupy their time. So Evie – as if being so far unmarried and having to live at home was not enough – was made to do the duty visits, give up her free afternoon. No wonder, Mrs Swan thought, that she looked as morose as a hen.

She herself had planned a busy afternoon and had brought from the garden a large striped marrow to be made into jam. It matched the white and amber cat who had settled beside it on the sofa, as if for company or camouflage. The cat slept most of its life – at night from custom and by day from boredom. On the sofa now he drowsed, had not quite dropped off, for his eyelids wavered. His front legs were folded under him, like a cow's, his whiskers curled down over his alderman's chains – the bib of white rings on his breast.

Mrs Swan, glancing regretfully at the marrow, noticed him and said mechanically, 'Isn't he a lovely Ginger, then?'

The cat at once feigned a deep sleep.

'He must be company,' Evie said.

Mrs Swan was often told this, and, although it was not true, she never disagreed. She was not a person who could make a friend of a cat, and had never found the necessity. They bored one another. She had had him to keep away the mice. Instead, he brought them in and played evil games with them on the hearthrug.

'He's no trouble,' she said.

Mrs Rippon passed the open door without glancing in, on her way back from the churchyard. The clock made a sudden rustling noise and struck four with an old-fashioned chime, and Mrs Swan got up and put the teapot by the kitchen range to warm. Evie racked her brains for something to say, and began a tedious description of the bridesmaids' dresses at a wedding she had been to. She thought her aunt could not fail to be grateful for this glimpse of the outside world.

While she waited for the kettle to boil, Mrs Swan took up her knitting. She was making a blanket from little squares sewn together, and there was already a carrier bag full of them knitted from oddments of drab-coloured wool – a great deal of khaki left over from the war. The needles clicked steadily and she let her eyes move about the room as her thoughts settled like moths on her possessions. She might wash the muslin curtains tomorrow if the weather held. Evie was dropping cigarette ash on to the rag hearthrug, she noticed. She would put it on the clothesline in the morning, and give it the devil's own beating.

'The two grown-up bridesmaids were in a sort of figured nylon organza,' Evie said. She tried hard to give an accurate picture, but her aunt did not understand the words. The water in the kettle had begun to stir, so she put aside the knitting and finished laying the table. She had some stewed raspberries to eat with the bread and butter. This was her last meal of the day and she always enjoyed it, but she knew that Evie would say 'Nothing for me, Auntie,' and light another cigarette.

'In a mauvy-pinky shade, lovely with the sweet peas,' she was saying.

The girl's clothes-mad, though it's only natural, her aunt thought as she poured out the tea and suffered boredom.

Evie lit another cigarette to stop herself yawning, remembering the freedom of stepping on to the bus after these visits, the wonderful release, and the glow of self-righteousness – duty done, sunshine bestowed, vistas widened.

Mrs Swan stood by the wall of her front garden, knitting, as Evie's bus drove off. It was a summer's evening, with a scent of blossom from the trees in the churchyard. The vicarage doves were strutting about the roof, making peaceful sounds, over the tiles white-splashed with their droppings.

Mrs Butcher from the Plough Inn had got off the bus before it turned to go back to the town, taking Evie on it. She walked slowly – looking angrily hot, as red-haired people often do – carrying a cardboard dress box. It was an awkward shape, and the string cut into her fingers. She had hoped to get into the pub without her husband, Eric, noticing it and, seeing him crossing the yard, she stopped to have a chat with Mrs Swan until he should have disappeared again.

'Lovely evening,' she said.

'Yes, very nice,' Mrs Swan responded cheerfully, although usually the woman passed by without speaking, intent on her own business, full of dissatisfactions and impatience. She drank too much at night and laughed for no reason, Charlie used to say when he returned from his evening glass of bitter. But all day long she was morose.

'You're busy.' Phyllis Butcher nodded at Mrs Swan's knitting, determined not to move on until Eric was back in the bar. She would leave the dress box in the outside Ladies, until after opening time. Her husband was more observant about parcels than about clothes. Once a dress was unwrapped, she was safe, and if a customer praised a new one and he glanced at it suspiciously, she would look quite surprised and say, 'Why, it's been hanging in my wardrobe for at least three years.'

'I've got lots of odd wool,' she said, when Mrs Swan explained about the blanket she was making. 'The sweaters and things I've started in my time. I'll bring it round tomorrow.'

'It's very good of you,' said Mrs Swan. 'A different colour makes a change.' I'll believe in it when I see it, she thought, knowing the sort of woman Mrs Butcher was.

Yet she was wrong, for the very next afternoon Mrs Butcher came to the cottage with a great assortment of brightly coloured wool. She sat down in the kitchen and drank a cup of tea. She had been crying, Mrs Swan thought, and presently she began to explain why, stretching her damp handkerchief from corner to corner, and sometimes dabbing her eyes with it.

Mrs Swan sorted the wool and untangled it. The colours excited her, particularly a turquoise blue with a strand of silver twisted in it, and her fingers itched to begin knitting a new square – an adventure she must put off until she had finished one of mottled grey.

Phyllis Butcher's mother was poorly. Listening, Mrs Swan thought it did the woman credit that she should weep.

'I'll have to go up there,' Mrs Butcher said. 'Up north. Real Geordie country,' she added scornfully. 'I hate it there.'

'I was in service in Scotland once,' said Mrs Swan. 'Nice scenery and all, but I was happier when I moved down south. I shouldn't care to go back.' The very thought was tiring. She visualised the road to Scotland, climbing steeply all the way, a long pull uphill, ending in a cold bedroom under the slated turret roof of a castle. 'I saw an eagle once,' she said. 'A wicked great bird. There were stags, too, and cattle with great horns. Five o'clock us girls got up, and some days I could have cried, my hands were so cold.'

'Oh, Consett's not romantic,' Phyllis Butcher said. 'It's all mining round there. I can't stand it, that's a fact, and never could. I know I ought to go more often, but you can't think how it depresses me.'

Eric had put it more strongly – hence the tears. 'Your

own mother,' he had said. 'You'll be old and lonely one day yourself, perhaps.' 'I'd rather be taken!' she had cried.

'Mother's not easy,' she told Mrs Swan. When she had drunk her tea, from habit she turned the cup upside down in the saucer and then lifted it up again and examined the tea leaves. There were always birds flying, and she had forgotten what they meant.

'What's her complaint?' Mrs Swan enquired, for she was interested in sickness, and when younger had longed to be a nurse.

'Oh, I don't know. If it's not one thing it's another. The house is full of bottles of medicine. Illness gives me the creeps. She's always been chesty, of course.' She was still studying the cup and, turning it in her hands, had found the promise of a letter and what she thought was a threatened journey. 'I'll go tomorrow,' she said. 'Get things straightened up here and set off in the morning. "Hello, stranger," she'll say when I walk in. That's enough for a start to make me want to turn round and go back the way I came. If she wasn't so catty, I'd go more often. I couldn't do enough for her, if she was only pleasant.'

'Why not go straight away?' Eric had said when she received the letter. 'She might be worse than she makes out.'

'I can't just walk out of the house like that,' she had told him. 'There are all the things I have to do here – arrangements to make.'

To escape his critical eye, she had slipped round with the wool – anything to get out of the house – and had sat in the peaceful little room for over half an hour, trying to improve her self-esteem.

'I should go and get it over with,' Mrs Swan advised, thinking of her niece, Evie, and her bright face when she said goodbye, and her quick, light step going toward the bus stop.

Phyllis did not see Mrs Swan again until she had returned from the funeral. She had delayed her journey too long, and, as she opened her mother's front gate, bracing herself for the usual sarcastic greeting, she had looked up and seen one of the neighbours drawing the blind over the bedroom window.

She went to stay in a small hotel rather than remain in the house. Eric came up to join her for the funeral, at which she knew the neighbours were watching her and whispering. Their eyes were lowered, their lips set together whenever she turned to look at them, but she guessed what they were saying. They had known her when she was a child, but she had forgotten all of them and their names meant nothing.

She had not pretended to grieve, not even in order to shelter herself from Eric's words of blame. 'You could just as easily have gone the day before,' he told her. 'I don't know what these people think of us.'

'And I'm sure I don't care,' she said. But she cared very much, and her face burned as she walked out of the chapel after the coffin, feeling the hostility of the other women, the neighbours who had sat with her mother and taken in her meals.

'You'll have to thank them properly,' Eric said. 'Do something to show your gratitude.'

She refused to speak to them. 'I know what they're like,' she said. 'They lean over one another's fences all day long and wag their wicked tongues. Wild horses wouldn't drag me to this place again.'

All the unspoken words had hurt her and those spoken ones of Eric's, too. She had such a different picture of herself from the one other people seemed to see, and she was frightened and astounded by glimpses of how she appeared to them, for they perceived traits she was sure she had never possessed – or only under the most serious provocation. She thought so much about herself that it was important to have the thoughts comfortable, and many desolate hours had been made more bearable by gazing at her own reflection. Warm-hearted, impulsive, she was sure she was – herself hardly considered, and then always last, as she bustled about the countryside doing good. 'No one knows what people in this village owe her.' The words were clear, though the person who said them was only dimly imagined. 'She herself would never tell, but I doubt if there's a cottage in the parish where there isn't someone with cause to be grateful. In this village, it's a funny thing, if anyone is in trouble, it's the pub they go to for help, not the vicarage.' From her bedroom window, she could look across at the churchyard and would imagine the procession of villagers winding up the pathway under the chestnut trees, in black for her own funeral. 'There wasn't a dry eye,' she told herself.

Then Eric's sharp phrases splintered the image – 'Your own mother.' 'You think only of yourself and what you are going to put on your back.'

She tried not to listen, and could soon comfort herself, just as when she looked in a mirror and the freckled skin and sandy hair were transfigured into alabaster and Titian red.

Sitting at lunch in the train, flying past dreary canals and grey fields, she endured her husband's sullen silence, and buttered bread rolls; buttering and nibbling, to comfort herself, she stared out at the sour-looking pastures.

She was glad to be back in her own picturesque village. The Thames valley consoled her, but uncertainty still hovered about her and she wondered if, after all, she had failed her own image of herself. She had not yet dared to unpack her new dress. It was too bright a colour and she dreaded Eric's comments. She kept it hidden on top of the wardrobe, although she knew that the pleasure of putting it on for the first time was perhaps the only way there was of dispelling her sadness.

To escape the atmosphere of disapproval, she unravelled one of her old sweaters and took the wool to Mrs Swan, not admitting to herself that, because of past aloofness, there was no other house in the village where she could drop in and exchange a word or two. In the past, an afternoon's shopping had always cured despondency, and, in the evenings, beer and backchat were even better distractions. However, deference to her bereavement seemed to have sobered customers for the time being – the last sort of behaviour to raise her spirits.

Mrs Swan was not alone. She had called Mrs Rippon in from the garden to give her a present of a pot of blackberry jelly, and they were sitting at the table, drinking tea.

Phyllis joined them, nervously praising the look of the jelly and everything else she could see.

'I was sorry to hear of your loss,' said Mrs Swan, whose neighbour kept her eyes averted and suddenly took up the pot of jelly and said goodbye.

'I brought some more wool.' Phyllis saw the half-finished blanket spread over the back of a horsehair sofa, and began to praise that, too, and got up to study it – the uneven stitches and the cobbled-together squares, the drabness already beginning to break into gaudiness since her last visit. She returned to her chair, feeling that the brightness she had brought was symbolic. 'Yes, poor Mother,' she said. She bowed her head and sighed and looked resigned. 'It sounds a dreadful thing to say, but I can't be sorry, for *her* sake. It really was a merciful release.'

That's what young Evie will say about me when I go, Mrs Swan thought. And so it will be, too, for her.

'It's peaceful here,' said Phyllis.

The cat lay asleep by the fender, moving his ears and beating the end of his tail rhythmically against the rug, as if he were in the midst of a dream that bored and angered him. Above the fireplace hung a strip of sticky paper, black with flies; some dead and some dying a wretched death. Others had evaded it, and circled the room slowly and warily.

Phyllis leaned forward and sniffed at a vase full of

nasturtiums edged with their little round leaves. The smell tantalised her, reminding her of something. Was it mustard, she wondered, or some medicine – or just nasturtiums? They had grown in Consett. Those and dusty, insect-bitten hollyhocks were all she could remember in the shabby strip of garden where her father had kept rabbits.

'Aren't they pretty?' she said, sniffing the flowers again, and then she determined not to praise another thing, lest she should sound condescending. 'That's your husband, isn't it?' she asked, nodding at an old photograph in a frame made of sea shells.

'He had that taken the day he joined up, when he was twenty-five. And he wore a moustache like that till he was fifty. Then he began to go bald, and that great bush looked silly then, he thought, so he shaved it off. He hadn't a hair between his head and heaven by the time he was sixty.'

'Yes, I remember,' Phyllis said. She supposed she did remember seeing him in the public bar, but she had never bothered to give him a name.

'It's a pity having to leave your mother all that long way away,' Mrs Swan said. 'My own mother's buried down in Bristol and the train fare's out of the question. I'd dearly like to go.' After a pause, she said, 'I expect the flowers were lovely, though it's not an easy time of the year. I find plenty of garden flowers for Charlie, but they're no use for a burial. Gladioli don't make up well and shop roses are exorbitant.'

'We sent carnations, Eric and I.'

She got up to go and stood looking down at the cat, whose dream seemed to have taken a better turn, for he lay relaxed now, with crossed paws and a smile on his face. Phyllis felt peaceful, too.

'Well, come again,' Mrs Swan said, from politeness.

'I really will,' Phyllis promised.

Enlivening Mrs Swan's life became an absorbing pastime

and something of which, for once, Eric could not disapprove. Phyllis was always dropping into the cottage, and found ingenious ways of giving presents tactfully, not knowing that the tact was wasted, since Mrs Swan had grace enough to be pleased with the gifts and to accept them simply, unbothered by motives. She thought of them as charity, and had no objection to that. She only wondered why there was so little of it about nowadays.

'The hens are laying like wildfire,' Phyllis would say. If she met anyone she knew on the way home, she always explained her outing. 'I was just taking a few eggs to poor old Mrs Swan.'

One day she asked her to go back to the Plough for a glass of sherry, but Mrs Swan thought it a mistake for widows to drink. 'I haven't taken any since Charlie died,' she said.

'You're very good to that old lady,' one of the customers told Phyllis.

'I'm not at all. I just like being with her. And she's got no one else. It means a lot to her and costs me nothing.'

'Most people wouldn't bother, all the same.'

'It's a terrible thing, loneliness.'

'There's no need to tell *me* that.'

The bar had only just opened for the evening, and he was the only customer so far. He was always the first to arrive, and although he came so regularly, Phyllis knew very little about him. He was middle-aged and not very talkative, and never stayed drinking for long. 'Very genuine,' she said, when other people mentioned him. It was an easy label and she made it sound utterly dull.

This evening, instead of opening his newspaper, he seemed inclined to talk. 'Living in lodgings palls in the end,' he said. 'I never married, and it gets lonely, the evenings and weekends. I sometimes think what I'd give to have some nice family where I could drop in when I wanted, and be one of them – remember the children's birthdays, give a hand with the gardening, that sort of thing. Everyone ought to have some family like that where they're just accepted and taken for granted, given pot luck, not a lot of fuss. It's tiring always being a guest. Well, I find it so.'

'It sounds to me as if there's a fairy godfather being wasted,' Phyllis said.

He smiled. 'You feel you'd like to have your stake in someone else's family if you haven't got one of your own. Will you have a drink with me?'

'Thank you very much,' she said brightly. 'I'd like a lager.'

'Well, please do.'

'What a lovely rose,' she said. 'I've always noticed what lovely roses you wear in your buttonhole, Mr . . . ' Her voice trailed off, as she couldn't remember his name. 'Well, here's all you wish yourself,' she said, and sipped the lager, then wiped her lips on her scented handkerchief.

He had taken the rose from his buttonhole and handed it to her across the bar. 'Out of my landlady's garden,' he said. 'I always look after them for her.'

'Oh, you are sweet!' She twirled the rose in her fingers and then turned to the mirrored panelling behind the bar and, standing on tiptoe to see her reflection above the shelf of bottles, tucked the rose into her blouse.

'That reminds me of that picture – "The bar at the *Folies Bergère*" – one of my favourites,' he said. 'All the bottles, and your reflection, and the rose.'

'Well, how funny you should say that. We had it for our Christmas card one year. Everyone liked it. "Well, we didn't realise they had Bass in those days" – that's what everyone said. "In Paris, too!" There's those bottles on the bar, if you remember. It makes the picture look a bit like an advertisement. Look at my lovely rose, Eric.'

'Good evening, Mr Willis,' Eric said, carrying in a crate of light ale. 'Yes, it's quite a perfect bloom, isn't it? I suppose she cadged it off you.'

'It's a pleasure to give Mrs Butcher something,' Mr Willis

replied. 'As far as I have seen, it's usually *she* who does it all.'

Phyllis was happier, gentler than she had been for years. In Mr Willis's eyes she saw her ideal self reflected.

'Oh, I haven't had time to powder my nose,' she would say, scrabbling through her handbag, which she kept on a shelf beneath the bar.

'I suppose you've been off on one of your errands of mercy,' said Mr Willis.

'Don't be silly. I've had a very nice tea party with my old lady in the almshouse. What errand of mercy is there about that? Oh, you really shouldn't. What a gorgeous colour!'

Every evening now, he brought her a rose. When he had left the bar to go back to his lodgings for supper, the other customers teased her. 'Your boy friend stayed late tonight,' Eric would say.

'He's sweet,' she protested. 'No truly. Such lovely old-world manners, and he's so genuine.'

The evening before her birthday, he came in as usual, admired her new blouse, and gave her a yellow rosebud. 'And that may be the last,' he said.

'Oh, you aren't going away!' she exclaimed, looking so disconcerted that he smiled with pleasure.

'No, but the roses have already gone. Unless we have another crop later on.'

'What a relief. You really frightened me. I can do without the roses at a pinch, but we couldn't do without you.'

'You're always kind. I enjoy our chats. I couldn't do without them, either.'

She turned her head away, as if she dared not meet his eyes.

'How's your old lady?' he asked. In the silence that had fallen he was conscious of his heart beating. It was a loud and hollow sound, like an old grandfather clock, and he spoke quickly lest she, too, should hear it. They were alone in the bar, as they so often were for the first quarter of an hour after opening time.

'My old lady?' she repeated, and seemed to be dragging her thoughts back from a long way away. Then she smiled at him. 'Oh, she's very well.'

'Have you seen her lately?'

'Well, not many days go by when I don't pop in.'

But she had not popped in for a long time. There had been other things to occupy her mind, and shopping had become a pleasure again.

'You must be sure to come in tomorrow and have a drink with me,' she said. 'It's my birthday.'

Instead of pinning the rosebud to her blouse, she put it in a glass of water. 'I'll keep it for tomorrow night,' she said.

He leaned across the bar and took the rose from the glass and wiped it carefully on his handkerchief Then, hoping he would not blush, he tucked it into her blouse.

The next morning, two dozen shop roses arrived by messenger.

When the bus turned round at the church and set off on its journey back to the town, Evie always felt marooned. Until it returned, in two hours' time, there was no escape.

It was three o'clock on a late autumn afternoon – soft, misty weather. In the churchyard, graves were lost under the fallen leaves. There were pockets of web on the brambles and unseen strands of it in the air. From the bus stop, Evie could see her great-aunt at work in the churchyard, raking leaves off the grave. She was wearing a forage cap of emerald-green wool that she had knitted herself, and she had tied a pinafore over her winter coat.

'Well, girl,' she said, when Evie joined her. 'I wasn't expecting you.'

'Mother thought the news ought to come from me,' Evie said. She sat down on a slab of polished granite and gazed at her aunt's astonishing hat. 'I'm getting engaged on Sunday,' she said. 'Norman's bringing his mother and father to tea, and giving me the ring then. It's a diamond with two amethysts.'

'And when's the wedding?'

Evie looked vague. 'Oh, I don't know about that. Both Norman and I favour long engagements.' She stood up quickly, hearing footsteps and not wanting to be seen sitting on a grave.

Phyllis Butcher was taking a short cut through the churchyard on her way from the post office. She nodded as she passed them, hurrying toward the lich gate.

'*She's* off hand,' Evie said. 'There were two women talking about her on the bus. She was in the telephone box outside the post office as we went by. They were saying that she goes down there nearly every afternoon to ring someone up, although they've got the phone at the pub. I must say she looks the type. Does she still keep pestering you?'

'She hasn't been in since the summer. Fill that vase from the tap over there, will you?'

Evie took the stone urn, which was inscribed 'In Loving Memory', and made her way between graves to the water tap by the church wall. When she came back, the grave was raked free of leaves and Mrs Swan was untying the string round a bunch of bronze chrysanthemums.

'I imagine her one of those people – gushing one moment and cutting you dead the next,' Evie said, her thoughts still on Phyllis Butcher. 'Every time I came last summer, she was stuck there in the kitchen. And putting you under an obligation with all those presents.'

'I didn't see any obligation in it.'

'I told Mother about her, and she was quite annoyed. It wasn't her place to carry on like that.'

'I was sorry for her,' Mrs Swan replied. 'She did me no harm.' She knelt down to arrange the flowers in the urn. 'There, that looks nice, I think. I'm always pleased when the chrysanthemums come. Charlie was so fond of them.'

She straightened her back and pushed stray ends of hair under her cap. 'If you bring the rake, I'll take the basket. We'll make a cup of tea, and you can tell me about your plans.'

They walked slowly to the lich gate. The last of the yellow leaves were drifting down. On some graves, the chestnut fans lay flat, like outspread hands.

A Dedicated Man

IN the dark, raftered dining-room, Silcox counted the coned napkins and, walking among the tables, lifted the lids of the mustard pots and shook salt level in the cellars.

At the beginning of their partnership as waiter and waitress, Edith had liked to make mitres or fleurs-de-lis or water-lilies of the napkins, and Silcox, who thought this great vulgarity, waited until after he had made his proposal and been accepted before he put a stop to it. She had listened meekly. 'Edwardian vulgarity,' he had told her. Taking a roll of bread from the centre of the petalled linen, he whipped the napkin straight, then turned it deftly into a dunce's cap.

Edith always came down a little after Silcox. He left the bedroom in plenty of time for her to change into her black dress and white apron. His proposal had not included marriage or any other intimacy and, although they lay every night side by side in twin beds, they were always decorous in their behaviour, fanatically prim, and he had never so much as seen her take a brush to her hair, as he himself might have said. However, there was no one to say it to, and to the world they were Mr and Mrs Silcox, a plain, respectable couple. Both were ambitious, both had been bent on leaving the hotel where they first met – a glorified boarding-house, Silcox called it. Both, being snobbish, were galled at having to wait on noisy, sunburnt people who wore freakish and indecent holiday clothes and could not pronounce *crêpes de volaille*, let alone understand what it meant.

By the time Silcox heard of the vacancy at the Royal George, he had become desperate beyond measure, irritated at every turn by the vulgarities of seaside life. The Royal George was mercifully as inland as anywhere in England can be. The thought of the Home Counties soothed him. He visualised the landscape embowered in flowering trees.

In his interview with the manageress he had been favourably impressed by the tone of the hotel. The Thames flowed by beyond the geranium-bordered lawns; there would be star occasions all summer – the Fourth of June, Henley, Ascot. The dining-room, though it was small, had velvet-cushioned banquettes and wine lists in padded leather covers. The ashtrays advertised nothing and the flowers had not come out of the garden.

'My wife,' he said repeatedly during the interview. He had been unable to bring her, from consideration to their employer. The manageress respected him for this and for very much else. She could imagine him in tails, and he seemed to wear the grey suit as if it were a regrettable informality he had been unable to escape. He was stately, eyes like a statue's, mouth like a carp's. His deference would have that touch of condescension which would make customers angle for his good will. Those to whom he finally unbent, with a remark about the weather or the compliments of the season, would return again and again, bringing friends to whom they could display their status. 'Maurice always looks after me,' they would say.

Returning to the pandemonium – the tripperish hotel, the glaring sky – he made his proposal to Edith. 'Married couple', the advertisement had stipulated and was a necessary condition, he now understood, for only one bedroom was available. 'It has twin bedsteads, I ascertained,' he said.

Marriage, he explained, could not be considered, as he was married already. Where the person in question (as he spoke of his wife) was at present, he said he did not know. She had been put behind him.

Until that day, he had never spoken to Edith of his personal affairs, although they had worked together for a year. She was reserved herself and embarrassed by this unexpected lapse, though by the proposal itself she felt deeply honoured. It set the seal on his approval of her work.

'I think I am right in saying that it is what matters most to both of us,' he observed, and she nodded. She spoke very little and never smiled.

The manageress of the Royal George, when Edith went for her separate interview, wondered if she were not too grim. At forty-five, her hair was a streaked grey and clipped short like a man's at the back. She had no make-up and there were deep lines about her mouth which had come from the expression of disapproval she so often wore. On the other hand, she was obviously dependable and efficient, would never slop soup or wear dirty cuffs or take crafty nips of gin in the still-room whenever there was a lull. Her predecessor had done these things and been flighty, too.

So Edith and Silcox were engaged. Sternly and without embarrassment they planned arrangements for bedroom privacy. These were simply a matter of one staying in the bathroom while the other dressed or undressed in the bed-room. Edith was first to get into bed and would then turn out the light. Silcox was meanwhile sitting on a laundry basket in his dressing gown, glancing at his watch until it was time to return. He would get into bed in the dark. He never wished her goodnight and hardly admitted to himself that she was there.

Now a week had gone by and the arrangements had worked so smoothly that he was a little surprised this evening that on the stroke of seven o'clock she did not appear. Having checked his tables, he studied the list of bookings and was pleased to note the name of one of his *bêtes noires*. This would put a spur to his pride and lift the evening out of the ordinary ruck. Pleasant people were not the same challenge.

Upstairs, Edith was having to hurry, something she rarely deigned to do. She was even a little excited as she darted about the room, looking for clean cuffs and apron, fresh dress preservers and some pewter-coloured stockings, and she kept pausing to glance at a photograph on the chest of drawers. It was postcard size and in a worn leather frame and was of an adolescent boy wearing a school blazer.

When she had gone back to the bedroom after breakfast she saw the photograph for the first time. Silcox had placed it there without a word. She ignored it for a while and then became nervous that one of the maids might question her about it, and it was this reason she gave Silcox for having asked him who it was.

'Our son,' he said.

He deemed it expedient, he added, that he should be a family man. The fact would increase their air of dependability and give them background and reality and solid worth. The boy was at a public school, he went on, and did not divulge to his friends the nature of his parents' profession. Silcox, Edith realised with respect, was so snobbish that he looked down upon himself.

'How old is he?' she asked in an abrupt tone.

'He is seventeen and working for the Advanced Level.'

Edith did not know what this was and wondered how she could manage to support the fantasy.

'We shall say nothing ourselves,' said Silcox, 'as we are

not in the habit of discussing our private affairs. But he is there if wanted.'

'What shall we . . . what is his name?'

'Julian,' Silcox said and his voice sounded rich and musical.

Edith looked with some wonder at the face in the photograph. It was a very ordinary face and she could imagine the maids conjecturing at length as to whom he took after.

'Who is he really?' she asked.

'A young relative,' said Silcox.

In Edith's new life there were one or two difficulties – one was trying to remember not to fidget with the wedding ring as if she were not used to wearing it, and another was being obliged to call Silcox 'Maurice'. This she thought unseemly, like all familiarities, and to be constant in it required continual vigilance. He, being her superior, had called her Edith from the start.

Sleeping beside him at night worried her less. The routine of privacy was established and sleep itself was negative and came immediately to both of them after long hours of being on their feet. They might have felt more sense of intimacy sitting beside one another in deckchairs in broad daylight, for then there would be the pitfalls of conversation. (How far to encroach? How much interest to show that could be shown without appearing inquisitive?)

Edith was one of those women who seem to know from childhood that the attraction of men is no part of their equipment, and from then on to have supported nature in what it had done for them, by exaggerating the gruffness and the gracelessness and becoming after a time sexless. She strode heavily in shoes a size too large, her off-duty coat and skirt were as sensible as some old nannie's walking-out attire. She was not much interested in people, although she did her duty towards them and wrote each week to her married sister in Australia; and was generous to her at Christmas. Her letters, clearly written as they were, were still practically unreadable – so full of facts and times: where she took the bus to on her day off and the whole route described, where this road forked and that branched off and what p.m. she entered this or that café to progress from the grapefruit to the trifle of the table d'hote (five and sixpence). Very poor service usually, she wrote – odd knives and forks left on the table while she drank her coffee, for no one took any pride nowadays.

Edith had no relations other than her sister; her world was peopled with hotel staff and customers. With the staff she was distant and sometimes grim if they were careless in their work, and with her customers she was distant and respectful. She hardly responded to them, although there were a very few – usually gay young men or courtly and jovial elderly ones – to whom she behaved protectively, as Nannie-ish as she looked when she wore her outdoor clothes.

The other person in her life – Silcox – was simply to her the Establishment. She had never worked with anyone she respected more – in her mind, he was always a waiter and she always thought of him dressed as a waiter. On his day off, he seemed lowered by wearing the clothes of an ordinary man. Having to turn her eyes away from him when she glimpsed him in a dressing gown was really no worse. They were not man and woman in one another's eyes, and hardly even human beings.

No difficulties they were beset with in their early days at the Royal George could spoil the pleasures of their work. The serenity of the dining-room, the elaborate food which made demands upon them (to turn something over in flaming brandy in a chafing-dish crowned Silcox's evening), the superiority of the clientele and the glacial table linen. They had suffered horrors from common people and this escape to elegance was precious to them both. The hazards that threatened were not connected with their work, over which both had mastery from the beginning, but with their private lives. It was agonising to Edith to realise that now they were expected to spend their free time together. On the first day off they took a bus to another hotel along the river and there had luncheon. Silcox modelled his behaviour on that of his own most difficult customers, and seemed to be retaliating by doing so. He was very lordly and full of knowledge and criticism. Edith, who was used to shopping ladies' luncheons in cafés, became nervous and alarmed. When she next wrote to her sister, she left this expedition altogether out of the letter and described instead some of the menus she had served at the Royal George, with prices. Nowadays, there was, for the first time in her life, an enormous amount that had to be left out of the letters.

She was dreading their next free day and was relieved when Silcox suggested that they should make a habit of taking the train to London together and there separating. If they came back on the same train in the evening, no suspicions would be roused.

In London, she enjoyed wandering round the department stores, looking without surprise or envy at all the frivolous extravagances. She made notes of prices, thinking that her sister would be interested to compare them with those in Melbourne, and she could spend a whole day over choosing a pair of gloves, going from shop to shop, studying the quality. One day, she intended to visit the zoo.

Silcox said that he liked to look in the jewellers' windows. In the afternoons, he went to a news cinema. Going home in the train, he read a newspaper and she looked at the backs of houses and little gardens, and later, fields or woods, staring as if hypnotised.

One morning, when she had returned to their bedroom after breakfast, he surprised her by following her there. This was the time of day when he took a turn about the garden or strolled along by the river.

When he had shut the door, he said quietly, 'I'm afraid I must ask you something. I think it would be better if you were less tidy in here. It struck me this morning that by putting everything away out of sight, you will give rise to suspicion.'

Once, he had been a floor waiter in a hotel and knew, from taking breakfast in to so many married people, what their bedrooms usually looked like. His experience with his own wife he did not refer to.

'I overheard Carrie saying what a tidy pair we were and she had never met anyone like it, not a pin in sight when she came into this room, she said.'

'I respect your intentions,' he said grandly, 'but the last thing to serve our purpose is to appear in any way out of the ordinary. If you could have one or two things lying about – your hairbrush, perhaps – well, I leave it to you – just a pot of something or other on the dressing table. A wife would never hide everything away in the drawers. Carrie's right, as it is there isn't even a pin to be seen. Nothing to show it's anyone's room at all, except for the photograph.'

Edith blushed and pressed her lips tightly together. She turned away and made no reply. Although she knew that it had been difficult for him to make the suggestion, and sensible and necessary as she saw it to be, she was angry with him. She wondered why his words had so humiliated her, and could find no reason. He had reproved her before about her work – the water-lily napkins, for instance – but he had never angered her.

She waited for him to leave her and then she removed from the drawer a large, harsh-bristled brush, a boxful of studs and safety pins and a pot of Vaseline which she used in cold weather when her lips were chapped. In the early evening, when she came up to change, she found Silcox's brushes beside hers, a shoe-horn dangled from the side of the mirror and his dressing gown had been taken from his clothes' cupboard and was hanging at the back of the door.

She felt very strange about it all and when she went downstairs she tried to direct all her thoughts towards her work.

'He couldn't be anyone else's,' said Carrie Hurt, the maid, looking at the photograph. She had the impertinence to take it up and go over to the window with it, to see it better.

'He is thought to take more after his father's side,' Edith said, tempted to allow the conversation to continue, then wondering why this should be.

'I expect it's his father's side that says it,' Carrie replied. 'Oh, I can see you. The way his hair grows on his forehead. His father's got quite a widow's peak.'

Edith found herself looking over Carrie's shoulder, as if she had never seen the photograph before.

'As a matter of fact, he is a little like my sister's eldest boy,' she conceded. 'His cousin,' she added, feeling wonder at the words.

'Well, you must be proud of him. Such an open face,' Carrie said, replacing the photograph in its right position and passing a duster over the glass.

'Yes,' said Edith. 'He's a good boy.'

She left Carrie and went downstairs and walked in the garden until it was time to go on duty. She went up and down the gravel paths and along by the river, but she could not overcome the excitement which lately disturbed her so, the sensation of shameful pleasure.

By the river's edge, she came upon Silcox, who had taken up fishing in his spare time – a useful excuse for avoiding Edith's company. He stood on the bank, watching the line where it entered the water, and hardly turned his head as Edith approached him.

'Where does he – where does Julian go to in the holidays?' she asked.

'He goes to relatives,' Silcox answered.

She knew that she was interrupting him and that she must move on. As she did, he heard her murmuring anxiously, 'I do so hope they're kind.'

He turned his head quickly and looked after her, but she had gone mooning back across the lawn. The expression of astonishment stayed on his face for a long time after that, and when she took up her position in the dining-room before lunch, he looked at her with concern, but she was her usual forbidding and efficient self again.

'Don't we ever go to see him?' she asked a few days later. 'Won't they think us strange not going?'

'What we do in our free time is no concern of theirs,' he said.

'I only thought they'd think it strange.'

He isn't real, none of it's true, she now constantly reminded herself, for sometimes her feelings of guilt about that abandoned boy grew too acute.

Sometimes, on Sunday outings from school, boys were brought by their parents to have lunch at the hotel, and Edith found herself fussing over them, giving them huge helpings, discussing their appetites with their parents.

'They're all the same at that age,' she would say. 'I know.'

It was so unlike her to chat with the customers and quite against Silcox's code. When he commented disdainfully upon her unusual behaviour, she seemed scarcely to listen to his words. The next Sunday, serving a double portion of ice cream to a boy, she looked across at his mother and smiled. 'I've got a son myself, madam,' she said. 'I know.'

Silcox, having overheard this, was too enraged to settle down to his fishing that afternoon. He looked for Edith and found her in the bedroom writing a letter to her sister.

'It was a mistake – this about the boy,' he said, taking up the photograph and glaring at it. 'You have not the right touch in such matters. You carry the deception to excess. You go too far.'

'Too far?' she said brightly, but busy writing.

'Our position is established. I think the little flourishes I thought up had their result.'

'But they were all *your* little flourishes,' she said, looking up at him. 'You didn't let me think of any, did you?'

He stared back at her and soon her eyes flickered, and she returned to her writing.

'There won't be any more,' he said. 'From me, or from you. Or any more discussion of our affairs, do you understand? Carrie in here every morning gossiping, you chatting to customers, telling them such a pack of lies – as if it were all true, and as if they could possibly be interested. You know as well as I do how unprofessional it is. I should never have credited it of you. Even when we were at that dreadful place at Paignton, you conducted yourself with more dignity.'

'I don't see the harm,' she said mildly.

'And I don't see the necessity. It's courting danger for one thing – to get so involved. We'll keep our affairs to ourselves or else we'll find trouble ahead.'

'What time does the post go?'

Without reading her letter through, she pushed it into an envelope. Goodness knows what she has written, he thought. A mercy her sister was far away in Australia.

The photograph – the subject of their contention – he pushed aside, as if he would have liked to be rid of it.

'You don't seem to be paying much attention,' he said. 'I only warn you that you'd better. Unless you hope to make laughing stocks of both of us.'

Before she addressed the envelope, she looked gravely at him for a moment, thinking that perhaps the worst thing that could happen to him, the thing he had always dreaded most, was to be laughed at, to lose his dignity. I used to be the same, she thought, taking up her pen.

'Yes, I made a mistake,' he said. 'I admit it freely. But we shall stand by it, since it's made. We can hardly kill the boy off, now we've got him.'

She jerked round and looked at him, her face even paler than usual, then seemed to gather her wits again and bent her head. Writing rather slowly and unsteadily, she finished addressing the envelope.

'I hope I shan't have further cause for complaint,' he said – rather as if he were her employer, as in fact he always felt himself to be. The last word duly spoken, he left her, but was frowning as he went downstairs. She was behaving oddly, something was not quite right about her and he was apprehensive.

Edith was smiling while she tidied herself before slipping out to the pillar box. 'That's the first tiff we've ever had,' she thought. 'In all our married life.'

'I find *her* all right,' Carrie Hurt said to the still-room maid. 'Not stand-offish, really, when you get to know her.'

'It's him I can't abide.'

'I'm sorry for her. The way he treats her.'

'And can't you tell he's got a temper? You get that feeling, don't you, that for two pins he'd boil over?'

'Yes, I'm sorry for her. When he's not there, she likes to talk. And dotes on that boy of theirs.'

'Funny life it must be, not hardly ever seeing him.'

'She's going to soon, so she was telling me, when it's his birthday. She was showing me the sweater she was knitting for him. She's a lovely knitter.'

Silcox found Edith sitting in a secluded place at the back of the hotel where the staff were allowed to take the air. It was a cobbled courtyard, full of empty beer crates and strings of tea towels hung to dry. Pigeons walked up and down the outhouse roofs and the kitchen cat sat at Edith's feet watching them. Edith was knitting a white, cable-stitch sweater and she had a towel across her lap to keep the wool clean.

'I have just overheard that Carrie Hurt and the still-room girl discussing you,' Silcox said, when he had looked round to make sure that there was no one to overhear him. 'What is this nonsense about going to see the boy, or did my ears deceive me?'

'They think we're unnatural. I felt so ashamed about it that I said I'd be going on his birthday.'

'And when is *that*, pray?'

'Next month, the eighteenth. I'll have the sweater done by then.'

She picked up the knitting pattern, studied it frowning.

'Oh, it is, is it? You've got it all cut and dried. But his birthday happens to be in March.'

'You can't choose everything,' she said. She was going on with her knitting and smiling.

'I forbid you to say any more about the boy.'

'You can't, you see. People ask me how he's getting on.'

'I wish I hadn't started the damn fool business.'

'I don't. I'm so glad you did.'

'You'll land us in gaol, do you realise that? And what is this you're knitting?' He knew, from the conversation he had overheard.

'A sweater for him, for Julian.'

'Do you know what?' he said, leaning towards her and almost spitting the words at her, one after the other, 'I think you're going out of your mind. You'll have to go away from here. Maybe we'd both better go, and it will be the parting of the ways.'

'I don't see any cause for that,' said Edith. 'I've never been so happy.'

*   *   *

But her happiness was nearly at an end; even before she could finish knitting the sweater, the spell had been broken.

A letter came from her sister, Hilda, in Melbourne. She wrote much less frequently than Edith and usually only when she had something to boast about – this time it was one of the boys having won a tennis tournament.

She has always patronised me, Edith thought. I have never harped on in that way about Julian. I don't see why I should have hidden his light under a bushel all these years.

She sat down at once and wrote a long letter about his different successes. Whatever Hilda's sons may have done, Julian seemed to find it easy to do better. 'We are sending him for a holiday on the Continent as a reward for passing his exams,' she finished up. She was tired of silence and modesty. Those qualities had never brought her any joy, none of the wonderful exhilaration and sense of richness she had now. Her attitude towards life had been too drab and undemanding; she could plainly see this.

She took her letter to the village and posted it. She imagined her sister looking piqued – not puzzled – when she read it.

Silcox was in the bedroom when she returned. A drawer slid quickly shut and he was suddenly busy winding his watch. 'Well, I suppose it's time to put my hand to the wheel,' he said in a voice less cold than it had been of late, as he went out.

Edith was suspicious of this voice, which was too genial, she thought, and she looked round to see if anything of hers had been tampered with. She was especially anxious about her knitting, which was so precious to her; but it was still neatly rolled up and hanging in a clean laundry bag in her cupboard.

She opened the drawer which Silcox had so smartly closed and found a letter lying on top of a pile of black woollen socks. A photograph was half out of the envelope. Though he had thrust it out of sight when she came into the room, she realised that he had been perfectly easy in his mind about leaving it where it was for it would be contrary to his opinion of her that she would pry or probe. He knows nothing about me, she thought, taking the photograph to the window so that she could see it better.

She was alarmed at the way her heart began to leap and hammer, and she pressed her hand to her breast and whispered, 'Hush' to its loud beating. 'Hush, hush,' she implored it, and sat down on her bed to wait for the giddiness to pass.

When she was steadier, she looked again at the two faces in the photograph. There was no doubt that one of them was Julian's, though older than she had imagined and more defined than in the other photograph – the one that stood always on the chest of drawers.

It was so much like the face of the middle-aged woman whom his arm encircled affectionately, who wore the smug, pleased smile of a mother whose son has been teasing her. She glowed with delight, her lips ready to shape fond remonstrances. She looked a pretty, silly woman and wore a flowered, full-skirted dress, too girlish for her, too tight across the bust. They were standing by the wooden fence of a little garden. Behind them, hollyhocks grew untidily and a line of washing, having flapped in the wind as the camera clicked, hung there, blurred, above their heads. Julian had stared at the photographer, grinning foolishly, almost pulling a face. 'It's all put on,' thought Edith. 'All for effect.'

When her legs stopped trembling, she went again to the drawer and fetched the letter. She could only read a little of it at a time, because the feeling of faintness and nausea came upon her in waves and she would wait, with closed eyes, till each receded. After seeing 'Dear Father' she was as still as a stone, until she could brace herself for more, for the rest of the immaturely written, facetious letter. It contained abrupt and ungracious thanks for a watch he had received for what he referred to as his twenty-first. He seemed, Edith thought, to have expected more. A good time had been had by all, with Mum pushing the boat out to the best of her ability. They were still living in Streatham and he was working in a car showroom, where, he implied, he spent his time envying his customers. Things weren't too easy, although Mum was wonderful, of course. When he could afford to take her out, which he only wished he were able to do more often, she enjoyed herself as if she were a young girl. It was nice of his father to have thought of him, he ended reproachfully.

Carrie Hurt pushed the bedroom door open at the same time as she rapped on it with her knuckles. 'I was to say would you come down at once, Edith. There's some people in the dining-room already.'

'I shan't be coming down,' Edith said.

'Don't you feel well?'

'Tell him I shan't be coming down.'

Edith turned her head away and remained like that until Carrie had gone. Quietly, she sat and waited for Silcox to arrive. He would do so, she knew, as soon as he could find the manageress or a maid to take his place for a moment. It would offend his pride to allow such a crisis, but he would be too seriously alarmed to prevent it.

Her hatred was now so heavy that it numbed her and she was able to sit, quite calm and patient, waiting for him, rehearsing no speeches, made quite incapable by the suddenness of the calamity and the impossibility of accepting the truth of it.

It was not so very long before she heard his hurrying footsteps. He entered the room as she had thought he would, brimming with pompous indignation. She watched this fade and another sort of anger take its place when he saw the letter in her hand, the photograph on the bed.

'No, your eyes don't deceive you,' she said.

At first, he could think of nothing better to say than 'How dare you!' He said this twice, but as it was clearly inadequate, he stepped forward and grasped her wrists, gripping them tightly, shook her back and forth until her teeth were chattering. Not for years, not since the days of his brief marriage, had he so treated a woman and he had forgotten the overwhelming sensations to be derived from doing so. He released her, but only to hit her across her face with the back of one hand then the other.

Shaken, but unfrightened, she stared at him. 'It was true all the time,' she said. 'He was really yours and you disowned him. Yet you made up that story just to have a reason for putting out the photograph and looking at it every day.'

'Why should I want to do that? He means nothing to me.' He hoped to disconcert her by a quick transition to indifference.

'And his mother – *I* was supposed to be his mother.'

He laughed theatrically at the absurdity of this idea. It was a bad performance. When he had finished being doubled-up, he wiped his eyes and said: 'Excuse me.' The words were breathed on a sigh of exquisite enjoyment.

Coming to the door for the second time, Carrie Hurt waited after knocking. She had been surprised to hear Silcox laughing so loudly as she came along the passage. She had never heard him laugh in any way before and wondered if he had gone suddenly mad. He opened the door to her, looking grave and dignified.

'Yes, I am coming now,' he said.

'They're very busy. I was told to say if you could please . . .'

'I repeat, I am coming now. Edith is unwell and we must manage for today as best we may without her. She will stay here and rest,' he added, turning and saying this directly to Edith and stressing his even tone by a steady look. He would have locked the door upon her if Carrie had not been standing by.

Edith was then alone and began to cry. She chafed her wrists that were still reddened from his grasp, and moved her head from side to side, as if trying to evade the thoughts that crowded on her.

Carrie Hurt returned presently with a glass of brandy. 'It can't do any harm,' she said. 'He told me to leave you alone, but there might be something she wants, I thought.'

She put the glass on the table beside the bed and then went over to draw the curtains. Edith sat still, with her hands clasped in her lap, and waited for her to go.

'My mother has these funny spells,' Carrie told her. Then, noticing the letter lying on the bed, she asked, 'Oh, you haven't had any bad news, have you?'

'Yes,' Edith said.

She leaned forward to take the glass, sipped from it and shuddered.

'Not your *boy*?' Carrie whispered.

Edith sighed. It seemed more than a sigh – a frightening sound, seeming to gather all the breath from her body, shuddering, expelling it

'He isn't ill, is he?' Carrie asked, expecting worse – though Silcox, to be sure, had seemed controlled enough. And what had his dreadful laughter meant?

Edith was silent for a moment and took a little more brandy. Then she said, in a forced and rather high-pitched voice: 'He is much worse than ill. He is disgraced.'

'Oh, my God!' said Carrie eagerly.

Edith's eyes rested for a second on the photograph lying beside her on the bed and then she covered it with her hand. 'For theft,' she said, her voice strengthening, 'thieving,' she added.

'Oh dear, I'm ever so sorry,' Carrie said softly. 'I can't believe it. I always said what an open face he'd got. Don't you remember – I always said that? Who could credit it? No one could. Not that I should breathe a word about it to a single soul.'

'Mention it to whoever you like,' Edith said. 'The whole world will know, and may decide where they can lay the blame.'

She drained the glass, her eyes closed. Then, 'There's bad blood there,' she said.

When Silcox had finished his duties, he returned, but the door was locked from inside, and there was no answer when he spoke, saying her name several times in a low voice, his head bent close to the keyhole.

He went away and walked by the river in his waiter's clothes, stared at by all who passed him. When he returned to the hotel, he was stared at there, too. The kitchen porter seemed to be re-assessing him, looked at him curiously and spoke insolently. The still-room maid pressed back against the passage wall as he went by. Others seemed to avoid him.

The bedroom door was still shut, but no longer locked. He stood looking at the empty room, the hairbrush had gone from the dressing table and only a few coat-hangers swung from the rail in the clothes' cupboard. He picked up the brandy glass and was standing there sniffing it when Carrie Hurt, who had enjoyed her afternoon, appeared in the doorway.

'I don't know if you know, she's packed and gone,' she said, 'and had the taxi take her to the train. I thought the brandy would pull her together,' she went on, looking at the glass in Silcox's hand. 'I expect the shock unhinged her and she felt she had to go. Of course, she'd want to see him, whatever happened. It must have been her first thought. I should like to say how sorry I am. You wouldn't wish such a thing on your worst enemy.'

He looked at her in bewilderment and then, seeing her glance, as it swerved from his in embarrassment, suddenly checked by something out of his sight, he walked slowly round the bed and saw there what she was staring at – the waste-paper basket heaped high with her white knitting, all cut into little shreds; even the needles had been broken in two.

*   *   *

Before the new couple arrived, Silcox prepared to leave. Since Edith's departure, he had spoken to no one but his customers, to whom he was as stately as ever – almost devotional he seemed in his duties, bowed over chafing-dish or bottle – almost as if his calling were sacred and he felt himself worthy of it.

On the last morning, he emptied his bedroom cupboard and then the drawers, packing with his usual care. In the bottom drawer, beneath layers of shirts, and rolled up in a damask napkin, he was horrified to discover a dozen silver-plated soup spoons from the dining-room.

from *The Devastating Boys*

The Devastating Boys

LAURA was always too early; and this was as bad as being late, her husband, who was always late himself, told her. She sat in her car in the empty railway-station approach, feeling very sick, from dread.

It was half-past eleven on a summer morning. The country station was almost spellbound in silence, and there was, to Laura, a dreadful sense of self-absorption – in herself – in the stillness of the only porter standing on the platform, staring down the line: even – perhaps especially – in inanimate things; all were menacingly intent on being themselves, and separately themselves – the slanting shadow of railings across the platform, the glossiness of leaves, and the closed door of the office looking more closed, she thought, than any door she had ever seen.

She got out of the car and went into the station walking up and down the platform in a panic. It was a beautiful morning. If only the children weren't coming then she could have enjoyed it.

The children were coming from London. It was Harold's

idea to have them, some time back, in March, when he read of a scheme to give London children a summer holiday in the country. This he might have read without interest, but the words 'Some of the children will be coloured' caught his eye. He seemed to find a slight tinge of warning in the phrase; the more he thought it over, the more he was convinced. He had made a long speech to Laura about children being the great equalisers, and that we should learn from them, that to insinuate the stale prejudices of their elders into their fresh, fair minds was such a sin that he could not think of a worse one.

He knew very little about children. His students had passed beyond the blessed age, and shades of the prison-house had closed about them. His own children were even older, grown up and gone away; but, while they were young, they had done nothing to destroy his faith in them, or blur the idea of them he had in his mind, and his feeling of humility in their presence. They had been good children carefully dealt with and easy to handle. There had scarcely been a cloud over their growing up. Any little bothers Laura had hidden from him.

In March, the end of July was a long way away. Laura, who was lonely in middle age, seemed to herself to be frittering away her days, just waiting for her grandchildren to be born: she had agreed with Harold's suggestion. She would have agreed anyway, whatever it was, as it was her nature – and his – for her to do so. It would be rather exciting to have two children to stay – to have the beds in Imogen's and Lalage's room slept in again. 'We could have two boys, or two girls,' Harold said. 'No stipulation, but that they must be coloured.'

Now *he* was making differences, but Laura did not remark upon it. All she said was, 'What will they do all the time?'

'What our own children used to do – play in the garden, go for picnics . . . '

'On wet days?'

'Dress up,' he said at once.

She remembered Imogen and Lalage in her old hats and dresses, slopping about in her big shoes, see-sawing on high heels, and she had to turn her head away, and there were tears in her eyes.

Her children had been her life, and her grandchildren one day would be; but here was an empty space. Life had fallen away from her. She had never been clever like the other professors' wives, or managed to have what they called 'outside interests'. Committees frightened her, and good works made her feel embarrassed and clumsy.

She *was* a clumsy person – gentle, but clumsy. Pacing up and down the platform, she had an ungainly walk – legs stiffly apart, head a little poked forward because she had poor sight. She was short and squarely built and her clothes were never right; often she looked dishevelled, sometimes even battered.

This morning, she wore a label pinned to her breast, so that the children's escort would recognise her when the train drew in; but she felt self-conscious about it and covered it with her hand, though there was no one but the porter to see.

The signal dropped, as if a guillotine had come crashing down, and her heart seemed to crash down with it. Two boys! she thought. Somehow, she had imagined girls. She was used to girls, and shy of boys.

The printed form had come a day or two ago and had increased the panic which had gradually been gathering. Six-year-old boys, and she had pictured perhaps eight- or ten-year-old girls, whom she could teach to sew and make cakes for tea, and press wild flowers as she had taught Imogen and Lalage to do.

Flurried and anxious entertaining at home; interviewing headmistresses; once – shied away from failure – opening a sale-of-work in the village – these agonies to her diffident nature seemed nothing to the nervousness she felt now, as the train appeared round the bend. She simply wasn't good with children – only with her own. *Their* friends had frightened her, had been mouse-quiet and glum, or had got out of hand, and she herself had been too shy either to intrude or clamp down. When she met children – perhaps the small grandchildren of her acquaintances, she would only smile, perhaps awkwardly touch a cheek with her finger. If she were asked to hold a baby, she was fearful lest it should cry, and often it would, sensing lack of assurance in her clasp.

The train came in and slowed up. Suppose that I can't find them, she thought, and she went anxiously from window to window, her label uncovered now. And suppose they cry for their mothers and want to go home.

A tall, authoritative woman, also wearing a label, leaned out of a window, saw her and signalled curtly. She had a compartment full of little children in her charge to be delivered about Oxfordshire. Only two got out on to this platform, Laura's two, Septimus Smith and Benny Reece. They wore tickets, too, with their names printed on them.

Benny was much lighter in complexion than Septimus. He was obviously a half-caste and Laura hoped that this would count in Harold's eyes. It might even be one point up. They stood on the platform, looking about them, holding their little cardboard cases.

'My name is Laura,' she said. She stooped and clasped them to her in terror, and kissed their cheeks. Sep's in particular was extraordinarily soft, like the petal of a poppy. His big eyes stared up at her, without expression. He wore a dark, long-trousered suit, so that he was all over sombre and unchildlike. Benny had a mock-suede coat with a nylon-fur collar and a trilby hat with a feather. They did not speak. Not only was she, Laura, strange to them, but they were strange to one another. There had only been a short train journey in which to sum up their chances of becoming friends.

She put them both into the back of the car, so that there should be no favouritism, and drove off, pointing out – to utter silence – places on the way. 'That's a café where we'll go for tea one day.' The silence was dreadful. 'A caff,' she amended. 'And there's the little cinema. Not very grand, I'm afraid. Not like London ones.'

They did not even glance about them.

'Are you going to be good friends to one another?' she asked.

After a pause, Sep said in a slow grave voice, 'Yeah, I'm going to be a good friend.'

'Is this the country?' Benny asked. He had a chirpy, perky Cockney voice and accent.

'Yeah, this is the countryside,' said Sep, in his rolling drawl, glancing indifferently at some trees.

Then he began to talk. It was in an aggrieved sing-song. 'I don't go on that train no more. I don't like that train, and I don't go on that again over my dead body. Some boy he say to me, "You don't sit in that corner seat. I sit there." I say, "You don't sit here. I sit here." "Yeah," I say, "You don't own this train, so I don't budge from here." Then he dash my comic down and tore it.'

'Yep, he tore his comic,' Benny said.

'"You tear my comic, you buy me another comic," I said. "Or else." "Or *else*," I said.' He suddenly broke off and looked at a wood they were passing. 'I don't go near those tall bushes. They full of snakes what sting you.'

'No, they ain't,' said Benny.

'My Mam said so. I don't go.'

'There aren't any snakes,' said Laura, in a light voice. She, too, had a terror of them, and was afraid to walk through bracken. 'Or only little harmless ones,' she added.

'I don't go,' Sep murmured to himself. Then, in a louder voice, he went on. 'He said, "I don't buy no comic for you, you nigger," he said.'

'He never said that,' Benny protested.

'Yes, "You dirty nigger," he said.'

'He never.'

There was something so puzzled in Benny's voice that Laura immediately believed him. The expression on his little monkey face was open and impartial.

'I don't go on that train no more.'

'You've got to. When you go home,' Benny said.

'Maybe I don't go home.'

'We'll think about that later. You've only just arrived,' said Laura, smiling.

'No, I think about that right now.'

Along the narrow lane to the house, they were held up by the cows from the farm. A boy drove them along, whacking their messed rumps with a stick. Cow pats plopped on to the road and steamed there, zizzing with flies. Benny held his nose and Sep, glancing at him, at once did the same. 'I don't care for this smell of the countryside,' he complained in a pinched tone.

'No, the countryside stinks,' said Benny.

'Cows frighten me.'

'They don't frighten me.'

Sep cringed against the back of the seat, whimpering; but Benny wound his window right down, put his head a little out of it, and shouted, 'Get on, you dirty old sods, or else I'll show you.'

'Hush,' said Laura gently.

'He swore,' Sep pointed out.

They turned into Laura's gateway, up the short drive. In front of the house was a lawn and a cedar tree. From one of its lower branches hung the old swing, on chains, waiting for Laura's grandchildren.

The boys clambered out of the car and followed her into the hall, where they stood looking about them critically; then Benny dropped his case and shot like an arrow towards Harold's golf bag and pulled out a club. His face was suddenly bright with excitement and Laura, darting

200

forward to him, felt a stab of misery at having to begin the
'No's' so soon. 'I'm afraid Harold wouldn't like you to
touch them,' she said. Benny stared her out, but after a
moment or two gave up the club with all the unwillingness
in the world. Meanwhile, Sep had taken an antique coach-
ing horn and was blowing a bubbly, uneven blast on it, his
eyes stretched wide and his cheeks blown out. 'Nor that,'
said Laura faintly, taking it away. 'Let's go upstairs and
unpack.'

They appeared not at all overawed by the size of this
fairly large house; in fact, rather unimpressed by it.

In the room where once, as little girls, Imogen and
Lalage had slept together, they opened their cases. Sep put
his clothes neatly and carefully into his drawer; and Benny
tipped the case into his – comics, clothes and shoes, and a
scattering of peanuts. I'll tidy it later, Laura thought.

'Shall we toss up for who sleeps by the window?' she
suggested.

'I don't sleep by no window,' said Sep. 'I sleep in *this* bed;
with *him*.'

'I want to sleep by myself,' said Benny.

Sep began a babyish whimpering, which increased into
an anguished keening. 'I don't like to sleep in the bed by
myself. I'm scared to. I'm real scared to. I'm scared.'

This was entirely theatrical, Laura decided, and Benny
seemed to think so, too; for he took no notice.

A fortnight! Laura thought. This day alone stretched
endlessly before her, and she dared not think of any following ones. Already she felt ineffectual and had an inkling
that they were going to despise her. And her brightness was
false and not infectious. She longed for Harold to come
home, as she had never longed before.

'I reckon I go and clean my teeth,' said Sep, who had
broken off his dirge.

'Lunch is ready. Afterwards would be more sensible,
surely?' Laura suggested.

But they paid no heed to her. Both took their tooth-brushes, their new tubes of paste, and rushed to find the bathroom. 'I'm going to bathe myself,' said Sep. 'I'm going to bathe all my skin, and wash my head.'

'Not *before* lunch,' Laura called out, hastening after them; but they did not hear her. Taps were running and steam clouding the window, and Sep was tearing off his clothes.

'He's bathed three times already,' Laura told Harold.

She had just come downstairs, and had done so as soon as she heard him slamming the front door.

Upstairs, Sep was sitting in the bath. She had made him a lacy vest of soapfroth, as once she had made them for Imogen and Lalage. It showed up much better on his grape-dark skin. He sat there, like a tribal warrior done up in warpaint.

Benny would not go near the bath. He washed at the basin, his sleeves rolled up; and he turned the cake of soap over and over uncertainly in his hands.

'It's probably a novelty,' Harold said, referring to Sep's bathing. 'Would you like a drink.'

'Later perhaps. I daren't sit down, for I'd never get up again.'

'I'll finish them off. I'll go and see to them. You just sit there and drink this.'

'Oh, Harold, how wonderfully good of you.'

She sank down on the arm of a chair, and sipped her drink, feeling stunned. From the echoing bathroom came shouts of laughter, and it was very good to hear them, especially from a distance. Harold was being a great success, and relief and gratitude filled her.

After a little rest, she got up and went weakly about the room, putting things back in their places. When this was done, the room still looked wrong. An unfamiliar dust seemed to have settled all over it, yet, running a finger over the piano, she found none. All the same, it was not the usual scene she set for Harold's homecoming in the evenings. It had taken a shaking up.

Scampering footsteps now thundered along the landing. She waited a moment or two, then went upstairs. They were in bed, in separate beds; Benny by the window. Harold was pacing about the room, telling them a story: his hands flapped like huge ears at either side of his face; then he made an elephant's trunk with his arm. From the beds, the children's eyes stared unblinkingly at him. As Laura came into the room, only Benny's flickered in her direction, then back at once to the magic of Harold's performance. She blew a vague, unheeded kiss, and crept away.

'It's like seeing snow begin to fall,' Harold said at dinner. 'You know it's going to be a damned nuisance, but it makes a change.'

He sounded exhilarated; clashed the knife against the steel with vigour, and started to carve. He kept popping little titbits into his mouth. Carver's perks, he called them.

'Not much for me,' Laura said.

'What did they have for lunch?'

'Fish cakes.'

'Enjoy them?'

'Sep said, "I don't like that." He's very suspicious, and that makes Benny all the braver. Then he eats too much, showing off.'

'They'll settle down,' Harold said, settling down himself to his dinner. After a while, he said, 'The little Cockney one asked me just now if this were a private house. When I said "Yes," he said, "I thought it was, because you've got the sleeping upstairs and the talking downstairs." Didn't quite get the drift.'

'Pathetic,' Laura murmured.

'I suppose where they come from, it's all done in the same room.'

'Yes, it is.'

'Pathetic,' Harold said in his turn.

'It makes me feel ashamed.'

'Oh, come now.'

'And wonder if we're doing the right thing – perhaps unsettling them for what they have to go back to.'

'My dear girl,' he said. 'Damn it, those people who organise these things know what they're doing.'

'I suppose so.'

'They've been doing it for years.'

'Yes, I know.'

'Well, then . . . '

Suddenly she put down her knife and fork and rested her forehead in her hands.

'What's up, old thing?' Harold asked, with his mouth full.

'Only tired.'

'Well, they've dropped off all right. You can have a quiet evening.'

'I'm too tired to sit up straight any longer.' After a silence, lifting her face from her hands, she said, 'Thirteen more days! What shall I do with them all that time?'

'Take them for scrambles in the woods,' he began, sure that he had endless ideas.

'I tried. They won't walk a step. They both groaned and moaned so much that we turned back.'

'Well, they can play on the swing.'

'For how long, how *long*? They soon got tired of that. Anyhow, they quarrel about one having a longer turn than the other. In the end, I gave them the egg timer.'

'That was a good idea.'

'They broke it.'

'Oh.'

'Please God, don't let it rain,' she said earnestly, staring out of the window. 'Not for the next fortnight, anyway.'

*   *   *

The next day, it rained from early morning. After breakfast, when Harold had gone off, Laura settled the boys at the dining-room table with a snakes-and-ladders board. As they had never played it, she had to draw up a chair herself, and join in. By some freakish chance, Benny threw one six after another, would, it seemed, never stop; and Sep's frustration and fury rose. He kept snatching the dice-cup away from Benny, peering into it, convinced of trickery. The game went badly for him and Laura, counting rapidly ahead, saw that he was due for the longest snake of all. His face was agonised, his dark hand, with its pale scars and scratches, hovered above the board; but he could not bring himself to draw the counter down the snake's horrid speckled length.

'I'll do it for you,' Laura said. He shuddered, and turned aside. Then he pushed his chair back from the table and lay, face-down on the floor, silent with grief.

And it's not yet ten o'clock, thought Laura, and was relieved to see Mrs Milner, the help, coming up the path under her umbrella. It was a mercy that it was her morning.

She finished off the game with Benny, and he won; but the true glory of victory had been taken from him by the vanquished, lying still and wounded on the hearthrug. Laura was bright and cheerful about being beaten, trying to set an example; but she made no impression.

Presently, in exasperation, she asked, 'Don't you play games at school?'

There was no answer for a time, then Benny, knowing the question wasn't addressed to him, said, 'Yep, sometimes.'

'And what do you do if you lose?' Laura asked, glancing down at the hearthrug. 'You can't win all the time.'

In a muffled voice, Sep at last said, 'I don't win *any* time. They won't let me win any time.'

'It's only luck.'

'No, they don't *let* me win. I just go and lie down and shut my eyes.'

'And are these our young visitors?' asked Mrs Milner, coming in with the vacuum cleaner. Benny stared at her; Sep lifted his head from his sleeve for a brief look, and then returned to his sulking.

'What a nasty morning I've brought with me,' Mrs Milner said, after Laura had introduced them.

'You brought a nasty old morning all right,' Sep agreed, mumbling into his jersey.

'But,' she went on brightly, putting her hands into her overall pockets, 'I've also brought some lollies.'

Benny straightened his back in anticipation. Sep, peeping with one eye, stretched out an arm.

'That's if Madam says you may.'

'They call me Laura.' It had been Harold's idea and Laura had foreseen this very difficulty.

Mrs Milner could not bring herself to say the name and she, too, could foresee awkwardnesses.

'No, Sep,' said Laura firmly. 'Either you get up properly and take it politely, or you go without.'

She wished that Benny hadn't at once scrambled to his feet and stood there at attention. Sep buried his head again and moaned. All the sufferings of his race were upon him at this moment.

Benny took his sweet and made a great appreciative fuss about it.

All the china had gone up a shelf or two, out of reach, Mrs Milner noted. It was like the old days, when Imogen's and Lalage's friends had come to tea.

'Now, there's a good lad,' she said, stepping over Sep, and plugging in the vacuum cleaner.

'Is that your sister?' Benny asked Laura, when Mrs Milner had brought in the pudding, gone out again, and closed the door.

'No, Mrs Milner comes to help me with the housework – every Tuesday and Friday.'

'She must be a very kind old lady,' Benny said.

'Do you like that?' Laura asked Sep, who was pushing jelly into his spoon with his fingers.

'Yeah, I like this fine.'

He had suddenly cheered up. He did not mention the lolly, which Mrs Milner had put back in her pocket. All the rest of the morning, they had played excitedly with the telephone – one upstairs in Laura's bedroom; the other downstairs, in the hall – chattering and shouting to one another, and running to Laura to come to listen.

That evening, Harold was home earlier than usual and could not wait to complain that he had tried all day to telephone.

'I know, dear,' Laura said. 'I should have stopped them, but it gave me a rest.'

'You'll be making a rod for everybody's back, if you let them do just what they like all the time.'

'It's for such a short while – well, relatively speaking – and they haven't got telephones at home, so the question doesn't arise.'

'But other people might want to ring you up.'

'So few ever do, it's not worth considering.'

'Well, someone did today. Helena Western.'

'What on earth for?'

'There's no need to look frightened. She wants you to take the boys to tea.' Saying this, his voice was full of satisfaction, for he admired Helena's husband. Helena herself wrote what he referred to as 'clever-clever little novels'. He went on sarcastically, 'She saw you with them from the top of a bus, and asked me when I met her later in Blackwell's. She says she has absolutely *no* feelings about coloured people, as some of her friends apparently have.' He was speaking in Helena's way of stresses and breathings. 'In fact,' he ended, 'she rather goes out of her way to be extra pleasant to them.'

'So she does have feelings,' Laura said.

She was terrified at the idea of taking the children to tea with Helena. She always felt dull and overawed in her company, and was afraid that the boys would misbehave and get out of her control, and then Helena would put it all into a novel. Already she had put Harold in one; but, luckily, he had not recognised his own transformation from professor of archaeology to barrister. Her simple trick worked, as far as he was concerned. To Harold, that character, with his vaguely left-wing opinions and opinionated turns of phrase, his quelling manner to his wife, his very appearance, could have nothing to do with him, since he had never taken silk. Everyone else had recognised and known, and Laura, among them, knew they had.

'I'll ring her up,' she said; but she didn't stir from her chair, sat staring wearily in front of her, her hands on her knees – a very resigned old woman's attitude; Whistler's mother. I'm *too* old, she thought. I'd be too old for my own grandchildren. But she had never imagined *them* like the ones upstairs in bed. She had pictured biddable little children, like Lalage and Imogen.

'They're good at *night*,' she said to Harold, continuing her thoughts aloud. 'They lie there and talk quietly, *once* they're in bed. I wonder what they talk about. Us, perhaps.' It was an alarming idea.

In the night she woke and remembered that she had not telephoned Helena. I'll do it after breakfast, she thought.

But she was still making toast when the telephone rang, and the boys left the table and raced to the hall ahead of her. Benny was first and, as he grabbed the receiver, Sep stood close by him, ready to shout some messages into the magical instrument. Laura hovered anxiously by, but Benny warned her off with staring eyes. 'Be polite,' she whispered imploringly.

'Yep, my name's Benny,' he was saying.

Then he listened, with a look of rapture. It was his first real telephone conversation, and Sep was standing by, shivering with impatience and envy.

'Yep, that'll be OK,' said Benny, grinning. 'What day?'

Laura put out her hand, but he shrank back, clutching the receiver. 'I got the message,' he hissed at her. 'Yep, he's here,' he said, into the telephone. Sep smiled self-consciously and drew himself up as he took the receiver. 'Yeah, I am Septimus Alexander Smith.' He gave his high, bubbly chuckle. 'Sure I'll come there.' To prolong the conversation, he went on, 'Can my friend, Benny Reece, come, too? Can Laura come?' Then he frowned, looking up at the ceiling, as if for inspiration. 'Can my father, Alexander Leroy Smith, come?'

Laura made another darting movement.

'Well, no, he can't then,' Sep said, 'because he's dead.'

This doubled him up with mirth, and it was a long time before he could bring himself to say goodbye. When he had done so, he quickly put the receiver down.

'Someone asked me to tea,' he told Laura. 'I said, "Yeah, sure I come."'

'And me,' said Benny.

'Who was it?' Laura asked, although she knew.

'I don't know,' said Sep. 'I don't know *who* that was.'

When later and secretly, Laura telephoned Helena, Helena said, 'Aren't they simply *devastating* boys?'

'How did the tea party go?' Harold asked.

They had all arrived back home together – he, from a meeting; Laura and the boys from Helena's.

'They were good,' Laura said, which was all that mattered. She drew them to her, one on either side. It was her movement of gratitude towards them. They had not let her down. They had played quietly at a fishing game with real water and magnetised tin fish, had eaten unfamiliar things, such as anchovy toast and brandy snaps, without any expression of alarm or revulsion; they had helped carry the tea things indoors from the lawn. Helena had been surprisingly clever with them. She made them laugh, as seldom Laura could. She struck the right note from the beginning. When Benny picked up sixpence from the gravelled path, she thanked him casually and put it in her pocket. Laura was grateful to her for that and proud that Benny ran away at once so unconcernedly. When Helena had praised them for their good behaviour, Laura had blushed with pleasure, just as if they were her own children.

'She is really very nice,' Laura said later, thinking still of her successful afternoon with Helena.

'Yes, she talks too much, that's all.'

Harold was pleased with Laura for having got on well with his colleague's wife. It was so long since he had tried to urge Laura into academic circles, and for years he had given up trying. Now, sensing his pleasure, her own was enhanced.

'When we were coming away,' Laura said, 'Helena whispered to me, "Aren't they simply *dev*astating?"'

'You've exactly caught her tone.'

At that moment, they heard from the garden, Benny also exactly catching her tone.

'Let's have the bat, there's a little pet,' he mimicked, trying to snatch the old tennis racquet from Sep.

'You sod off,' drawled Sep.

'Oh, my dear, you shake me rigid.'

Sep began his doubling-up-with-laughter routine; first, in silence, bowed over, lifting one leg then another up to his chest, stamping the ground. It was like the start of a tribal dance, Laura thought, watching him from the window; then the pace quickened, he skipped about, and laughed, with his head thrown back, and tears rolled down his face. Benny looked on, smirking a little, obviously proud that his wit should have had such an effect. Round and round went Sep, his loose limbs moving like pistons. 'Yeah, you shake me rigid,' he shouted. 'You shake me entirely rigid.' Benny, after hesitating, joined in. They circled the lawn, and disappeared into the shrubbery.

'She *did* say that. Helena,' Laura said, turning to Harold. 'When Benny was going on about something he'd done she said, "My dear, you shake me entirely rigid."'

Then Laura added thoughtfully, 'I wonder if they are as good at imitating *us*, when they're lying up there in bed, talking.'

'A sobering thought,' said Harold, who could not believe he had any particular idiosyncrasies to be copied. 'Oh, God, someone's broken one of my sherds,' he suddenly cried, stooping to pick up two pieces of pottery from the floor. His agonised shout brought Sep to the french windows, and he stood there, bewildered.

As the pottery had been broken before, he hadn't bothered to pick it up, or confess. The day before, he had broken a whole cup and nothing had happened. Now this grown man was bowed over as if in pain, staring at the fragments in his hand. Sep crept back into the shrubbery.

The fortnight, miraculously, was passing. Laura could now say, 'This time next week.' She would do gardening, get her hair done, clean all the paint. Often, she wondered about the kind of homes the other children had gone to – those children she had glimpsed on the train; and she imagined them staying on farms, helping with the animals, looked after by buxom farmers' wives – pale London children, growing gratifyingly brown, filling out, going home at last with roses in their cheeks. She could see no difference in Sep and Benny.

What they had really got from the holiday was one another. It touched her to see them going off into the shrubbery with arms about one another's shoulders, and to listen to their peaceful murmuring as they lay in bed, to hear their shared jokes. They quarrelled a great deal, over the tennis racquet or Harold's old cricket bat, and Sep was constantly casting himself down on the grass and weeping, if he were out at cricket, or could not get Benny out.

It was he who would sit for hours with his eyes fixed on Laura's face while she read to him. Benny would wander restlessly about, waiting for the story to be finished. If he interrupted, Sep would put his hand imploringly on Laura's arm, silently willing her to continue.

Benny liked her to play the piano. It was the only time she was admired. They would dance gravely about the room, with their bottles of Coca Cola, sucking through straws, choking, heads bobbing up and down. Once, at the end of a concert of nursery rhymes, Laura played 'God Save the Queen' and Sep rushed at her, trying to shut the lid down on her hands. 'I don't like that,' he keened. 'My Mam don't like 'God Save the Queen' neither. She say "God save *me*".'

'Get out,' said Benny, kicking him on the shin. 'You're shaking me entirely rigid.'

On the second Sunday, they decided that they must go to church. They had a sudden curiosity about it, and a yearning to sing hymns.

'Well, take them,' said liberal-minded and agnostic Harold to Laura.

But it was almost time to put the sirloin into the oven. 'We did sign that form,' she said in a low voice. 'To say we'd take them if they wanted to go.'

'Do you *really* want to go?' Harold asked, turning to the boys, who were wanting to go more and more as the discussion went on. 'Oh, God!' he groaned – inappropriately, Laura thought.

'What religion are you, anyway?' he asked them.

'I am a Christian,' Sep said with great dignity.

'Me, too,' said Benny.

'What time does it begin?' Harold asked, turning his back to Laura.

'At eleven o'clock.'

'Isn't there some kids' service they can go to on their own?'

'Not in August, I'm afraid.'

'Oh, God!' he said again.

Laura watched them setting out; rather overawed, the two boys; it was the first time they had been out alone with him.

She had a quiet morning in the kitchen. Not long after twelve o'clock they returned. The boys at once raced for the cricket bat, and fought over it, while Harold poured himself out a glass of beer.

'How did it go?' asked Laura.

'Awful! Lord, I felt such a fool.'

'Did they misbehave, then?'

'Oh, no, they were perfectly good – except that for some reason Benny kept holding his nose. But I knew so many people there. And the vicar shook hands with me afterwards and said, "We are especially glad to see *you*." The embarrassment!'

'It must have shaken you entirely rigid,' Laura said, smiling as she basted the beef. Harold looked at her as if for the first time in years. She so seldom tried to be amusing.

At lunch, she asked the boys if they had enjoyed their morning.

'Church smelt nasty,' Benny said, making a face.

'Yeah,' agreed Sep. 'I prefer my own country. I prefer Christians.'

'Me, too,' Benny said. 'Give me Christians any day.'

'Has it been a success?' Laura asked Harold. 'For them, I mean.'

It was their last night – Sep's and Benny's – and she wondered if her feeling of being on the verge of tears was entirely

213

from tiredness. For the past fortnight, she had reeled into bed, and slept without moving.

A success for *them*? She could not be quite sure; but it had been a success for her, and for Harold. In the evenings, they had so much to talk about, and Harold, basking in his popularity, had been genial and considerate.

Laura, the boys had treated as a piece of furniture, or a slave, and humbly she accepted her place in their minds. She was a woman who had never had any high opinions of herself.

'No more cricket,' she said. She had been made to play for hours – always wicket keeper, running into the shrubs for lost balls while Sep and Benny rested full-length on the grass.

'He has a lovely action,' she had said to Harold one evening, watching Sep taking his long run up to bowl. 'He might be a great athlete one day.'

'It couldn't happen,' Harold said. 'Don't you see, he has rickets?'

One of her children with rickets, she had thought, stricken.

Now, on this last evening, the children were in bed. She and Harold were sitting by the drawing-room window talking about them. There was a sudden scampering along the landing and Laura said. 'It's only one of them going to the toilet.'

'The *what*?'

'They ticked me off for saying lavatory,' she said placidly. 'Benny said it was a bad word.'

She loved to make Harold laugh, and several times lately she had managed to amuse him, with stories she had to recount.

'I shan't like saying goodbye,' she said awkwardly.

'No,' said Harold. He got up and walked about the room, examined his shelves of pottery fragments. 'It's been a lot of work for you, Laura.'

She looked away shyly. There had been almost a note of praise in his voice. Tomorrow, she thought. I hope I don't cry.

At the station, it was Benny who cried. All the morning he had talked about his mother, how she would be waiting for him at Paddington Station. Laura kept their thoughts fixed on the near future.

Now they sat on a bench on the sunny platform, wearing their name-labels, holding bunches of wilting flowers, and Laura looked at her watch and wished the minutes away. As usual, she was too early. Then she saw Benny shut his eyes quickly, but not in time to stop two tears falling. She was surprised and dismayed. She began to talk brightly, but neither replied. Benny kept his head down, and Sep stared ahead. At last, to her relief, the signal fell, and soon the train came in. She handed them over to the escort, and they sat down in the compartment without a word. Benny gazed out of the further window, away from her, rebukingly; and Sep's face was expressionless.

As the train began to pull out, she stood waving and smiling; but they would not glance in her direction, though the escort was urging them to do so, and setting an example. When at last Laura moved away, her head and throat were aching, and she had such a sense of failure and fatigue that she hardly knew how to walk back to the car.

It was not Mrs Milner's morning, and the house was deadly quiet. Life, noise, laughter, bitter quarrelling had gone out of it. She picked up the cricket bat from the lawn and went inside. She walked about, listlessly tidying things, putting them back in their places. Then fetched a damp cloth and sat down at the piano and wiped the sticky, dirty keys.

She was sitting there, staring in front of her, clasping the cloth in her lap, when Harold came in.

'I'm taking the afternoon off,' he said. 'Let's drive out to Minster Lovell for lunch.'

She looked at him in astonishment. On his way across the room to fetch his tobacco pouch, he let his hand rest on her shoulder for a moment.

'Don't fret,' he said. 'I think we've got them for life now.'

'Benny cried.'

'Extraordinary thing. Shall we make tracks?'

She stood up and closed the lid of the keyboard. 'It was awfully nice of you to come back, Harold.' She paused, thinking she might say more; but he was puffing away, lighting his pipe with a great fuss, as if he were not listening. 'Well, I'll go and get ready,' she said.

Flesh

PHYL was always one of the first to come into the hotel bar in the evenings, for what she called her *aperitif*, and which, in reality, amounted to two hours' steady drinking. After that, she had little appetite for dinner, a meal to which she was not used.

On this evening, she had put on one of her beaded tops, of the kind she wore behind the bar on Saturday evenings in London, and patted back her tortoiseshell hair. She was massive and glittering and sunburnt – a wonderful sight, Stanley Archard thought, as she came across the bar towards him.

He had been sitting waiting for her. They had found their own level in one another on about the third day of the holiday. Both being heavy drinkers drew them together. Before that had happened, they had looked one another over warily as, in fact, they had all their fellow-guests.

Travelling on their own, speculating, both had watched and wondered. Even at the airport, she had stood out from the others, he remembered, as she had paced up and down in her emerald-green coat. Then their flight number had been called, and they had gathered with others at the same channel, with the same pink labels tied to their hand luggage, all going to the same place; a polite, but distant little band of people, no one knowing with whom friendships were to be made – as like would no doubt drift to like. In the days that followed, Stanley had wished he had taken more notice of Phyl from the beginning, so that at the end of the holiday he would have that much more to remember. Only the emerald-green coat had stayed in his mind. She had not worn it since – it was too warm – and he dreaded the day when she would put it on again to make the return journey.

Arriving in the bar this evening, she hoisted herself up on a stool beside him. 'Well, here we are,' she said, glowing, taking one peanut; adding, as she nibbled, 'Evening, George,' to the barman. 'How's tricks?'

'My God, you've caught it today,' Stanley said, and he put his hands up near her plump red shoulders as if to warm them at a fire. 'Don't overdo it,' he warned her.

'Oh, I never peel,' she said airily.

He always put in a word against the sun-bathing when he could. It separated them. She stayed all day by the hotel swimming pool, basting herself with oil. He, bored with basking – which made him feel dizzy – had hired a car and spent his time driving about the island, and was full of alienating information about the locality, which the other guests – resenting the hired car, too – did their best to avoid. Only Phyl did not mind listening to him. For nearly every evening of her married life she had stood behind the bar and listened to other people's boring chat: she had a technique for dealing with it and a fund of vague phrases. 'Go on!' she said now, listening – hardly listening – to Stanley, and taking another nut. He had gone off by himself and found a place for lunch: *hors d'œuvre*, nice-sized slice of veal, two veg, *crème caramel*, half bottle of rosé, coffee – twenty-two shillings the lot. 'Well, I'm blowed,' said Phyl, and she took a pound note from her handbag and waved it at the barman. When she snapped up the clasp of the bag it had a heavy, expensive sound.

One or two other guests came in and sat at the bar. At this stage of the holiday they were forming into little groups, and this was the jokey set who had come first after Stanley and Phyl. According to them all sorts of funny things had happened during the day, and little screams of laughter ran round the bar.

'Shows how wrong you can be,' Phyl said in a low voice, 'I thought they were ever so starchy on the plane. I was wrong about you, too. At the start, I thought you were . . . you know . . . one of *those*. Going about with that young boy all the time.'

Stanley patted her knee. 'On the contrary,' he said, with a meaning glance at her. 'No, I was just at a bit of a loose end, and he seemed to cotton on. Never been abroad before, he hadn't, and didn't know the routine. I liked it for the first day or two. It was like taking a nice kiddie out on a treat. Then it seemed to me he was sponging. I'm not mean, I don't think; but I don't like that – sponging. It was quite a relief when he suddenly took up with the Lisper.'

By now, he and Phyl had nicknames for most of the other people in the hotel. They did not know that the same applied to them, and that to the jokey set he was known as Paws and she as the Shape. It would have put them out and perhaps ruined their holiday if they had known. He thought his little knee-pattings were of the utmost discretion, and she felt confidence from knowing her figure was expensively controlled under her beaded dresses when she became herself again in the evenings. During the day while sun-bathing, she considered that anything went – that, as her mind was a blank, her body became one also.

The funny man of the party – the awaited climax – came into the bar, crabwise, face covered slyly with his hand, as if ashamed of some earlier misdemeanour. 'Oh, my God, don't look round. Here comes trouble!' someone said loudly, and George was called for from all sides. 'What's the poison, Harry? No, my shout, old boy. George, if you *please*.'

Phyl smiled indulgently. It was just like Saturday night with the regulars at home. She watched George with a professional eye, and nodded approvingly. He was good. They could have used him at the Nelson. A good quick boy.

'Heard from your old man?' Stanley asked her.

She cast him a tragic, calculating look. 'You must be joking. He can't *write*. No, honest, I've never had a letter from him in the whole of my life. Well, we always saw each other every day until I had my hysterectomy.'

Until now, in conversations with Stanley, she had always referred to 'a little operation'. But he had guessed what it was – well, it always was, wasn't it? – and knew that it was the reason for her being on holiday. Charlie, her husband, had sent her off to recuperate. She had sworn there was no need, that she had never felt so well in her life – was only a bit weepy sometimes late on a Saturday night. 'I'm not really the crying sort,' she had explained to Stanley. 'So he got worried, and sent me packing.' 'You clear off to the sun,' he had said, 'and see what that will do.'

What the sun had done for her was to burn her brick-red, and offer her this nice holiday friend. Stanley Archard, retired widower from Hove.

She enjoyed herself, as she usually did. The sun shone every day, and the drinks were so reasonable – they had many a long discussion about that. They also talked about his little flat in Hove; his strolls along the front; his few cronies at the club; his sad, orderly and lonely life.

This evening, he wished he had not brought up the subject of Charlie's writing to her, for it seemed to have fixed her thoughts on him and, as she went chatting on about him, Stanley felt an indefinable distaste, an aloofness.

She brought out from her note case a much-creased

cutting from *The Morning Advertiser*. 'Phyl and Charlie Parsons welcome old friends and new at the Nelson, Southwood. In licensed hours only!' 'That was when we changed houses,' she explained. There was a photograph of them both standing behind the bar. He was wearing a dark blazer with a large badge on the pocket. Sequins gave off a smudged sparkle from her breast, her hair was newly, elaborately done, and her large, ringed hand rested on an ornamental beer handle. Charlie had *his* hands in the blazer pockets, as if he were there to do the welcoming, and his wife to do the work: and this, in fact, was how things were. Stanley guessed it, and felt a twist of annoyance in his chest. He did not like the look of Charlie, or anything he had heard about him – how, for instance, he had seemed like a fish out of water visiting his wife in hospital. 'He used to sit on the edge of the chair and stare at the clock, like a boy in school,' Phyl had said, laughing. Stanley could not bring himself to laugh, too. He had leaned forward and taken her knee in his hand and wobbled it sympathetically to and fro.

No, she wasn't the crying sort, he agreed. She had a wonderful buoyancy and gallantry, and she seemed to knock years off his age by just *being* with him, talking to him.

In spite of their growing friendship, they kept to their original, separate tables in the hotel restaurant. It seemed too suddenly decisive and public a move for him to join her now, and he was too shy to carry it off at this stage of the holiday, before such an alarming audience. But after dinner, they would go for a walk along the sea front, or out in the car for a drink at another hotel.

Always, for the first minute or two in a bar, he seemed to lose her. As if she had forgotten him, she would look about her critically, judging the set-up, sternly drawing attention to a sticky ring on the counter where she wanted to rest her elbow, keeping a professional eye on the prices.

When they were what she called 'nicely grinned-up', they liked to drive out to a small headland and park the car, watching the swinging beam from a lighthouse. Then, after the usual knee-pattings and neck-strokings, they would heave and flop about in the confines of the Triumph Herald, trying to make love. Warmed by their drinks, and the still evening and the romantic sound of the sea idly turning over down below them, they became frustrated, both large, solid people, she much corseted and, anyhow, beginning to be painfully sunburnt across the shoulders, he with the confounded steering wheel to contend with.

He would grumble about the car and suggest getting out on to a patch of dry barley grass; but she imagined it full of insects; the chirping of the cicadas was almost deafening.

She also had a few scruples about Charlie, but they were not so insistent as the cicadas. After all, she thought, she had never had a holiday romance – not even a honeymoon with Charlie – and she felt that life owed her just one.

After a time, during the day, her sunburn forced her into the shade, or out in the car with Stanley. Across her shoulders she began to peel, and could not bear – though desiring his caress – him to touch her. Rather glumly, he waited for her flesh to heal, told her 'I told you so'; after all, they had not forever on this island, had started their second, their last week already.

'I'd like to have a look at the other island,' she said, watching the ferry leaving, as they sat drinking nearby.

'It's not worth just going there for the inside of a day,' he said meaningfully, although it was only a short distance.

Wasn't this, both suddenly wondered, the answer to the too small car, and the watchful eyes back at the hotel. She had refused to allow him into her room there. 'If anyone saw you going in or out. Why, they know where I live.

What's to stop one of them coming into the Nelson any
time, and chatting Charlie up?'

'Would you?' he now asked, watching the ferry starting
off across the water. He hardly dared to hear her answer.

After a pause she laughed. 'Why not?' she said, and took
his hand. 'We wouldn't really be doing any harm to anyone.'
(Meaning Charlie.) 'Because no one could find out, could
they?'

'Not over there,' he said, nodding towards the island.
'We can start fresh over there. Different people.'

'They'll notice we're both not at dinner at the hotel.'

'That doesn't prove anything.'

She imagined the unknown island, the warm and starlit
night and, somewhere, under some roof or other, a large
bed in which they could pursue their daring, more than
middle-aged adventure, unconfined in every way.

'As soon as my sunburn's better,' she promised. 'We've
got five more days yet, and I'll keep in the shade till then.'

A chambermaid advised yoghurt, and she spread it over her
back and shoulders as best she could, and felt its coolness
absorbing the heat from her skin.

Damp and cheesy-smelling in the hot night, she lay awake,
cross with herself. For the sake of a tan, she was wasting her
holiday – just to be a five minutes' wonder in the bar on
her return, the deepest brown any of them had had that
year. The darker she was, the more *abroad* she would seem
to have been, the more prestige she could command. All
summer, pallid herself, she had had to admire others.

Childish, really, she decided, lying rigid under the sheet,
afraid to move, burning and throbbing. The skin was taut
behind her knees, so that she could not stretch her legs; her
flesh was on fire.

Five more days, she kept thinking. Meanwhile, even this
sheet upon her was unendurable.

* * *

On the next evening, to establish the fact that they would not always be in to dinner at the hotel, they complained in the bar about the dullness of the menu, and went elsewhere.

It was a drab little restaurant, but they scarcely noticed their surroundings. They sat opposite one another at a corner table and ate shellfish briskly, busily – he, from his enjoyment of the food; she, with a wish to be rid of it. They rinsed their fingers, quickly dried them and leaned forward and twined them together – their large placid hands, with heavy rings, clasped on the tablecloth. Phyl, glancing aside for a moment, saw a young girl, at the next table with a boy, draw in her cheekbones to suppress laughter then, failing, turn her head to hide it.

'At *our* age,' Phyl said gently, drawing away her hands from his. 'In public, too.'

She could not be defiant; but Stanley said jauntily, 'I'm damned if I care.'

At that moment, their chicken was placed before them, and he sat back, looking at it, waiting for vegetables.

As well as the sunburn, the heat seemed to have affected Phyl's stomach. She felt queasy and nervy. It was now their last day but one before they went over to the other island. The yoghurt – or time – had taken the pain from her back and shoulders, though leaving her with a dappled, flaky look, which would hardly bring forth cries of admiration or advance her prestige in the bar when she returned. But, no doubt, she thought, by then England would be too cold for her to go sleeveless. Perhaps the trees would have changed colour. She imagined – already – dark Sunday afternoons, their three o'clock lunch done with, and she and Charlie sitting by the electric log fire in a lovely hot room smelling of oranges and the so-called hearth littered with peel. Charlie – bless him – always dropped off amongst a confusion of newspapers, worn out with banter and light ale, switched off, too, as he always was with her, knowing that he could relax – be nothing, rather – until seven o'clock, because it was Sunday. Again, for Phyl, imagining home, a little pang, soon swept aside or, rather, swept aside *from*.

She was in a way relieved that they would have only one night on the little island. That would make it seem more like a chance escapade than an affair, something less serious and deliberate in her mind. Thinking about it during the day-time, she even felt a little apprehensive; but told herself sensibly that there was really nothing to worry about: knowing herself well, she could remind herself that an evening's drinking would blur all the nervous edges.

'I can't get over that less than a fortnight ago I never knew you existed,' she said, as they drove to the afternoon ferry. 'And after this week,' she added, 'I don't suppose I'll ever see you again.'

'I wish you wouldn't talk like that – spoiling things,' he said heavily, and he tried not to think of Hove, and the winter walks along the promenade, and going back to the flat, boiling himself a couple of eggs, perhaps; so desperately lost without Ethel.

He had told Phyl about his wife and their quiet happiness together for many years, and then her long, long illness, during which she seemed to be going away from him gradually; but it was dreadful all the same when she finally did.

'We could meet in London on your day off,' he suggested.

'Well, maybe.' She patted his hand, leaving that disappointment aside for him.

There were only a few people on the ferry. It was the end of summer, and the tourists were dwindling, as the English community was reassembling, after trips 'back home'.

The sea was intensely blue all the way across to the island. They stood by the rail looking down at it, marvelling, and feeling like two people in a film. They thought they saw a dolphin, which added to their delight.

'Ethel and I went to Jersey for our honeymoon,' Stanley said. 'It poured with rain nearly all the time, and Ethel had one of her migraines.'

'I never had a honeymoon,' Phyl said. Just the one night at the Regent Palace. In our business, you can't both go away together. This is the first time I've ever been abroad.'

'The places I could take you to,' he said.

They drove the car off the ferry and began to cross the island. It was hot and dusty, hillsides terraced and tilled; green lemons hung on the trees.

'I wouldn't half like to actually *pick* a lemon,' she said.

'You shall,' he said, 'somehow or other.'

'And take it home with me,' she added. She would save it for a while, showing people, then cut it up for gin and tonic in the bar one evening, saying casually, 'I picked this lemon with my own fair hands.'

Stanley had booked their hotel from a restaurant, on the recommendation of a barman. When they found it, he was openly disappointed; but she managed to be gallant and optimistic. It was not by the sea, with a balcony where they might look out at the moonlit waters or rediscover brightness in the morning; but down a dull side street, and opposite a garage.

'We don't *have* to,' Stanley said doubtfully.

'Oh, come on! We might not get in anywhere else. It's only for sleeping in,' she said.

'It *isn't* only for sleeping in,' he reminded her.

An enormous man in white shirt and shorts came out to greet them. 'My name is Radam. Welcome,' he said, with confidence. 'I have a lovely room for you, Mr and Mrs Archard. You will be happy here, I can assure you. My wife will carry up your cases. Do not protest, Mr Archard. She is quite able to. Our staff has slackened off at the end of the season, and I have some trouble with the old ticker, as

you say in England. I know England well. I am a Bachelor of
Science of England University. Once had digs in Swindon.'

A pregnant woman shot out of the hotel porch and
seized their suitcases, and there was a tussle as Stanley
wrenched them from her hands. Still serenely boasting, Mr
Radam led them upstairs, all of them panting but himself.

The bedroom was large and dusty and overlooked a
garage.

'Oh, God, I'm sorry,' Stanley said, when they were left
alone. 'It's still not too late, if you could stand a row.'

'No. I think it's rather sweet,' Phyl said, looking round
the room. 'And, after all, don't blame yourself. You couldn't
know any more than me.'

The furniture was extraordinarily fret-worked, as if to
make more crevices for the dust to settle in; the bedside-
lamp base was an old gin bottle filled with gravel to weight
it down, and when Phyl pulled off the bed cover to feel the
bed she collapsed with laughter, for the pillowcases were
embroidered 'Hers' and 'Hers'.

Her laughter eased him, as it always did. For a moment,
he thought disloyally of the dead – of how Ethel would
have started to be depressed by it all, and he would have
hard work jollying her out of her dark mood. At the same
time, Phyl was wryly imagining Charlie's wrath, how he
would have carried on – for only the best was good enough
for him, as he never tired of saying.

'He's quite right – that awful fat man,' she said gaily. 'We
shall be very happy here. I dread to think who he keeps
"His" and "His" for, don't you?'

'I don't suppose the maid understands English,' he said,
but warming only slightly. 'You don't expect to have to
read off pillowcases.'

'I'm sure there *isn't* a maid.'

'The bed is very small,' he said.

'It'll be better than the car.'

He thought, she is such a woman as I have never met.

She's like a marvellous Tommy in the trenches – keeping everyone's pecker up. He hated Charlie for his luck.

I shan't ever be able to tell anybody about 'Hers' and 'Hers', Phyl thought regretfully – for she dearly loved to amuse their regulars back home. Given other circumstances, she might have worked up quite a story about it.

A tap on the door, and in came Mr Radam with two cups of tea on a tray. 'I know you English,' he said, rolling his eyes roguishly. 'You can't be happy without your tea.'

As neither of them ever drank it, they emptied the cups down the hand basin when he had gone.

Phyl opened the window and the sour, damp smell of new cement came up to her. All round about, building was going on; there was also the whine of a saw-mill, and a lot of clanking from the garage opposite. She leaned farther out, and then came back smiling into the room, and shut the window on the dust and noise. 'He was quite right – that barman. You *can* see the sea from here. It's down the bottom of the street. Let's go and have a look as soon as we've unpacked.'

On their way out of the hotel, they came upon Mr Radam, who was sitting in a broken old wicker chair, fanning himself with a folded newspaper.

'I shall prepare your dinner myself,' he called after them. 'And shall go now to make soup. I am a specialist of soup.'

They strolled in the last of the sun by the glittering sea, looked at the painted boats, watched a man beating an octopus on a rock. Stanley bought her some lace-edged handkerchiefs, and even gave the lacemaker an extra five shillings, so that Phyl could pick a lemon off one of the trees in her garden. Each bought for the other a picture postcard of the place, to keep.

'Well, it's been just about the best holiday I ever had,' he said. 'And there I was in half a mind not to come at all!' He had for many years dreaded the holiday season, and only went away because everyone he knew did so.

'I just can't remember when I last had one,' she said. There was not – never would be, he knew – the sound of self-pity in her voice.

This was only a small fishing village; but on one of the headlands enclosing it and the harbour was a big new hotel, with balconies overlooking the sea, Phyl noted. They picked their way across a rubbly car-park and went in. Here, too, was the damp smell of cement; but there was a brightly lighted empty bar with a small dance floor, and music playing.

'We could easily have got in here,' Stanley said. 'I'd like to wring that bloody barman's neck.'

'He's probably some relation, trying to do his best.'

'I'll best him.'

They seemed to have spent a great deal of their time together hoisting themselves up on bar stools.

'Make them nice ones,' Stanley added, ordering their drinks. Perhaps he feels a bit shy and awkward, too, Phyl thought.

'Not very busy,' he remarked to the barman.

'In one week we close.'

'Looks as if you've hardly opened,' Stanley said, glancing round.

It's not *his* business to get huffy, Phyl thought indignantly, when the young man, not replying, shrugged and turned aside to polish some glasses. Customer's always right. He should know that. Politics, religion, colour-bar – however they argue together, they're all of them always right, and if you know your job you can joke them out of it and on to something safer. The times she had done that, making a fool of herself, no doubt, anything for peace and quiet. By the time the elections were over, she was usually worn out.

Stanley had hated her buying him a drink back in the hotel, but she had insisted. 'What all that crowd would think of me!' she had said; but here, although it went much against her nature, she put aside her principles, and let him pay; let him set the pace, too. They became elated, and she was sure it would be all right – even having to go back to the soup-specialist's dinner. They might have avoided that; but too late now.

The barman, perhaps with a contemptuous underlining of their age, shuffled through some records and now put on *Night and Day*. For them both, it filled the bar with nostalgia.

'Come *on*!' said Stanley. 'I've never danced with you. This always makes me feel . . . I don't know.'

'Oh, I'm a terrible dancer,' she protested. The Licensed Victuallers' Association annual dance was the only one she ever went to, and even there stayed in the bar most of the time. Laughing, however, she let herself be helped down off her stool.

He had once fancied himself a good dancer; but, in later years, got no practice, with Ethel being ill, and then dead. Phyl was surprised how light he was on his feet; he bounced her round, holding her firmly against his stomach, his hand pressed to her back, but gently, because of the sunburn. He had perfect rhythm and expertise, side-stepping, reversing taking masterly control of her.

'Well, I never!' she cried. 'You're making me quite breathless.'

He rested his cheek against her hair, and closed his eyes, in the old, old way, and seemed to waft her away into a different dimension. It was then that he felt the first twinge, in his left toe. It was doom to him. He kept up the pace, but fell silent. When the record ended, he hoped that she would not want to stay on longer. To return to the hotel and take his gout pills was all he could think about. Some intuition made her refuse another drink. 'We've got to go back to the soup-specialist some time,' she said. 'He might even be a good cook.'

230

'Surprise, surprise!' Stanley managed to say, walking with pain towards the door.

Mr Radam was the most abominable cook. They had – in a large cold room with many tables – thin greasy chicken soup, and after that the chicken that had gone through the soup. Then peaches; he brought the tin and opened it before them, as if it were a precious wine, and no hanky-panky going on. He then stood over them, because he had much to say. 'I was offered a post in Basingstoke. Two thousand pounds a year, and a car and a house thrown in. But what use is that to a man like me? Besides, Basingstoke has a most detestable climate.'

Stanley sat, tight-lipped, trying not to lose his temper, but this man, and the pain, were driving him mad. He did not – dared not drink any of the wine he had ordered.

'Yes, the Basingstoke employment I regarded as not *on*,' Mr Radam said slangily.

Phyl secretly put out a foot and touched one of Stan's – the wrong one – and then thought he was about to have a heart attack. He screwed up his eyes and tried to breathe steadily, a slice of peach slithering about in his spoon. It was then she realised what was wrong with him.

'Oh, sod the peaches,' she said cheerfully, when Mr Radam had gone off to make coffee, which would be the best they had ever tasted, he had promised. Phyl knew they would not complain about the horrible coffee that was coming. The more monstrous the egoist, she had observed from long practice, the more normal people hope to uphold the fabrication – either for ease, or from a terror of any kind of collapse. She did not know. She was sure, though, as she praised the stringy chicken, hoisting the unlovable man's self-infatuation a notch higher, that she did so, because she feared him falling to pieces. Perhaps it was only fair, she decided, that weakness should get preferential treatment.

Whether it would continue to do so, with Stanley's present change of mood, she was uncertain.

She tried to explain her thoughts to him when, he leaving his coffee, she having gulped hers down, they went to their bedroom. He nodded. He sat on the side of the bed, and put his face into his hands.

'Don't let's go out again,' she said. 'We can have a drink in here. I love a bedroom gin, and I brought a bottle in my case.' She went busily to the wash basin, and held up a dusty tooth glass to the light.

'You have one,' he said.

He was determined to keep unruffled, but every step she took across the uneven floorboards broke momentarily the steady pain into burning splinters.

'I've got gout,' he said sullenly. 'Bloody hell, I've got my gout.'

'I thought so,' she said. She put down the glass very quietly and came to him. 'Where?'

He pointed down.

'Can you manage to get into bed by yourself?'

He nodded.

'Well, then!' she smiled. 'Once you're in, I know what to do.'

He looked up apprehensively, but she went almost on tiptoe out of the door and closed it softly.

He undressed, put on his pyjamas, and hauled himself on to the bed. When she came back, she was carrying two pillows. 'Don't laugh, but they're "His" and "His",' she said. 'Now, this is what I do for Charlie. I make a little pillow house for his foot, and it keeps the bedclothes off. Don't worry, I won't touch.'

'On this one night,' he said.

'You want to drink a lot of water.' She put a glass beside him. '"My husband's got a touch of gout," I told them down there. And I really felt quite married to you when I said it.'

She turned her back to him as she undressed. Her body, set free at last, was creased with red marks, and across her shoulders the bright new skin from peeling had ragged, dirty edges of the old. She stretched her spine, put on a transparent nightgown and began to scratch her arms.

'Come here,' he said, unmoving. 'I'll do that.'

So gently she pulled back the sheet and lay down beside him that he felt they had been happily married for years. The pang was that this was their only married night and his foot burned so that he thought that it would burst. And it will be a damn sight worse in the morning, he thought, knowing the pattern of his affliction. He began with one hand to stroke her itching arm.

Almost as soon as she had put the light off, an ominous sound zig-zagged about the room. Switching on again, she said, 'I'll get that devil, if it's the last thing I do. You lie still.'

She got out of bed again and ran round the room, slapping at the walls with her *Reader's Digest*, until at last she caught the mosquito, and Stanley's (as was apparent in the morning) blood squirted out.

After that, once more in the dark, they lay quietly. He endured his pain, and she without disturbing him rubbed her flaking skin.

'So this is our wicked adventure,' he said bitterly to the moonlit ceiling.

'Would you rather be on your own?'

'No, no!' He groped with his hand towards her.

'Well, then . . . '

'How can you forgive me?'

'Let's worry about you, eh? Not me. That sort of thing doesn't matter much to me nowadays. I only really do it to be matey. I don't know . . . by the time Charlie and I have locked up, washed up, done the till, had a bit of something to eat . . . '

Once, she had been as insatiable as a flame. She lay and

remembered the days of her youth; but with interest, not wistfully.

Only once did she wake. It was the best night's sleep she'd had for a week. Moonlight now fell over the bed, and on one chalky whitewashed wall. The sheet draped over them rose in a peak above his feet, so that he looked like a figure on a tomb. If Charlie could see me now, she suddenly thought. She tried not to have a fit of giggles for fear of shaking the bed. Stanley shifted, groaned in his sleep, then went on snoring, just as Charlie did.

He woke often during that night. The sheets were as abrasive as sandpaper. I knew this damn bed was too small, he thought. He shifted warily on to his side to look at Phyl who, in her sleep, made funny little whimpering sounds like a puppy. One arm flung above her head looked, in the moonlight, quite black against the pillow. Like going to bed with a coloured woman, he thought. He dutifully took a sip or two of water and then settled back again to endure his wakefulness.

'Well, *I* was happy,' she said, wearing her emerald-green coat again, sitting next to him in the plane, fastening her safety belt.

His face looked worn and grey.

'Don't mind me asking,' she went on, 'but did he charge for that tea we didn't order?'

'Five shillings.'

'I *knew* it. I wish you'd let me pay my share of everything. After all, it was me as well wanted to go.'

He shook his head, smiling at her. In spite of his prediction, he felt better this departure afternoon, though tired and wary about himself.

'If only we were taking off on holiday now,' he said, 'not coming back. Why can't we meet up in Torquay or somewhere? Something for me to look forward to,' he begged her, dabbing his mosquito-bitten forehead with his handkerchief.

'It was only my hysterectomy got me away this time,' she said.

They ate, they drank, they held hands under a newspaper, and presently crossed the twilit coast of England, where farther along grey Hove was waiting for him. The trees had not changed colour much and only some – she noticed, as she looked down on them, coming in to land – were yellower.

She knew that it was worse for him. He had to return to his empty flat; she, to a full bar, and on a Saturday, too. She wished there was something she could do to send him off cheerful.

'To me,' she said, having refastened her safety belt, taking his hand again. 'To me, it was lovely. To me it was just as good as if we had.'

Sisters

ON a Thursday morning, soon after Mrs Mason returned from shopping – in fact she had not yet taken off her hat – a neat young man wearing a dark suit and spectacles, half gold, half mock tortoiseshell, and carrying a rolled umbrella, called at the house, and brought her to the edge of ruin. He gave a name, which meant nothing to her, and she invited him in, thinking he was about insurance, or someone from her solicitor. He stood in the sitting-room, looking keenly about him, until she asked him to sit down and tell her his business.

'Your sister,' he began. 'Your sister Marion,' and Mrs Mason's hand flew up to her cheek. She gazed at him in alarmed astonishment, then closed her eyes.

In this town, where she had lived all her married life, Mrs Mason was respected, even mildly loved. No one had a word to say against her, so it followed there were no strong feelings either way. She seemed to have been made for widowhood, and had her own little set, for bridge and coffee mornings, and her committee meetings for the better known charities – such as the National Society for the Prevention of Cruelty to Children, and the Royal Society for the Prevention of Cruelty to Animals.

Her husband had been a successful dentist, and when he died she moved from the house where he had had his practice, into a smaller one in a quiet road nearby. She had no money worries, no worries of any kind. Childless and serene, she lived from day to day. They were almost able to set their clocks by her, her neighbours said, seeing her leaving the house in the mornings, for shopping and coffee at the Oak Beams Tea Room, pushing a basket on wheels, stalking rather on high-heeled shoes, blue-rinsed, rouged. Her front went down in a straight line from her heavy bust, giving her a stately look, the weight throwing her back a little. She took all of life at the same pace – a sign of ageing. She had settled to it a long time ago, and all of her years seemed the same now, although days had slightly varying patterns. Hers was mostly a day-time life, for it was chiefly a woman's world she had her place in. After tea, her friends' husbands came home, and then Mrs Mason pottered in her garden, played patience in the winter, or read historical romances from the library. 'Something light,' she would tell the assistant, as if seeking suggestions from a waiter. She could never remember the names of authors or their works, and it was quite a little disappointment when she discovered that she had read a novel before. She had few other disappointments – nothing much more than an unexpected shower of rain, or a tough cutlet, or the girl at the hairdresser's getting her rinse wrong.

Mrs Mason had always done, and still did, everything expected of women in her position – which was a phrase she often used. She baked beautiful Victoria sponges for bring-and-buy sales, arranged flowers, made *gros-point* covers for her chairs, gave tea parties, even sometimes, daringly, sherry parties with one or two husbands there, much against their will – but this was kept from her. She was occasionally included in other women's evening gatherings for she made no difference when there was a crowd, and it was an easy kindness. She mingled, and chatted about other people's holidays and families and jobs. She never drank more than two glasses of sherry, and was a good guest, always exclaiming appreciatively at the sight of canapés, 'My goodness, *someone*'s been busy!'

Easefully the time had gone by.

This Thursday morning, the young man, having mentioned her sister, and seen her distress, glanced at one of the needlework cushions, and rose for a moment to examine it. Having ascertained that it was her work (a brief, distracted nod), he praised it, and sat down again. Then, thinking the pause long enough, he said, 'I am writing a book about your sister, and I did so hope for some help from you.'

'How did you know?' she managed to ask with her numbed lips. 'That she was, I mean.'

He smiled modestly. 'It was a matter of literary detection – my great hobby. My life's work, I might say.'

He had small, even teeth, she noticed, glancing at him quickly. They glinted, like his spectacles, the buttons on his jacket and the signet ring on his hand. He was a hideously glinty young man she decided, looking away again.

'I have nothing to say of any interest.'

'But anything you say will interest us.'

'Us?'

'Her admirers. The reading public. Well, the world at large.' He shrugged.

'The world at large' was menacing, for it included this town where Mrs Mason lived. It included the Oak Beams Tea Room, and the Societies of Prevention.

'I have nothing to say.' She moved, as if she would rise.

'Come! You had your childhoods together. We know

238

about those only from the stories. The beautiful stories. That wonderful house by the sea.'

He looked at a few shelves of books beside him, and seemed disappointed. They were her late husband's books about military history.

'It wasn't so wonderful,' she said, for she disliked all exaggeration. 'It was a quite ordinary, shabby house.'

'Yes?' he said softly, settling back in his chair and clasping his ladylike hands.

The shabby, ordinary house – the Rectory – had a path between cornfields to the sea. On either side of it now were caravan sites. Her husband, Gerald, had taken her back there once when they were on holiday in Cornwall. He, of course, had been in the know. She had been upset about the caravans, and he had comforted her. She wished that he were here this morning to deal with this terrifying young man.

Of her childhood, she remembered – as one does – mostly the still hot afternoons, the cornflowers and thistles and scarlet pimpernels, the scratchy grass against her bare legs as they went down to the beach. Less clearly, she recalled evenings with shadows growing longer, and far-off sounding voices calling across the garden. She could see the picture of the house with windows open, and towels and bathing costumes drying on upstairs sills and canvas shoes, newly whitened, drying too, in readiness for the next day's tennis. It had all been so familiar and comforting; but her sister, Marion, had complained of dullness, had ungratefully chafed and rowed and rebelled – although using it all (twisting it) in later years to make a name for herself. It had never, never been as she had written of it. And she, Mrs Mason, the little Cassie of those books, had never been at all that kind of child. These more than forty years after, she still shied away from that description of her squatting and peeing into a rock pool, in front of some little boys Marion had made up. 'Cassie! Cassie!' her sisters had cried, apparently, in consternation. But it was Marion herself who had done that, more like. There were a few stories she could have told about Marion, if she had been the one to expose them all to shame, she thought grimly. The rock-pool episode was nothing, really, compared with some of the other inventions – 'experiments with sex', as reviewers had described them at the time. It was as if her sister had been compelled to set her sick fancies against a background that she knew.

Watching Mrs Mason's face slowly flushing all over to blend with her rouged cheekbones, the young man, leaning back easily, felt he had bided his time long enough. Something was obviously being stirred up. He said gently – so that his words seemed to come to her like her own thoughts – 'A few stories now, please. Was it a happy childhood?'

'Yes. No. It was just an ordinary childhood.'

'With such a genius amongst you? How *awfully* interesting!'

'She was no different from any of the rest of us.' But she *had* been, and so unpleasantly, as it turned out.

'Really *extraordinarily* interesting.' He allowed himself to lean forward a little, then, wondering if the slightest show of eagerness might silence her, he glanced about the room again. There were only two photographs – one of a long-ago bride and bridegroom, the other of a pompous-looking man with some sort of chain of office hanging on his breast.

It was proving very hard-going, this visit; but all the more of a challenge for that.

Mrs Mason, in her silvery-grey wool dress, suddenly seemed to him to resemble an enormous salmon. She even had a salmon shape – thick from the shoulders down and tapering away to surprisingly tiny, out-turned feet. He imagined trying to land her. She was demanding all the skill and tenacity he had. This was very pleasurable. Having let him in, and sat down, her good manners could find no way of getting rid of him. He was sure of that. Her good manners were the only encouraging thing, so far.

'You know, you are really not at all what I expected,' he said boldly, admiringly. 'Not in the very least like your sister, are you?'

What he had expected was an older version of the famous photograph in the Collected Edition – that waif-like creature with the fly-away fringe and great dark eyes.

Mrs Mason now carefully lifted off her hat, as if it were a coronet. Then she touched her hair, pushing it up a little. 'I was the pretty one,' she did not say; but, feeling some explanation was asked for, told him what all the world knew. 'My sister had poor health,' she said. 'Asthma and migraines, and so on. Lots of what we now call allergies. I never had more than a couple of days' illness in my life.' She remembered Marion always being fussed over – wheezing and puking and whining, or stamping her feet up and down in temper and frustration, causing scenes, a general rumpus at any given moment.

He longed to get inside her mind; for interesting things were going on there he guessed. Patience, he thought, regarding her. She was wearing opaque grey stockings; to hide varicose veins, he thought. He knew everything about women, and mentally unclothed her. In a leisurely fashion – since he would not hurry anything – he stripped off her peach-coloured slip and matching knickers, tugged her out of her sturdy corselette, whose straps had bitten deep into her plump shoulders, leaving a permanent indentation. He did not even jib at the massive, mottled flesh beneath, creased, as it must be, from its rigid confinement or the suspender imprints at the top of her tapering legs. Her navel would be full of talcum powder.

'It was all so long ago. I don't want to be reminded,' she said simply.

'Have you any photographs – holiday snapshots, for instance? I adore looking at old photographs.'

There was a boxful upstairs, faded sepia scenes of them all paddling – dresses tucked into bloomers – or picnicking, with sandwiches in hand, and feet out of focus. Her father, the rector, had developed and printed the photographs himself, and they had not lasted well. 'I don't care to live in the past,' was all she said in reply.

'Were you and Marion close to one another?'

'We were sisters,' she said primly.

'And you kept in touch? I should think that you enjoyed basking in the reflected glory.' He knew that she had not kept in touch, and was sure by now that she had done no basking.

'She went to live in Paris, as no doubt you know.'

Thank heavens, Mrs Mason had always thought, that she *had* gone to live in Paris, and that she herself had married and been able to change her name. Still quite young, and before the war, Marion had died. It was during Mr Mason's year as mayor. They had told no one.

'Did you ever meet Godwin? Or any of that set?'

'Of course not. My husband wouldn't have had them in the house.'

The young man nodded.

Oh, that dreadful clique. She was ashamed to have it mentioned to her by someone of the opposite sex, a complete stranger. She had been embarrassed to speak of it to her own husband, who had been so extraordinarily kind and forgiving about everything connected with Marion. But that raffish life in Paris in the thirties! Her sister living with the man Godwin or turn and turn about with others of her set. They all had switched from one partner to the other; sometimes – she clasped her hands together so tightly that her rings hurt her fingers – to others of the same sex. She knew about it; the world knew; no doubt her friends knew, although it was not the sort of thing they would have discussed. Books had been written about that Paris lot, as Mrs Mason thought of them, and their correspondence published. Godwin, and Miranda Braun, the painter, and Grant Opie, the American, who wrote obscene books; and many of the others. They were all notorious: that was Mrs Mason's word for them.

'I think she killed my father,' she said in a low voice, almost as if she were talking to herself. 'He fell ill, and did not seem to want to go on living. He would never have her name mentioned, or any of her books in the house. She sent him a copy of the first one – she had left home by then, and was living in London. He read some of it, then took it out to the incinerator in the garden and burned it. I remember it now, his face was as white as a sheet.'

'But *you* have read the books surely?' he asked, playing her in gently.

She nodded, looking ashamed. 'Yes, later, I did.' A terrified curiosity had proved too strong to resist. And, reading, she had discovered a childhood she could hardly recognise, although it was all there: all the pieces were there, but shifted round as in a kaleidoscope. Worse came after the first book, the stories of their girlhood and growing up and falling in love. She, the Cassie of the books, had become a well-known character, with all her secrets laid bare; though they were really the secrets of Marion herself and not those of the youngest sister. The candour had caused a stir in those far-off days. During all the years of public interest, Mrs Mason had kept her silence, and lately had been able to bask indeed – in the neglect which had fallen upon her sister, as it falls upon most great writers at some period after their death. It was done with and laid to rest, she had thought – until this morning.

'And you didn't think much of them, I infer,' the young man said.

She started, and looked confused. 'Of what?' she asked, drawing back, tightening his line.

'Your sister's stories.'

'They weren't true. We were well-brought-up girls.'

'Your other sister died, too.'

He *had* been rooting about, she thought in dismay. 'She died before all the scandal,' Mrs Mason said grimly. 'She was spared.'

The telephone rang in the hall, and she murmured politely and got up. He heard her, in a different, chatty voice, making arrangements and kind enquiries, actually laughing. She rang off presently, and then stood for a moment steadying herself. She peered into a glass and touched her hair again. Full of strength and resolution, she went back to the sitting-room and just caught him clipping a pen back into the inside of his jacket.

'I'm afraid I shall have to get on with some jobs now,' she said clearly, and remained standing.

He rose – had to – cursing the telephone for ringing, just when he was bringing her in so beautifully. 'And you are sure you haven't even one little photograph to lend me,' he asked. 'I would take enormous care of it.'

'Yes, I am quite sure.' She was like another woman now. She had been in touch with her own world, and had gained strength from it.

'Then may I come to see you again when you are not so busy?'

'Oh, no, I don't think so.' She put out an arm and held the door handle. 'I really don't think there would be any point.'

He really felt himself that there would not be. Still looking greedily about him, he went into the hall towards the front door. He had the idea of leaving his umbrella behind, so that he would have to return for it; but she firmly handed it to him. Even going down the path to the gate, he seemed to be glancing from side to side, as if memorising the names of flowers.

*   *   *

'I said nothing, I said nothing,' Mrs Mason kept telling herself, on her way that afternoon to play bridge. 'I merely conveyed my disapproval.' But she had a flustered feeling that her husband would not have agreed that she had done only that. And she guessed that the young man would easily make something of nothing. 'She killed my father.' She had said that. It would be in print, with her name attached to it. He had been clever to ferret her out, the menacing young man, and now he had something new to offer to the world – herself. What else had she said, for heaven's sake? She was walking uphill, and panted a little. She could not for the life of her remember if she had said any more. But, ah yes! How her father had put that book into the incinerator. Just like Hitler, some people would think. And her name and Marion's would be linked together. Ex-mayoress, and that rackety and lustful set. Some of her friends would be openly cool, others too kind, all of them shocked. They would discuss the matter behind her back. There were even those who would say they were 'intrigued' and ask questions.

Mrs Oldfellow, Mrs Fitch and Miss Christy all thought she played badly that afternoon, especially Mrs Oldfellow who was her partner. She did not stay for sherry when the bridge was over but excused herself, saying that she felt a cold coming on. Mrs Fitch's offer to run her back in the car she refused, hoping that the fresh air might clear her head.

She walked home in her usual sedate way; but she could not rid herself of the horrible idea they were talking about her already.

Hôtel du Commerce

THE hallway, with its reception desk and hat stand, was gloomy. Madame Bertail reached up to the board where the keys hung, took the one for Room Eight, and led the way upstairs. Her daughter picked up the heavier suitcase, and begun to lurch lopsidedly across the hall with it until Leonard, blushing as he always (and understandably) did when he was obliged to speak French, insisted on taking it from her.

Looking offended, she grabbed instead Melanie's spanking-new wedding-present suitcase, and followed them grimly, as *they* followed Madame Bertail's stiffly corseted back. Level with her shoulder-blades, the corsets stopped and the massive flesh moved gently with each step she took, as if it had a life of its own.

In Room Eight was a small double bed and wallpaper with a paisley pattern, on which what looked like curled-up blood-red embryos were repeated every two inches upon a sage-green background. There were other patterns for curtains and chair covers and the thin eiderdown. It was a depressing room, and a smell of some previous occupier's *Ambre Solaire* still hung about it.

'I'm so sorry, darling,' Leonard apologised, as soon as they were alone.

Melanie smiled. For a time, they managed to keep up their spirits. 'I'm so tired, I'll sleep anywhere,' she said, not knowing about the mosquito hidden in the curtains, or the lumpiness of the bed, and other horrors to follow.

They were both tired. A day of driving in an open car had made them feel, now they had stopped, quite dull and drowsy. Conversation was an effort.

Melanie opened her case. There was still confetti about. A crescent-shaped white piece fluttered on to the carpet, and she bent quickly and picked it up. So much about honeymoons was absurd – even little reminders like this one. And there had been awkwardnesses they could never have foreseen – especially that of having to make their way in a foreign language. (*Lune de miel* seemed utterly improbable to her.) She did not know how to ask a maid to wash a blouse, although she had pages of irregular verbs somewhere in her head, and odd words, from lists she had learned as a child – the Parts of the Body, the Trees of the Forest, the Days of the Week – would often spring gratifyingly to her rescue.

When she had unpacked, she went to the window and leaned out, over a narrow street with lumpy cobbles all ready for an early-morning din of rattling carts and slipping hooves.

Leonard kept glancing nervously at her as he unpacked. He did everything methodically, and at one slow pace. She was quick and untidy, and spent much time hanging about waiting for him, growing depressed, then exasperated, leaning out of windows, as now, strolling impatiently in gardens.

He smoked in the bedroom: she did not, and often thought it would have been better the other way about, so that she could have had something to do while she waited.

He hung up his dressing gown, paused, then trod heavily across to his suitcase and took out washing things, which he arranged neatly on a shelf. He looked at her again. Seen from the back, hunched over the windowsill, she seemed to be visibly drooping, diminishing, like melting wax; and he knew that her mood was because of him. But a lifetime's habit – more than that, something inborn – made him feel helpless. He also had a moment of irritation himself, seeing her slippers thrown anyhow under a chair.

'Ready, then,' he said, in a tone of anticipation and decision.

She turned eagerly from the window, and saw him take up his comb. He stood before the glass, combing, combing his thin hair, lapsing once more into dreaminess, intent on what he was doing. She sighed quietly and turned back to look out of the window.

'I can see a spire of the cathedral,' she said presently; but her head was so far out of the window – and a lorry was going by – that he did not hear her.

Well, we've *had* the cathedral, she thought crossly. It was too late for the stained glass. She would never be able to make him see that every minute counted, or that there should not be some preordained method but, instead, a shifting order of priorities. Unpacking can wait; but the light will not.

By the time they got out for their walk, and saw the cathedral, it was floodlit, bone-white against the dark sky, bleached, flat, stagey, though beautiful in this unintended and rather unsuitable way. Walking in the twisting streets, Leonard and Melanie had glimpsed the one tall spire above rooftops, then lost it. Arm in arm, they had stopped to look in shop windows at glazed pigs' trotters, tarts full of neatly arranged strawberries, sugared almonds on stems, in bunches, tied with ribbons. Leonard lingered, comparing prices of watches and cameras with those at home in England; Melanie, feeling chilly, tried gently to draw him on. At last, without warning, they came to the square where the cathedral stood, and here there were more shops, all full of little plaster statues and rosaries, and antiques for the tourists.

'Exorbitant,' Leonard kept saying. 'My God, how they're out to fleece you!'

Melanie stood staring up at the cathedral until her neck ached. The great rose window was dark, the light glaring on the stone façade too static. The first sense of amazement and wonder faded. It was part of her impatient nature to care most for first impressions. On their way south, the sudden, and far-away sight of Chartres Cathedral across the plain, crouched on the horizon, with its lopsided spires, like a giant hare, had meant much more to her than the close-up details of it. Again, for *that*, they had been too late. Before they reached the town, storm clouds had gathered. It might as well have been dusk inside the cathedral. She, for her part, would not have stopped to fill up with petrol on the road. She would have risked it, parked the car anywhere, and run.

Staring up at *this* cathedral, she felt dizzy from leaning backwards, and swayed suddenly, and laughed. He caught her close to him and so, walking rather unevenly, with arms about the other's waist, moved on, out of the square, and back to the hotel.

Such moments, of more-than-usual love, gave them both great confidence. This time, their mood of elation lasted much longer than a moment.

Although the hotel dining-room was dark, and they were quite alone in it, speaking in subdued voices, their humour held; and held, as they took their key from impassive Madame Bertail, who still sat at the desk, doing her accounts; it even held as they undressed in their depressing room, and had no need to hold longer than that. Once in bed, they had always been safe.

*　　*　　*

'Don't tell me! Don't tell me!'

They woke at the same instant and stared at the darkness, shocked, wondering where they were.

'Don't tell me! I'll spend my money how I bloody well please.'

The man's voice, high and hysterical, came through the wall, just behind their heads.

A woman was heard laughing softly, with obviously affected amusement.

Something was thrown, and broke.

'I've had enough of your nagging.'

'I've had enough of *you*,' the woman answered coolly.

Melanie buried her head against Leonard's shoulder and he put an arm round her.

'I had enough of *you*, a very long time ago,' the woman's voice went on. 'I can't honestly remember a time when I *hadn't* had enough of you.'

'What I've gone through!'

'What *you've* gone through?'

'Yes, that's what I said. What *I've* gone through.'

'Don't shout. It's so common.' She had consciously lowered her own voice, then said, forgetting, in almost a shout, 'It's a pity for both our sakes, you were so greedy. For Daddy's money, I mean. That's all you ever cared about – my father's money.'

'All *you* cared about was getting into bed with me.'

'You great braggart. I've always loathed going to bed with you. Who wouldn't?'

Leonard heaved himself up in bed, and knocked on the damp wallpaper.

'I always felt sick,' the woman's voice went on, taking no notice. She was as strident now as the man; had begun to lose her grip on the situation, as he had done. 'And God knows,' she said, 'how many other women you've made feel sick.'

Leonard knocked louder, with his fist this time. The wall seemed as soft as if it were made from cardboard.

'I'm scared,' said Melanie. She sat up and switched on the light. 'Surely he'll kill her, if she goes on like that.'

'You little strumpet!' The man slurred this word, tried to repeat it and dried up, helplessly, goaded into incoherence.

'Be careful! Just be careful!' A dangerous, deliberate voice hers was now.

'Archie Durrant? Do you think I didn't know about Archie Durrant? Don't take me for a fool.'

'I'll warn you; don't put ideas into my head, my precious husband. At least Archie Durrant wouldn't bring me to a lousy place like this.'

She then began to cry. They reversed their roles and he in his turn became the cool one.

'He won't take you anywhere, my pet. Like me, he's had enough. *Un*like me, *he* can skedaddle.'

'Why doesn't someone *do* something!' asked Melanie, meaning, of course, that Leonard should. 'Everyone must be able to hear. And they're English, too. It's so shaming, and horrible.'

'Go on, then, skedaddle, skedaddle!' The absurd word went on and on, blurred, broken by sobs. Something more was thrown – something with a sharp, hard sound; perhaps a shoe or book.

Leonard sprang out of bed and put on his dressing gown and slippers.

Slippers! thought Melanie, sitting up in bed, shivering.

As Leonard stepped out into the passage, he saw Madame Bertail coming along it, from the other direction. She, too, wore a dressing gown, corded round her stout stomach; her grey hair was thinly braided. She looked steadily at Leonard, as if dismissing him, classing him with his loose compatriots, then knocked quickly on the door and at once tried the door handle. The key had been turned in the lock. She knocked again, and there was silence inside the room. She knocked once more, very loudly, as if to make sure of this silence, and then, without a word to Leonard, seeming to feel satisfied that she had dealt successfully with the situation, she went off down the corridor.

Leonard went back to the bedroom and slowly took off his dressing gown and slippers.

'I think that will be that,' he said, and got back into bed and tried to warm poor Melanie.

'You talk about your father's money,' the man's voice went on, almost at once. 'But I wouldn't want any truck with that kind of money.'

'You just want it.'

Their tone was more controlled, as if they were temporarily calmed. However, although the wind had dropped they still quietly angled for it, keeping things going for the time being.

'I'll never forget the first time I realised how you got on my nerves,' he said, in the equable voice of an old friend reminiscing about happier days. 'That way you walk upstairs with your bottom waggling from side to side. My God, I've got to walk upstairs and downstairs behind that bottom for the rest of my life, I used to think.'

Such triviality! Melanie thought fearfully, pressing her hands against her face. To begin with such a thing – for the hate to grow from it – not nearly as bad as being slow and keeping people waiting.

'I wasn't seriously loathing you then,' the man said in a conversational tone. 'Even after that fuss about Archie Durrant. I didn't seriously *hate* you.'

'Thank you very much, you . . . cuckold.'

If Leonard did not snore at that moment, he certainly breathed sonorously.

During that comparative lull in the next room, he had dropped off to sleep, leaving Melanie wakeful and afraid.

'She called him a cuckold,' she hissed into Leonard's ear.

'No, the time, I think,' said the man behind the wall, in the same deadly flat voice, 'the time I first really hated you, was when you threw the potatoes at me.'

'Oh, yes, that was a *great* evening,' she said, in tones chiming with affected pleasure.

'In front of my own mother.'

'She seemed to enjoy it as much as I did. Probably longed for years to do it herself.'

'That was when I first realised.'

'Why did you stay?' There was silence. Then, 'Why stay now? Go on! Go now! I'll help you to pack. There's your bloody hairbrush for a start. My God, you look ridiculous when you duck down like that. You sickening little coward.'

'I'll kill you.'

'Oh God, he'll kill her,' said Melanie, shaking Leonard roughly.

'You won't, you know,' shouted the other woman.

The telephone rang in the next room.

'Hallo?' The man's voice was cautious, ruffled. The receiver was quietly replaced. 'You see what you've done?' he said. 'Someone ringing up to complain about the noise you're making.'

'You don't think I give a damn for anyone in a crumby little hotel like this, do you?'

'Oh, my nerves, my nerves, my nerves,' the man suddenly groaned. Bedsprings creaked, and Melanie imagined him sinking down on the edge of the bed, his face buried in his hands.

Silence lasted only a minute or two. Leonard was fast asleep now. Melanie lay very still, listening to a mosquito coming and going above her head.

Then the crying began, at first a little sniffing, then a quiet sobbing.

'Leonard, you must wake up. I can't lie here alone listening to it. Or *do* something, for heaven's sake.'

He put out a hand, as if to stave her off, or calm her, without really disturbing his sleep, and this gesture infuriated her. She slapped his hand away roughly.

'There's nothing I can do,' he said, still clinging to the

253

idea of sleep; then, as she flounced over in the bed, turning her back to him, he resignedly sat up and turned on the light. Blinking and tousled, he stared before him, and then leaned over and knocked on the wall once more.

'*That* won't do any good,' said Melanie.

'Well, their door's locked, so what else can I do?'

'Ring up the police.'

'I can't do that. Anyhow, I don't know how to in French.'

'Well, try. If the hotel was on fire, you'd do something, wouldn't you?'

Her sharp tone was new to him, and alarming.

'It's not really our business.'

'If he kills her? While you were asleep, she called him a cuckold. I thought he was going to kill her then. And even if he doesn't, we can't hope to get any sleep. It's perfectly horrible. It sounds like a child crying.'

'Yes, with temper. Your feet are frozen.'

'Of course, they're frozen.' Her voice blamed him for this.

'My dear, don't let *us* quarrel.'

'I'm so tired. Oh, that – damned mosquito.' She sat up, and tried to smack it against the wall, but it had gone. 'It's been such an awful day.'

'I thought it was a perfectly beautiful day.'

She pressed her lips together and closed her eyes, drawing herself away from him, as if determined now, somehow or other, to go to sleep.

'Didn't you like your day?' he asked.

'Well, you must have known I was disappointed about the cathedral. Getting there when it was too dark.'

'I didn't know. You didn't give me an inkling. We can go first thing in the morning.'

'It wouldn't be the same. Oh, you're so hopeless. You hang about, and hang about, and drive me mad with impatience.'

She lay on her side, well away from him on the very edge of the bed, facing the horribly patterned curtains, her

mouth so stiff, her eyes full of tears. He made an attempt
to draw her close, but she became rigid, her limbs were
iron.

'You see, she's quietening down,' he said. The weeping had
gone through every stage – from piteous sobbing, gasping,
angry moans, to – now – a lulled whimpering, dying off,
hardly heard. And the man was silent. Had he dropped
senseless across the bed, Melanie wondered, or was he still
sitting there, staring at the picture of his own despair.

'I'm so sorry about the cathedral. I had no idea . . . ' said
Leonard, switching off the light, and sliding down in bed.
Melanie kept her cold feet to herself.

'We'll say no more about it,' she said, in a grim little
voice.

They slept late. When he awoke, Leonard saw that Melanie
was almost falling out of bed in her attempt to keep away
from him. Disquieting memories made him frown. He tried
to lay his thoughts out in order. The voices in the next room,
the nightmare of weeping and abuse; but worse, Melanie's
cold voice, her revelation of that harboured disappointment; then, worse again, even worse, her impatience with
him. He drove her nearly mad, she had said. Always? Since
they were married? When?

At last Melanie awoke, and seemed uncertain of how to
behave. Unable to make up her mind, she assumed a sort
of non-behaviour to be going on with, which he found most
mystifying.

'Shall we go to the cathedral?' he asked.

'Oh, I don't think so,' she said carelessly. She even turned
her back to him while she dressed.

There was silence from the next room, but neither of
them referred to it. It was as if some shame of their own
were shut up in there. The rest of the hotel was full of
noises – kitchen clatterings and sharp voices. A vacuum

cleaner bumped and whined along the passage outside, and countrified traffic went by in the cobbled street.

Melanie's cheeks and forehead were swollen with mosquito bites, which gave her an angry look. She scratched one on her wrist and made it water. They seemed the stigmata of her irritation.

They packed their cases.

'Ready?' he asked.

'When you are,' she said sullenly.

'Might as well hit the trail as soon as we've had breakfast,' he said, trying to sound optimistic, as if nothing were wrong. He had no idea of how they would get through the day. They had no plans, and she seemed disinclined to discuss any.

They breakfasted in silence in the empty dining-room. Some of the tables had chairs stacked on them.

'You've no idea where you want to go, then?' he asked.

She was spreading apricot jam on a piece of bread and he leaned over and gently touched her hand. She laid down the knife, and put her hand in her lap. Then picked up the bread with her left hand and began to eat.

They went upstairs to fetch their cases and, going along the passage, could see that the door of the room next to theirs now stood wide open. Before they reached it, a woman came out and hesitated in the doorway, looking back into the room. There was an appearance of brightness about her – her glowing face, shining hair, starched dress. Full of gay anticipation as it was, her voice, as she called back into the room, was familiar to Melanie and Leonard.

'Ready, darling?'

The other familiar voice replied. The man came to the doorway, carrying the case. He put his arm round the woman's waist and they went off down the passage. Such a well-turned-out couple, Melanie thought, staring after them, as she paused at her own doorway, scratching her mosquito bites.

'Let's go to that marvellous place for lunch,' she heard the man suggesting. They turned a corner to the landing, but as they went on downstairs, their laughter floated up after them.

Miss A. and Miss M.

A NEW motorway had made a different landscape of that part of England I loved as a child, cutting through meadows, spanning valleys, shaving off old gardens and leaving houses perched on islands of confusion. Nothing is recognisable now: the guest-house has gone, with its croquet lawn; the cherry orchard; and Miss Alliot's and Miss Martin's weekend cottage. I should think that little is left anywhere, except in *my* mind.

I was a town child, and the holidays in the country had a sharp delight which made the waiting time of school term, of traffic, of leaflessness, the unreal part of my life. At Easter, and for weeks in the summer, sometimes even for a few snatched days in winter, we drove out there to stay – it wasn't far – for my mother loved the country, too, and in that place we had put down roots.

St Margaret's was the name of the guest-house, which was run by two elderly ladies who had come down in the world, bringing with them quantities of heavily riveted Crown Derby, and silver plate. Miss Louie and Miss Beatrice.

My mother and I shared a bedroom with a sloping floor and threadbare carpet. The wallpaper had faint roses, and a powdery look from damp. Oil lamps or candles lit the rooms, and, even now, the smell of paraffin brings it back, that time of my life. We were in the nineteen twenties.

Miss Beatrice, with the help of a maid called Mabel, cooked deliciously. Beautiful creamy porridge, I remember, and summer puddings, suckling pigs and maids-of-honour and marrow jam. The guests sat at one long table with Miss Louie one end and Miss Beatrice the other, and Mabel scuttling in and out with silver domed dishes. There was no wine. No one drank anything alcoholic, that I remember. Sherry was kept for trifle, and that was it, and the new world of cocktail parties was elsewhere.

The guests were for the most part mild, bookish people who liked a cheap and quiet holiday – schoolmasters, elderly spinsters, sometimes people to do with broadcasting who, in those days, were held in awe. The guests returned, so that we had constant friends among them, and looked forward to our reunions. Sometimes there were other children. If there were not, I did not care. I had Miss Alliot and Miss Martin.

These two were always spoken of in that order, and not because it was easier to say like that, or more euphonious. They appeared at luncheon and supper, but were not guests. At the far end of the orchard they had a cottage for weekends and holidays. They were schoolmistresses in London.

'Cottage' is not quite the word for what was little more than a wooden shack with two rooms and a veranda. It was called Breezy Lodge, and draughts did blow between its ramshackle clap-boarding.

Inside, it was gay, for Miss Alliot was much inclined to orange and yellow and grass-green, and the cane chairs had cushions patterned with nasturtiums and marigolds and ferns. The curtains and her clothes reflected the same taste.

Miss Martin liked misty blues and greys, though it barely mattered that she did. She had a small smudged-looking face with untidy eyebrows, a gentle, even submerged nature. She was a great – but quiet – reader and never seemed to wish to talk of what she had read. Miss Alliot, on the other hand, would occasionally skim through a book and find enough in it for long discourses and an endless supply of allusions. She wrung the most out of everything she did or saw and was a great talker.

That was a time when one fell in love with who ever was *there*. In my adolescence the only males available to me for adoration were such as Shelley or Rupert Brooke or Owen Nares. A rather more real passion could be lavished on prefects at school or the younger mistresses.

Miss Alliot was heaven-sent, it seemed to me. She was a holiday goddess. Miss Martin was just a friend. She tried to guide my reading, as an elder sister might. This was a new relationship to me. I had no elder sister, and I had sometimes thought that to have had one would have altered my life entirely, and whether for better or worse I had never been able to decide.

How I stood with Miss Alliot was a reason for more pondering. Why did she take trouble over me, as she did? I considered myself sharp for my age; now I see that I was sharp only for the age I *lived* in. Miss Alliot cultivated me to punish Miss Martin – as if she needed another weapon. I condoned the punishing. I basked in the doing of it. I turned my own eyes from the troubled ones under the fuzzy brows, and I pretended not to know precisely what was being done. Flattery nudged me on. Not physically fondled, I was fondled all the same.

In those days before – more than forty years before – the motorway, that piece of countryside was beautiful, and the word 'countryside' still means there to me. The Chiltern Hills. Down one of those slopes below St Margaret's streamed the Cherry Orchard, a vast delight in summer of marjoram and thyme. An unfrequented footpath led through it, and every step was aromatic. We called this walk the Echo Walk – down through the trees and up from the valley on its other side to larch woods.

Perched on a stile at the edge of the wood, one called out messages to be rung back across the flinty valley. Once, alone, I called out, 'I love you', loud and strong, and 'I love you' came back faint, and mocking. 'Miss Alliot,' I added. But that response was blurred. Perhaps I feared to shout too loudly, or it was not a good echo name. I tried no others.

On Sunday mornings I walked across the fields to church with Miss Martin. Miss Alliot would not join us. It was scarcely an intellectual feast, she said, or spiritually uplifting, with the poor old vicar mumbling on and the organ asthmatic. In London, she attended St Ethelburga's in the Strand, and spoke a great deal of a Doctor Cobb. But, still more, she spoke of the Townsends.

For she punished Miss Martin with the Townsends too.

The Townsends lived in Northumberland. Their country house was grand, as was to be seen in photographs. Miss Alliot appeared in some of these shading her eyes as she lay back in a deckchair in a sepia world or – with Suzanne Lenglen bandeau and accordion-pleated dress – simply standing, to be photographed. By whom? I wondered. Miss Martin wondered, too, I thought.

Once a year, towards the end of the summer holiday (mine: theirs) Miss Alliot was invited to take the train north. We knew that she would have taken that train at an hour's notice, and, if necessary, have dropped everything for the Townsends.

What they consisted of – the Townsends – I was never really sure. It was a group name, both in my mind and in our conversations. 'Do the Townsends play croquet?' I enquired, or 'Do the Townsends change for dinner?' I was avid for information. It was readily given.

*　　*　　*

'I know what the Townsends would think of *her*,' Miss Alliot said, of the only common woman, as she put it, who had ever stayed at St Margaret's. Mrs Price came with her daughter, Muriel, who was seven years old and had long, burnished plaits, which she would toss – one, then the other – over her shoulders. Under Miss Alliot's guidance, I scorned both Mrs Price and child, and many a laugh we had in Breezy Lodge at their expense. Scarcely able to speak for laughter, Miss Alliot would recount her 'gems', as she called them. 'Oh, she *said* . . . one can't believe it, little Muriel . . . Mrs Price *insists* on it . . . changes her socks and knickers twice a day. She likes her to be nice and fresh. And . . . ' Miss Alliot was a good mimic, '"she always takes an apple for recess". What in God's name is recess?'

This was rather strong language for those days, and I admired it.

'It's "break" or . . . ' Miss Martin began reasonably. This was her mistake. She slowed things up with her reasonableness, when what Miss Alliot wanted, and I wanted, was a flight of fancy.

I tried, when those two were not there, to gather foolish or despicable phrases from Mrs Price, but I did not get far. (I suspect now Miss Alliot's inventive mind at work – rehearsing for the Townsends.)

All these years later, I have attempted, while writing this, to be fair to Mrs Price, almost forgotten for forty years; but even without Miss Alliot's direction I think I should have found her tiresome. She boasted to my mother (and no adult was safe from my eavesdropping) about her hysterectomy, and the gynaecologist who doted on her. 'I always have my operations at the Harbeck Clinic.' I was praised for that tidbit, and could not run fast enough to Breezy Lodge with it.

I knew what the medical words meant, for I had begun to learn Greek at school – Ladies Greek, as Elizabeth Barrett Browning called it, 'without any accents'. My growing knowledge served me well with regard to words spoken in lowered tones. 'My operations! How Ralph Townsend will adore that one!' Miss Alliot said.

A Townsend now stepped forward from the general family group. Miss Martin stopped laughing. I was so sharp for my years that I thought she gave herself away by doing so, that she should have let her laughter die away gradually. In that slice of a moment she had made clear her sudden worry about Ralph Townsend. Knowing as I did then so much about human beings, I was sure she had been meant to.

Poor Miss Martin, my friend, mentor, church-going companion, mild, kind and sincere – I simply used her as a stepping stone to Miss Alliot.

I never called them by their first names, and have had to pause a little to remember them. Dorothea Alliot and Edith Martin. 'Dorothea' had a fine ring of authority about it. Of course, I had the Greek meaning of that too, but I knew that Miss Alliot was the giver herself – of the presents and the punishments.

My mother liked playing croquet and cards, and did both a great deal at St Margaret's. I liked going across the orchard to Breezy Lodge. There, both cards and croquet were despised. We sat on the veranda (or, in winter, round an oil stove which threw up petal patterns on the ceiling) and we talked – a game particularly suited to three people. Miss Alliot always won.

Where to find such drowsy peace in England now is hard to discover. Summer after summer through my early teens the sun shone, bringing up the smell of thyme and marjoram from the earth – the melting tar along the lane and, later, of rotting apples. The croquet balls clicked against one another on the lawn, and voices sounded lazy and far away. There were droughts, when we were on our honour to be careful with the water. No water was laid on at Breezy Lodge, and it had to be carried from the house. I took this duty from Miss Martin, and several times a day stumbled through the long grass and buttercups, the water swinging in a pail, or slopping out of a jug. As I went, I disturbed clouds of tiny blue butterflies, once a grass snake.

Any excuse to get to Breezy Lodge. My mother told me not to intrude, and I was offended by the word. She was even a little frosty about my two friends. If for some reason they were not there when we ourselves arrived on holiday I was in despair, and she knew it and lost patience.

In the school term I wrote to them and Miss Martin was the one who replied. They shared a flat in London, and a visit to it was spoken of, but did not come about. I used my imagination instead, building it up from little scraps as a bird builds a nest. I was able to furnish it in unstained oak and hand-woven rugs and curtains. All about would be jars of the beech leaves and grasses and berries they took back with them from the country. From their windows could be seen, through the branches of a monkey-puzzle tree, the roofs of the school – Queen's – from which they returned each evening.

That was their life on their own where I could not intrude, as my mother would have put it. They had another life of their own in which I felt aggrieved at not participating: but, I was not invited to. After supper at St Margaret's, they returned to Breezy Lodge, and did not ask me to go with them. Games of solo whist were begun in the drawing-room, and I sat and read listlessly, hearing the clock tick and the maddening mystifying card words – 'Misère', 'Abundance' – or 'going a bundle', 'prop and cop', and 'Misère Ouverte' (which seemed to cause a little stir). I pitied them and their boring games, and I pitied myself and my boring book – imposed holiday reading, usually Sir Walter Scott, whom I loathed. I pecked at it dispiritedly and looked about the room for distraction.

Miss Louie and Miss Beatrice enjoyed their whist, as they enjoyed their croquet. They really were hostesses. We paid a little – astonishingly little – but it did not alter the fact that we were truly guests, and they entertained us believing so.

'Ho . . . ho . . . hum . . . hum,' murmured a voice, fanning out a newly dealt hand, someone playing for time. 'H'm, h'm, now let me see.' There were relaxed intervals when cards were being shuffled and cut, and the players leaned back and had a little desultory conversation, though nothing amounting to much. On warm nights, as it grew later, through the open windows moths came to plunge and lurch about the lamps.

Becoming more and more restless, I might go out and wander about the garden, looking for glow-worms and glancing at the light from Breezy Lodge shining through the orchard boughs.

On other evenings, after Miss Beatrice had lit the lamps, Mrs Mayes, one of the regular guests, might give a Shakespeare recital. She had once had some connection with the stage and had known Sir Henry Ainley. She had often heard his words for him, she told us, and perhaps, in consequence of that, had whole scenes by heart. She was ageing wonderfully – that is, hardly at all. Some of the blonde was fading from her silvery-blonde hair, but her skin was still wild rose, and her voice held its great range. But most of all, we marvelled at how she remembered her lines. I recall most vividly the balcony scene from *Romeo and Juliet*. Mrs Mayes sat at one end of a velvet-covered *chaise-longue*. When she looped her pearls over her fingers, then clasped them to her bosom, she was Juliet, and Romeo when she held out her arms, imploringly (the rope of pearls swinging free). Always she changed into what, in some circles, was then called semi-evening dress, and rather old-fashioned dresses they were, with bead embroidery and loose panels hanging from the waist. Once, I imagined, she would have worn such dresses *before* tea and have changed again later into something even more splendid. She had lived through grander days: now, was serenely widowed.

Only Mrs Price did not marvel at her. I overheard her say to my mother, 'She must be forever in the limelight, and I for one am sick and tired, *sick* and *tired*, of Henry Ainley. I'm afraid I don't call actors "Sir". I'm like that.' And my mother blushed, but said nothing.

Miss Alliot and Miss Martin were often invited to stay for these recitals; but Miss Alliot always declined.

'One is embarrassed, being recited *at*,' she explained to me. 'One doesn't know where to look.'

I always looked at Mrs Mayes and admired the way she did her hair, and wondered if the pearls were real. There may have been a little animosity between the two women. I remember Mrs Mayes joining in praise of Miss Alliot one day, saying, 'Yes, she is like a well-bred race horse,' and I felt that she said this only because she could not say that she was like a horse.

Mrs Price, rather out of it after supper, because of Mrs Mayes, and not being able to get the hang of solo whist, would sulkily turn the pages of the *Illustrated London News*, and try to start conversations between scenes or games.

'*Do* look at *this*.' She would pass round her magazine, pointing out something or other. Or she would tiptoe upstairs to see if Muriel slept, and come back to report. Once she said, *à propos* nothing, as cards were being re-dealt, 'Now who can clasp their ankles with their fingers? Like *that* – with no gaps.' Some of the ladies dutifully tried, but only Mrs Price could do it. She shrugged and laughed. 'Only a bit of fun,' she said, 'but they do say that's the right proportion. Wrists, too, that's easier, though.' But they were all at cards again.

One morning, we were sitting on the lawn and my mother was stringing redcurrants through the tines of a silver fork into a pudding basin. Guests often helped in these ways. Mrs Price came out from the house carrying a framed photograph of a bride and bridegroom – her son, Derek, and daughter-in-law, Gloria. We had heard of them.

'You don't look old enough,' my mother said, 'to have a son that age.' She had said it before. She always liked to make people happy. Mrs Price kept hold of the photograph, because of my mother's stained fingers, and she pointed out details such as Gloria's veil and Derek's smile and the tuberoses in the bouquet. 'Derek gave her a gold locket, but it hasn't come out very clearly. Old enough! You are trying to flatter me. Why my husband and I had our silver wedding last October. Muriel was our little after-thought.'

I popped a string of currants into my mouth and sauntered off. As soon as I was out of sight, I sped. All across the orchard, I murmured the words with smiling lips.

The door of Breezy Lodge stood open to the veranda. I called through it, 'Muriel was their little after-thought.'

Miss Martin was crying. From the bedroom came a muffled sobbing. At once, I knew that it was she, never could be Miss Alliot. Miss Alliot, in fact, walked out of the bedroom and shut the door.

'What is wrong?' I asked stupidly.

Miss Alliot gave a vexed shake of her head and took her walking stick from its corner. She was wearing a dress with a pattern of large poppies, and cut-out poppies from the same material were appliquéd to her straw hat. She was going for a walk, and I went with her, and she told me that Miss Martin had fits of nervous hysteria. For no reason. The only thing to be done about them was to leave her alone until she recovered.

We went down through the Cherry Orchard and the scents and the butterflies were part of an enchanted world. I thought that I was completely happy. I so rarely had Miss Alliot's undivided attention. She talked of the Townsends, and I listened as if to the holy intimations of a saint.

'I thought you were lost,' my mother said when I returned.

Miss Alliot always wore a hat at luncheon (that annoyed Mrs Price). She sat opposite me and seemed in a very good humour, taking trouble to amuse us all, but with an occasional allusion and smile for me alone. 'Miss Martin has one of her headaches,' she explained. By this time I was sure that this was true.

The holidays were going by, and I had got nowhere with *Quentin Durward*. Miss Martin recovered from her nervous hysteria, but was subdued.

Miss Alliot departed for Northumberland, wearing autumn tweeds. Miss Martin stayed on alone at Breezy Lodge, and distempered the walls primrose, and I helped her. Mrs Price and Muriel left at last, and a German governess with her two little London pupils arrived for a breath of fresh air. My mother and Mrs Mayes strolled about the garden. Together they did the flowers, to help Miss Louie, or sat together in the sunshine with their *petit point*.

Miss Martin and I painted away, and we talked of Miss Alliot and how wonderful she was. It was like a little separate holiday for me, a rest. I did not try to adjust myself to Miss Martin, or strive, or rehearse. In a way, I think she was having a well-earned rest herself; but then I believed that she was jealous of Northumberland and would have liked some Townsends of her own to retaliate with. Now I know she only wanted Miss Alliot.

Miss Martin was conscientious; she even tried to take me through *Quentin Durward*.

She seemed to be concerned about my butterfly mind, its skimming over things, not stopping to understand. I felt that knowing things ought to 'come' to me, and if it did not, it was too bad. I believed in instinct and intuition and inspiration – all labour-saving things.

Miss Martin, who taught English (my subject, I felt), approached the matter coldly. She tried to teach me the logic of it – grammar. But I thought 'ear' would somehow teach me that. Painless learning I wanted, or none at all. She would not give up. She was the one who was fond of me.

We returned from our holiday, and I went back to school. I was moved up – by the skin of my teeth, I am sure – to a higher form. I remained with my friends. Some of those had been abroad for the holidays, but I did not envy them.

Miss Martin wrote to enquire how I had got on in the *Quentin Durward* test, and I replied that as I could not answer one question, I had written a general description of Scottish scenery. She said that it would avail me nothing, and it did not. I had never been to Scotland, anyway. Of Miss Alliot I only heard. She was busy producing the school play – *A Tale of Two Cities*. Someone called Rosella Byng-Williams was very good as Sidney Carton, and I took against her at once. 'I think Dorothea has made quite a discovery,' Miss Martin wrote – but I fancied that her pen was pushed along with difficulty, and that she was due for one of her headaches.

Those three 'i's' – instinct, intuition, inspiration – in which I pinned my faith were more useful in learning about people than logic could be. Capricious approach to capricious subject.

Looking back, I see that my mother was far more attractive, lovable, than any of the ladies I describe; but there it was – she was my mother.

Towards the end of that term, I learned of a new thing, that Miss Alliot was to spend Christmas with the Townsends. This had never been done before: there had been simply the early autumn visit – it seemed that it had been for the sake of an old family friendship, a one-sided one, I sharply guessed. Now, what had seemed to be a yearly courtesy became something rather more for conjecture.

Miss Martin wrote that she would go to Breezy Lodge alone, and pretend that Christmas wasn't happening – as lonely people strive to. I imagined her carrying pails of cold water through the wet, long grasses of the orchard, rubbing her chilblains before the oil stove. I began to love her as if she were a child.

My mother was a little flustered by my idea of having Miss Martin to stay with us for Christmas. I desired it intensely, having reached a point where the two of us, my mother and I alone, a Christmas done just for me, was agonising. What my mother thought of Miss Martin I shall never know now, but I have a feeling that school mistresses rather put her off. She expected them all to be what many of them in those days were – opinionated, narrow-minded, set in their ways. She had never tried to get to know Miss Martin. No one ever did.

She came. At the last moment before her arrival I panicked. It was not Miss Alliot coming, but Miss Alliot would hear all about the visit. Our house was in a terrace (crumbling). There was nothing, I now saw, to commend it to Miss Martin except, perhaps, water from the main and a coal fire.

After the first nervousness, though, we had a cosy time. We sat round the fire and ate chinese figs and sipped ginger wine and played paper games which Miss Martin could not manage to lose. We sometimes wondered about the Townsends and I imagined a sort of Royal-Family-at-Sandringham Christmas with a giant tree and a servants' ball, and Miss Alliot taking the floor in the arms of Ralph Townsend – but then my imagination failed, the picture faded: I could not imagine Miss Alliot in the arms of any man.

After Christmas, Miss Martin left and then I went back to school. I was too single-minded in my devotion to Miss Alliot to do much work there, or bother about anybody else. My infatuation was fed by her absence, and everything beautiful was wasted if it was not seen in her company.

The Christmas invitation bore glorious fruit. As a return, Miss Martin wrote to ask me to stay at Breezy Lodge for my half-term holiday. Perfect happiness invaded me, remembered clearly to this day. Then, after a while of walking on air, the bliss dissolved. Nothing in the invitation, I now realised, had been said of Miss Alliot. Perhaps she was off to Northumberland again, and I was to keep Miss Martin company in her stead. I tried to reason with myself that even that would be better than nothing, but I stayed sick with apprehension.

At the end of the bus ride there on a Saturday morning, I was almost too afraid to cross the orchard. I feared my own disappointment as if it were something I must protect myself and – incidentally Miss Martin – from. I seemed to become two people – the one who tapped jauntily on the door, and the other who stood ready to ward off the worst. Which did not happen. Miss Alliot herself opened the door.

She was wearing one of her bandeaux and several ropes of beads and had a rather gypsy air about her. 'The child has arrived,' she called back into the room. Miss Martin sat by the stove mending stockings – an occupation of those days. They were Miss Alliot's stockings – rather thick and biscuit-coloured.

We went over to St Margaret's for lunch and walked to the Echo afterwards returning with branches of catkins and budding twigs. Miss Alliot had a long, loping stride. She hit about at nettles with her stick, the fringed tongues of her brogues flapped – she had long, narrow feet, and trouble with high insteps, she complained. The bandeau was replaced by a stitched felt hat in which was stuck the eye-part of a peacock's feather. Bad luck, said Miss M. Bosh, said Miss A.

We had supper at Breezy Lodge, for Miss Alliot's latest craze was for making goulash, and a great pot of it was to be consumed during the weekend. Afterwards, Miss Martin knitted – a jersey of complicated Fair Isle pattern for Miss Alliot. She sat in a little perplexed world of her own, entangled by coloured wools, her head bent over the instructions.

Miss Alliot turned her attention to me. What was my favourite line of poetry; what would I do if I were suddenly given a thousand pounds; would I rather visit Rome or Athens or New York; which should I hate most – being deaf or blind; hanged or drowned; are cats not better than dogs, and wild flowers more beautiful than garden ones, and Emily Brontë streets ahead of Charlotte? And so on. It was heady stuff to me. No one before had been interested in my opinions. Miss Martin knitted on. Occasionally, she was included in the questions, and always appeared to give the wrong answer.

I slept in their bedroom, on a camp bed borrowed from St Margaret's. (And how was I ever going to be satisfied with staying *there* again? I wondered.)

Miss Alliot bagged (as she put it) the bathroom first, and was already in bed by the time I returned from what was really only a ewer of water and an Elsan. She was wearing black silk pyjamas with D.D.A. embroidered on a pocket. I bitterly regretted my pink nightgown, of which I had until then been proud. I had hastily brushed my teeth and passed a wet flannel over my face in eagerness to get back to her company and, I hoped, carry on with the entrancing subject of my likes and dislikes.

I began to undress. 'People are kind to the blind, and impatient with the deaf,' I began, as if there had been no break in the conversation. 'You are so right,' Miss Alliot said. 'And people matter most.'

'But if you couldn't see . . . well, this orchard in spring,' Miss Martin put in. It was foolish of her to do so. 'You've already seen it,' Miss Alliot pointed out. 'Why this desire to go on repeating your experiences?'

Miss Martin threw in the Parthenon, which she had *not* seen, and hoped to.

'Still people matter most,' Miss Alliot insisted. 'To be cut off from them is worse than to be cut off from the Acropolis.'

She propped herself up in bed and with open curiosity watched me undress. For the first time in my life I realised what dreadful things I wore beneath my dress – lockknit petticoat, baggy school bloomers, vest with Cash's name tape, garters of stringy elastic tied in knots, not sewn. My mother had been right . . . I should have sewn them. Then, for some reason, I turned my back to Miss Alliot and put on my nightgown. I need not have bothered, for Miss Martin was there between us in a flash, standing before Miss Alliot with Ovaltine.

On the next day – Sunday – I renounced my religion. My doubts made it impossible for me to go to church, so Miss Martin went alone. She went rather miserably, I was forced to notice. I can scarcely believe that any deity could have been interested in my lack of devotion, but it was as if, somewhere, there was one who was. Freak weather had set in and, although spring had not yet begun, the sun was so warm that Miss Alliot took a deckchair and a blanket and sat on the veranda and went fast asleep until long after Miss Martin had returned. (She *needed* a great deal of sleep, she always said.) I pottered about and fretted at this waste of time. I almost desired my faith again. I waited for Miss Martin to come back, and, seeing her, ran out and held a finger to my lips, as if Miss Alliot were royalty, or a baby. Miss Martin nodded and came on stealthily.

It was before the end of the summer term that I had the dreadful letter from Miss Martin. Miss Alliot – hadn't we both feared it? – was engaged to be married to Ralph

Townsend. Of course, that put paid to my examinations. In the event of more serious matters, I scrawled off anything that came into my head. As for questions, I wanted to answer them only if they were asked by Miss Alliot, and they must be personal, not factual. As usual, if I didn't know what I was asked in the examination paper, I did a piece about something else. I imagined some *rapport* being made, and that was what I wanted from life.

Miss Martin's letter was taut and unrevealing. She stated the facts – the date, the place. An early autumn wedding it was to be, in Northumberland, as Miss Alliot had now no family of her own. I had never supposed that she had. At the beginning of a voyage, a liner needs some small tugs to help it on its way, but they are soon dispensed with.

Before the wedding, there were the summer holidays, and the removal of their things from Breezy Lodge, for Miss Martin had no heart, she said, to keep it on alone.

During that last holiday, Miss Martin's face was terrible. It seemed to be fading, like an old, old photograph. Miss Alliot, who was not inclined to jewelry ('Would you prefer diamonds to Rembrandts?' once she had asked me), had taken off her father's signet ring and put in its place a half hoop of diamonds. Quite incongruous, I thought.

I was weeks older. Time was racing ahead for me. A boy called Jamie was staying at St Margaret's with his parents. After supper, while Mrs Mayes's recitals were going on, or the solo whist, he and I sat outside the drawing-room on the stairs, and he told me blood-chilling stories, which I have since read in Edgar Allan Poe.

Whenever Jamie saw Miss Alliot, he began to hum a song of those days – 'Horsy, keep your tail up'. My mother thought he was a bad influence, and so another frost set in.

Sometimes – not often, though – I went to Breezy Lodge. The Fair Isle sweater was put aside. Miss Martin's having diminished, diminished everything, including Miss Alliot.

Nothing was going on there, no goulash, no darning, no gathering of branches.

'Yes, she's got a face like a horse,' Jamie said again and again.

And I said nothing.

'But he's *old*.' Miss Martin moved her hands about in her lap, regretted her words, fell silent.

'Old? How old?' I asked.

'He's seventy.'

I had known that Miss Alliot was doing something dreadfully, dangerously wrong. She could not be in love with Ralph Townsend; but with the Townsends entire.

On the day they left, I went to Breezy Lodge to say good-bye. It looked squalid, with the packing done – something horribly shabby, ramshackle about it.

Later, I went with Jamie to the Echo and we shouted one another's names across the valley. His name came back very clearly. When we returned, Miss Alliot and Miss Martin had gone for ever.

Miss Alliot was married in September. Miss Martin tried sharing her London flat with someone else, another school-mistress. I wrote to her once, and she replied.

Towards Christmas my mother had a letter from Miss Louie to say that she had heard Miss Martin was dead – 'by her own hand,' she wrote, in her shaky handwriting.

'I am HORRIFIED,' I informed my diary that night – the five-year diary that was full of old sayings of Miss Alliot, and descriptions of her clothes.

*   *   *

I have quite forgotten what Jamie looked like – but I can still see Miss Alliot clearly, her head back, looking down her nose, her mouth contemptuous, and poor Miss Martin's sad, scribbly face.

Uncollected Stories

Husbands and Wives

THAT pity may be felt quite genuinely at a distance is
well known; and, when Eric joined up, Alison was pitied
enormously by all sorts of people, who could not bear to
think of her alone in her house so far beyond the village. She
was quiet and solitary there. Woods – great woods, which
stretched away over the hills and ran into other woods
– came up to the fence on two sides, stretched branches down
over the roof and in autumn shed their leaves, which came
down steadily and relentlessly as snow, across paths and
lawns and cabbage patch.

This first autumn he was away, the leaves fell suddenly.
It was disappointing. For a day or two, sunlight struck the
great tan-coloured woods, wavered as if falling through
water. Then the winds brought destruction. The ash leaves
came down in bunches, still softly green, but the beech leaves
swirled in the air, flat, like coins, or curled and convoluted
like sea shells.

It was like a painting by Monet, Alison thought, standing
at the sitting-room window and watching. Leaves. They

dripped, cascaded; they mounted up in columns like something from the Old Testament or fell like a fountain. Inside, they would lisp drily along the passage or sail in and float in the soup. In the morning she would find them in bed with her.

It was the sort of house which seemed always conscious of the outside world, which doors could not shut out, nor drawn curtains quite conceal. There was the feeling that, left on its own for a year or so, the woods would reclaim their territory; grass would grow, leaves pile up, owls fly in and out of the windows. Then Eric's house, his effort to impose civilisation where it was despised, would be ruined, mocked at, even by the beetle crossing his hearth.

He was an architect. 'I want to live in the country,' he had explained to his wife, 'but I will not have lavatories down the garden path and hot water carried in cans.' He wanted it to be a healthy and pleasant house in which to bring up their children.

When war broke out, they had the house, but were still without the children. It had cost too much, felling trees, digging and levelling. It was, however, as comfortable as could be, Eric would think, turning the hot shower to cool, then to cold, reaching for warm towels. Now – as Trooper Watson – he must accustom himself to something less. Naturally, children were no longer a possibility.

Alison was not really to be pitied, for down there in the wood she was neither happy nor unhappy. She was never nervous, as other women thought she must be and men considered that she should be. No one came to see her. They liked to sympathise by telephone or, at all events, without the walk home afterwards.

She was busy, though, in the house and working in the garden until dark. There were all the leaves to be swept, the wrecked lurching rows of runner beans to be cleared away, logs to be sawn. She was keeping the house beautiful for Eric's first leave, looking towards that and no further.

By tea-time now, the garden grew muffled and drips of moisture fell furtively from leaves. Through the mist and bonfire smoke the great sunflowers turned their faces at her. Day by day, their heads dropped lower. Then they were collapsed and were done for and she brought them into the shed and strung them up to dry for chickens' food.

Inside, spread on window-sills to ripen, were flat baskets of green and yellow tomatoes, waxen-looking and with highlights which reminded her of fruit she had painted at school. Marrows of a deep saffron colour with lemon stripes lay on the dresser. In the evenings, with the curtains drawn, it seemed as if part of the garden had crept inside. She would sit knitting or writing her daily letter to Eric, her report on the garden and the house. When she had listened to the nine o'clock news, she would get ready for bed. Lying flat on her back, looking out at mist or stars, listening to the endless fidgeting of the leaves, she would feel a sense of achievement, her hard, strong body aching from the day's work. Only occasionally would a breath of defeatism ruffle her tranquillity. 'Surely,' the small voice breathed – or was it the leaf upon the floorboards? 'Surely?' But that was enough. On that word, she slept.

His leave grew nearer and now his letters ended – 'In eight days . . . ' 'In five . . . ' They were like children towards Christmas, throwing one pebble each night from a window. Towards the end was a little rush of excitement, polishing, baking, airing his clothes.

On the last day but one, she washed her long bright hair and stood at the window in the sun drying it. She watched Rose, the gypsy woman, coming up with her copper bucket for water, watched her crossing the little orchard from the woods, a baby on her shoulders, the bucket on her arm, a young child with its hand on her skirt. Every other day she came for one bucket of water. They never wash, then, Alison thought, fluffing her hair. They had lived for three months down in the wood, in a tent under a clump of holly trees.

281

Once she had seen the woman pushing the pram – a deep and dirty one – without a hood – back from the village. At each end of the pram, a child, between them a stack of bread.

Now, she wrapped her head in the towel, and went out to the back door. The woman stood there smiling. The children, fat, dirty and backward for their ages, recoiled from Alison towards their mother, who held out in her rough hand a present – four clothes pegs, newly made, the wood white and gleaming as the kernel of a nut.

Alison took them and felt them damp. For a second, she saw the hand in contrast to them – ridged with dirt, scaly, and heavy with thick gold rings – the family wealth.

As the baby was hoisted up higher on the woman's shoulders, its bare bottom was exposed, bare, blue with cold, tinted like a ripe plum, and the firm thighs.

Oh, God, the dirt! she thought, fascinated.

That they were truly gypsies she could not be sure. Their hair was darkly yellow, their skin fair: and the names of the children – Leonard and Kathleen – were incongruous and absurd. Only once had Alison seen the father – a short, swarthy man, a knife-grinder. He went about the countryside, sharpening scissors; his eyes, when he had lifted them from the turning wheel and the knife's edge, were dark and keen and his manner suggested a strange combination, of courtesy and contempt. At night, he returned to the holly bushes, covering the grinding machine carefully with a tarpaulin – a better one than the children had. Sometimes drawing the curtains after tea, Alison would think of them down in the wood with their long night begun.

Now, as she lifted the copper can to the tap, she thought that the woman was all courtesy but no contempt. She was timid as a squirrel, but not so clean. Human beings need so many bits and pieces in order to keep themselves clean, that when they are living in the wild state they cannot compare with animals.

The can was heavy and she lifted it with two hands. For a moment it linked the two women together – their hands lay side by side and their eyes were on the swinging water. But it was impossible to imagine that they had anything in common, anything even as general as sex or race, that they had been born in the same way and would one day share the same death, the same earth.

'Goodbye.'

'Goodbye, Miss.'

The children, with their hands, their clinging ways, seemed to influence their mother away from the house and the stranger. Across the grass, slowly, she returned with the filled bucket, the baby and the child, who stumbled in the tussocky grass and held her skirt bunched in its fist. And Alison took her four clothes pegs and laid them on the window-sill in the sun and began to brush her hair. It fell cool and sweet-smelling before her face and in this dark and fragrant tent she was smiling to herself.

That night it was still and frosty. She opened the windows and got into bed – This is the last night, she thought. It is true that seven days' leave will not last for ever, but with the end of it she had not begun to concern herself. Outside, a rimed leaf loosened itself and fell, some creatures rustled in the wood, an owl hooted. The branches stood motionless as if printed upon the sky. Half a moon with a scarred face freed itself from the curd-like cloud. Her eyes, filled with that vision of laced branches, closed and she slept.

Swung in a hammock of sleep, she rocked, warm, suspended, slipping into darkness and warmth, curved with crossed arms and knees drawn up, the first attitude of humanity.

Into this safety came something alien. At first, she accepted it and then her mind refused the sound, it became strange, unearthly, she denied it, she awoke. I screamed in my sleep, she thought. But while she lay, still in bed, the screaming continued. It could not be a woman screaming, for there was no woman to scream. Yet it was. Very close to the house it sounded in the frosty air, and there was nothing else, not a rustle, nor any movement, nor another voice

If it had been tomorrow, she thought foolishly and suddenly. Then Eric would have been here. The sweat had sprung from her hands and back and was damp on the sheet beneath her. The cold struck her body sharply as she crept out of bed and went to the window.

The horrifying sound went on – a woman who tried to mouth words as she screamed. Each cry chilled the blood, was uncontrolled, instinct with horror and bestiality. There was no other sound, except that Alison suddenly and boldly, so that she amazed herself, called out: 'Is anyone in trouble?' Inadequate! the cool part of her noted, the unfrightened part. At once, the scream seemed to form into words, which came from the fence on the wood side. 'It's my man. All night he's been beating me. Can't I have no peace? Can't I have no peace?'

These words came brokenly again and again, grew fainter, receded, were accompanied now by plungings, rustlings, twig-snappings. She was going away. It was as if she had gained an objective. Still she cursed, her voice clotted with hatred and fear, but growing fainter.

Alison crept back to bed, lay rigid and shivering. Her reason still seemed to refuse what her ears told it – that Rose, that quiet, timid squirrel, to whom the children clung, who spoke softly and gave presents shyly and silently, should become so transformed, so horrifying.

She was too cold now to sleep. The sea roared in her ears and the sound of a leaf moving startled her. She lay rigid and alert, but now could hear nothing.

The police, she thought: and then, but the police could do nothing. For a man – she remembered that much of the law – must be allowed to beat his own wife. It is not for the police to interfere. She tried to sleep, desiring desperately that dawn should come, for that pallor to creep over the furniture and lighten the curtains and restore her to common sense, to the proportions proper to the day. It did not come. The world was caught up and frozen in darkness and the moon is an illumination which does not inspire common sense. As soon as the silence had settled once more, it was broken again into fragments by a small cry, lower than the first, but more heartbroken, little agonised bleatings.

'Oh, no God, no!' she cried, sitting up in bed, covering her ears with her hands. Now that the mother had wandered away had he begun to beat his children?

'Then I can't bear it,' she sobbed. Sickened by that sound she crawled from the bed and began to look for clothes. There was nothing else for her to do. One grown-up cannot lie in bed while another is hurting little children. Over her pyjamas, she pulled slacks and a jersey. Forcing her shoes on, she became desperately frightened. I must go quickly, she thought, before I am too afraid. She stood in the room, thinking, No one will come if I scream. There is no one to hear me! She had no weapon. Things like pokers seemed too foolish to take. She crept down the stairs thinking of Eric, not knowing what she was going to do; then she let herself out of the back door. The cold solid air filled her throat and chest.

I won't creep, she thought, I will run. I will go loudly, be aggressive. Then, perhaps, she would not hear the beating of her heart, feel all the platitudes coming true – the blood being frozen, the limbs turned to stone. So she broke through the undergrowth, leapt the fence, tore her way through brambles and plunged knee-deep sometimes into ditches of leaves. She could hear clearly now the strangled, reedy sound of the children crying and as she went she called 'Stop it. Stop it.' She felt, like a soldier going into battle, that it was only possible to act in hatred and with the ears filled with some noise other than the whispers of fear.

And now she saw how big the woods were, how different from the day-time and she thought – and the thought irrelevant as it was silenced her and checked her – It is always like this at night when I am in bed – large, menacing, watchful. From each tree – watchful.

She stood there facing the great dark clump of holly bushes and listened, but there was no sound – until one of the trees seemed to detach itself and step forward. It did not spray up leaves on all sides as she had done, yet it was a man. He came closer to her – in the moonlight she saw the dark, level eyes, even a faint shine on the dark suit over his thighs, a belt of plaited leather with a bright buckle. She watched the buckle as it came towards her, and then up went her eyes to meet his. I must speak first, she thought. Her instinct told her this. At the same time, she saw that his hands were towards his back and thought of knives, remembering his way of getting a living.

'You can stop this,' she cried loudly. The wood echoed, the sound was shocking. 'If I hear one more sound from those children I shall call the police.' He smiled, but she had a feeling that she mustn't let him speak, that she could not endure to hear his voice. 'You see?' she cried. 'You see? That's what I shall do. I will not be disturbed in this way and I will not have those children hurt.'

He said nothing, but now his bare hands came forward, the thumbs were stuck inside the plaited belt. She felt only partial relief at this, for the difficulty was now to go. She could not. Courage to turn she had not.

'Now remember,' she challenged him, but it was ridiculous, like a child's game. He would not answer. In his eyes, she saw what she was – hysterical, shrill, a woman; middle-class, so taking for granted comforts he knew nothing about; trying to make temper hide fear, but he knew and she knew through him that there was no anger, only terror.

At last – only just in time – for she was at the point of dropping to her knees and sobbing for mercy, for permission to go – he turned slightly and listened, having heard what she had not. It was someone coming up through the wood. It was Rose. As she approached them she came more slowly. A man's jacket was buttoned to her throat over her long dress, her hair on one side had fallen to her shoulder.

'Come here,' he said softly. And then nodding sideways at Alison, 'Friend of yours,' he added and slouched off, spitting into the leaves, his hands on his belt.

The wide timid eyes sought Alison's in the moonlight. 'I'm sorry Miss.'

'Not you,' she said quickly. 'Are you all right?'

'Oh, yes, Miss.'

'And the children?'

'Oh yes.'

Shocked, the eyes looked back. 'He's ever so good really – I think he . . . ' she whispered, glanced, ducked her head, buttoned and unbuttoned, brushed back her hair.

'All right,' said Alison sternly. 'I'm going now.'

He had stopped and was standing looking back, his head on one side, mocking her, she thought, listening. Then, 'I can't think why you're not in the army,' she suddenly called out, and turned and went, trying not to scramble or run, but there was no dignity in how she went. (She felt fingers locked round her ankles, daggers between her shoulder blades.) Across her own lawn she ran without pretence and let herself in. Now the house frightened her. She bolted and barred, and put on lights, then she went into the living-room and sat by the clock with *The Diary of a Nobody* in her lap, and her eyes on the door.

In the morning they were gone. Eric came home at tea-time. There was the log fire, the home-made cakes, the little sandwiches, the book he had brought for her, his approval, his kindness, their quiet intellectual understanding. They had a serene pleasant evening, talking, listening to the gramophone, supper by the fire, with chops and a little omelette laced with rum. Everything went peacefully as of old, until he said: 'Our minds are like brother and sister, close, sympathetic. Nothing could ever part us' and she burst into tears.

The Blossoming

MISS Partridge came back to the house after the funeral, with her solicitor walking on one side of her and the family doctor on the other – although he could scarcely now be called a 'family' doctor as, apart from her, the family had gone.

'You should take a holiday,' Dr Jenkins said, looking round the dingy drawing-room, feeling depressed for her. 'You've had a long stretch of . . . ' As his voice trailed off, he was thinking of all the old-age pensioners looking after aged parents. This was the way it was going. Soon they would be looking after grandparents.

'A holiday?' Miss Partridge looked startled, but she gave a little smile as if the doctor had made a naughty suggestion. 'I couldn't afford it.' Because it was out of her reach, she could daringly consider it. She had not had a holiday for twenty years.

Dr Jenkins looked at the solicitor, who leaned back as far as he could in his frail chair, said, 'Ellie, my dear, you're a rich woman now – a comparatively rich woman. You can go wherever you wish.'

She became at once alarmed, shrugged her wealth away, shuddering. 'Too late,' she said.

Having no servants, when she asked: 'Tea, or whisky?' her voice seemed to urge whisky on them. It was less trouble, and she was quite exhausted.

Even when they agreed to drink whisky, she was obliged to go through the hall and down a passage to the kitchen to fetch water.

In the sink squatted a large spider. He seemed to own the place. We'll be alone together tonight, she thought – the spider and I! She suddenly contorted her face and turned on the tap with a gush, washing the poor thing – all broken legs and frantic reluctance – down the plug hole. It was as if that long-bedridden mother upstairs had protected her from such horrors until now when, untrained and unprepared, and full of a new brutality, Miss Partridge must face them on her own.

She returned, trembling, with the jug of water. The drawing-room conversation of low voices broke off as she crossed the hall.

'Quite a number in church,' Mr Mavory, the solicitor, was saying as she came through the door.

But five wreaths only! she thought. It was a disgrace really. If she died, *when* she died, there would be only four.

'So a little holiday, then,' Dr Jenkins said robustly. 'I practically insist. You deserve it if anyone does.'

After a very short time they set down their glasses and stood up.

'Oh, don't, don't go!' she cried.

'I'll be back within a day or two about business matters,' Mr Mavory said.

She stood at the front door and watched them walk down the drive. Across the road was the church: and Mother in her new grave. The church clock struck four, although it was nearly half-past.

She turned back into the house, closed the door softly,

290

and stood looking about her, hoping not to see spiders, for it was the time of year when they did their house-invading, as if finding their way back to a place of ancestry.

'I am a rich – a comparatively rich woman,' she said aloud. All the things she did not want and had not wanted, for many years, lay now within her grasp.

The night was no more dreadful than she had foreseen. Her little luminous bedside clock took her slowly towards morning through her snatches of sleep.

'Why not move to a more convenient place?' asked Mr Mavory. 'This must be an expensive house to keep up.'

'Oh, *no*!' she said. 'It hasn't cost us a *penny*, for years.'

He looked at a great dark patch of damp on the faded William Morris wallpaper.

Following his glance, she looked, too, and saw the stains as if for the first time. Those powdery willow leaves had been there all her life. There were familiar Morris wallpapers elsewhere in the house – of honeysuckle, or of white and bile green chrysanthemums. It was true that nothing had been spent on the house for years; but not, she realised, because nothing had needed to be spent. Paint had flaked off window-frames and sills, the high ceiling was dark and shadowy – with dirt, perhaps.

Mr Mavory watched her looking about the room, and held his tongue. He wondered if the house were clean, thought probably not. Miss Partridge *knew* that it was not. Cross-patch Mrs Murphy came up from the village twice a week, and flicked about with dusters, but would never climb steps or move furniture because of dropped womb trouble. She was always in such a temper that Miss Partridge shut herself in her bedroom until she had gone.

Apart from the doctor's and Mr Mavory's occasional

visits, no one else came. Mrs Partridge, before and during her illness, had not encouraged visitors.

The house was not large, but had rooms into which no one went. Sometimes, Miss Partridge's sense of isolation seemed to become a physical thing, pressing into her ears, and choking her. 'I will have a glass of Dutch courage,' she would say – for she often thought aloud. She drank the whisky in gulps, as if it were medicine; but felt better afterwards.

She was lonely, though did not know it, having been too busy for years, with the trays for upstairs, and the bell ringing, and the afternoon readings-aloud, the bothers with bowels and bedsores, the staving-off of unwanted callers. To go shopping had been an adventure; but there was little she now needed to buy, eating frugally, absent-mindedly.

She passed her time drifting about the rooms, or making little forays into the webbed-over, tangled garden.

Now, the wallpapers worried her. Mr Mavory, drinking *his* glass of whisky without shuddering, saw thoughts come and go on her anxious little face.

Rummaging in her mind, oblivious to him, she put a hand to her mouth, then touched her frizzy hair. Her home – her life-long home – was creeping into decay. She saw the signs of it about her, and remembered others in other parts of the house.

Mr Mavory had come to the conclusion that she would never move from here, would not know how to. He discarded that idea, and began to talk instead about the improvement of property. The word 'house' he never used. He threw in suggestions, which seemed to bounce back from the walls. Money no impediment, he so constantly reaffirmed.

'But I could not have men traipsing about the house. And everything would have to be moved. I couldn't bear it.'

Mason & Toope would take over, Mr Mavory assured her.

'Oh, *they* came once when we had a burst pipe, and made such a noise, and charged us so much. Mother was quite upset.'

'Then do as Dr Jenkins advised you. Take a holiday. Have a rest. Let others do things for you for a change.'

He went on to tell her of a nice guest-house where his aunt sometimes stayed. It was in Hove, in a quiet street away from the sea. The food was excellent, he said; but food meant nothing to Miss Partridge.

'I don't think I could,' she said: he saw a flicker of doubt on her face; she was beginning to recover from shock and fatigue.

The next day he called again, with a book of wallpaper patterns he had borrowed from Mason & Toope. Turning the leaves, she murmured with pleasure and surprise, at the beauty of entwined roses, lovers' knots, satin stripes and embossed fleurs-de-lis. She was almost as enthusiastic as if any part of it were to do with her.

When he went away, he left the book. And, in the evening, having nothing better to do, she took it on her lap and began to turn the great pages. Again and again, she went back to the pink roses latticed on pearly grey. It was her favourite, she decided.

Then, at last, she looked up, and gazed for a long while at the yellowing willow leaves upon the wall.

So, after a short time, Miss Partridge took herself off to the Fernhurst Guest Home in Hove, and Mason & Toope moved in to deal with the decorating.

Fernhurst was all that Mr Mavory had described. The food was simple and light, and the service was hushed. No one spoke to Miss Partridge. At first, she sat at a table by the door but, later, as guests departed, was promoted to one by the window, overlooking a hedge of golden privet and a quiet road. The season was nearly over and she walked along an almost deserted front, or sat in an empty shelter listening to the sea on the pebbles, sometimes thinking about the rose wallpaper, and wondering how far Mason

& Toope had got with it. Real roses, they looked. She had felt that they might almost be scented.

After a week of Hove she began to be restless, to wonder what on earth she was doing at the Fernhurst. After ten days, she paid her bill, packed her suitcase, got on the train and went home.

It was a warm, sunny afternoon when she arrived back. She took a cab from the station, and the driver came with her to the front door with her suitcase. The door was wide open, and the house smelled of paint: no one was about.

She went into the drawing-room. Furniture was pushed into the middle of it and covered with a dust sheet. On one wall the roses blossomed, brightened by sunshine from an uncurtained window. The other walls still showed only grey plaster.

Miss Partridge stood entranced before the rose-covered wall, and could imagine the whole room in bloom. It would be quite beautiful. Her mother would have been horrified – at the change, at the expense. She had always been careful about money.

After a time, Miss Partridge became conscious of men's voices coming from the garden at the back. She went out of the front door and round the house, and discovered two young men in white overalls sitting in the last of the sun on the old garden seat. They were drinking tea, and on the iron table before them were paper bags and thermos flasks.

'Good afternoon, Miss,' one said. He was George Toope, younger son of *the* Toope. The other she recognised as Sandy Wright, who had once delivered newspapers.

'We wasn't expecting you,' George said. He did not rise, but shifted along the seat, patting the space beside him.

Miss Partridge, with hardly any hesitation, sat down. 'I found my holiday very tiring,' she said. 'I walked about too much, for there was nothing else to pass the time.'

'You could do with this, I reckon,' George said, for he

seemed to be the spokesman. He unscrewed the top of his thermos flask and poured tea into it.

'Oh, how kind! I could,' Miss Partridge said.

He offered sugar in a screw of paper, and she watched him shake some into her cup; then he took a pencil from behind his ear and stirred her tea with it.

'You needn't have brought your own sugar,' she said. 'There is plenty of it in the larder. You should have helped yourself.'

'And have that old bitch Murphy after us?' Sandy said, speaking at last. '*No thanks.*' Miss Partridge flushed. 'It is not Mrs Murphy's sugar,' she said, with unusual firmness. Of course, she would not have said that to, or before, Mrs Murphy.

Sandy held out a meat sandwich on a crumpled paper bag.

'I can't take your . . . tea,' she said, confused as to what time of day it was. He wagged the paper bag up and down in the palm of his hand, commandingly. She took a thick triangle of sandwich and began to nibble it and twist it about her mouth. Doing so, she looked at the forlorn garden.

'Fag?' asked Sandy, when she had at last finished the sandwich.

'Fag? Oh, no, no; thank you.'

She wondered about this relaxed time they were having, for in less than an hour they would knock off work. But, though wondering at it, she approved of it, and she felt peaceful sitting there with them in the sun.

When they went back to their work, she went on sitting there, listening to them treading about the bare and creaking floorboards in the drawing-room, their voices echoing excitingly. When they left at five o'clock, the house seemed very silent.

Miss Partridge sat out the days which followed in the crowded dining-room, amongst the sickly green and white chrysanthemums, which did not seem to her at all like real flowers, and were soon to be replaced by poppies, cornflowers and intersecting ears of corn. Every now and then – drawn there – she would peep in at the nearly finished room with its mass of roses, and marvel at its beauty. Twice a day she made tea for her 'boys', as she thought of them. They were no trouble – nothing like the nuisance she had imagined they would be.

'Here we are then!' Miss Partridge called out gaily, waiting for the drawing-room door to be opened, lest there should be a can of paint, or George or Sandy on a ladder on the other side. At once there was a subdued hustle: the door was opened, and George took from her the heavy tray with the silver teapot, and freshly made scones.

'Quite a party!' he said, winking at Sandy.

'When I was a child, I longed for a party,' Miss Partridge said. 'Did you ever have one?'

'Oh, the various old rave-up.'

She nodded, and turned back to the door.

'Only *two* cups?' George asked. 'We can't have parties on our tod – not just me and Sandy. I'll get another one out the kitchen.' She sat down on a dust-sheeted sofa, and smiled. She had not allowed herself to expect to be asked.

George returned with the extra cup and saucer. 'Shall I do the honours?' he asked. He lifted the tarnished teapot questioningly, his little finger quirked. 'Shall I be Mother?'

He is never at a loss for words, Miss Partridge thought, as Sandy went off into a fit of laughter.

'Is this real silver?' George asked, sobered by the pale amber stream coming from the spout.

'It is hall-marked seventeen hundred something.'

'Might be worth a fortune.'

'It is rather dented, as you can see.'

'Never mind: silver's silver. It could be melted down.'

And why not? Miss Partridge wondered placidly.

'It *could* be an antique,' Sandy said slowly, feeling that it was time he should speak. 'It could be worth its weight in gold.'

'Bloody nit,' George said, cramming a scone into his mouth.

Miss Partridge – hardly drinking, not eating – looked at the walls, and said, 'It's just like a garden. With *real* flowers, I mean. A bee could fly in here, and feel quite confused.'

'It could feel b. well confused,' said Sandy, who rarely rose to such heights of humour.

'Well, back to work! Do a bit more,' George commanded. 'Tomorrow we begin on the second reception room.'

The second reception room was really the dining-room, where the received, during the last half century, could be counted on the fingers of two hands. It was papered with the white and green chrysanthemums, gone dark now, against a darker ground.

'Have you ever seen chrysanthemums like them?' Miss Partridge asked, as George and Sandy began to scrape them away.

'I never thought of them as chrysanths. Just flowers like.'

'Some of those flowers, as you call them, have over forty petals,' Miss Partridge said. 'When I didn't feel up to what was given me for lunch, I'd be obliged to sit there all afternoon, until whatever it was was gone. Forty-something petals, I counted them through my tears.'

'My dad just used to larrup me if I didn't finish my greens,' Sandy said. Miss Partridge twisted her hands together. 'I can't bear to think about that,' she said.

'Did me no harm. I learned to like my greens all right in the end,' Sandy said in a loaded voice, for the benefit of George, who laughed briefly, as he worked.

'Oh, if only I *could*!' Miss Partridge said, in an imploring voice. The scraping down of those walls was so wonderful to her that she felt she must be part of it. She looked at the discoloured rubbish on the floor in excitement.

'Look!' said George sternly, 'it was your Mr Mavory got the estimate: he won't let up on it. Every second we let slide, not working up to our full capacity, Sandy and me, costs *my* dad money. Real money.'

She thought of the dreamy interludes in the garden, with thermos flasks and sandwiches, and their lack of hurry and bustle. Perhaps now the autumn had set seriously in.

Sandy made a frowning face at George, who then handed over the scraper to Miss Partridge. 'OK. But I don't want this about the village, or everyone will be wanting to have a go. Might have Union bother. So please keep it to yourself.'

But to this Miss Partridge scarcely listened. Flushed with enthusiasm – and at the honour of such responsibility – she scraped away at the background of her childhood, her life.

In the evening, she walked about the flowered drawing-room, entranced by its beauty, and, because there was no longer silence all day, she did not mind the silence of these lonely hours. She knew that the next day would bring the clanking pail of handles, the snatches of talk, the whistling of 'Galway Bay'. Weekends, however, were long enough to remind her of the past deprivations.

Mrs Murphy grumbled about the upheaval. She said that the white paint would show the dirt; and said it in a hope-less way, as if there would be nothing she could do about it. She detested George and Sandy, and told tales behind their backs. When it came the turn for Miss Partridge's bedroom to be decorated, she stood in front of the sprays of forget-me-nots and said that her and her sister Gladys's bedroom had been done like that when they were in service. 'It was thought good enough for kitchen-maids,' she added.

But George and Sandy were enthusiastic. It was they who chose the violets for the landing, and Sandy said he intended to have the same if he married, which George said his mother would never let him do.

Mr Mavory, feeling slightly responsible for the changes, thought them all unbearably crude; but Dr Jenkins, seeing the results in Miss Partridge herself, approved. 'If she'd had strings of upside-down baboons eating bananas, I'd have been for it,' he told Mavory. 'Her circulation has improved.'

When the cold weather came, George and Sandy were glad of their indoor work. As one room was finished, they moved on to another. It became such a long-drawn-out job that George's father, Mr Toope, was obliged to ask Miss Partridge for 'a little something down', as he embarrassedly put it. She was stretching the work far beyond the matter of the original estimate, he explained. He was glad of the business, but there were difficulties. Miss Partridge wrote a cheque for three hundred pounds and – for the days of taking cheques upstairs for her mother to sign were over – wrote 'Elinor Partridge' on it with a flourish. She had waited a long time for that much authority.

George and Sandy brought with them each day all the gossip of the village, so that she began to feel set in her surroundings and a part of them for the first time. When she went shopping she *knew* about the people she met – knew that the girl at the grocer's had won twenty pounds at Bingo, which was a good thing, Sandy said, as although she didn't show yet she had an expensive time coming up: the butcher's wife was expecting, too, forlornly awaiting her fifth daughter – 'wishing it on herself,' George said. 'She needs to talk herself into a son.' And Miss Partridge knew who was out of work, and would be glad of a little job of upholstery or window-cleaning. Such simple jobs as unblocking a sink, or mending a fuse George and Sandy, those marvellous men about the house, would do for her.

It was late autumn. The beech woods had a brief glory, then frosts, followed by high winds, bared the branches. A foggy, mushroomy, pre-Christmas smell filled the air.

By Christmas, George and Sandy had finished, were promised elsewhere – up at the Hall, in fact, where Lady Leadbetter was having all the rooms done with William Morris wallpaper – an aberration which amused the three of them as they discussed it at tea-time.

Miss Partridge was of course alone for Christmas. Her four expected Christmas cards arrived and were set up on the chimney-piece. On Christmas Eve, when she was feeling at her most depressed – even wishing her mother was still upstairs to run up to with a warm mince pie – she found another card lying on the doormat. She opened the envelope excitedly.

A boozy old Santa Claus was holding up a cocktail glass and saying 'Complimentsh of the Sheashon'. Inside, signed in two different hands, was, 'All the best, Sandy and George'. Smiling, she set it in a central place between those of distant relations and the printed one from Mr and Mrs C. E. Mavory, with that crossed out and 'Charles and Margery' written above it – a friendly and informal touch Miss Partridge thought.

But in spite of the unexpected card and the fire crackling busily in her bright new room, she could not fight off her depression. Christmas is always a bad time, she reminded herself; but it will pass. And after Christmas, what? she wondered – with George and Sandy up at Lady Leadbetter's pasting on all those hideous wallpapers. She did not know Lady Leadbetter, but was positively cross with her, and positively jealous, too. 'She won't make scones for them,' she said aloud. 'Or china tea. They'll find a difference.'

Apart from the cards, there was nothing Christmassy about the house. In the meat safe were two lamb chops; one for Christmas dinner, the other for Boxing Day. No one would ever make a mince pie for herself; and she had not.

Pacing about the room, grasping at anything which

might help her state, she began to wonder if Mr Mavory might drop in for a minute or two after church in the morning. In her mother's day, he sometimes had. If he did, there was plenty of sherry. It became important to her that he should call: otherwise no one would – all day, and the next. Dr Jenkins, dressed up as Father Christmas, would, she knew, be carving turkeys at the hospital.

She remembered the holly tree in the garden, and decided to go out to pick a sprig or two in case of her visitors.

It was almost dark. She took a torch, and stepped out into the damp air. It was warm, un-Christmassy. I'll pick the holly and arrange it nicely, she thought: and then it will be time for a drink. Tomorrow really depended on Mr Mavory coming.

Such a tangle of old, dying apple trees and high nettles. The torch beam wavered amongst it, as she stumbled over rank grass, determined on her holly. It was a poor winter for berries, but she tore off a few twigs. Making her way back she thought of the garden of the Sleeping Princess, the stinging leaves, the arched, branched briars. It seemed sadly out of place with her bright house. Coming round the side of the house, by softly dripping hydrangeas, she suddenly stopped, swung the torch about, over high-grown hedges and recidivist flowerbeds. She was tense, like an explorer on the edge of new terrain.

The words *landscape gardeners* had come into her head – an idea which dawned wonderfully in her.

After a while, she went indoors and arranged the meagre holly in a vase. 'That's better,' she said. She read again 'All the best from George and Sandy'. She poured herself out a glass of whisky, and put a knob of coal on the fire, then, remembering her new financial position, another and another. I am a comparatively rich woman, she thought, sipping her whisky. She went to the window and drew aside the curtain, but of course, could see nothing but blackness. In her mind, though, she saw men out there – two men, probably – gum-booted, rain-coated, clumping about, measuring, digging, planting, sitting on the old seat drinking pale tea, eating hot scones. She would hear them all day, calling out to one another, joking and whistling. At night silence would fall; but in the morning they would come again.

The Wrong Order

IT was the year that the white lilac came up to expectations. This evening, against a thundery sky and amongst tenderly green leaves, the blossom crowded up as white as paper. In a freshening wind, the sky darkened, thickened, and the lilac heads jostled together, nudging each other.

Branches of other trees swayed, as if they were strange plants at the bottom of the sea.

'It has paid for lopping,' Hilda Warfield said, pausing by the sitting-room window as she so often did. 'It has never been more beautiful.'

She had her back to the two men who watched her.

Then lightning cracked the sky, and the rain came hissing down, bouncing off the marble-topped garden table.

'I'm so glad it's been good *this* year,' Hilda went on, almost as if she were talking to herself.

Oh, God! her friend, Tom, thought, she is going to say 'As it's my last.'

He got up, and went into the kitchen, so that he should not hear her saying it. She insisted on talking about her death, referred to it constantly and casually, as if it were some familiar pet of hers, running always at her heels, like Charlie, her Bedlington terrier.

'It's that damn doctor,' her husband Hector – a mild man, despite his name – had said to Tom, later on that dreadful day when she had returned from London with her news.

They had lived, the three of them, in amity and comfort until this terrible thing had settled down in their midst, always tagging along with them, now, so never to be entirely ignored. When Hector woke in the night, it was on his mind in a leap. Sometimes he crept into Hilda's room, could not rest until he had done so; but she was always sleeping peacefully. He went back to his bed and lay marvelling at that.

He could not properly settle to work in his office by day; his alarmed thoughts accompanied him up in the train in the morning and down in the evening. Looking out at villas set in gardens, golf courses and new motor roads, he saw nothing: his hands holding his newspaper up for protection sometimes suddenly trembled, and fellow commuters looked at him stealthily. It was no secret about Hilda. 'I like and respect the truth,' she had told the specialist, and he had talked to her of her inoperable condition: 'but it will be for your heart to decide how long,' he had said finally, thinking her an amazing woman. She thanked him calmly for her death sentence, shook hands firmly, and went away . . . she, too, back past the villas and the golf courses and all the budding trees. On that journey a certain peace, and disbelief, had fallen over her, strangely, at the same time and, presumably, from the same source.

Because of her respect for the truth everybody knew, and everyone seemed to be waiting with her, and watching her. She had become special, and set aside.

Her husband, in spite of those middle-of-the-night peeps into her room, now hated being left alone with her. Tom was a great help to him, and this evening of the storm, Hector was cross with him for going off to the kitchen just as Hilda said those dreaded words. He had to listen to them all by himself.

He drank whisky, passed a hand over his tired face, yawned. Getting past all this travelling up and down, he thought. He was to retire next year. But that was the forbidden future, and his mind swerved away from it. He drank more whisky, loosened his tie, leaned back in his chair, very red across his cheeks and forehead, dark and crumpled in his London clothes, unlike the other two so comfortably dressed.

And now the lilac was full of rain, the blossom like sodden sponges too heavy to be tossed about any more. Tiny, star-like florets had been shaken down on to the grass. When the shower was over, the garden dripped steadily. A rainbow appeared against the mulberry-coloured sky and all the trees were sharply green. 'How beautiful!' said Hilda.

In the kitchen, Tom snipped chives into the soup, carried the bowls into the dining-room. Mrs Clarebut had left everything ready.

He was glad to be out here, pottering about, and, apart from his own wishes, thought that Hector should have a little time with Hilda. He, Tom, was with her all day long.

At supper, Hilda asked, 'Shall we have some music after? Or those old holiday slides?' A silence from the other two, bent over soup. Neither wanted either – harking back to the châteaux on the Loire and themselves there, or picnicking on the banks of the Cher, brought back what had been – which, in view of what was to be, was overwhelmingly too much. Also, those rather old, blurred Chopin and Schumann records were of a twilight sadness they could no longer abide. Hector especially hated them. Never knowing what to look at when they were going on, he always closed his eyes. My nerves! he thought; then dozed. He would have liked to have been like other businessmen at the end of a day's work, slumped down uncritically before a television set. Hilda would not have one in the house. She said that they barred conversation, became an addiction, and only coronations and royal weddings were any good on them.

Tom took up the soup plates and went to fetch the chicken pie. 'You choose, Hilda,' he said on his way. Hector looked out of the window at a rather awkward backwards angle for him, and crushed up toast melba.

'Then I choose neither,' Hilda said, with a shrug. '*Ça ne fait rien.*'

While she was waiting for Tom to return, she took off some heavy Celtic-like jewelry from her breast, laid it on the table and studied it carefully, as if she were loth to waste the briefest chance of looking at something lovely. She arranged the chain on the table, and peered at the milky stones set in silver, gathering it up quickly and reclasping it to her when Tom came in and handed her a plate.

After dinner, she went into the garden and threw a ball for her dog, Charlie, who tore across the squelching lawn, but knew better than to dive into flowerbeds. Breathing heavily, Hilda stooped and retrieved the ball from amongst dripping leaves.

'How has she been?' Hector asked Tom.

'The same. Not much lunch. She had her rest.'

They talked then of other things, not thinking of them, though. Hector spoke of his city day, Tom of sowing radish seed.

I used to ask him about his painting, Hector remembered guiltily. But we were younger then.

From a window, they caught glimpses of Hilda wandering in the garden. Charlie looked like a bedraggled sheep. Tom saw her looking up into the lilac tree, her hands clasped above, resting on her large bosom. 'Rapt' was the word which came into his mind. He remembered reading about Colette on her death-bed, her absorbed and heightened passion for the little things about her, and he wondered if he could stand much more of the same thing. On weekdays, Mrs Clarebut came at nine-thirty, with her little boy, Rupert – Rupe the Terrible, as he was known to Hilda and Tom. He did not do much damage, except to nerves; nor did he tear about: but he insinuated himself, was always *there*, and talked incessantly. Tom went shopping for as long as he could, pottering about the village, collecting gossip. Hilda, who was supposed to love children, and to grieve that she had none of her own, was obliged to stay at home and endure Rupe, only occasionally lapsing into asperity – as when he addressed her as 'Auntie'.

'Why are you looking out of that window all the time, Auntie?'

'Mrs Warfield.'

'I can't say that.'

'Then "Hilda". But *not* Auntie.'

'Why?'

'To answer your other question, I was looking at the white lilac tree – because this is the very best time for it; soon the flowers will topple over and die.'

'Everybody will topple over and die one of these days,' Rupe said, watching her. 'In an emergency,' he added, because it was his newest long word.

'So true,' said Hilda coldly.

In the mornings, she wore a hessian apron with a large pocket across its front, her kangaroo pouch, she told Rupe, who gave her a sideways, scornful glance. Into this pocket, to save her journeys, went everything she might need – scissors and bast and secateurs, pencils and spectacles. She had a walking stick with a rubber tip, and leaned on it heavily as she went about the garden, making mental notes of little jobs for Tom when he returned from his interminable shopping.

The garden was beautiful, and very hardly kept up – with its lawns on different levels; the iris lawn, the cedar lawn, the lower lawn, the tea lawn. There were box hedges and bowers, grass walks and borders, and the famous lilac tree.

Beyond the lower lawn was a white-painted wooden building, which Tom had once used for a studio; still thought he did. He had become, under Hilda's expert direction, less and less of a painter, more and more a gardener.

On her slow perambulating round the paths, Rupe attended Hilda, talking usually of death, since it seemed to him to be a forbidden subject. One 'hush' from his mother was enough to commit him to it. He touched on the idea of Charlie's death quite cheerfully, and, then, with his sideways glance through sandy lashes, on Hilda's.

'We all come to it,' she said.

'And go to God.'

'That's as may be.'

'Do you mind dying?'

'It looks as if we haven't much choice.'

She poked with her stick at a bit of new spring groundsel. 'Pull it up, like a good boy.'

He snapped it off and left the root.

'Oh, dear, now I shall have to ask Mr Bonchurch to do it.'

'Why can't *you* do it?' Again that steady, sideways look.

'I become giddy if I bend down.'

'You might die of being giddy.'

'I might. What a bore you are with your small talk.'

'What's that?'

She sighed and turned back towards the house. By now, she was waiting impatiently for Tom's return. Such lots of little jobs she had for him to do, now that she no longer could. When old Stack, her gardener, had died, she had really felt bereft – her great partner and ally gone. Together, they had made the garden, from nothing more promising than a piece of sloping parkland and a damaged cedar tree.

She had begun to train Tom as her assistant, not knowing then that he must be her successor; for Hector did nothing in the garden beyond snoozing in a deckchair, said he would be just as happy in public gardens doing that – and much less expensive, he added. At weekends, he played golf, and drank.

Hilda deplored the golf course, for she would have preferred real country. Beyond the lower lawn, a green could be glimpsed, and the sort of people she would wish to avoid grouped about, or trundling golf-bag trolleys. Even this morning, an acquaintance, looking for a lost ball, parted the top of the hedge and peered through. 'Hi! Hilda!' she called. 'Garden's looking great. You too.'

Hilda nodded without smiling. The hedge was one of her failures. Nothing made it put on growth.

Meanwhile, Tom had come back. He unpacked his basket on the kitchen table, and told Mrs Clarebut of news from the butcher's.

In the village, he was known as Hilda's 'fancy man'. Mrs Clarebut had often given out that the three slept in different bedrooms, that she had never seen any sign of what she called 'hanky-panky'. The village, though, could not take in the strangeness of a woman living with two men, one of them related to her in no way, yet her slave. Mrs Clarebut, knowing more than most, had a glimmering of the way in which Hilda was able to claim a man's allegiance without sexuality. She wondered if it had not been rather like training a dog – a matter of getting the whip-hand from the start.

As Tom was gossiping and unpacking the basket, Hilda came to the kitchen door. 'Mrs Clarebut won't mind doing that,' she said. 'I wondered if you could give me a hand with something in the garden.'

She was dogged by her ginger-haired familiar, who said, 'If she bent down she might die.'

Like lightning, Mrs Clarebut streaked across the kitchen, seized him in a frightful grip above his thin elbow, shook him, hissed at him, making matters a hundred times worse.

'Groundsel,' Hilda said to Tom, as if nothing else were happening. 'Will you come and see?'

They went into the garden, soon to be followed by a snivelling Rupe.

As they walked down a grass path, Hilda said, taking a pencil and pad from her apron pocket, 'I'd like those delphiniums out when they're finished: they're too much on top of the phloxes. Perhaps it's a good thing poor old Stack died. He can't be faced with all these weeds. Although, of course, if *he* were here, *they* wouldn't be. All the same, I sometimes feel that I've betrayed him. Can't seem to help doing that. No doubt he'll understand.' And, belying the doubts she had earlier implied to Rupe of the existence of an after-life, she sent a rueful smile heavenwards.

In spite of the soft earth, plantains broke off at roots, groundsel snapped, as Tom cursed them. 'All right,' Hilda said. 'If you fetch my kneeling mat, my little fork, and help me down, I'll manage. I'm sorry that I bothered you.'

The future of the garden – her realm – was threatened with incompetence and indifference.

'Do they have gardens in heaven?' Rupe inquired.

'How the hell do *I* know?' Hilda asked.

'When Charlie goes to heaven, Jesus might mistake him for a sheep.'

'He may well do that.'

'But *I* know a sheep when I see one.'

'So you're one up on Jesus.'

'You're not allowed to say that.'

Tom returned with a small garden fork, and a trug, but no kneeling mat, and he applied himself to the weeds.

'Because it's rude,' said Rupe.

*   *   *

310

It was not illness that imposed the pattern of Hilda's days. She had always liked to do the same things at the same time – mornings, out and about in her apron; afternoons a rest, lying on a *chaise-longue* with – still – her little possessions at hand, for there was a table drawn up with her favourite gardening books, shells and pebbles in a bowl, kaleidoscopes to divert her, pills, spectacles, a fan, large amber worry beads and alabaster hand-coolers. Tom had once brought for her from Greece a lump of Parian marble; when she was feverish she held it against her brow. All these treasures were within a hand's reach, so that she need not stir.

Rupe, tagging along as usual, sometimes sat beside her, staring at the drooping face as Hilda napped and his mum washed up. He would quietly take up a large freckled shell and hold it to his freckled ear, and try to imagine the crashing, then dragging, rattling sound of the sea on the pebbles at Brighton, where once he had been for a day, sitting a lot of the time in a dampish shelter with a comic to shut him up. Shaking the shell about, clamping it to his ear, he simply felt that something had gone muffled in his head. It was annoying like catarrh; not at all like the sea. He yawned, quickly remembered to say 'Pardon me', and then, even more polite he thought, he leaned forward and whispered, 'This is very nice. Can I have it when you are dead?'

Behaving beautifully – memorably, she faintly hoped – Hilda opened her eyes, looked at the shell, and gently said, 'Yes, you may. But it is not really good manners to ask for things.' She had trained herself to pitch her voice very low, and it seemed to give her an advantage over others.

After Rupe and his mother had gone, Tom would bring her a cup of tea. At five-thirty, she went up for her bath, and he roamed about the landing, dreading a sudden splash or a long silence.

And then it was evening. As time went on, she became

311

too tired to go into the garden again. She lay on the *chaise-longue*, arranging the shells on their dish, examining each minutely; or turning her kaleidoscopes.

'What I like about the patterns,' she once said, 'is that they don't stay. Everything should vanish. And, of course, everything does.'

Hector roused himself, got up for more whisky. 'Oh, I dunno,' he said vaguely.

'I find that a comfort.'

He refilled her glass of campari, and she fished out the lump of ice and sucked it, then held it in her hand, and studied it, as if she had never seen ice before. 'Very strange,' she said, in a puzzled voice.

The lilac was over, and cut back again for another spring.

'I hope it will be lovely for you again next year,' Hilda said in her intolerable way.

'I wouldn't notice if *you* weren't here,' her husband said glumly. 'This whole place is the last place I could put up with. If anything happened, which I'm damn sure it won't, I'd skedaddle.'

Hilda looked at him, appalled.

'The garden,' she said.

'P'raps shouldn't've said that,' Hector mumbled.

'But the *garden*!'

'Of course, whatever you say.'

Tom, followed by Charlie, came into the room, and saw her face. She was trembling.

He thought, at last her courage has gone. It had been a great wonder to him that it had lasted so long. He looked at Hector, who shook his head slowly.

Hilda said to Tom, 'Would *you* leave this garden – for it to go to rack and ruin?'

'Just put me foot in it,' Hector said. He waited for Tom to take over the situation. All his life, he had been used to ordering things, and had done so with calm and mastery; but not in this house.

After dinner, Tom went to fetch the slides and the screen, because conversation was becoming impossible. They looked – and Hector sipped while looking – at the wide and shallow Loire; at men fishing, bone-white châteaux, themselves. Hilda smiled at last. '*En pays connus*,' she said. 'Weren't they the loveliest holidays of all?'

It was not Hector's lucky evening. 'We can't live in the past,' he said; became furious, had fallen into another trap, of which there were so many.

Tom quickly slipped in a photograph of Hilda standing in the garden of an *auberge* in front of a trellis of morning glories.

'A beautiful, simple flower. *They* do the vanishing trick, too. Though I love field daisies more. What's your favourite, Tom?'

'I think those striped camellias.'

'Oh, clever you. Hector?'

Was he forgiven? He stirred suspiciously. 'Red roses,' he said in a staunch voice. 'From a shop.'

Her ripple of laughter was a relief to the other two, whether it was sarcastic or not. She felt – though had no reason to feel – that she had won her way, and that the future of her garden was secure.

'Bed-time,' Hector said.

'Oh, no! There's a lot more left to this day,' Hilda protested.

'Well, I'll push off,' her husband said. He got up stiffly from his chair.

The time had come when Hilda went about the garden in a wheelchair. By now, Tom had forgotten that he had ever been a painter. The little he had always paid, from a private income, towards the running of the house was now inadequate, he knew; but he could not bring up the matter. He worked harder with the weeds, and the shopping, and brushing Charlie and taking him for walks, and sometimes he wondered about his life when Hilda was dead. He determined to serve her till the end.

'Hector, you look so fagged,' Hilda said on a Saturday morning. 'Why *must* you go to golf?'

'Do me good, d'you know.'

'But after a hard week. . . . '

'The only exercise I get.'

'If it's exercise you want, you could push me down to the village. I should like that.'

He reddened and hesitated.

Tom knew how much Hector counted on his golf, and on his friends at the club as an escape from work and worries.

'I'm going to the village, Hilda; I'll take you,' he said quickly. 'You've always refused when I've asked you before.'

'There's been the garden to think about, but today I felt like a little holiday.'

'We can have a drink in the garden at the Red Lion.'

'It would be nice,' Hilda said coolly, 'but I begin to wonder if I shan't change my mind.'

She changed her mind, and, sitting at home waiting, it seemed to her that Tom was an absurd time buying a few things for Sunday lunch.

Tom, it was true, had lingered about the village, gazing in shop windows without seeing anything, reading all the advertisements at the post office – for daily help, and help in gardens, for babysitters and second-hand prams; so many cries for aid, none offering any. He considered buying a cracked soup tureen at the junk shop. He stopped to chat to people about dogs and babies and the weather, gave news of Hilda and received messages for her, though she had never been popular, and her protracted and much-talked-about dying seemed to have made her less so. Mitchell, the butcher, would be his last call, because a leg of lamb is heavy to carry. The butcher's was the source of all gossip, the very spring-head, from which information dribbled to the general stores, the ironmonger and the barber.

There was a little queue, and it turned at once to stare at Tom. The shop was at a standstill with incredulity, and then feet shuffled in the sawdust, glances veered away. A leader seemed needed, and Mr Mitchell came round the chopping block in his bloodied apron, steel swinging from waist, a knife in hand. He looked alarming, and said in a low voice, to be remembered and described by everybody present, 'A word with you outside, Mr Bonchurch, if I may.'

Tom meekly left the shop with him, and at once some-one else came in and took his place in the queue, to be immediately informed of the morning's happenings.

'On the first green,' one said, already half into the story.

'It's Mr Warfield. He's dead,' another said, filling the gap.

'They were looking all round the village for Mr Bonchurch to tell him. Only just walked in here.'

'Heart attack, I suppose. It usually is. What about *her*? Likely she's had one by now, too.'

'No, we'd have heard.' (Standing in this place, they thought.)

'Mr Mitchell out there telling him.'

The newcomer stepped quickly back and looked over her shoulder out of the shop window, but Tom and Mr Mitchell were out of sight.

So that was how Tom learned of Hector's death – incredulously, in a lean-to full of bits of carcasses and hanging birds.

'I must go,' was all that he could say, with dread in his heart.

Mr Mitchell said kindly, 'Len can drive you back in the van.'

Indeed, Tom's legs felt too weak for walking. He nodded distractedly. Mr Mitchell was too kind.

'And don't worry about tomorrow's dinner,' Mr Mitchell said. 'I'll get Len to pop a little something through the back door this afternoon. A small shoulder, I should think.'

The shop was full of concern when Mr Mitchell returned. No one complained of having been kept waiting. All felt braced – eye witnesses almost.

'He didn't get his joint,' some silly, practical woman said.

When Tom got back to the house, Mrs Clarebut was standing by Hilda with a glass of brandy. The doctor was awaited, and she wished him to know, when he came, that she had done the right thing. Rupe had been shut in the kitchen and was hollering.

Hilda stared at Tom, and he went across the room and stood by her, but could only mumble her name – no other words came to him. At last, she put out a hand and took the brandy and drank it steadily, as if it were a glass of milk. Mrs Clarebut took the empty glass to the kitchen where she gave Rupe a clout. He was too outraged to care. He, who had always been so interested in people dying, was now excluded from the excitement of it. This seemed to him to be intolerably unfair.

After a time, staring before her, Hilda whispered, 'I told him not to go.'

In the next days, having to arrange the cremation, Tom was in a state of great bewilderment. He kept thinking, absurdly, that this was the sort of thing he would have left to Hector.

Hilda rarely spoke. She ate little, and she looked afraid – not sad, or grief-stricken, but terrified. At night Tom, who could not sleep himself, knew that her light was on.

When he was forced to speak to her of things to be done, she shuddered, her lips pressed together. She wheeled herself out to the garden, but almost at once turned restlessly back.

Death, which had seemed like a fantasy to her, was at her heels now, with the reality of menace to herself. Here was the truth she had said she loved.

Hector was now a non-person, though his things still lay about. Disregarding all her suffering – she thought – Tom kept asking her for decisions, such as the time of the funeral, the fitting-in of Hector's disposal in a tight crematorium schedule. ('We could manage it at eleven-thirty, or two o'clock. Well, two o'clock would be splendid for us,' the undertakers had said.) Then, long-ignored relations Hilda must be hostess to, it seemed. And police, solicitor, doctor, vicar were all bothering her, who should not, she felt, be bothered at all. Not as a rule a tearful person, she began to cry a great deal, hopelessly, with the tears trickling between the trembling fingers she spread over her face, her mouth, when glimpsed, squared and ugly, like a furious baby's.

Tom felt like running away. I'm in for it now, he kept thinking – trapped, alone with her.

Although he could never have imagined that she would be so inconsolable about the loss of Hector, he now wondered if she could recover from it, and yet sometimes he felt that it was fear, rather than bereavement, which made her start and pale and open wide her eyes.

'Then there's the question of flowers,' he said timidly.

'Yes, yes.' She spoke with impatience.

'I'll order yours for you, shall I? What do you think?'

'Red roses. I remember he said. . . . '

'All right, I'll see to it. Then there's a Cousin Gertrude Stubbings. She wrote after the notice in *The Times*, if you remember. Oughtn't something to be done about *her*?'

'Ask her to luncheon if you wish.'

After all, it's *her* cousin, he thought.

*   *   *

Mrs Clarebut enjoyed a brief importance in the village, and what *she* said in the shops her husband repeated in the Red Lion. 'Very quiet,' he told them. 'Just the relations – an Honourable among them, so I hear. The missus will be officiating, sending Rupe to my sister for the day: no spirits, or beer. Just sherry, and sandwiches and so on. Some people have funny ideas about funerals. They're meeting the deceased at the crematorium; he'll be there before they arrive.'

No coffin carried from the house, as of yore. No lowered blinds. Many of those in the pub remembered the old days, and were sad, passingly, for their children.

Hilda was not going to the funeral. Her doctor, unnecessarily, forbade it.

'Would you like your wreath sent here first, so that you can see it?' Tom asked.

'No, no, no, no!' She shook her head, looking distraught. Those red shop roses he had said were his favourites, she remembered: her own favourites, the morning glories and the meadow daisies – what sort of funeral garland would *they* make? She began to cry hysterically.

On the funeral day, after the sherry and sandwiches, the undertaker arrived. He had a relaxed, but sympathetic manner; he kept an eye on his watch, and at last gave a nod to Tom. To be too early was distressing for the mourners, who then had to hang about until a different set of mourners had gone – though there was a waiting-room, with magazines: to be late was unprofessional, besides putting the next lot out. The undertaker's timing was appreciated at the crematorium.

Hilda was kissed by a cluster of stifling relations. Under the circumstances, they found little to say, some of them wondering how long it would be before they were summoned back again. All had come from a distance, and none was young, and they would be glad to be on the homeward road.

The house was so quiet when they had gone. Mrs Clarebut, appreciating the occasion, did a sort of muffled washing-up.

Hilda lay on the *chaise-longue*, her hands in her lap. Presently, she took up one of her kaleidoscopes, but found that she resented the shifting patterns. She touched all the dead things about her, shells, marbles, pebbles. She fanned herself, exasperatedly, with a paper fan, waiting for Tom's return.

It was not long. He came in, looking strange in his dark suit. The relations had gone on their ways – to London, Hove and Bournemouth. He felt unreal, for he had had to do things for which he was not cut out, and was likely to have to do a great many more of the same kind.

Hilda did not refer to where he had been.

In the evening, to Tom's relief, the doctor called. He talked to Hilda while Tom prepared a supper tray. The dining-room, since Hector's death, was unused. Meals had become picnics on laps.

Tom, who had never wanted marriage, now knew that he had got the worst of someone else's. He began to blame other people in his mind – a girl who long ago had refused his half-hearted proposal, his father for leaving enough money to save him from starving as a painter; but especially he blamed Hilda for turning him into a slave without his knowing it until too late. He thought about running away, but only as a daydream. To deserve his own – and universal – condemnation would make life not worth living. Between daydreams and nightmares, his comfort was Mrs Clarebut. She often stood as a buffer between him and Hilda, coaxing her with hot drinks, while allowing him to go shopping – his greatest pleasure now.

The business of Hector's estate seemed involved and endless. Tom hated money and the affairs connected with it, was utterly bored and scarcely listened. Hilda simply moaned, while the solicitor inched round the subject of her own will.

'If *you* should die,' he began lightly, as if such a thing were hardy likely to happen.

'Oh, I am sure you will sort it out.'

Everyone found her difficult, but Tom most of all.

One day, something seeming miraculous to him happened. A journalist, interested in art, wrote to him of one of his paintings he had come across. He had done it years before. The gallery had quite forgotten him, but had found his address and forwarded the letter. The painting – he remembered it – was simply of rain: a window-pane, with the different-sized drops coming down it. He had done it as a difficult exercise. Perhaps all his life he had tried to make things difficult for himself.

All day, after getting the letter, he was abstracted, did not much want to talk. Were there any more paintings? the letter asked. Could they be seen? An article might be written.

Hilda repeated something she had said, and he looked both blank and glum, hadn't heard her.

'I'm sorry, I was thinking of something else.'

'Then I'm sorry, to have interrupted you.'

He still took no notice of her, but went across the room and looked out of the window.

'I may be outstaying my welcome,' Hilda said softly, as if to herself.

But, for once, he didn't bother to listen.

The next day he went down to the studio in the garden. He hadn't been inside it for months. But he only glanced about him, moved a canvas or two, and felt a great weight upon him. Then he locked the door, and went away. He kept the letter, but did not reply to it. The writer assumed that he had gone away, or died.

That evening was terrible to Tom; but all the evenings were terrible now. He suffered claustrophobia in that room with her, made any excuse to be out of it. And they were long evenings, for she would not go to bed. He was always tired, and he thought that she might as well be in bed upstairs, as doing simply nothing downstairs. But at the suspicion of his trying to bend her will, she would cry; and it did not become her to cry.

'Why wash up at night?' she asked him, as he came back into the sitting-room one evening. 'We used always to leave it for Mrs Clarebut to do in the morning.'

'She has plenty to do.'

'No more than before. Less, in fact.' She dabbed her handkerchief to her mouth. 'These evenings on our own upset you, I know; but they upset me, too, I can tell you. They're no joke to me.' She began to smooth out her hand-kerchief now, turn it about in her hands as women do when they are quarrelling. She pulled out all the lace edges and examined them, pouting. But she was not – never had been – that kind of woman. He stood helplessly by.

'The least you could do. . . . '

'What? What?'

'You make it clear you think I'm an unconscionable time a-dying. Oh, *yes*!'

'Please, Hilda. . . . '

'It's not my fault I don't die . . . and all these dreadful nights going on and on, when I can't sleep, and you always trying to pack me off to bed, so that they can begin earlier and earlier. . . . ' Her voice had started to rise, but from habit she drew it down again. She was like some querulous, disappointed bride, had fallen into the behaviour as to the manner born. Tom was amazed.

'Would you like to play bézique?'

'No, I would *not* like to play bézique. It might keep you from your beloved kitchen.'

'You really are not yourself this evening,' was all he could think of saying.

So she began to cry in earnest. There was nothing he

could do, but try to remember good times in the past and fondness for one another when they were younger: and to try to keep his patience. He reminded himself – as he so often did – that time would pass, and then he supposed that by this he could only mean that *she* would pass, and he had come to look on her as indestructible.

When at last she consented to go to bed, he went up first, as usual, to get her room ready, and took two sleeping-pills from her bottle for his own store, his escape route. He drew the curtains and arranged her pillows.

She could manage the stairs, leaning on him. On the small half-landing there was a chair for her to rest before the last few stairs.

She sat, breathing with effort, with her hands spread over her knees. She gasped, 'Led you a bit of a dance. Sorry.'

'Nothing to be sorry *for*,' he said breezily.

'Always seem to lead you a dance these days. Good of you to bear with me, I s'pose. Don't know what . . . ' she fanned herself with her hand, her breathing coming back more steadily, 'don't know quite what I'd do without you.'

Tom wondered this all the time, woke in the night and wondered it.

'No reason why you should have to,' he said, as they began to go on upstairs.

Unpublished Stories

A Responsibility

DIRTY confetti and the petals of cherry blossom edged the church path. When Jessie arrived, the path and porch were deserted. The building itself, the purple bricks and leaden windows, seemed to rock and swoon in the sudden thundery heat: though she herself was probably rocking more. She walked nervously towards the porch; but, as soon as she reached its cool shadow, began to shiver.

Never having been to a christening before, not even one of her own, she was angry at having let Gwen persuade her to come. That morning, in the bar, the prospect of being a godmother had fascinated her. ('My godchild,' she would be able to say.) Gwen knew no more than Jessie of procedure and etiquette, and with the smallest idea of what lay ahead, Jessie had acquiesced; had shut up the bar promptly at two o'clock and hurried to the church without having a bite to eat.

She opened her bag a little and peered in, not liking to be seen prinking outside a church, even if it was Roman Catholic. Her face looked veined and puffy, her eyes quite bloodshot. Screened by the handbag, she patted her nose and chin with a grubby puff; but now nothing would restore her but a cup of tea and a lie down.

The smell of the church terrified her. It was chilling, like the smell of a hospital. She settled her fox-fur on her shoulders and tried to stand in a casual attitude, at the same time drawing in her stomach muscles. Posture, she thought vaguely.

Then a group of people came down the path, all in black except for a dazzling white baby. They approached the church with calm authority. The men glanced briefly at Jessie and followed the women and the baby inside. She could hear their boots clanging on some gratings, and the sound added to her terror. Perhaps I shall have to say things in Latin! she suddenly thought. The glaring heat of the dead Sunday afternoon, the unmoving trees, the shop windows with drawn blinds, the Guinness she had drunk, produced a feeling of stifled fury towards Gwen.

At last, she saw them coming along the street, three heads above the brick wall; Gwen, her Polish husband Nicky, and Frederick his friend.

Jessie faced them with hostility and fear. Frederick she had not bargained for. Six weeks ago, they had argued and parted from one another, never to meet again, they had said: though obviously in a little town such as this they must continually meet, for any turn in the street was likely to bring them face to face.

Gwen looked frail. She wore her pale blue wedding suit, and the skirt was creased from having the baby on her lap. Her shoes were down-at-heel and one stocking laddered. When she had come into the bar with Nicky before they were married, she had always been neat and smart. Her marriage had changed that. She was not yet twenty, but looked already a down-trodden housewife.

'Why is Frederick here?' Jessie asked when they came near.

The two Poles looked like brothers, both blond, wide-shouldered, and wearing pale suede shoes and silvery raincoats.

'He's a godparent,' Gwen said uncertainly.

'You promised for me to be that. Otherwise, why the hell am I here?'

'There can be more than one.'

'Of course,' Nicky said. He smiled and bowed. Frederick began to whistle softly through his teeth and stare up at the church roof.

'We better get inside,' Gwen said.

'Don't say you are not Catholic,' Nicky warned Jessie. He put a hand under his wife's elbow and, looking with solemn fondness at the baby, went towards the porch.

'This is no fault of mine,' Jessie said. Even her furs seemed outraged, their white-tipped hairs bristling.

'Nor mine,' Frederick shrugged.

'You're always shrugging or bowing, like a bloody penguin.'

'I am sorry to offend.'

'Oh, you don't offend *me*. You can do a Highland fling or fall flat on your back for all I care,' Jessie said, now in the church porch.

'What is this – a mass christening?' Frederick asked, looking at the knot of black-clad people and their baby, who with purpling face arched its back and snatched at the air with spidery hands, letting out frail sounds as a prelude to something louder.

At one end of the church, the two groups huddled, ostensibly opposed. Our sort of people seem so flimsy, Jessie thought. For one thing, we don't have any relations. On an occasion like this anyone has to do, grab up a god-mother out of the bar at the last minute. She sat very straight, holding the card with the Order of Service printed on it. Inside, she felt queasy, uneasy. The enemy baby (as she now thought of it) comforted her a little by beginning to wail. Curdled milk ran out of the side of its mouth.

Gwen's baby slept. His bare, mottled feet stuck out of the shawl, and when Gwen moved him his head bobbed weakly on his thin neck, but he did not open his eyes.

My godson! Jessie thought. It is a responsibility. I'll buy him a silver tankard with his name on and when he goes up to Oxford or Cambridge, I'll visit him and he'll take me round the colleges. Then, looking at Gwen's laddered stocking, the skirt hanging on her (after all, she was six months gone when she bought it, though no one would have known, Jessie thought), this seemed all too improbable, even for daydreaming. Glad I came, though, she decided. Can lie down any afternoon.

Frederick sat bolt upright, too, with his arms folded across his chest, as if he were on trial. Jessie tried to give him a look of contempt, to direct waves of animosity towards him, but he gazed blandly ahead. She thought: Whatever we may say about Nicky, he did marry poor Gwen. She was lucky about that, and doesn't have to go to work any more.

Gwen, watching the other family, passed the baby along to Jessie, who held it self-consciously. When the ceremony was over, she carried it from the church, anxious to be out in the air again, and believing that the others were following her. Frederick caught up with her in the porch. 'A little child has brought us together,' he said, smiling at the distance.

Vexed, she walked ahead of him into the sunshine. The warmth of the afternoon wafted towards them. The street glittered and shimmered and some yellow wallflowers in the churchyard agonised the eye.

He followed her down the path.

'What a pleasant surprise!' she said, not able to leave things as they were. 'Who'd have thought, when I woke up this morning *this* would happen?'

'Do you still drink as much?' he asked in a polite voice.

Nicky came running out of the church and down the path towards them.

'Will you please tell me your name?' he asked Jessie. 'We

are to write down the godparents.' He had always known Jessie too well to have considered her surname. Jessie was nervous of being committed in any way, and believed that the less she put her name to things the better.

'Gutteridge,' she said reluctantly. The feeling of being on alien ground, which she had cast off on leaving the church, returned.

'Please will you spell this for me?'

Sullenly, she spelt it.

Nicky ran back to the church, his lips moving busily.

A taxi was waiting at the gates and Frederick opened the door and curtly signalled Jessie to get in.

'I ordered this,' he said, and sat down beside her. All of his movements, the way he crossed one leg over the other, and flicked a speck of dust off his knee, demonstrated his contempt for her, and his own ease and relaxation.

I wonder what I did wrong, she thought. He liked me at first and I thought he enjoyed the quarrelling.

She had wondered for weeks, but reached no conclusion, afraid that because she was middle-aged men would always slip through her fingers.

'Oh, go on, say something, or I shall scream,' she said, shaking with exasperation.

'What am I to say?' he asked courteously.

'Shut up!'

She stroked the baby's cheek with the tip of her finger, feeling ridiculous sitting there beside Frederick with the baby in her arms.

Gwen and Nicky came down the path.

'I ordered the taxi,' Frederick said again, opening the door for them. They climbed in and sat on the little tip-up seats, and Gwen, her hands loose in her lap, glanced across at the baby.

'Like me to have him?' she asked.

'No, he's all right.'

She looked useless and idle now, as if she were nothing when the baby was taken from her.

'They couldn't make anything of your name,' Nicky told Jessie. 'Tomorrow I must go back with it written down.'

'I should forget it,' Jessie said.

When the taxi stopped, Frederick got out first. 'I'll see to this,' he told them. 'This is on me.'

He always knew how to behave, Jessie thought. She could not help but admire him. The first time he had come into the bar, she had noticed his manner. When he had paid for his drink, he had taken a great handful of silver from his pocket and slapped it down on the bar for her to sort out what he owed. When his friends came in – Nicky perhaps, and Gwen – he would let them order their drinks and then he would push the money across to Jessie. 'I'm taking care of that,' he would say.

Awkwardly, Jessie stepped out of the car, holding the baby, who with blue eyes now wide open placidly surveyed the sky, and turned its fist hungrily against its mouth.

Gwen and Nicky lived in two rooms above a butcher's shop. When Nicky unlocked the street door, there was a cool smell of meat and scrubbed wood. Against the window hung sheaves of clean wrapping paper on hooks. Pots of ferns stood in the shadows, and shining knives and cleavers. Jessie held her breath, fastidiously, and followed Gwen up the narrow stairs.

The rooms were sparsely furnished and the men, throwing off their raincoats, sank down as if exhausted in the only two chairs. In the bedroom, Jessie laid the baby in his cradle, which was a large wooden box from the greengrocer's. There was none of the equipment – the lined baskets and the powder puffs and enamel bowls – that Jessie had so envied her married sister. A waste of a baby, she decided.

'He's wet his frock,' she told Gwen. 'I'll change it, if you like.' She felt rather condescending and capable with the baby now, quite used to him.

'It's the only one he's got,' Gwen said. 'He just stays in his nightgown other days.'

In the morning, Jessie thought that she would go to the draper's and buy a heap of baby linen.

'I'm glad it's over,' Gwen said, as she combed her hair. 'Nicky was all for it. He was christened himself, you see.'

When she heard her husband calling, she dropped the comb at once and ran into the other room where the men lolled in their chairs, their arms trailing over the sides as if they were drifting in a punt on the river.

They are a heartless pair, Jessie thought.

'A pity if either of you over-taxed yourself. You want to take things quiet at your age,' she said. The other three could see the reason why she had never married, and, a second or two later, she saw it herself, looking at Gwen complying for all she was worth handing them cups of tea, perching on the arm of her husband's chair in a grateful way.

'Where am I supposed to sit?' she asked.

Frederick folded his arms across his chest, as he had in church, and shut his eyes. She sat on the arm of his chair.

'Such beautiful manners,' she murmured. 'Very lucky, Gwen, us having these two polite gents.'

'*You* haven't got *me*,' Frederick said.

'Gwen, get the bottle of port out of the cupboard,' Nicky said. 'We should drink the baby's health.'

Port on top of tea! Jessie thought. She glanced at Frederick, as if to share with him her surprise at this idea, but his eyes seemed to her transparent, without any *look* in them. His manner was transparent, too; but nothing was behind it to be revealed. He was quite negative; just *not hers*.

'To Nicholas!' Nicky said. They stood and raised their glasses, and tears rushed to Jessie's eyes. She always cried easily – when 'God Save The King' was played, or when she saw a bride. Gwen looked tearful, too, but from fatigue. While the others were drinking, she fetched the baby and sat down, opening her blouse to feed him. Once, Jessie saw her brush her lashes with her fingers. The baby fed steadily, then less steadily, then nodded; full, blissful, his eyelids at half-mast and a line of eye showing beneath.

'He's too tired to shut his eyes even,' Jessie said.

'A very tiring day,' Frederick said.

'He's just good,' Gwen said, and she buttoned her blouse and dried her eyes finally.

Nicky said: 'What about filling our glasses?'

She hurried to do so, the baby asleep over her shoulder.

'I must go,' Frederick said, when he had emptied his glass.

'Yes,' said Jessie, standing up, too. She hoped, still, that she would not be obliged to spend the evening on her own. To walk along quarrelling with Frederick would be better.

Frederick took a pound note, smoothed it flat and put it behind the clock. 'Buy the baby something,' he said to Gwen.

Nicky saw them downstairs and through the shop. He locked the door behind them, and they were left standing in the hot deserted streets.

'Never anyone much about on Sundays,' Jessie said conversationally.

He was silent.

'Going to thunder, I think,' she went on, looking at the lowering, cloudless sky, and drawing her furs round her, trying to provoke him into some response, she said: 'It's my birthday tomorrow.'

He smiled and tightened the belt of his raincoat, buckling it neatly.

'That is no concern of mine,' he said, and walked briskly away, whistling through his teeth. One after another, enormous spots of rain began to fall upon the pavement.

Violet Hour at the Fleece

THEY were the first in. The landlord followed them into the little side bar with two pints of stout and mild on a tin tray, then rattled with a poker at the fire which had been quenched with a welter of coal. It was an empty gesture, a mere pass made in the direction of hospitality. When he had gone: 'Well!' she said, turning from a picture of Lord Kitchener, tears in her eyes.

'You haven't been in here since I went,' he said.

'How did you know?'

'Because you walked up to that picture as if you were saying: "Ah, Lord Kitchener, my old friend!" If you were here every night you wouldn't have done that.' He handed her a glass of beer and went to the window. The cobbles outside, between pub and church, were full of shadows, the sun struck only the gilt weather vane on the steeple. Now the quarter was marked with rounded leaden notes. Thrushes sang from gravestones and umbrella trees.

'The violet hour. Who said that? Sappho?'

'Sappho. I like the sound of Sappho. The last time I was in here . . . '

'The day before war. A Saturday. They were all here – the man in the bowler hat and his wife. . . . '

'The one in the corner with the paste sandwiches, reading. . . . '

'One moment!' She flicked her fingers. '*Extinct Civilisations*! That was it.'

'Over there,' she pointed, 'two girls drinking. *Good* girls! There hadn't started to be tarts about then. Not here, I mean.'

'Are there now?'

She laughed. 'And *you* said: "We'll always remember this because it is a Date. It is something children will have to learn for history."'

'Poor little sods.'

'"When I am eighty," you said, "I shall tell people I remember that day. I sat drinking at the Fleece with Sarah Fletcher . . . "'

'So I shall tell my children that.'

'And they will be madly bored, and you will say "That stout old woman who lives now, I believe, at Tunbridge Wells."'

'No. I shall say, "I was drinking with Sarah Fletcher, a beautiful lady and my very dear friend."'

'No one has talked like that to me for four years.'

She sat down at the table and he came and sat down beside her. They slipped into the old habit of drinking together, elbow against elbow, their beer going down level as it used.

'How've you been for . . . ?' he tapped the glass.

'I haven't much. . . . '

'Nor me. How does it go down?'

'It seems no different, though I suppose it is.'

'How is your son?' he asked politely.

'His milk teeth are coming out. Funny and touching when he grins. I love it in him. Not in other children, though.'

'And your daughter?'

'You speak very stiffly.' She laughed.

'Say "silly sod" as you used.'

'No. I've stopped saying that.'

As he tapped the table with a half-crown, he was thinking how grimy his hand looked, and curled the nails into his palm, against the coin.

'I hated all the maleness, chaps undressing together, being hearty,' he said suddenly. 'I always felt thin and blue. Good luck!' he lifted his filled glass.

'But the worst thing was Christmas dinners. All sitting there being pleased and cheery with our nice dinners and the officers being decent, but each one of us his own private self. "Poor men and soldiers unable to rejoice." Perhaps not, though. Perhaps all enjoying themselves like hell. God, this is boring. Before I came tonight, I thought I wouldn't tell any soldier stories. You see, you don't like me to talk like it.'

She wiped a little moustache of froth from her mouth. 'I want you to tell me some time, but it separates me from you, and just now it is hard enough to get back again.'

'I thought we were doing fine.'

'I thought so too.'

'And then there always *were* things to separate us. Your posh friends and your political notions. These endureth for ever, but being a soldier soon stops.'

'I can think of the fighting and your being hungry and the hospital all right, but I can't hear about the Christmas dinner. I can't think about that.'

'I enjoyed it like mad really. Look, now the fire's going to burn for us.'

The coals shuddered and collapsed and a few flames, pale like irises, grew up between them.

'Do you still cry as much as you used?'

'No.' At once, the tears rushed up into her eyes.

The landlord came in now, and placed a log on top of

the flames, which wavered and sank down. It was a damp green log, with ivy still clinging to its bark.

'Tell me more, then, about being a soldier.'

'No, it's just madly boring and stupid, living miles below the subsistence level, and the chaps being so coarse, much worse even than the way posh girls like you are coarse. And when they're not being coarse, they're bloody touching and have S.W.A.K. on the backs of their letters and make you feel ashamed. It's only all being together. Then office jobs – copy lists of numbers on to ration cards, so boring you make mistakes ... do a pile and then say Oh, God! October has only thirty days, correct them all, smudges and blots and then, Oh damn! it's November has thirty. And being in a sort of dirty post-office place, dust, broken nibs, ink bottles empty, falling over and full of fluff. And stuffy. You're not listening. Let's have some more beer. Darling, what are you looking at?'

'I was watching the ivy on that log turning bronze.'

'I hate ivy. Christ! The trouble is, I've no more money.'

She felt in her coat pockets. It was a thick white coat with a fine bloom of dirt upon it.

'Angel! I do like taking money from a nice girl.'

'Ivy. My mother's favourite. She used to like to spend two or three hours fixing it all up in a jar against a white wall.'

'Your mother did do the hell of a lot of high-class things, but don't go on about *her*. You'll only cry.'

'I remember her doing that, in a long dress and *she* was crying because her mother and father had gone away for ever. I saw the back of her. I was eight. Her hair was shiny black and soft and done up like a Japanese woman's. It would be a good thing to paint. How tired I am of the fronts of people! Particularly bosoms. The back could be most expressive. You could tell by the arms and the listless way of holding the ivy that she was weeping because her father had left her in an ugly house with a nasty husband.

The Victorians would have gone round to the other side and left an opened letter lying on the table and written "Parting" on the frame – or "Solitude". But Toulouse-Lautrec and I like it best the other way round . . . and *you* don't like it at all. You've had your bellyful of it, in fact.'

'No, but I'm always afraid of you crying when you speak about your mother, and when you begin to harp on bosoms and your inferiority. It worries me when you cry. It must be a thing you do a lot in your family. It's all right now while you're young and beautiful, but very uncomfortable for everyone once you're past forty.'

A woman came in and drew red serge curtains and switched on the light. It rained cruelly down on them. He curled his fingers out of sight again.

'Mike!' he suddenly cried with false *bonhomie*.

She put up her cheek for her husband to kiss, which he would not do in a pub.

'How are you, old man?'

'Fine. Fine, thanks.'

'Quite fit again?'

'Rather! You?'

'Pretty good.'

'What to drink?'

'No. Can't stop. Coming Sarah?'

'One for the road?'

'No, nor the ditch. Many thanks, all the same. OK Sarah?'

She looked at them both with a feeling of contempt. Men together. Or, perhaps, just men before a woman. They speak symbols, she thought. It isn't a language at all. They make strange, half-savage noises at one another.

She said goodbye and the two of them went out into the last few moments of the violet hour. Her husband held open the car door. She sank back into the seat, watching sullenly the road before her, regretting the bright pub.

'OK?' He fidgeted at the dashboard and they were away.

The buildings made strange shapes against the darkening sky.

'Oh, crying!' he protested. 'Oh, stop for God's sake. Oh, Christ!'